Transformed . . .

She felt like heaven in his arms. And she was quiet. Blissfully quiet. Meltingly quiet. Responsive. Delightful.

Until she pushed herself away from him. Her hand flew up to her mouth and she pressed the back of it against lips still moist from his kiss. He held out a hand, wishing she would take it and return to him . . .

HEAVEN'S PROMISE

RACHEL WILSON

JOVE BOOKS, NEW YORK

HAUNTING HEARTS is a registered trademark of Berkley Publishing Corporation.

HEAVEN'S PROMISE

A Jove Book / published by arrangement with the author

PRINTING HISTORY
Jove edition / November 1998

The Penguin Putnam Inc. World Wide Web site address is
http://www.penguinputnam.com

ISBN: 0-515-12405-2

A JOVE BOOK®
Jove Books are published by The Berkley Publishing Group,
a member of Penguin Putnam Inc.,
375 Hudson Street, New York, New York 10014.
JOVE and the "J" design are trademarks belonging to
Jove Publications, Inc.

PRINTED IN THE UNITED STATES OF AMERICA

10 9 8 7 6 5 4 3 2 1

A while back, an old dancing buddy, Art Aratin, sent a letter telling me I should write a book featuring Danilo, the Gypsy King, in honor of Daniel Matousek. Danny was a dancer, too, as well as the founder and director of Zena, a womans' Balkan chorus based in the Los Angeles area. He was brilliant at what he did, and loved the folk music and dances of Eastern Europe. Art and Danny, this one's for you.

I hope my Mainiac relatives, descendants of the Homsteads, will forgive me for changing the shape of the Homstead monument. I had to do it, or the poor characters wouldn't have had anything to sit on! I also rearranged the geography of Palmyra to make it negotiable on foot and gave it a hotel and a saloon.

HEAVEN'S PROMISE

Prologue

Alone. Immobile. Frozen in time. Nowhere. Emptiness upon emptiness upon emptiness. Abandoned in infernal limbo. Locked in a wretched, voiceless, soundless, soulless void.

Oh, my love, where are you? Why did you forsake me? Where are you? Where are you?

No answer. No answer. Would there never be an answer?

Chapter
One

Susanna Clement sat on a boulder, her elbows resting on the book on her knees, her chin in her hands. She stared at a mossy tombstone, studying the name engraved thereon and moodily mulling over everything the marker represented.

She wasn't sad exactly, but the knowledge that the headstone marked an empty grave made her insides quiver with the tiniest degree of melancholy. No one knew what had happened; that's what bothered Susanna. She wanted to unlock the stone's secrets, to learn what had really transpired all those years ago, to discover why the body that should be resting in that grave wasn't there.

Maple and elm trees shaded this section of the Spring Hill Cemetery, and a soft breeze blew, tickling the skin on her arms into gooseflesh. She glanced up into the trees and smiled. Late afternoon sunlight filtered through their leaves and dappled the grass at her feet.

3

Except for a hint of claustrophobia engendered by so much vegetation and civilization, Susanna loved Maine. The landscape was so different from what she was used to. Back home, a person could see just about forever. Nothing stood in the way of her and the distant horizon. She grew up knowing exactly why people used to believe the world was flat. It was easy to imagine a body walking to the edge of the earth and falling off. Here in Maine, a person could only see as far as the next clump of trees or twist in the road.

And green! Susanna had never seen so much green in one place in her life. On the dry, brown, windswept plains of her home, the first anemic shoots of yellowish green rendered everyone nearly hysterical with spring fever. That usually happened in March, although sometimes those faint signs of new life appeared later in the year. The green here in Maine was so brilliant it had hurt her eyes at first.

Her glance slid back to the tombstone, and she sighed. The soulful sound of her exhalation seemed fitting to her as she sat in the graveyard where a hundred years' worth and more of her ancestors lay buried. All of those other graves, filled as they were with the bones of those who'd been wept over, loved, parted with sadly, made this one empty grave seem especially forlorn to her.

They'd never found the body. Magdalena Bondurant, whose name was carved on the headstone, had simply disappeared one day in her thirtieth year, thus assuring that the end of her life would generate almost as much controversy as the rest of it. Susanna sighed again and decided she'd best not dent the diary on her lap with her pointy elbows any longer. After all, the book was almost forty years old, and she intended to take extremely good care of it.

Picking it up, she carefully turned to the page she'd marked with an embroidered bookmark. Susanna hadn't worked the embroidery herself, since she had ten thumbs and scorned such delicate work—''woman's work,'' people called it. Susanna did not approve of labors being categorized in such a manner.

Her mother had crafted the bookmark for her, however, and Susanna appreciated it. She loved her mother very much, even though Susanna believed her to be much too concerned about the world's opinion than she ought to be. Her mother hadn't told Susanna a single solitary thing about Magdalena Bondurant. Everything Susanna knew about her maternal great-aunt she'd gleaned from this one slender volume. She didn't know much.

"Some things are best forgotten, Susanna," her mother had said every time Susanna had asked a question.

Easy for her mother to say. How could Susanna forget something she'd never been privileged to know? It was all very exasperating. She considered Great-Aunt Magdalena the most interesting member of the Bondurant family. Her mother considered her a blot on the family history.

Susanna hadn't been able to stop thinking about Magdalena Bondurant since she discovered the diary in her mother's cedar chest. She'd been rummaging for edging fabric, and had unearthed a mystery instead.

Magdalena Bondurant, until Susanna found the diary, had been merely a name in the family Bible—a name no one talked about. The woman fascinated Susanna. She haunted her dreams. Susanna kept rereading the diary, hoping that somewhere in there was the key to understanding the enigma that was her great-aunt.

The work continues, Susanna read from the diary. It was a passage she'd read over and over again these past several days. *I feel a grand elation to be allowed a small part in it. The storage facility is ready. I shall not fail. The work is too important for failure.*

Now what, Susanna wondered, was *the work*? And what was *the storage facility*? Susanna had her suspicions, and they thrilled her. But what had her great-aunt's part been in it? There were so many things

Susanna longed to find out. Living in Artesia, New Mexico Territory, she'd been at a terrible disadvantage since Magdalena Bondurant had lived and, one presumed, died at the other end of the country.

That's one of the reasons Susanna had been so happy when her aunt Winnie invited her to spend the summer here in Palmyra. Palmyra had been Magdalena's home when she wasn't touring with her theatrical company, and it was in Palmyra, Susanna presumed, that her secrets resided. She hoped she'd be able to discover even a few of them.

Susanna had graduated with honors from the Women's Teaching Seminary in Springfield, Missouri, in May. She planned to begin teaching school in her hometown of Artesia after the new year. Miss Elliott, the woman who had been the Artesia schoolmistress for almost twenty years, would be retiring then.

This summer might well be the last one Susanna would ever have to savor as a girl. Soon she'd take up the burdens of a woman. She aimed to do right by them, too. She had no intention of taking up the pallid, uninspiring role of shadow to some masterful man. Not on her life. No, Susanna intended to shine, if not as brightly as her great-aunt Magdalena, at least a little. She intended to scatter the seeds of enlightenment. To address the issue of women's suffrage and the abysmal laws of this so-called land of freedom that rendered women no better than chattel.

Perhaps that's why she appreciated the mysterious Magdalena so much. Magdalena had *lived*. Magdalena hadn't allowed the constraints of society to thwart her. She'd grabbed life by the lapels and shaken it until it rattled. As an actress and a free spirit, she'd shocked people, certainly, but she had *lived*.

Susanna frowned. Magdalena had shocked her family so much that they wouldn't talk about her to this day. Drat them! It was so frustrating. Susanna longed to know everything about the fascinating Magdalena. She wanted to know who she really was, how she really lived, and how she really died.

Susanna was looking forward to this summer in Maine. She wanted to investigate her great-aunt's life, to probe into Magdalena's exciting adventures and unlock the mystery of her disappearance.

Unfortunately, her mother's sister, Aunt Winnie Dexter, was even less forthcoming about Magdalena Bondurant than Susanna's mother had been. These Maine folks were a tight-lipped bunch. "Close," her father had called it, laughing. Susanna sniffed. Stuffy is how she saw it, and she didn't think the characteristic was the least bit funny.

"Well, well, well. What have we here?"

Susanna was so caught up in her own thoughts that the hearty baritone voice at her back startled her. She jumped, and jerked her head around to see who had spoken. She was surprised to find a tall young man standing there, garbed in a lightweight summer suit. His summer straw hat was tilted at a cocky angle. He didn't remove it, either. He was as handsome as the devil, with dark blond hair; blue eyes; a clean-shaven, tanned face; and a wicked grin. Susanna felt herself color, and hated it.

She didn't admire his insouciant air or the way his gaze raked her from her head to her toes, as if he were undressing her with his mind's eye. He didn't so much as bow and beg her pardon, either, but stood there, grinning like a cat who'd just cornered a mouse. The bounder.

"I didn't expect to find anyone like you in this backwater of a place—especially in the graveyard."

He spoke to her as if they'd been formally introduced aeons ago and were now best friends. The nerve of some people!

Susanna had it in her head to ignore him, but the fellow flopped down on Magdalena Bondurant's headstone, stuck his long legs out in front of him, crossed his ankles, leaned back, peered at her from half-closed eyes, and heated his grin up a degree or two. Susanna was not amused.

"You're sitting on a headstone," she pointed out, her voice chilly.

The man made a show of glancing at his seat and arching his brows, as if he were astonished to discover she was right. Then he shrugged and grinned again. "So what? Whoever it belonged to is past caring now."

She felt her lips purse up and made an effort to smooth them out. Her mother pinched her lips together like that, and she'd gotten herself a fine set of wrinkles because of it. Although Susanna didn't consider herself vain, she didn't particularly want to wrinkle. Besides, pursing her lips made her look priggish, and she didn't wish to be considered a prig even more than she didn't want wrinkles.

"You may well be wrong there, sir. That headstone marks the grave of my own great-aunt, Magdalena Bondurant, and it's quite possible that she's still alive."

That didn't sound right. Before Susanna could figure out how to correct it without making herself sound like a fool, the man stood up again. He glanced down at the headstone.

"Well, I'll be damned!"

Susanna did not approve of his language. Nor did she approve of the faint whiff of distilled spirits she detected on his person. She wrinkled her nose. Here was an example of just the sort of male she despised. Arrogant, rude, and indifferent to the sensibilities of his fellow man. And woman.

"As to *that*, I wouldn't be at all surprised," she said tartly.

The fellow gave a bark of laughter. Susanna wished he wasn't so blasted handsome. When he laughed, his eyes sparkled and crinkled up at the edges, and he looked very young and quite appealing. Susanna had often wished that people's exteriors more accurately reflected their interiors, but they seldom did. She considered it a design flaw, and spoke to God about it sometimes. Thus far He hadn't spoken back.

"So you're related to this flashy bit of goods, are you?" He looked down at the headstone again and evidently didn't hear Susanna's gasp of outrage—or didn't care.

"You're talking about my own great-aunt, sir, and I'll thank you to do so with respect! She was a great lady and an important actress."

"That's not what I've heard."

He winked at her. He actually had the audacity to *wink* at her! Susanna was mightily offended. She stood in a huff, held her great-aunt's diary out so the cad could see it, and tapped it with the finger of her other hand. "Do you see this book, sir? This is the diary written by the woman you so vilely disparage. She was embarked upon a noble enterprise and cared deeply about righting society's wrongs."

His eyebrows wiggled suggestively. Susanna itched to slap his handsome face, but suspected him of deliberately trying to provoke her. She wouldn't give him the satisfaction of knowing he'd succeeded.

"*I* believe," she said stoutly, love for this unknown great-aunt of hers propelling her, "that Magdalena Bondurant was an underground operative helping the abolitionists!" So there. Let him chew on *that* for a while. She hoped he choked on his shame.

He laughed at her. Susanna could scarcely believe her eyes and ears when he threw back his head and bellowed with laughter. His stomach made a perfect target, but she didn't punch him in it and was proud of herself. She was a lady, after all, even if he was about as far from being a gentleman as a man could get.

She continued to glower at him as he grabbed a white handkerchief from the breast pocket of his summer coat and wiped his streaming eyes. "Oh, me," he said. "Oh, my."

"Spoken like a true egoist," she muttered.

He looked down at her and stuffed his handkerchief back into his pocket. He hadn't done it neatly at all, but let the ends dangle down as if he didn't care a whit. Susanna got the feeling he didn't.

"And just what would a little girl like you know about egoism?"

A little girl? Susanna drew herself up to her full five feet, four inches and eyed him with loathing. *"I,"* she said distinctly, "am a college graduate. *With* honors. And I know a good deal about the egoism rampant in the male of the species."

She had hoped to daunt him with her firm speech and obvious education. Instead she only succeeded in winning herself another broad grin.

"Well, Miss College Graduate, I must say it's a pleasure to meet you. I didn't know there were any women like you here in Palmyra." He stuck out his right hand. "Julian Kittrick here, ma'am, reporter for the *Denver Post.*"

"Denver? Whatever are you doing here in Maine if you're from Denver?" *And why don't you go back there?* Susanna refrained from asking the latter only with an effort.

"I'll answer that question if you'll answer one for me." His hand didn't waver.

She ignored it and squinted up at him. She didn't trust him an inch and didn't know if she should be answering his questions. Before she could say so, he continued.

"I told you who I am. Now it's your turn. I'll answer any of your questions if you'll honor me with your name."

She hesitated. Since he seemed genuinely interested in who she was, she didn't want to tell him. On the other hand, her curiosity—either her besetting sin or her greatest virtue, depending on whether her mother or she was describing herself—was intense.

Feeling outmaneuvered and grumpy, she finally said, "Susanna Clement." Then, after eyeing his outstretched hand for long enough that any right-thinking man would have withdrawn it—Julian Kittrick didn't—she picked

up two of his fingers in two of hers and gave them a
little twitch.

"Oh, no, you don't. You're not getting away with
that."

With yet another loud laugh, he engulfed her hand in
his and shook it vigorously.

His touch was warm, his hand hard with calluses, and
Susanna couldn't quell the thrill that shot through her
from the contact. Good heavens. She hadn't held a
man's naked hand—ever. Even when she'd gone to
dances back home, the ladies had worn gloves. This was
shocking. It was intimate. She tried to suppress the admission that it was also exciting and quite, quite wick-
edly delicious.

"Miss Susanna Clement. Lovely name for a lovely
lady."

He bowed over her hand. Susanna's eyes popped open
in surprise at the gallantry. Then he straightened again,
and she knew his bow had been a mockery. Whether he
was mocking her or society at large, she couldn't tell,
but she was irked. His attitude freed her, though, in a
way. At least she didn't have to beat about the bush or
be scrupulously polite. She snatched her hand back.

"All right, Mr. Kittrick. I've told you my name. Now
you tell me why you're here in Palmyra, Maine, when
you belong in Denver, Colorado."

He flopped down on Magdalena's headstone once
more, again offending Susanna. "Ah, Miss Clement,
you're out there. I do so belong here in Palmyra, because
I'm researching a story."

Irked that he should be sprawling in that impolite
way—after all, she, a lady, remained standing and he
should, therefore, wait until she'd seated herself before
doing so himself, even in a cemetery—Susanna frowned
at him. It didn't help that he persisted in sitting on her
great-aunt's tombstone, either. He really was too insolent.

"Well, then, why are you here?" Because she was so
annoyed with him, she crossed her arms over her chest

and tapped her foot. When she caught his gaze straying to her bosom, which her crossed arms emphasized, she dropped her arms to her side. He was truly intolerably awful!

"Actually, Miss Clement, it looks like I'm here for the same reason you are."

"I sincerely doubt that."

"I'll bet you're wrong."

His grin made Susanna long to kick him in the shins. But she was no longer ten years old and in a battle of strength with the neighbor boy. She was a well-educated young woman who fought with her wits when it proved necessary. Through gritted teeth, she said, "We'll never know, will we, until you honor your pledge and tell me why you're here."

"*Touché.*" He winked again. She fought her impulse to slap his brazen face. "All right, Miss Clement, I'll tell you why I'm here. I'm doing research into a piece I'm going to write about this female." He patted the headstone. "Miss Magdalena Bondurant. Your great-aunt."

Susanna's mouth dropped open.

"But I'm afraid you won't like my angle much."

Her mouth snapped shut again. "I'm not surprised. What's your angle, pray tell?"

He reached inside his suit coat and withdraw a small notebook. Susanna looked at it curiously. Could this dreadful man actually be what he claimed to be? She itched to get her hands on that notebook of his. Susanna herself had always harbored a secret passion for journalism. She hated it that it was the beastly Julian Kittrick who was fulfilling her own dreams.

"Several months ago," he went on, "I read about a beautiful Yankee actress who led a secret life. Rumor had it that she was helping slaves escape from bondage in the South. She cut quite a swath across the eastern seaboard forty years ago. She wasn't as prudish as her latter-day relatives, I gather."

He honored Susanna with another broad wink. She

refused to give him the indignant reaction she knew he craved, but merely muttered, "Go on."

"And then, one late June day in 1857, here in Palmyra, Maine, *poof*!" He snapped his fingers. "She up and vanished."

"Yes, yes, yes. Everything you've said is common knowledge." She hoped he hadn't unearthed anything new. Susanna wanted to be the one to discover her great-aunt's secrets. She didn't want this awful creature, who respected nothing and no one, to do it.

"Yeah, but there's more."

She eyed him malevolently, wishing her great-aunt's ghost would swoop down and snatch him away for his effrontery. Not that she believed in such things as ghosts.

"Her disappearance wouldn't be any more than merely interesting if that's all there was to it, though."

"For people who possess humane instincts, my great-aunt's disappearance was far more than merely *interesting,* Mr. Kittrick. It was tragic."

She thought she detected a flicker of compassion in his eyes, but she wasn't sure. It would have surprised her if it had been there.

He did tilt his head, however, as if acknowledging the justice of her caustic observation. "Granted."

Well, that was something.

"However, did you know that a fortune in precious gems disappeared with her?"

There went his blasted grin again. It flashed across his tanned face like a beam of sunshine. Susanna wasn't astonished, now that she thought about it, to know that he was from Denver, where people were more apt to sport sunburns than these Maine natives, who lived in the rain and fog.

"Again, Mr. Kittrick, you have failed to amaze me or to produce information that isn't already widely known. A fortune in precious gems disappeared *at about the same time* my great-aunt did. There is no connection between the two events."

"Ha! You really believe that, do you?"

"Yes, I do."

"Then you're more of a fool than I took you for."

Seething inside, Susanna chose not to respond.

He sat up straighter on the tombstone. "Face it, Miss Clement, there may be such a thing as coincidence, but it only shows up in novels. In real life, coincidences are as rare as finding a civilized man in the New Mexico Territory." He laughed at his comparison.

"*I* was reared in New Mexico Territory, Mr. Kittrick, by people whom I assure you are extremely civilized. I am visiting my maternal aunt here in Palmyra, Maine, for the summer." She had the satisfaction of seeing Mr. Kittrick's eyes open wide with surprise this time.

"You're joshing me!"

"I am doing no such thing."

"Whereabouts do you live? In Santa Fe or Albuquerque? You couldn't live in any other place in the territory, because you speak in complete grammatical sentences. There's not another town in the territory that's sophisticated enough for grammar." He laughed again.

Until his sarcastic jibe about her home, Susanna hadn't believed she could become more indignant. She discovered she'd been wrong. "That's what you think. I happen to live with my family in Artesia. My parents own and run a mercantile establishment there, and I can assure *you*, Mr. Kittrick, my family is sophisticated." Slightly.

He relaxed again. "Well, I'll be damned."

"Yes. We've already established that point."

His laugh grated on her nerves like a rusty nail. "At any rate, I don't believe in coincidences, sweetheart. I'll lay you odds that Miss Magdalena Bondurant and those jewels left town together. And I'm here to prove it."

"You can't."

"Want to bet?"

"No! You simply can't do that, Mr. Kittrick. It's not true, and you can't print such a scurrilous story."

"Tell that to my editors. Messrs. Bonfils and Tammen

think I can. In fact, they're paying all my expenses here in Maine just so I can get that story.''

Horrified by his avowed plan, Susanna sank back down on the boulder she'd lately deserted, her heart thudding sickeningly. "Oh, but Mr. Kittrick, it's not true. My great-aunt was a truly noble woman bent upon a great cause. She was helping slaves to escape, for heaven's sake. You can't blacken her memory in such a despicable way. You can't!''

"Not even if it's true?''

"But it's *not* true!''

He cocked his head to one side. Susanna disapproved of the way his eyes gleamed and of the cynical expression on his face.

"How do you know it's not true?''

She threw out her arms. "It can't be! My great-aunt was a courageous lady who was assisting with the Underground Railroad.''

"I don't buy that for a minute. Anyway, so what if she was?'' He crossed his arms over his chest and gazed at her steadily. His straight look disconcerted her, and her heart began to ache.

"But—but why would a woman whose whole life had been devoted to a great cause suddenly throw all her scruples away, desert her cause, and steal a fortune in gems?''

"I have no idea.'' His negligent shrug made Susanna want to push him off of that headstone, flat onto his insolent back.

"If you have no idea, you can't write it, then.'' Even as she said the words, she suspected they weren't true. Mr. Julian Kittrick didn't appear to her to be the type of journalist who cared very much about the truth. In fact, she had a disagreeable hunch that he might be one of those unscrupulous "yellow" journalists she'd heard so much about in college.

His cocky smile warned her. "Miss Clement, I'm a newspaperman. My newspaper, the *Post*, doesn't hold with whitewashing stories. My editors like to print the exciting stuff. They don't flinch from the truth, even if the truth turns out to be shocking—even sordid. If a story has a little dirt clinging to it, they don't shy away from it.'' He brushed a fleck of dust from his lapel in a show of false modesty. "They thrive on excitement, in fact. Not unlike Denver itself.''

"You work for a sensational press, in other words.''

He cocked his head and twinkled at her. "You might put it that way.''

Almost frozen with indignation and impotent rage, Susanna said, "And you're as happy to make up stories as to find real ones.''

His smile vanished. "No! By God, Miss Clement, you're really something, you know that? To condemn a fellow you don't even know isn't very polite, you know.''

She huffed her contempt.

"Journalism is my profession. I don't make stories up. I seek out the truth.''

"What if you can't find the truth?'' Her jaw ached from clenching it so tightly.

There went that blasted grin of his again. Another insouciant shrug. Another twinkle. "I've got a lively imagination.''

Susanna took several deep, sustaining breaths and held them, unwilling to shout and give him the impression she was a flighty woman with more emotion than intelligence. She let her breath out slowly, hoping her rage would abate. It didn't.

"Imagination.'' She ground the word out and gave it the emphasis she believed it deserved.

"Don't you like imagination, Miss Clement? Don't you have an imagination?'' The words were spoken sweetly, as if he'd dipped them in honey before offering them to her.

Susanna was not fooled. "No, Mr. Kittrick. I've been told I possess neither humor nor imagination. I do, how-ever, possess a great deal of integrity and a healthy conscience. I prefer to discover the facts, not to make them up.''

He held his hands up in a gesture begging peace. ''I'm not about to make up any facts, Miss Clement. What I plan to do is dig up all the facts I can find. Then and only then, unless I find specific proof of what really happened—which I may well do—I will draw studied conclusions from them.''

''And then use them to blacken my great-aunt's name.''

He shrugged, as if to tell her that none of this was his fault. Susanna hated him in that instant more than she'd hated the anchovies her aunt Winnie had tried to feed her last Saturday.

''It sounds to me as though you've already convicted my great-aunt of theft.''

''Not at all.'' His broad smile belied his words. ''Why, who knows? I may discover that she wasn't a light-skirt and shady character at all.''

Susanna's gasp frightened a bird who'd been observing them from the branch of a spreading maple tree. It squawked and flew away. Susanna glared after it. Julian laughed again.

''How dare you! You great oaf! To sully the character of a great lady with your vile calumnies! You ought to be horsewhipped, Mr. Kittrick!''

His eyebrows lifted in mock hurt. ''Why, Miss Clement, how you talk. I think your great-aunt was a peach. In fact, she's the most interesting thing about Palmyra, Maine. I like the old girl.'' He patted the headstone. ''And I think she was clever as the devil to pull the wool over so many people's eyes.''

Although her wrath was all but smothering her by this time, Susanna managed to grind out, ''What do you mean by that?''

He gave her another wink. ''Why, look at you. She's even got *you,* a college-educated female with a puritan-ical streak, believing she was an abolitionist and a saint.'' He threw his head back and roared with laughter.

"I think she's great! Imagine her getting away with a whole bag of precious gems and still making people think she had some kind of morals. It makes me laugh!"

Susanna couldn't stand to listen to another second of this man's filthy slanders. It would have been easy for her to shove him off of her great-aunt's tombstone, but she didn't. She was a lady. Just as Magdalena had been.

Clutching Magdalena Bondurant's diary in her right hand so tightly that her fingers hurt, Susanna whirled around and marched away from Julian Kittrick. She left him laughing. Her great-aunt would have been proud of her.

Evidently he realized he'd lost his audience, because Susanna heard his startled, "Hey! Hey, don't run away! I don't bite. Honest! Come back here!"

She didn't turn around.

Chapter
Two

Julian wiped his eyes and stared at the retreating form of Susanna Clement. More accurately, he stared at her swaying bottom, which he appreciated more than he could say—more than he *would* say, at any rate.

A last couple of chuckles bubbled up in his chest and escaped into the still atmosphere of the cemetery. Ah, sweet Prudence. Quite a find, Miss Susanna Clement. He'd had a good time chatting with her. Or riling her. He chuckled again, then burped and slapped his chest. Beer bubbles, he reckoned. Julian was glad he hadn't burped in front of Miss Prudence; she'd have been even more appalled with him than she already was.

He leaned back and let the sun's rays caress his face. He preferred being out of doors in the fresh air than hanging out in the saloon, breathing in stale cigar smoke and drinking his afternoons away. Since he had an image as a hard-living, devil-may-care journalist to uphold, he wouldn't admit it to a soul.

Still, he was glad to know there was more to Palmyra, Maine, than old fogies in the saloon and stiff-necked

Puritans. Not that Miss Susanna Clement wasn't puritanical.

She was sure pretty, though. Too bad she was such a stick. On the other hand, it had been fun irritating her.

He sat up again and watched her pick her way past a couple of the larger tombstones, admiring the play of the sun's rays on her fine auburn hair. Her eyes had reminded Julian of really good, aged bourbon. He should have told her so and watched her reaction. She'd undoubtedly have been offended. He chuckled again. Next time he met up with her—he knew there would be a next time, since Palmyra was such a small place—he'd try to see if he could goad her into slapping him. Then he could pretend moral outrage. He was sure that would make her feel guilty.

He wondered if he was drunk. He didn't think so, but he couldn't account for his reaction to Susanna Clement any other way. As a rule, Julian was not a fellow who anticipated meetings with fine, upstanding ladies with pleasure. His kind of female was the type Miss Clement wouldn't be caught dead in the same room with. Or the same cemetery. He laughed again.

So Magdalena Bondurant was a saint, was she? Julian rose and peered down at the headstone that marked Magdalena's empty grave. He sincerely doubted her sanctity. Julian had met up with only one saint in his life, and he'd lived damned near everywhere.

As if pulled by a magnetic force, he found himself turning again, hoping to catch a last glimpse of Miss Clement. She was gone. He sighed his disappointment. He wondered where she lived, and wished he'd followed her.

"Don't be an ass, Kittrick."

Julian stuffed his hands into his trousers pockets and kicked at some pebbles at his feet. So, what should he do now? He guessed he could always go back to the saloon and drink some more, but he didn't want to. His vocation notwithstanding, Julian really didn't care for drinking.

He pulled out his notebook, glanced at the notes he'd taken, and shook his head. Hell. He really hadn't discovered very much at all about Magdalena Bondurant's early life. He should probably do some more research. This town had a courthouse. Maybe he'd visit the courthouse and see if there were any legal records he could peruse. How boring. He'd rather argue with Miss Clement some more.

With a grin, Julian set out to find the courthouse. He might even be able to discover the address of one Susanna Clement. Now there was a worthy goal.

The long summer twilight guided Susanna's feet as she moped back to the cemetery that evening after supper. Her mood was unsettled—had been ever since she stormed away from Julian Kittrick earlier in the day.

At supper she'd tried to draw her aunt Winnie out on the subject of Magdalena Bondurant, but Aunt Winnie wouldn't be drawn.

"I don't know why you want to go digging up old scandals, Susanna."

"I want to discover the truth."

Aunt Winnie had sniffed. "The truth is that Magdalena Bondurant is the only skeleton the Bondurant family closet has ever contained, Miss Truth, and the rest of us would just as soon you leave her there."

Susanna had wanted to argue, but didn't. She owed Aunt Winnie a good deal and liked her a lot. She didn't want to upset her. Yet she didn't understand the family's reluctance to discuss Great-Aunt Magdalena, either. As for Susanna, she thought Magdalena was no skeleton; she thought she was wonderful. She also subscribed to Ralph Waldo Emerson's theory that there is properly no history, only biography.

Unfortunately, Magdalena Bondurant's biography was a big, black blank, at least at the end.

And now that wretched journalist, Mr. Julian Kittrick, was planning to create a biography for her. Susanna's heart squinched painfully and her hand bunched into a fist she wished she could swing at his arrogant nose.

She wanted to discover the truth herself—the *real* truth; not some made-up scandal that would titillate the readers of the *Denver Post*. Unfortunately, she hadn't a clue as to how to go about it. Her aunt Winnie was certainly no help. And her uncle Cyrus was even worse. Susanna got the feeling he didn't so much deplore Magdalena's shady character as simply not care. Uncle Cyrus was even more silent than the rest of her Maine kin.

Susanna had found most of these state of Mainers polite, but they certainly weren't as expansive and friendly as the folks back home. She sighed deeply, and reminded herself that this was what she'd craved. She'd longed to experience the civilized East, and now she was doing so. It merely took some getting used to, was all.

Oh, she knew Palmyra, Maine, wasn't New York, New York, but at least it was more settled than New Mexico Territory, which was generally outrageous and totally unfit for a woman of her education and ambition, with its hordes of cowboys and bands of scruffy Indians and roving bandit gangs. Still, she wouldn't have minded if the folks here in Palmyra weren't such an uncommunicative bunch.

She'd wandered to her great-aunt's empty grave by this time, sank down on the boulder she'd deserted earlier in the day, and contemplated matters. They looked pretty grim. She couldn't abide the notion of her great-aunt's memory being tarnished by that brash, unprincipled journalist. Yet unless Susanna herself turned up information to contradict the conclusions Mr. Kittrick was sure to leap to, that looked like what was going to happen.

"Oh, dear," she murmured into the gathering shadows.

An answering sigh from nearby startled her into glancing up. She blinked, certain her eyes were deceiving her. They couldn't possibly be seeing what they were showing her. She rubbed them hard. She stared. She tried to stand, but her legs had turned to water and she couldn't. A scream froze in her throat.

"No," she whispered past the panic surging inside her. "No."

The ghost—it had to be a ghost, because Susanna knew good and well that regular, everyday people weren't transparent—seemed to shrug. The gesture looked self-deprecatory, almost diffident, and Susanna rubbed her eyes again.

She'd gone 'round the bend. Over the edge. Fallen off the deep end. Oh, Lord, what a dismal end to an intelligent woman's life—and she was only twenty-two years old! She spared a moment to feel sorry for herself.

The ghost cleared its throat. Susanna was astonished that a ghost could do such a thing.

"I didn't mean to startle you," it said.

Susanna opened her mouth but couldn't force anything out. She stared at the apparition. It didn't seem to be coming any closer, thank God, but it wasn't going away, either. Whatever would her aunt Winnie write to her parents back home? How could she break the news to them that their only daughter had lost her mind? Tears welled in her eyes at the thought.

The ghost spoke again. *"Please don't be frightened."*

Easy for it to say. Susanna swallowed her terror. At least this figment didn't appear to be threatening her at the moment. What would happen if she turned her back on it? She wondered if she could simply rise and walk away and be troubled no more with spirits. Now she knew what Ebenezer Scrooge must have felt when first faced with Marley's ghost. Scrooge was such a miserable old sinner that she hadn't felt any compassion for him at all until right this minute.

"I'd never have disturbed you if I hadn't overheard your conversation with that dreadful newspaperman this afternoon."

Susanna blinked at the ghost. He'd overheard her conversation with Julian Kittrick? And it had inspired him to appear to her? She wished she'd kept silent earlier in the day if this is what her passionate defense of her great-aunt had wrought.

She said, "Go away. Please." Her voice quivered. It sounded pathetic. She felt pathetic.

The thought occurred to her that if she stared hard enough, this alarming specter would go away, so she did. Maybe it was a trick of the light or an optical illusion occasioned by her own fevered imagination. Not that she had an imagination. And optical illusions didn't speak to one, did they? Oh, dear.

Staring didn't work, so she shut her eyes, hoping that would. Immediately the unpleasant notion struck her that the thing might creep up on her while she wasn't looking, so she opened them again and tried staring at it once more. It didn't move. Oh, sweet heaven, what was she supposed to do now?

It looked to her as if this fellow—if it wasn't a figment—had been flamboyant in life. In an odd—indeed, a ghostly—way, he still was. Although she could see through him, she could yet detect the colors of his translucent garments. The cloak he had flung over his shoulders in a dramatic manner had what she would swear was a red silk lining. Had been a red silk lining. Once. In life. If a cloak could have life.

She shook her head hard, trying to get her thoughts to settle down. Whatever this thing was, it wore a tall black beaver hat, like the kind Susanna had seen in photographs and paintings of Abraham Lincoln.

Perhaps some schoolchildren had rigged up this phantasm as a joke. Maybe they were hiding in the bushes, hoping to amuse themselves by frightening the wits out of visitors to the cemetery. The thought appealed to Susanna, who scanned the area around the apparition, hoping to espy ropes and pulleys. She didn't see any. She also couldn't recall, off the top of her head, of any fabric that would lend itself to such perfect transparency. Maybe it was a new one, recently invented back here in Maine where there were scores of fabric mills. Maybe this was a test effort to see if it worked, although it betokened mighty shady business practices if it was.

"I mean you no harm."

It was too late for that, since it had already scared her out of ten years of her life at least. She scowled at the thing, and feeling the tiniest bit stronger, stood up. Her knees shook.

"Who—what are you?" Again, she remembered Scrooge, and his asking Marley's ghost if it could sit down. Fat lot of good remembering did her now. As much as she enjoyed reading Mr. Dickens's books, she'd just as soon her mind would cease wandering. She might need her wits about her if this thing lunged or did one of the other things ghosts were purported to do.

The Headless Horseman galloped through her brain, and her heart sped up, as if trying to run away from it. This was Ichabod Crane territory if there ever was such a place. Brom Bones. Maybe this was a late-nineteenth-century personification—ghostonification?—of Brom Bones. She didn't see a horse anywhere.

That's only a story, she reminded herself firmly, which didn't help. This thing standing—was it standing?—in front of her wasn't a story. It was a *thing,* and it terrified her.

"I am Danilo, the Gypsy King," the thing said, sounding self-important.

Susanna narrowed her eyes. Danilo, the Gypsy King? Who was he trying to trifle with, anyway? Danilo, the Gypsy King, her foot. She frowned at it. "Go away. You've had your fun. Now go away and leave me alone."

"But—"

From out of nowhere, Susanna's grit returned, propelled by lingering terror. She stamped her foot. "No! You just go away now. You've had your little joke and frightened me quite enough already. I'm tired of your silly, childish prank and don't want to have any more to do with it. Or you. Now *go!*" She pointed in the direction of the forest that abutted the graveyard.

To her utter astonishment, the ghost let out with a wail

of sorrow, collapsed onto a headstone, and began weeping piteously. She gaped at it, wondering what its game was now.

"I knew it," the thing said with a sob. *"I knew I'd make a botch of this in death, as I botched everything in life. Oh, woe! Oh, alas! Oh, alack!"*

Although the words were overly theatrical and made Susanna's sensible nature recoil, his terrible grief seemed genuine. In fact, Susanna had never witnessed such a spectacle of anguish before. She didn't know what to do. Now that the thing's attention had been diverted, she supposed she could run away. Yet, Susanna had never been unkind, and this entity's sorrow touched her.

Because she still didn't trust it, she said, "Stop that." Although she tried to sound firm, her command lacked authority.

The ghost only shook its head and continued weeping. Disconsolate. Susanna understood the meaning of the word now as she never had before. This poor ghost was disconsolate, and its unhappiness made her unhappy. "Here," she said, trying again. "Stop that. There's no need to cry. Please."

It looked up at her. Susanna saw that its transparent face was streaked with transparent tears.

This was no schoolyard prank. The knowledge jarred her. There's no way on the face of this green earth that schoolchildren could have rigged up such a thing.

Her thoughts turned to Julian Kittrick. Was he behind this? It was difficult for her to feature even the clever, care-for-nobody Mr. Kittrick coming up with this sophisticated a prank. Susanna had seen a moving image projected onto a screen when she was in college, but this was too advanced for the technology that had produced that image.

This was—this was a ghost.

Oh, dear. Still unsure of herself, she said, "I beg your pardon if I offended you."

It shook its head. *"I'm used to it."*

"I can imagine you must be." The statement came out sounding more tart than she'd intended, and it produced another wail of melancholy.

"I thought you'd understand," the ghost cried thickly. *"I thought, when I heard you defend Magdalena this afternoon, that if there was anyone alive on the earth who'd understand, it would be you. I should have known better."* The words and the tone in which he said them were as bitter as gall.

Susanna swallowed. She still didn't really believe this. Not really. Although when she thought about it, it made as much sense to find a ghost in a graveyard as to think she'd suddenly lost her mind. She'd never shown a single hint of mental instability before that she could recollect.

Because she didn't fancy being made a fool of and still couldn't quite believe the evidence of her senses, she asked cautiously, "What—what do you mean?"

The ghost stood and took a step—or a waft—toward her. She backed up an equal distance. She didn't want that thing any closer to her than it already was. It stopped, looking aggrieved. Too bad. Susanna wasn't about to relax her guard yet.

"I mean you no harm," it repeated.

"So you've said." Skepticism dripped from her words.

The ghost heaved an enormous sigh. *"Ah, cruel beauty. I should have known."*

"What should you have known?" Was he referring to *her* as a beauty? Or was the beauty to which he referred a generic expression meant to be applied to women in general or, perhaps, the entire human race? She wished she knew, because she'd be flattered if he thought she was pretty, but she didn't feel up to asking.

"I should have known that a relative of Magdalena Bondurant would be as cruel as she was."

Susanna straightened indignantly. "My great-aunt was not cruel! She was a splendid lady endeavoring to serve a glorious cause."

The ghost eyed her caustically. *"Yes. That's what she used to say, too."*

He certainly had a melodramatic way of expressing himself. Susanna tilted her head to one side and studied him. All in all, she did have to admit that he didn't *seem* dangerous. He appeared rather effete, actually.

Not that Susanna knew much about effete men. The only men she'd been exposed to before her train arrived in Maine three weeks ago had been rugged frontiersmen and cowboys. She seen a vicious gang of bank robbers riding away from the scene of their crime once, but that was all. Effete individuals, Susanna supposed, didn't travel west and settle new territories. They stayed where they were, back here in the already settled East, which made sense to her.

"Exactly who are you, and what do you know about Magdalena Bondurant?" she asked, her tone sharp.

If he were a corporeal being, he might be said to have slapped a hand to his breast. As it was, his hand went partially through his ghostly body, and the effect wasn't quite as stirring. If she hadn't still been frightened, Susanna might have giggled.

"Magdalena Bondurant and I were engaged to be married."

Susanna's eyes popped open. "Really?"

He nodded. *"I loved her more than life itself."*

It occurred to her to wonder if his love had contributed to Magdalena's disappearance and his own death in what looked as though it had been his prime, but she couldn't think of a tactful way of asking. After a moment's thought she said cautiously, "Would you be willing to tell me about it?"

He inclined his head in a regal gesture. *"If you are willing to listen. That is why I appeared to you tonight."*

"I'm willing." Actually, now that her terror had abated somewhat, Susanna found herself almost eager. Almost. She still didn't understand this Danilo character, couldn't quite reconcile herself to his being a ghost, and wasn't ready to relax in his presence. She felt compelled to admit, "I don't really believe in ghosts, you know."

He sighed. *"I know."*

"But I'll listen." She didn't add that she'd suddenly decided to listen as the means of discovering exactly what sort of trick was being played on her.

"May I come closer?" he asked.

She hesitated too long for politeness, and he sighed again, more heavily this time. *"Never mind. I'll rest here."* He sank down onto another tombstone, this one a large, flat monument marking the final resting place of a family called Homstead.

"I beg your pardon, Mr. Danilo, but I'm not accustomed to dealing with . . ." She paused, wondering how to phrase her statement without giving offense. Then she decided she might as well be honest. "Ghosts."

"No one is," Danilo said glumly. *"And the name isn't Mr. Danilo. It's Danilo, the Gypsy King. I,"* he added with a dramatic lilt, *"was an actor in life. I have assumed the persona of my greatest role in death."*

Susanna frowned as she racked her brain, trying to recall the name of a play that contained a character named Danilo, the Gypsy King. "Um, what play is that from, Mr.—er—Danilo? I don't seem to remember."

He frowned, too. *"No. You wouldn't, of course. I died before Danilo could join the ranks of such immortal characters as Hamlet or Henry V."*

Susanna refrained from pointing out that Henry V had been a successful, if rather encroaching, English king and might, therefore, have been remembered even without Shakespeare's help. She did say, "How sad," because it seemed appropriate.

Danilo appeared to appreciate her sentiment. He nodded his head in acknowledgment and sighed again. *"Yes. It was terribly sad."* He lifted his head, which had been drooping in a pose of artistic melancholy. *"I was good, you know. I was a brilliant actor and an exceptional playwright. Magdalena's greatest performances were in roles that I created for her."*

Brilliant and exceptional and not exactly modest. Susanna fought a grin and focused on his last statement. "You wrote roles for her?"

He gazed at her for several seconds before saying, *"I loved her."*

His simple words touched Susanna, perhaps because he'd not adorned them with exalted emotions or dramatic inflection. She sighed. How romantic. How sad. How utterly fascinating.

"Er, you must have died not long after she disappeared." She waved her hand in his direction. "I mean, you—you don't look very old." Was that presumptuous? Was it rude? Susanna's curiosity had risen in direct proportion to the slackening of her fright. Even though she still wasn't *quite* sure she believed this fellow was actually a ghost—in fact, a rational part of her mind scoffed at the very notion—she was enchanted by his story.

"Alas, no. I was not old. I am forever the age I was that dark, evil night."

"Um, how old is that?" How rude of her! Still, she seemed unable to suppress her curiosity now that it had been stirred.

"Thirty-five. Thirty-five years old, and in the first flower of the achievement of my talents. Thirty-five years of life, of learning, of observation. I had only begun to bring my gifts to fruition. My creative capacity was burgeoning. My first two plays had been received to almost universal acclaim. A brilliant career lay ahead of me. I was cut down in the very prime of my life. Before I had been given a chance to show the world what lay within my fertile brain."

He almost tapped his head with a finger, but the digit seemed to slide right through his skull. Susanna had the fanciful thought that he'd meant to scratch his brain. She wondered why she couldn't see his internal organs.

She stared at him, rapt. She'd never heard anyone speak about himself with such a lack of modesty. She wondered if all actors were like Danilo, or if he'd been a special case. He'd mentioned a dark and evil night, and she considered asking him how he'd met his end, but she couldn't make herself do it. She guessed he'd tell her if he wanted to.

He looked up abruptly, and Susanna jumped.

"I mean you no harm," he said for what seemed like the hundredth time. *"But you must prevent that young man from blackening the reputation of the finest woman who ever walked the earth."*

The finest woman who ever walked the earth. Susanna, who had forgotten all about why she'd come to the cemetery this evening, cudgeled her brain. "Oh! You mean Magdalena Bondurant."

"Of course that's who I mean. Who did you think I meant?" Danilo sounded peeved.

Susanna took exception to his tone of voice. "Well, I beg your pardon, but I'm not in the habit of meeting ghosts in graveyards. Whatever customs prevail in *Maine,* we don't have such things in New Mexico Territory." At least she hoped they didn't. As interesting as this was, she didn't want it to become a habit, as it was too unnerving.

He sniffed as if he, too, were miffed. *"Believe me, it's no more fun appearing to people than it is being appeared to. It took me hours to find the fortitude. I was bracing myself for a hideous scream, and I have ex-*tremely *sensitive nerves."*

Susanna could have sworn he didn't have any nerves at all after having been staring straight through him for several minutes now, but she didn't argue. Since she wanted the matter cleared up once and for all, she said, "I am not in the habit of screaming, Mr.—what should I call you? I can't call you Danilo."

"Why ever not?" He looked at her as if she'd said something irrational.

"Why *not*? Because it's impolite and unseemly, is why not! Why, we haven't even been properly introduced."

She saw him roll his eyes. She hadn't known ghosts could do that.

"Oh, for heaven's sake. Young women of today are so much more prudish than they were in my day."

"I don't believe that for an instant. In fact, my great-aunt Magdalena even wrote about how stuffy her contemporaries were. Her own family was shocked when she took to the stage."

"You make it sound as if she took to crime," Danilo observed sourly.

"Whatever *you* might think, it was shocking at the time." Susanna lifted her chin. "In fact, it would be shocking today, if I were to do so."

"You? Never!"

Of all the nerve! As much as she knew he was right, still more did Susanna resent him coming right out and saying so. Besides, why should *he* automatically assume she wouldn't take to the stage? She wouldn't, of course, because she was a rotten actress, but he couldn't know that. The only reason *she* knew it was because of the class play she'd been in. A shudder rattled her when she recalled that awful experience. She'd been so scared. And so bad. Susanna wasn't accustomed to failing at the things she attempted, and she hadn't enjoyed the experience one little bit.

"Oh, don't look so angry, Miss Clement. It takes a certain indefinable quality—an ineffable something *—to be a success on the stage. Your great-aunt had it."* He sighed again with exaggerated melancholy and shook his head. *"She had it."*

"I'm sure she did. Her diary indicates she was a woman of rare sensibilities and talent."

"She was."

"That still doesn't solve the problem of what I should call you. Don't you have a last name?"

He scowled at her. *"I began life as Daniel Matteucci,"* he said stiffly.

Susanna brightened. "What an interesting name, Mr.—Matteucci, was it?"

"Yes." It didn't sound as though Danilo shared her enthusiasm for his surname.

"It sounds foreign."

He slanted her an exasperated glance. *"All persons living in these United States and its territories—barring the Indians—are foreign, if it comes to that."*

"I suppose so. But where is the surname Matteucci from?"

"Italy."

Italy. Sunny Italy. Land of many feudal—and feuding, if all Susanna'd read about them was true—states. Land of grapes and olives and great Renaissance artists and hot, passionate, Latin blood. Brooding, dangerous, dark-eyed men. Beautiful, sloe-eyed women. Spaghetti. Susanna had eaten spaghetti once. It had seemed deliciously, daringly exotic to her.

"Are you from Italy?"

He shook his head. *"New York City."*

"Oh." That didn't sound anywhere near as romantic as Italy. Still, she could detect an Italianate air about Danilo now that she knew it was there. He'd obviously had dark hair and eyes when he was alive, and she thought she detected a hint of olive in his complexion, although it was difficult to tell, what with being able to see trees, bushes, and headstones through it.

"Were your parents from Italy?"

He nodded.

"Can you say something in Italian to me?"

He glared at her, and she guessed she'd asked the wrong thing. Evidently Mr. Matteucci wasn't interested in reliving his youth. She cleared her throat. "Er, so what is it you want me to do? Exactly."

"I want you to discover the Truth." He made *truth* sound like the Holy Grail.

Susanna knitted her brows. "I'd like to do that, Mr. Matteucci. In fact, that was one of my primary reasons for visiting Maine this summer. I *want* to discover the truth. But I don't know how to do it." Injustice rose in her breast and flooded her with indignation. "That awful man is going to make up something scandalous if I can't, though."

She saw him nod. *"Exactly. That's why you, who believes in the goodness of my* cara, *must discover the truth first."*

Feeling pressured and more than a little exasperated, Susanna said, "Yes, yes, that's all well and good, but *how*? *How* am I supposed to discover the truth? It all happened so long ago, and nobody's around who remembers any longer. Even if people who were young then are still alive, wouldn't somebody have said something before now if they knew anything?"

"Not necessarily."

Recalling her own frustration with trying to draw her Maine relatives out on the subject of Magdalena, Susanna grumbled. "You're right. They're not exactly chatty here, are they."

"No, they're not. And taciturnity is not the only roadblock to the truth, either."

Danilo glowered ominously, and Susanna had the feeling he knew more than he'd divulged so far. She clasped her hands to her bosom. "You know something! You have a lead for me!"

"Perhaps."

"Well, then, *tell* me! Stop being coy, for heaven's sake!"

He eyed her with disapproval. *"Some people,"* he said scathingly, *"have no flair."*

"Oh, bother flair! I don't care about high drama. I care about my great-aunt's good name."

It didn't look to Susanna as though Danilo appreciated her commonsensical attitude. Too bad. She wanted to get to the bottom of Magdalena Bondurant's disappearance, not waste time on theatrics.

"I believe," he said slowly, as if savoring the moment and wanting to draw it out, *"that you could do much worse than to look up the descendants of a beastly man named Philip Sedgewick*. That *man knew more than he ever told anyone about Magdalena's disappearance. I believe this latest abomination of a Sedgewick is named Phineas."*

"Really? There was a Philip Sedgewick involved in all this?" Having just been given her first solid lead, Susanna was almost breathless with excitement.

Danilo nodded. *"He was a suitor for her hand, but she wouldn't have him. He was a miser and a Philistine. He'd have made her leave the stage if she'd favored his suit, but she didn't. She wanted me."*

"What makes you think he'd know anything?"

Staring off into the forest, which was fast getting dark, Danilo muttered blackly, *"Because I followed him one dark and stormy night. I know he was involved somehow in her disappearance."*

Susanna chewed that tidbit over for a moment or two. "If you're so sure about it, why didn't you ask him yourself forty years ago?"

Danilo's expression turned murderous. If Susanna weren't already used to him, she'd have been frightened. *"Because he died the same night I did. Two days after Magdalena disappeared."*

Then, to the accompaniment of Susanna's gasp of astonishment and in a thrilling poof that left her blinking, Danilo disappeared.

Chapter Three

Something. No. Nothing. But . . . Yes. Something. Or someone. Caring. Loving. Oh, please, please, come to me! Find me. Set me free.

Alone. So, so alone. Utterly alone. Frozen. Trapped. Imprisoned. Oh, please. Please. Please . . .

Susanna Clement was not a shy girl. Having taken to heart the teachings of her idol, Mrs. Susan B. Anthony, she knew that if women expected to take their rightful places in the world, they couldn't be timid about demanding their rights. She therefore did not flinch from her purpose this morning, but boldly walked down the path to Mr. Phineas G. Sedgewick's house, trod up the steps, and rapped on the door with vigor and purpose.

A sour-looking housekeeper opened the door and scowled at her. Undaunted, Susanna asked in a firm voice, "May I please see Mr. Sedgewick?"

The older woman looked as if she'd been eating pickles for breakfast. Finally she said, "The old sinner has somebody else with him right now."

The old sinner? My goodness. Although the woman's words didn't exactly warm Susanna's heart, she smiled brightly. "I shall be happy to wait until he is free, thank you."

"Free?" The housekeeper laughed unpleasantly. "Fat chance."

"Er, may I wait for him?"

Because she didn't want the door shut in her face, Susanna took a brash step toward the housekeeper, who frowned at her but backed up, as Susanna had expected she would. She'd learned during her suffragist days in college that people didn't expect one to behave with intrepidity and that, when one did, they generally fell back. It was battle strategy, and Susanna had learned it well. It had even gotten her arrested. Although she'd never said so to her parents, she accounted her brief stint in jail, uncomfortable as it had been, as one of the highlights of her life.

"May I wait here in the hallway?" she asked with a friendly smile.

The older woman looked her up and down and scowled. "I suppose so." The housekeeper gave her one last hard look and waddled off again.

The faint aroma of baking bread assaulted Susanna's senses and made her mouth water. There was nothing quite as wonderful as the smell of bread baking. She lifted her head and breathed deeply—and almost choked to death.

Good heavens! That voice! Clearly, from down the hall, she recognized that voice. Fury rose in her. Her brow furrowed. Her lips pursed, in spite of her mother's wrinkles.

How dare he!

Julian Kittrick, that vile, despicable, *wicked* man, had stolen the march on her! He'd somehow discovered Phineas Sedgewick's connection to Magdalena Bondurant—something even Susanna hadn't known about until last night—and had sneaked in here like the snake he was, ahead of her. And he was undoubtedly, right this minute, prying precious information out of the old man—information he planned to keep to himself, the deceitful fiend.

Well, he wouldn't get away with it. Following the sound of those voices, Susanna marched down the hall to a closed door and shoved it open as if she belonged there. Two men—an old, mean-looking one and a young, diabolically handsome one—gave starts of surprise and turned to see who had invaded their privacy.

"You foul *fiend*!" Susanna cried, glaring at Julian and ignoring the other man.

To her fury, a delighted grin replaced Julian's initial expression of surprise. "Miss Clement!"

"Who the devil are you, and what the devil do you mean by barging into my library?"

Susanna turned on the codger who'd snarled the question, and her fury dissipated. Oh, dear. She'd forgotten this was his house. After clearing her throat, she decided to continue as she'd begun. She walked boldly over to him and held out her hand.

"I am Miss Susanna Clement. I'm very pleased to meet you, Mr. Sedgewick. It *is* Mr. Sedgewick?" She'd seen her favorite teacher, Miss Clara Mae Amberly, speak very much like this to people whom she was attempting to intimidate into compliance. It didn't work with Mr. Sedgewick, who eyed her hand as if it were a repellent serpent.

"What the devil do you mean, walking in on us like that, girl? Didn't your mother teach you any manners?"

Susanna stiffened. "I beg your pardon, Mr. Sedgewick, but I believe this gentleman is encroaching into my own family's business, and I am here to see that he doesn't get away with it."

"You are, are you?" Sedgewick looked her up and down with the same contempt he might display for a grubby schoolchild.

Susanna tried to maintain a demeanor of calm authority, but it was a struggle.

"I'm not either encroaching."

At Julian's words, she turned to frown at him. He

shrugged and continued to grin as if she were providing the best show he'd seen in ages. Which was probably true, blast him.

"Well, I'm not, you know," he continued. "I'm here for a story. It's my job, and I aim to do it right. This is research." He shot a glance around the library.

"*Right,* according to you, is raking up old scandals and making up new ones when you can't find the truth," Susanna said flatly. "*I* aim to unearth the truth."

Phineas Sedgewick's irritated glance shot back and forth between Susanna and Julian. "I don't care what either one of you aims to do, as long as you do it somewhere besides my library. I allowed you in this morning, young man, because you said you could pay me for information. What do *you* have to offer, girl? I don't care who looks at a bunch of dusty old family papers as long as they pay me for the privilege." He pointed at Susanna with a gnarled, yellowish finger.

Susanna swallowed. Pay? Mr. Kittrick was going to *pay* this horrid monster for information? About her own great-aunt? Susanna's heart seemed to shrivel in her chest. "Well, I—I . . ." She swallowed again. "I don't know how much money I can come up with, sir, but—"

"Fine." Sedgewick turned away as if she held no further interest for him, and confronted Julian. "All right, young man. I don't hold with people rummaging around in other people's papers, but since you say you can pay whatever I aim to charge, I reckon it'll be worth my while. Don't know what you expect to find in the Sedgewick family archives about that Bondurant female, but you can go through them to your heart's content for a dollar an hour."

A dollar an hour? Susanna, who had been trying to figure out how she could stretch her allowance to pay this miserable old goat a dollar or two for the privilege of searching through his family papers, gulped audibly.

Julian had the audacity to wink at her. Indignation all but swallowed her whole. The beast! The scoundrel! The devil! With the entire resources of the *Denver Post* at his disposal, he was going to outmaneuver her yet. It wasn't fair.

"Wait," she said, unwilling to let these two men best her. "I'll have to check into the financial arrangements, but I may be able to come up with something."

That was a flat-out lie, but she wasn't about to give up without a fight. She ignored Julian's wicked expression and concentrated on holding Mr. Sedgewick's eye. She refused to back down in the face of his overt skepticism. At last he looked away first.

"Oh, very well. Just don't come back unless you have the money, because I'm not running a charity here."

She felt like expelling a breath of relief, but didn't for fear Julian would know she'd been faking. Not that he didn't know it already, from the look of him. Susanna could recall few times in her life when she'd been more offended by a man's appearance. Not only was he more handsome than a man had any right to be, but he looked as if it was all he could do to keep from bursting into shouts of laughter.

The transaction Julian had been working out with Mr. Sedgewick didn't take too many more minutes. Susanna watched, silent, while Sedgewick showed Julian where his research was to begin.

"There's some more stuff in the attic from around the same time, I think. I'll have Mrs. Glick bring the boxes down and set 'em on the table over there." Sedgewick sounded as though he considered this a major concession and a terrible inconvenience. "I expect you can rummage through them all you want there."

"Thank you very much, Mr. Sedgewick."

Susanna was surprised that Julian Kittrick could sound so gracious.

"May I open the curtains over there so I can read the papers better?"

Sedgewick looked at the curtains and back at the table. Then he eyed Julian. "A dollar an hour ain't going to pay to replace the carpet if it fades, you know." His voice held an edge of mistrust, as if he suspected Julian of wanting to ruin his household belongings for some fell purpose beyond his present understanding.

Susanna glanced down at the carpet. It looked as if it hadn't been replaced for a hundred years or more. She repressed a chuff of indignation. She had no business being indignant for Julian Kittrick's sake. A dollar an hour, indeed.

"I'm sure it won't take me so long to go through everything that the sunlight will fade the carpets, Mr. Sedgewick."

How that disreputable newspaperman could remain sanguine in the face of Sedgewick's miserly suspicion was a mystery to Susanna. If it had been anyone but Julian Kittrick displaying such admirable forbearance, she might have been impressed. As it was, she decided his attitude bespoke indifference, and she despised him for it.

Her dislike did not prevent her from following him out of Sedgewick's house, however, or from pursuing him down the path toward the road.

"Wait!" she called as she hurried to catch up with him. The only reason she had to do so was that *she,* unlike Julian, had paused at the door to shake Mr. Sedgewick's hand and thank him for his time and trouble. Sedgewick hadn't appreciated her courtesy, but had only grumbled out a dour, "Humph," and slammed the door in her face. Some people were simply too rude for words.

Julian pretended not to hear her. He was whistling a music-hall tune—which figured. He was undoubtedly a dissolute drunkard who whiled away his evenings at such tawdry entertainments.

"Wait!" she called again, running after him. Thank goodness Miss Amberly had drummed into her head the idiocy of lacing her corset tightly or she'd probably have fainted from lack of air.

As it was, she was puffing hard by the time she finally reached out and grabbed his coattail. Such behavior was shocking but Susanna was angry, and she didn't think

Mr. Kittrick deserved any consideration from her. She almost fell on her face when he kept walking for another pace or two and her arm jerked with the strain.

When he turned, his eyebrows had lifted in mock surprise, and he was looking down at her as if he'd only that moment realized she'd been pursuing him. She pressed a hand to her heart because it was racing and she was having a hard time catching her breath. She dropped her hand when she realized he was gazing at her bosom.

She wanted to shriek at him for being rude and horrid and having more money at his disposal than anyone with a modicum of respectability ought to have. But since she was out of breath, she didn't. Besides, she could think of only one way to profit by the knowledge he was sure to find at that ghastly Mr. Sedgewick's house, and it didn't include riling Julian Kittrick. She even managed not to frown.

"Did you wish to speak to me, Miss Clement?" His tone was cool and polite, as if he didn't already know precisely what she wanted. It made her want to slap his insolent face.

"Yes," she said with a gasp. "Yes."

He smiled down at her with the expression an indulgent parent might use on a child who'd done something amusing. She considered stomping on his fancy, highly polished shoes, but rejected the notion. She needed his cooperation, and she sure wouldn't get it that way.

Oh, my, she wished she could catch her breath! In New Mexico she generally went about her daily activities without any corset at all. Since she was summering in the civilized East, she'd been donning the instrument of torture every morning. Now she wished she hadn't been such a slave to convention, since it was constricting her middle and making the recovery of normal breathing difficult.

"I'm all ears, Miss Clement."

Actually this wasn't true. His ears were quite as handsome as the rest of him. Susanna wished she hadn't noticed. "May I walk along with you?" she asked, still fighting for breath.

His right eyebrow arched ironically. "Why, I don't believe I've ever received quite such an—interesting— offer, Miss Clement. I'd be delighted to have your company, as long as you don't expect me to run a footrace with you." He laughed.

The cad! His reference to her having galloped after him infuriated Susanna. A gentleman would have pretended not to notice. A *true* gentleman would have negated the necessity of her having to undertake such an undignified pursuit in the first place. She endeavored to ignore her own anger because she needed his cooperation. That knowledge alone galled her.

She pasted on a smile that she hoped didn't betray her inner turmoil. "Thank you, Mr. Kittrick."

"You're welcome, Miss Clement."

He resumed whistling as they continued down the road. As intent as she was on bending this man to her will, Susanna couldn't help but glance around with interest. The scenery here in Maine was so different from what she was used to in the territory that it might have been part of a different country altogether. A different planet, even.

The path under their feet this fine July morning was strewn with leaves left over from autumns past. The forest rose on either side of them. Branches met over their heads, creating the effect that they were walking through a tunnel. The words *into the woods* reverberated in Susanna's head. If she didn't know better, she'd have supposed this road would lead them into a deep, primeval forest where no man had ventured before them. She did know better, however. This road led through a stretch of woods and emptied out onto a village lane that crossed it at the other end. It seemed much too prosaic an end to such a romantic and lovely walk.

The scenery was beautiful, though, and brought snippets of fairy tales to Susanna's mind. She thought of Hansel and Gretel, hand in hand, walking into the woods all unsuspecting of the terrors awaiting them there. Witches. Ovens. Goose bones. Children fashioned from gingerbread.

She frowned and decided she didn't need to think about grim—or, rather, Grimm—fairy tales. One overly theatrical ghost in the Spring Hill Cemetery was quite enough for her; she'd leave witches to others and concentrate instead on the beauty surrounding her.

A moist, earthen smell with which she was unfamiliar, living as she did in the bone-dry, dusty plains of southeastern New Mexico Territory, kissed her nostrils. When her breathing returned to normal, she sniffed deeply of the fresh, damp smell. It was glorious.

Wagons had rutted the road on both sides, but grass grew in the middle. She and Julian kept to the ruts, which were flat and as smooth as a paved road. She wondered how many years it had taken for wagon wheels to so thoroughly pack the earth thus. European immigrants had lived in this part of Maine for two hundred years and more. The knowledge infused her with a sense of awe. The earliest white settlers had begun arriving in Artesia fewer than fifty years ago. These Palmyra woods were her history, and they gave her a feeling bordering on reverence.

As she glanced into the forest, she saw ferns growing under the leafy trees. She'd never seen a fern until she came to Maine. Aunt Winnie had cooked some of the sprouts for supper last evening, calling them fiddleheads. They'd been delicious. Until she visited her eastern kin, Susanna hadn't known one could eat ferns.

Her aunt and uncle had taken her to what they had referred to as a pond last week, where she'd donned her voluminous bathing costume and swum happily for hours. The pond was a body of water so large that it had looked like an ocean to Susanna—not that she'd ever seen an ocean, either, until this visit. But in New Mexico Territory, anything larger than a bathtub was a lake. Here in Maine that enormous expanse of water had been a mere pond. It was difficult for Susanna to conceive of how much water it would take to keep that "pond" filled year-round, or to keep this much vegetation green.

And then, after Susanna and Uncle Cyrus had become tired from swimming, they'd dined on lobsters and clams, two more foods she'd never tasted before and wished she could find in the territory. Aunt Winnie had told her about how sometimes the neighbors would all get together for what she called a clambake, and Susanna thought it sounded like ever so much fun. Rather like what a barbecue would be back home in New Mexico, only with shellfish and corn and people who talked funny. She sighed wistfully.

"Anything the matter, Miss Clement?"

She looked up to find Julian Kittrick grinning at her, as if he found her an object of fun. She'd forgotten all about him. Although his expression and the sarcastic lilt in his voice sparked her irritation, she chose not to react. She needed him, more's the pity.

"I was enjoying the scenery, Mr. Kittrick. I find it charming. It's very different from what I'm used to and I think it's beautiful."

He looked around, too. "Yeah. It is pretty."

It was a beginning. Endeavoring to sound interested, Susanna said, "I understand Denver is a lovely place, too. It's in the mountains, isn't it?"

"Sort of."

Hmmm. An uninspiring response for a man who made his living by the written word. Susanna deplored his reserve, but she didn't give up. "Is there this much greenery there?"

He squinted down at her, as if he suspected her of ulterior motives—which she had, although she didn't want him to know it. To hide her intentions, she gave him the smile that used to make Billy Poe, back home in Artesia, buy her ice-cream sodas. Billy was sweet on her, in spite of what some people stigmatized as her prickly disposition. *Billy* said he thought she was beautiful. Not that there was much to choose from in Artesia by way of beauty, but it was a comment she selected to consider now in order to bolster her courage.

Her smile didn't work the same way with the wretched Mr. Kittrick as it had with Billy Poe. Julian's grin only broadened, as if he were on to her. Susanna maintained her sweet smile in spite of his obvious doubt. *Blast* him!

"Yeah, I reckon it's this green in Denver. But the trees are different. It's a lot rockier back there. Quite a bit more rugged. This is—pretty."

It sounded to Susanna as if the admission came out reluctantly. She cleared her throat and tried once more. "Er, have you ever visited back East before, Mr. Kittrick?"

He didn't answer immediately, but stuffed his hands in his pockets. Susanna could swear his shoulders hunched over a little bit, but he straightened at once and she thought it might have been her imagination.

"Yeah."

"In pursuit of a story?"

Another pause. Another possible hunch. "No. I was born back here."

"Oh? Are you from Maine originally?"

He looked around, as if suddenly fascinated by the scenery. "New York."

"My goodness." Susanna would give her eyes to see New York—except that would defeat the purpose. She'd love to visit New York, though. It was the center of culture and civilization in the United States, for heaven's sake; unlike New Mexico Territory, which seemed to be the center for everything depraved and uncouth. Unless that was Denver. "Um, what part of New York, Mr. Kittrick?"

His grin had vanished. He appeared to be annoyed when he glanced down at her this time. "Nosy bit of goods, aren't you?"

Susanna gasped. "Well, I like that! Why, you—"

She remembered her purpose in time to clip her assessment of his character and morals short. She sucked in a deep breath and clamped her teeth together. When she'd regained her composure, if not her temper, she said sweetly, "I'm only trying to get to know you better, Mr. Kittrick. After all, *I* am interested in investigative journalism, too." That wasn't much of a lie, she decided. Even if it was, a prevarication in the pursuit of honor could be tolerated. At least she hoped it could.

"I'm from New York City, Miss Clement. The ugly part. The part where the poor people live. It's not pretty like this where I come from, no."

His words and the bitterness with which he pronounced them surprised her. She glanced up and discovered that he was looking at the forest surrounding them, too, and seemed as taken with it as she. She didn't want to feel anything approaching compassion or empathy for him, and she resented her sympathetic reaction to his announcement almost as much as she resented his evident appreciation of nature's work. She also didn't know what to say.

"It's very nice here," he continued, his tone softer. "Much prettier than New York City. I suppose you could even call it beautiful."

"Yes. Yes, it is." She hoped her reluctance to agree with anything he had to say didn't come across in her tone. She *needed* him.

Julian stopped walking and drew his hands out of his pockets. He continued to peer around, so Susanna, unsure what this new development meant, did likewise.

Birds sang from the treetops. She saw a small tortoise at the edge of the road, waddling into the woods. Woodland creatures scuttled here and there; she could hear them, although they weren't bold enough come out into the open. She'd heard that moose lived in these woods. And cougars. And bears. But she didn't want to think about those kinds of creatures. A prickling at the back of her neck made her glance up. Julian Kittrick was gazing at her intently.

His wicked grin warned her. "I don't bite, Miss Clement, whatever you might think. I'm here after a story. I'm sorry if you don't approve, but there you go.

Whatever purpose you had in chasing me down this morning, I'm not going to give up my story.''

Here it was: He'd cottoned on to her purpose in seeking his company, and had just declared war. Now it was her turn. She could return his volley or wave a white flag in surrender. What to do, what to do . . .

Her lips pursed, and she relaxed them with effort. "It's not merely a story, Mr. Kittrick. It's the story of my own great-aunt, and, well, I fear that you do not mean to do right by her memory.''

"Now, now, we don't know that. For a little while I'm only going to be doing a bit of research. Neither of us knows what that research will turn up.''

This was the time. It was now or never. She had to ask for his help. It galled her to beg, but she'd do it for the sake of Magdalena Bondurant. And Danilo, the man who'd loved her. "Well, then, if you won't be deterred from pursuing this story, let me help you. Please, Mr. Kittrick. I'm sure I can be of use to you.''

His eyes widened for a moment before he broke into a perfectly evil smile. "I'm sure you can, Miss Clement, but not in the way you think.''

"Oh!'' Now, what in the name of Glory did he mean by that? Nothing good, she feared.

She'd never before seen anyone who could appear to lounge in the middle of a beaten path in the middle of the woods, but lounge he did. He looked her up and down in a way that made her face heat up and gave her a very uncomfortable feeling.

"You're not bad-looking for a moralist, you know that?''

Through lips that were so stiff they barely moved, Susanna, who had only moments before been thinking about Billy Poe's assessment of her putative beauty, said, "No. I didn't know that.''

"Well, it's true.'' He tilted his head back and watched her through slitted eyes. "I might be willing to let you help me, Miss Clement.''

Her heart soared in spite of her distaste for his attitude.

"What'll you give me if I do?"

That same heart crashed at her feet.

She felt like a pure fool when she felt tears burn her eyes. She wouldn't allow this awful man to make her cry. She wouldn't. She looked away from him, into the woods again, swallowed hard, and blinked to keep her tears contained. Blast it! Blast *him*! Why did he have to come here and try to spoil everything with his newspaper and his money?

A finger caressed her cheek, and she uttered a sharp shriek, then blushed hotly.

"I didn't mean to make you cry, Miss Clement."

No honey was sweeter than his tone of voice. It drizzled into Susanna's brain, and her momentary fit of weakness vanished in a flash of pure rage.

"I'm not crying!"

"Of course you're not," he said gently.

His finger worked its way to her chin and nudged her head up. The devil take him! He was the most handsome man Susanna had ever seen. She knew good and well that he was accustomed to bending unsuspecting females to his will. Miss Amberly had told her often enough about the vile ways of men. Well, by Jupiter, he'd learn a lesson from Susanna Clement!

"I must say I find your insistence upon discovering scandals off-putting, however, particularly since the scandals you're trying to discover in this case affect my family."

"If there's a scandal, Miss Clement, it's forty years old. That shouldn't bother anyone too much at this point."

Forgetting herself and her determination to soften this man's hard heart, Susanna threw out her arms and cried, "But there *isn't* a scandal! My great-aunt was an honorable woman. A *noble* woman!"

His finger dropped, leaving a cold spot where the

breeze licked Susanna's chin. He shrugged. "In that case you have nothing to worry about."

"Nothing to worry about? I have *you* to worry about! An unscrupulous journalist who works for a sensational newspaper, who's just *longing* to rake up dirt about my relative! And to make it up if you can't find any! Ohhhh!"

"Nonsense. My aim is to uncover the truth. Nothing more than that. Your great-aunt's story is interesting. I'm sure the good folks in Denver will be fascinated by it."

"I don't believe you."

"Why not? I think the tale of a beautiful Yankee actress who worked with the abolitionists until she was overcome by greed, stole a fortune in jewels, and vanished as if into thin air with them will make a great story."

"She didn't!"

"How do you know?"

His nonchalant shrug coupled with his gorgeous grin sent her over the edge. She threw caution to the wind. "How *dare* you! You're a scoundrel! You're interested in her story only if it turns out to be lurid. You're nothing but a weasel, Mr. Kittrick! A weasel and a leech. You don't want me to help you because you're afraid I *will* find information vindicating Magdalena Bondurant! You're afraid I'll discover the truth, and then you won't be able to blacken her name! Why, I'd wager any amount of money that if you found something indicating Magdalena Bondurant was a saint on earth, you'd burn it and make up a filthy scandal instead, because a scandal would *sell,* and no one wants to read about goodness and right and nobility and—and—oh, you simply *infuriate* me!"

Too enraged for more words, Susanna whirled around, crossed her arms over her breasts, and fumed.

Susanna Clement's accusation kicked Julian in the guts like an army mule. Make up a story? He, Julian

Kittrick? For sensation's sake? For the sake of the *Denver Post*'s readership? And sacrifice the truth. *He?* He'd sooner have the skin flayed from his back and then be crucified upside down, like St. Peter.

"Miss Clement," he ground out, furious, "I can take a lot of guff from people, especially from women, since they're such experts at dishing it out, but *nobody* disparages my journalistic ethics. Nobody!"

She whirled to confront him again. Her face was red with anger, and her eyes looked like red-hot copper pennies, burning with rage. She was a tidy bundle, Miss Susanna Clement, but she was spitting mad now.

So was Julian. She'd touched him on his most sensitive spot. For years—decades—he'd struggled to overcome his past. And he'd done it, dammit! He was no longer the scruffy street urchin who used to cadge pennies from unsuspecting passersby on the filthy streets of the East Side slum where he'd been abandoned. He was no longer the little boy who hadn't known the difference between right and wrong but only whether his belly cramped with hunger.

Ever since Father Patrick had plucked him out of the gutter in his sixth year and recognized that Julian possessed a brain and a creative streak under his layers of filth and ignorance, Julian had been striving to better himself. Against all odds, he'd done it. He'd graduated from school and gone to college. He'd worked his way across the vastness of the growing United States, and he'd been offered a job—because he was *good,* dammit—with the *Denver Post*.

And now this female—this chit of a foul-tempered bluestocking shrew—had the audacity to call his integrity into question. Integrity he'd learned the hard way. Integrity he valued more than life itself.

Julian owed Father Patrick his best, and while there was breath in his body, he'd give it. Seething, he repeated, "*Nobody* questions my integrity."

"*I* do!" she all but shrieked at him. "*I* call your journalistic integrity into question! You're *trying* to blacken my great-aunt's name. You're trying to do that, Mr. Kittrick! You're not looking for the truth! You're looking for disgrace! Dishonor! Shame! You won't be satisfied until you can make up something that will show the world that Magdalena Bondurant was a trollop and a thief!''

''What if she was? What then, Miss Clement? If I discover that she was a thief, what do you want me to do? Hide the truth?''

''No! You *won't* discover that, because she wasn't, and you can't!''

''How do you know?''

''Because I *know*!''

''Folderol!''

''It's *not* folderol! You only hope it is because that dreadful *rag* you work for feeds on sensation like a guttersnipe feeds on rubbish. I know all about those kinds of newspapers, Mr. Kittrick. They grow fat on other people's tragedies and furnish titillation to their reading public, and the truth be hanged!''

Julian couldn't deny the first part of her observation. He could, however, clear up the latter part. ''The *Denver Post* may print news that's of interest to the public, Miss Clement, and it may print notorious stories that other newspapers shy away from—which I call censorship, whatever you might choose to call it—but it's honest scandal! We do not make up the stories we print!''

''I don't believe you!''

He leaned over, planted his fists on his hips, and looked her straight in the eye. ''So now you're calling me a liar. Is there anything else you'd like to say to besmirch my character, Miss Clement? Please! Feel free. Want to accuse me of—of murder? Blackmail? Embezzlement? Rapine? Arson? Go ahead. Evidently your puritanical moral rectitude doesn't flinch from reviling people you don't know as long as your damned great-aunt's reputation remains spotless.'' He straightened again. ''Not that it *is* spotless. Her name's already as shady as that forest over there.''

"Oh! Oh! You—"

Apparently she could think of nothing bad enough to say to him. She looked like she wanted to throw something. Or hit him. He felt exactly the same way about her. He turned and stomped down the road for several paces, away from her. Then he turned and stomped back again. He couldn't remember the last time he'd been this angry.

What made him really mad was that, until she began insisting that he was lower than the slimiest snake, Julian had actually liked her. Sure, she was a Puritan. Sure, she was stiff-necked and stuffy. But she was really pretty, and she had seemed to have a brain in that head of hers somewhere. At first he'd thought she was honorable, even if she seemed misguided. He wasn't so sure about that any longer, damn her.

When he'd first seen her sitting in that graveyard, studying Magdalena Bondurant's headstone, his reaction to her had been immediate—and physical. He hadn't realized she was a bluestocking suffragist and a harpy at the time.

Unfortunately, the physical attraction remained. Even now, when he wanted to wring her neck, he'd as soon do it in bed, naked. It made him almost as mad as she did.

They'd both been breathing hard for several moments, trying to get their rampaging emotions under control. Julian was still in a temper when Susanna spoke into the fulminating atmosphere.

"I beg your pardon."

Her words surprised him. He glowered down at her. She didn't look contrite. He didn't detect even one tiny, itsy-bitsy ounce of contrition in her expression. She looked instead as if she still wanted to batter him to death.

Nevertheless, as he watched, she took a deep breath—which thrust her bosom out in an extremely appealing way—and used it to repeat, "I beg your pardon. I have no proof of my accusations against you or your newspaper.''

Well, what do you know? That took the wind out of his sails. He relaxed slightly, pushed his straw hat back on his head, cocked his head to one side, and wasn't sure what to say.

Her expression intensified. Her big, beautiful brown eyes peered up at him with the passion of a crusader. ''But, *please,* Mr. Kittrick. *Please* let me help you. I know I can be of use to you in your research.''

He considered her closely for a moment. She started wringing her hands. He narrowed his eyes. ''If I let you help, you have to *help.* Not just pay attention to the material in your great-aunt's favor and throw the rest away.''

She bowed her head. ''I know. I will.''

He sensed she meant it. He still had a feeling she was honest, whatever else she was.

''If we find something that impugns her name, I'll print it. You have to understand that, or I won't let you anywhere near my sources.''

She nodded. ''I know.''

For several tense moments, he considered her request. Then he decided *Aw, what the hell.*

''All right, Miss Clement. I guess I have myself an assistant.''

She gave a leap of joy and threw her arms in the air. ''Oh, *thank* you, Mr. Kittrick!''

For the barest second or two, he thought she was going to kiss him. He was disappointed when she didn't.

Chapter Four

"And we're going to begin searching through his old family papers tomorrow." Susanna, too full of nervous excitement to sit still, paced the cemetery. She shot glances over her shoulder at the ghost who drooped on Magdalena Bondurant's headstone, looking discouraged.

"Search carefully," he advised gloomily. *"I don't know this Sedgewick, but if he's anything like his late uncle, he's a miser and a cad. And quite possibly worse."*

Susanna stopped pacing and stared at him, fascinated. "Really?"

"Really."

"Oh, this is so exciting!" With renewed vigor she resumed marching among the headstones.

"You think so, do you?"

"Indeed, I do! Just think, Mr. Matteucci, we may uncover the one piece of evidence that will clear Magdalena Bondurant's name forever. We may even discover what happened to her!"

Danilo sighed heavily. *"I hope you do."*

"So do I."

"There's something wrong with the whole thing."

He threw his arms out, making his cape flutter like a bird's wings. The gesture was very effective, and Susanna appreciated it. "You can say that again."

"No. I mean, if she's dead, where is her spirit? I don't understand why we haven't made contact here, on the other side."

Susanna contemplated that for a moment. "Er, I don't know much about spirits. Do they all wander?" Not that she'd ever thought much about it since, until Danilo, she hadn't believed in ghosts.

He shrugged. *"No, not all of us. That blasted Sedgewick, whom I know is dead, hasn't wandered anywhere near me, for example. Of course, he probably wouldn't dare. Still, Magdalena and I loved each other, Miss Clement. You'd think we'd have met up in this dimension—or that I'd have found her if she was still alive. I fear something sinister may have happened to her."*

"Sinister?"

"Sinister." Danilo's frown lengthened.

Susanna didn't like the sound of that, and her pacing intensified. The only thing they could hear for several minutes after that was the gentle evening breeze sloughing through the boughs over their heads and the crunch, crunch, crunch of her nervous footsteps.

After some little time Danilo said sourly, *"You're walking on my grave."*

Susanna stopped striding and glanced down at her feet. Then she saw the small headstone engraved *Danilo, the Gypsy King. Actor and Playwright.* "Oh, I beg your pardon." She took a couple of steps sideways. "It's hard to tell sometimes, you know."

Danilo humphed.

Out of curiosity, she asked, "Who placed the stone there?"

"A theatrical friend and fellow actor. He appreciated me, if no one else did."

"Oh, I'm sure others appreciated you."

Danilo gave out another grouchy humph. *"You might look through old newspaper clippings, too. They won't tell you much, but perhaps you can piece together enough information that you can determine where to investigate next."*

"Good idea." She stared hard at the ghost for a moment. "You know, Mr. Matteucci, you seem awfully glum this evening. Aren't you glad that Mr. Kittrick and I are finally doing what you had hoped somebody would do one day? Aren't you eager to discover what happened to Magdalena?"

He let out another sigh, even deeper than his last several. *"I suppose so."*

A little peeved, Susanna said, "Well, you don't seem very enthusiastic."

He threw out his arms in another dramatic gesture. *"I don't mean to seem discouraging, Miss Clement. It's only—it's only that it's been so long, and I fear you may meet with failure. If you fail, that man will make up something evil about Magdalena, and her name will be forever besmirched."*

Susanna took a deep breath. "Yes. I know. That's exactly why I made Mr. Kittrick let me help him."

"Humph."

Susanna tried to maintain an air of gravity, but it didn't last long. Her insides bubbled like champagne in a glass. She'd never felt this elated. She couldn't quite account for it either because, while it was true she wanted to keep an eye on Julian Kittrick and make sure he didn't ignore—or, worse, destroy—any evidence that might clear her great-aunt's name once and for all, she had a feeling her elation couldn't be accounted for on solely journalistic reasons. Deep down in her heart, she knew that Julian Kittrick himself played a role in her excitement.

Apparently Danilo was worried about that as well. He peered up at her, a frown on his face. *"Don't let that journalist turn your head, Miss Clement. He's got a pretty face, but he has no heart.''*

Danilo's words struck very close to her own innermost fears, and Susanna stopped pacing and glared at him. "I'd never!"

He humphed again.

Although Susanna raced down the staircase, her feet making a wholly undignified tattoo on the uncarpeted stairs, Aunt Winnie reached the front door before her. Drat! If Susanna hadn't wasted a good fifteen minutes primping, she'd have been there first. Primping for Julian Kittrick. She could hardly believe it of herself.

"May I help you, young man?" Aunt Winnie asked Julian, eyeing him curiously.

Susanna screeched to a halt behind her aunt. She wondered if she was out of breath from running, or if the sight of Julian Kittrick standing on her aunt's front porch, his straw hat in his hand, his blond hair gleaming in the morning sunlight, his blue eyes sparkling, had taken her breath away.

She told herself not to be foolish; she was out of breath from running, of course.

He held out a hand and said with magnificent affability, "Good morning. My name is Julian Kittrick. You must be Mrs. Dexter. Your niece, Miss Clement, has told me a lot about you."

That was a lie, but it was a pleasant one designed to put her aunt's suspicions, if she had any, to flight. And it worked. Aunt Winnie's attitude relaxed, and two patches of pink appeared on her cheeks. "Are you that newspaper fellow Susanna's been telling us about?"

Behind her aunt's back, Susanna frowned. Aunt Winnie made it sound as if Susanna'd been talking about Julian at the supper table or something. Which she had, but only with reference to the research they were undertaking, not as if she considered him a possible beau. She didn't appreciate Julian's sly grin when he spotted her. Nor did she appreciate the deprecating attitude he adopted for Aunt Winnie's benefit. The rat! He could charm the wings off a fly if he put his devious mind to it.

"I reckon that'd be me, all right, ma'am. It's a pleasure to meet you."

"Well, it's nice to meet you, too, Mr. Kittrick. Won't you come in for a cup of tea?"

Enough of this. Susanna marched to the front door and elbowed her way past her plump aunt, smiling at her to make up for it. "That won't be necessary, Aunt Winnie. Mr. Kittrick and I have decided to collaborate on an article, and we must get busy. We have lots of papers to look through."

Her aunt looked startled. Susanna knew she was taken aback by Susanna having usurped her neighborliness. But Susanna didn't want Mr. Kittrick to get any ideas. Or any *more* ideas, at least. Thanks to Aunt Winnie's artless speech, Susanna was sure he'd already gotten several.

In her most businesslike voice she said, "Let us be off, Mr. Kittrick. We have work to do."

"Yes, ma'am," he said meekly.

She squinted up at him, mistrusting that mild tone. His eyes held the most devilish twinkle she'd ever beheld, and she felt her cheeks get hot. Blast! Now Aunt Winnie would surely think he was a potential suitor.

"Don't work too hard. You're supposed to be having a holiday, Susanna."

"I won't let her tire herself out, Mrs. Dexter," Julian assured her.

As if she needed *his* protection. Ha! Setting Julian Kittrick to protect a nubile female would be akin to setting a tiger to protect a tasty lamb. Not that Susanna was a lamb or needed protection.

Deliberately, just to make certain her aunt knew what was what, she turned and said, "If you need me for any reason, Aunt Winnie, we'll be at Mr. Phineas Sedgewick's house, going through some old papers."

Her aunt's eyes opened wide. "Sedgewick? My goodness! I'm surprised that old miser would let you set foot inside his house, unless you paid him first.''

''Oh, we had to pay him, all right,'' Julian told her with a wink and a laugh.

Aunt Winnie laughed, too, thereby astonishing Susanna, who'd always believed her aunt to be above succumbing to a young man's wiles. Interesting. One learned something every day, she guessed. Today she had learned that her own aunt, Winifred Bondurant Dexter, had feet of clay.

Susanna felt very testy as she set off down the road with Julian Kittrick at her side. But her mood softened all too soon. The day was gorgeous: a perfect, soft summer day filled with sunlight, shadows, birdsong, and the tender green of new life everywhere. It was impossible to remain unaffected by the beauty surrounding her. Susanna breathed deeply as she peered into the forest alongside the road.

She wished they had woods like this in Artesia. She'd love to go exploring in them, to feel the moist, springy soil under her feet as she inhaled the loamy scent of them. In Artesia they had flat, dry plains covered with grama grass, dirt, and greasewood. When the wind blew, which it did constantly, she inhaled dust.

Her sigh caught Julian's attention. ''Thinking again, Miss Clement?''

He made it sound as though thinking must be a novel activity for her, and Susanna resented it.

''I'm comparing this landscape to the landscape back home, if you must know.''

''And are you discovering any differences?''

She shot him a suspicious glance, decided he was teasing her, and her mood did not improve. ''Of course I am.''

His grin was so beautiful Susanna couldn't stand looking at it, so she turned her head quickly. It didn't seem fair that any one man—especially this one—should be so blasted handsome.

''I was in the territory once, about five years ago,''

he said. "Santa Fe's kind of a nice place. Pretty, in a wild kind of way."

"Artesia is nothing like Santa Fe." *Pretty* was not, unfortunately, the first word that sprang to Susanna's mind when she contemplated her hometown.

"I know."

She glanced up at him again, suspicious. "You've been to Artesia?" She didn't believe it.

"No. But I went to Roswell once, for a story."

"Oh." Roswell was relatively close to Artesia and was just about as ugly. Only bigger. Roswell had one or two amenities to call its own. Artesia had—nothing. "The landscape around Roswell is like that in Artesia."

He laughed. "If you can call it landscape."

"I like it." The words fell from Susanna's lips like tiny, pointy icicles.

"You do, do you?"

"Yes. I do. It's—it's vast. It's unrestricted. It's—it's free."

"It's free, all right. That's why all the criminals run out there to escape prosecution in the States."

"They do not!"

"You're right. I beg your pardon."

Surprised, Susanna decided to be gracious. She inclined her head in an attitude of forgiveness.

"I suppose some of 'em get caught before they make it into the territory." He gave out with one of his big laughs.

Blast him! Furious, Susanna said coldly, "You're entitled to your opinion, Mr. Kittrick, however misguided."

His laugh made her itch to scratch his eyes out. Before she could succumb to her urge, they arrived at the Sedgewick place.

Like the home of her aunt and uncle, this house was a large, old one. Aunt Winnie had told Susanna that the Dexter house had been hauled across the frozen Sebasticook River by a team of oxen sometime in the late eighteenth or early nineteenth century. She wondered if

Mr. Sedgewick's ancestors had carted this house here
around the same time. Maybe they'd built it right on this
very spot. Heaven knew, there was wood enough in
Maine—unlike in Artesia, where lumber was a rare and
pricey commodity, and people were apt to start out life
there in soddies. And end life in soddies, too.

A barn, bigger than the main house, stood to the
south. Unlike her aunt and uncle's house, which had a
covered storage structure leading from the living quar-
ters to the barn, the Sedgewick barn sat apart, all by
itself. It was run-down and appeared lonely to Susanna.
Also unlike her aunt and uncle's place, the Sedgewick
barn had once been painted white, the same color as the
house. Both were peeling now.

Susanna wondered if Mr. Sedgewick, purported by all
to be a miser, resented the cost of paint. Uncle Cyrus
had no such scruples and had painted the Dexter barn a
bright, pretty red, which made it seem much friendlier
than this one. Nothing about the Sedgewick place looked
friendly to her.

"Hope he meant what he said about letting us search
his old records," Julian muttered as they walked up the
steps to the big porch.

"I'm sure he did. After all, a dollar an hour is quite
a sum." It was one she envied him, too.

Julian knew it, and laughed again. "You're right. The
old poop will probably welcome us with open arms."

He was wrong there. Mr. Sedgewick didn't welcome
them at all. His housekeeper, Mrs. Glick, however, was
not at all happy to see them.

"Come in," she said, her attitude grudging. "The old
man said you'd be coming here today to make a mess
in the study."

"We'll pick up after ourselves," Susanna assured her.

Mrs. Glick did not appear to be convinced. She
grunted something Susanna didn't catch, and walked
down the hall without another word.

Taking this as an invitation to follow her, they did.
Susanna felt uncomfortable and out of place in this big,

old home. She looked around and decided that, while this house probably dated from about the same time as did the Dexter house, the atmosphere in the two structures couldn't have been more different. It was the first time she wondered if houses could assume the personalities of their owners.

This drafty old mausoleum felt cold and forbidding, as if it had held generations' worth of unhappy people. Her aunt and uncle's house always felt welcoming, as if it had played host to happy souls and had taken on their good cheer.

They walked through a pocket of ice-cold air that made gooseflesh rise on her arms, and she shivered. She began to get a creepy feeling about this morning's enterprise.

Julian gave her a quick hug, and she almost screamed.

"Don't be alarmed, Miss Clement. It's a spooky old place, but it's not haunted. Anyway, if it is, I'm here to protect you."

He laughed again, and she resented it.

"Here." Mrs. Glick stopped at the study door and pushed it open. She didn't go inside, but gestured them to enter, as if she didn't care to take one step more than she absolutely had to. "The old man made me bring two boxes down from the attic. Don't leave any trash around for me to clean up."

Without another word, she turned and stomped off. She didn't even offer to bring them a pot of tea, a lapse Susanna begrudged for Julian's sake. After all, for a dollar an hour, they should at least be given refreshments. Not that Susanna would want to eat or drink anything that came from *that* woman's kitchen. She sniffed her disapproval and preceded Julian into the study.

In a trice, she forgot her miff. "Oh, look!" She pointed at the two huge cartons sitting on the floor next to the big old desk. "I wonder what they contain."

"Only one way to find out."

She turned to find Julian stripping off his jacket. She blinked when she realized his tailored shirt hugged a very well-muscled body. His shirt pulled across a chest that appeared solid as a rock, and the sleeves stretched over tautly developed biceps and triceps. She wondered what he'd done in his life to build up his musculature like that. Perhaps he was one of those young men who fancied the sport of boxing as exercise. Susanna had always deplored boxing. Until this minute. She realized she'd been staring, blinked, and looked away again.

"Like what you see?" His tone was warm and provocative, and it made Susanna blush.

She deliberately pretended to misunderstand him. "Yes. I do hope we can find something useful in these cartons."

He chuckled, and she knew she hadn't fooled him. Conceited beast. He was probably used to females falling all over him. Well, he'd have to wait a long time before Susanna Clement would succumb to his wicked charms.

It wasn't a long time at all, however, before she got so lost in reading forty-year-old correspondence and newspaper clippings that she forgot all about how irritating Julian Kittrick could be. She also forgot about his charm, his muscles, and his blond good looks. She was, in fact, engrossed.

Julian watched, beguiled, as Susanna read to him from an old recipe she'd discovered.

"Listen to this: 'Take an pumyon.' I suppose that must be a pumpkin, don't you think? 'Take an pumyon and boil it hard until the flesh peeleth away from the rind.' My goodness, Mr. Kittrick, I believe this recipe must date from Colonial times. Imagine that."

"I didn't know the town was even here in Colonial times."

"It wasn't incorporated until the early 1800s, but people lived in this area back then." Susanna spoke with authority.

"Interesting," he murmured.

In truth, he found it exceedingly interesting, but for a

reason unrelated to the recipe's relative age and old-
fashioned spellings. He was fascinated by the way Susanna's eyes sparkled with joy as she read to him from
her discovery. The sunlight playing in her hair and making it shine like gold in spots and copper in others was
charming, too. And the way her flushed cheeks betrayed
the pleasure she was taking in their activity appealed to
him as well.

She had an open notebook at her side, and several
sharpened pencils. She'd come prepared, and was de-
tailing anything they found that might bear even a re-
mote connection to their inquiry. Organized little thing,
Susanna Clement. Julian approved.

In fact, everything about the prissy Miss Susanna
Clement pleased him except, occasionally, her prickly
personality. He sighed and wondered if his attraction to
her was a legacy from some long-dead Puritan ancestor.
Since Julian didn't even know who his mother and father
were, much less more distant antecedents, the question
was destined to remain unanswered.

Susanna sighed, her breath ruffling the paper in her
hand and jerking Julian to attention. When she glanced
up at him, he had managed to subdue what he was sure
must have been a moony-eyed stare and hoped he looked
merely interested.

"I suppose I shouldn't waste time reading old recipes,
no matter how much fun they are. We have a task before
us." She gazed at the stacks and stacks of papers surrounding her.

They'd taken everything out of the two crates and
separated the papers into piles organized, as well as they
could do it, by date. Since there wasn't room enough on
the desk for all the piles, they'd set them on the floor.

Unlike most of the proper ladies he'd known in his
day, Susanna hadn't thought twice about plopping herself down among them. Then she'd dug right in, as if
she found this research problem of theirs as intriguing
as he did. Julian got the feeling she'd have enjoyed it

even if she didn't have a stake in the results. He decided her enthusiasm was refreshing.

"So you're interested in history, are you?" he asked, keeping his avid curiosity from leeching into his voice.

"Oh, yes. History was my favorite subject in school. I was accounted an excellent researcher, by the way."

Pride. Julian could hear it, and it tickled him. "You were, were you?"

"Yes, I was. In fact, it was I who discovered that the founder of our college had been divorced." She giggled. "It was quite a shocking revelation, too. The dean and headmistress tried to suppress the truth, but I wouldn't let them do it. I wrote an article about it and published it in the school newspaper."

"You did?"

"Yes. I was the editor, you see." She lifted her chin. Julian could tell she was triumphant of her achievements. He couldn't fault her for her attitude. Women had a hard go of it in this world unless they wanted to marry, sit at home, and rear children. Julian sensed Susanna's ambitions ran deeper than that. Not that there was anything wrong with rearing children and keeping house. Somebody had to do it, after all.

The mere thought of children made a shiver run through him. Not that he didn't like kids. He'd even like some of his own one day. But whenever he thought about children, he pictured himself as a boy huddling with all those other children on those mean New York City streets.

He and the others hadn't been proper playmates, but associates, as Susanna was his associate now. They'd all been trying to stay alive without benefit of homes or families. He'd wager most of those children were dead now. There had been hundreds, perhaps thousands, of them, and not nearly enough Father Patricks to go around.

"I expect the dean and headmistress weren't awfully happy about your article."

Her brow wrinkled, and her eyebrows dipped over her

pretty eyes, which began to snap with anger. Julian thought it was cute, the way she got so worked up about these things.

"No, they were not. In fact, they gave me a very stern lecture. Why, they even threatened to withhold my diploma!"

Her indignation tickled him. He said, "No!" in a shocked-sounding voice and could tell he'd irked her. What a surprise.

"It was a shocking threat, Mr. Kittrick. They were attempting to suppress my Constitutional right to free speech! I told them so, too."

"I bet you did."

"And I also told them that Mrs. Fitzgibbon's divorce was not to be deplored, but rather to be applauded as a reasoned answer to a troubling problem."

"Her old man was a problem, was he?"

She set aside the paper at which she'd been glancing and frowned at him. "Don't you dare patronize me, Mr. Kittrick."

"I wouldn't dream of it."

She eyed him skeptically.

"I mean it," he said for fear she wouldn't finish her story. "I'm curious, Miss Clement. Why was Mrs. Fitzgibbon justified in divorcing Mr. Fitzgibbon?"

Her steady gaze pierced him for several more seconds. At last she seemed to decide he deserved to hear the rest of the story. She picked up another paper and said, "Mr. Fitzgibbon was a drunkard and a dissolute gambler. If Mrs. Fitzgibbon had remained his wife, he would have dragged her down into the same gutter he seemed determined to wallow in. Instead she took a valiant stand, divorced him, moved to Missouri, and established a school. A *fine* school, I might add."

She gave a sharp nod. Julian grinned. She was cute as a button, really. And passionate. He appreciated passion in a person, as long as it was directed. He didn't fancy wild, emotional displays like those favored by females who had nothing better to do with their time than shriek and faint every time they turned around. But Susanna Clement's kind of passion, the kind that spurred her to do useful things, he valued. Quite highly, in fact.

He did feel he ought to point out something that had struck him as inconsistent, however. "You know, Miss Clement, for all your zeal in writing about a circumstance that might have been considered shocking in Mrs. Fitzgibbon, you remain singularly steadfast in your refusal to think your great-aunt might have done something society would disapprove of."

She sat up straight, her posture indicative of her firm opinions on this issue. "The two cases are entirely dissimilar, Mr. Kittrick."

"Are they?"

"They are. Mrs. Fitzgibbon divorced her husband. I don't consider that a sin, but some moralists who believe women should stay married, no matter how vicious and depraved their husbands are, do. My great-aunt did nothing to earn her shady reputation." She looked down and sniffed. "The only thing even remotely shocking about my great-aunt's behavior was her choice to pursue an acting career."

"I see."

She shot him a keen look. He expected her to continue her lecture, but she was distracted by something written on the paper she'd picked up.

"Oh, look! I think this may be something we can use. 'Spoke with McKenzie about the jewels today. The fool is inclined to waste the money he could get for their sale, but I shall speak with him again tomorrow. Rubies, sapphires, emeralds, diamonds. They're worth a fortune, and I aim to have them.' "

Her eyes blazed with fervor when she looked up from the paper. "Oh, Mr. Kittrick, do you suppose he's talking about the jewels that disappeared with Magdalena?"

"Could be. What else does it say. Is it a letter?"

Susanna turned the paper over in her hand, studying it closely. "It looks more like a memorandum whoever wrote it made to himself. Maybe it's part of a diary."

She reached into her skirt pocket and withdrew the same leatherbound volume she'd showed him the first time he'd met her. "I brought my great-aunt's diary with me so we'd be able to verify dates."

"Good thinking." Very good thinking, as a matter of fact. Julian was finding more to like about Susanna Clement as the hours passed. He wasn't sure that was a good thing.

She flipped through the small book until she came to a certain page, then pointed at it. "There! It *is* the same relative date. This reference to *gems* in Magdalena's diary is dated April sixth, and that paper I read from was dated the eleventh. Oh, I'll bet this is it!"

" 'It,' what? What exactly do you think it all means?"

"Well, that this Mr. McKenzie character, whoever he was, had some jewels, and that Mr. Sedgewick here"— she stabbed the paper in her lap—"wanted McKenzie to sell them to him. I'll wager that McKenzie was contemplating giving them to Great-Aunt Magdalena to help fund her Underground Railroad work."

"All right. That's a reasonable assumption. But first you're going to have to convince me that Magdalena Bondurant was actually working with the Underground Railroad. Do you have any solid proof?"

"Yes. No. That is, I sort of have proof." She fidgeted uncomfortably. "In a way."

"You sort of have proof. In a way? What does that mean, pray tell?"

Her expression had turned stormy when she glared up at him. "It's common knowledge! Even *you,* who seem to want to vilify her morals, character, and reputation, said you'd heard that she worked for the Underground Railroad."

He shrugged. "That's all based on innuendo and rumor. I only told you what I'd heard. Granted, it's what got me curious about her story, but I don't know if any of it's true."

Her brow wrinkled up again. It seemed to do that

when she was thinking hard, and Julian thought it was an endearing characteristic. For a few seconds he thought for sure she was going to explode with righteous wrath on her great-aunt's behalf. Then she straightened her shoulders, an activity that showed her wonderful figure off to advantage, and said, "There's only one way to discover the truth, and that is to keep searching. Surely we'll be able to find *something* that will confirm Magdalena Bondurant's involvement in such a worthy cause."

Julian cleared his throat. He guessed now was as good a time as any to give her the tidbit he'd been withholding. "You know, Miss Clement, before I left Denver, I corresponded with an elderly gentleman in Virginia who'd been involved in helping slaves escape back before the War Between the States began."

"Really? You did? What did he say?"

He loved the way her eyes opened up wide, got round, and glowed when she was excited. She had the most expressive face. Nine tenths of the time it expressed disapproval of him, but every once in a while—like now, for instance—it expressed powerful interest. He grinned, then shook his head and reminded himself he was supposed to be working.

"Yes, I really did. And he told me that as far as he knew, there was a house up in Maine somewhere—he thought it was either in Palmyra or Newport—where slaves used to be hidden before they could be transported to Canada."

"Oh, how exciting! I *know* Magdalena Bondurant was involved now. That only confirms it!" Her breathless exclamation hit Julian rather lower in his anatomy than he wanted it to. He began to harden, and busied himself with his own stack of papers. Damn, he wished he'd stop having these indelicate reactions to his research partner.

"It confirms nothing," he said more curtly than he'd intended to. "It only means there *may* have been a hide-out house up here somewhere."

"That's not true. Great-Aunt Magdalena makes reference in two places in this diary to a storage facility."

"Where is this storage facility of hers?"

Susanna looked down and frowned. "She didn't write that part."

"That figures. The old man didn't know or couldn't remember the names of anyone in this area who was involved in the operation."

"No names at all?"

He hated to hear the disappointment in her voice. He cleared his throat again. "None."

When he glanced up, Susanna's dashed hopes were so obvious, he could feel them where he sat. They lodged in his nether parts, too. Damn. He had to get over this.

"You know, Miss Clement, it makes sense that people were discreet about making reference to the work, if it was the Underground Railroad. If the authorities had found out, they'd have been in real trouble."

"I suppose that's true." Her shoulders drooped in concert with her voice.

He couldn't bear to see her unhappy. To make up for having made her so, he said, "The old geezer did say that he remembered there was a woman involved, though."

"He did?"

Her expression brightened so much that Julian felt as though he'd just rescued her favorite puppy from the jaws of catastrophe. He nodded. "He said he remembered that part specifically, because he thought it was strange that a woman would risk her life and reputation for such a cause."

That did it. At once, Susanna's expression hardened. She sniffed with indignation. "Well, I like that! It's just like a man to believe only *men* can get involved in noble causes!"

Julian was so charmed by Susanna's mercurial mood flips, he laughed out loud. She heaved a wadded-up piece of paper at him.

Chapter Five

Susanna made Julian help her pick up Mr. Sedgewick's study before they left at the end of the day. He, of course, expected her to do it alone, but she wouldn't let him get away with it.

"Why is it that men always leave the tidying-up to women?" she asked, miffed.

"Because it's their job?"

She scowled at him. "Nonsense! I've done every bit as much work as you have today. You can do as much work as I in cleaning up after us."

"I wouldn't dream of leaving all the tidying-up to you, Miss Clement," he said in an uncommonly meek— for him—voice.

Taking note of the hint of a twinkle in his eyes, she wondered if he'd balked at first just to rile her. She wouldn't put it past him. He really was the very devil of a fellow.

Their day together had confirmed her opinion of him as such. It had also showed her that he was as intense about his work as she, and she wasn't happy to have discovered it. It was easy to remain neutral to him when she believed him to be a wastrel and a scamp. It was more difficult when she realized that his devil-may-care exterior hid less frivolous depths.

Bother. Wasn't that just the way things always worked? Every time she thought she had something— or, in this case, someone—figured out, they went and proved they weren't one-dimensional after all.

Well, never mind. She hugged her notebook to her breast as they walked together down the lane. Her mind spun with the information they'd gleaned during their hard day's work.

"We have so much material here, Mr. Kittrick. It's quite gratifying to have had our first full day of work prove so fruitful."

"Yes. We'll still have to put it together with the other things we know and then try to make sense of it all, don't forget."

"Of course. But if we spend only another several hours in that dismal study of Mr. Sedgewick's, we should be through there. Then we can move on to other sources. For one thing, I've confirmed enough dates to look up clippings in the newspaper's archives now."

"Right. And then there's the public library here, and the one in Newport. They might have some old records there."

"True. And the Palmyra courthouse. I'd love to discover the whereabouts of the house where they hid the slaves."

"You sure it's a house?"

She looked up at him, stricken by the common sense of his question. "Actually, no. I don't know what it was."

"Hmmm. Well, it would be quite a find, all right. Assuming that old gent in Virginia was right about the location."

"I'm sure he was. Don't forget the references to a storage facility in Magdalena's diary."

"I'm not forgetting them, Miss Clement."

He smiled down at her in a way that made Susanna blush. She looked away and cleared her throat but couldn't think of anything to say. Then she remembered Danilo, and excitement drove the effect of Julian's expression from her mind. She'd bet anything that Danilo could help sort out all these notes. He might even know where the hideout facility was located. "I wish it were evening so I could go to the cemetery."

She realized her mistake as soon as the words were out of her mouth. She looked up guiltily and found Julian gazing down at her. She wasn't surprised to see the look of inquiry in his perfectly gorgeous blue eyes. Drat! She wished she'd stop seeing him as a man. This would be so much easier if she could think of him as merely a colleague.

"Why in the name of all that's holy do you want to visit the graveyard?"

"I, er, find contemplating Magdalena's headstone— um—relaxing. Inspiring. Conducive to thought. It's quiet there."

She saw him take a glance around. "Hell, it's quiet everywhere around here."

That was true. Palmyra, Maine, wasn't a hotbed of excitement.

"I mean, I find it easy to—to meditate there. To consider matters and sort them out."

"I see."

He didn't believe her; she could tell. Well, that was just too bad for him. She notched her chin up to show him that what he thought didn't matter to her. She only wished her appearance of disinterest told the truth.

That evening Susanna was all set to visit the cemetery when a sudden imperative hunch drove her up into her aunt's attic instead. By rights, this was the old Bondurant house, although people had taken to calling it the Dexter place since her uncle Cyrus had married Winnie Bondurant and moved in. There were no Bondurants left in Palmyra, Maine.

"Why do you want to go digging around in that dusty old place?" Aunt Winnie asked her after Susanna had grabbed a kerosene lantern and explained her mission.

"I'm trying to find information about Great-Aunt Magdalena."

"Hmph. I wish you'd let sleeping dogs lie, Susanna. No good will ever come of you digging around in old scandals."

Susanna paused at the foot of the narrow staircase leading up into the attic. "I don't believe there should be any scandal attached to Magdalena Bondurant's name, Aunt Winnie. I believe her memory has been viciously maligned through the years, and I aim to discover the truth!"

"Hmph," her aunt said again. "I just hope you don't unearth something none of us wants to know, is all I have to say about it."

Susanna knew better. Her Aunt Winnie, while a dear woman, seldom finished explaining her opinion about anything, but went on and on and on. Before her aunt could hold her captive with a lengthy discourse on the merits of leaving well enough alone, Susanna gave her a quick kiss on the cheek, said, "I love you, Aunt Winnie," and scooted up the stairs while her aunt was still gaping after her in astonishment.

Holding the lantern high, Susanna peered around in the dusty attic. She was glad she'd thought to don an apron, although she doubted whether it was going to save her skirt from the piles of dust and ribbons of cobwebs that had accumulated up here over the years.

"I'm glad I changed into my old blue dress, too," she muttered. Carefully, so as not to stir up a cloud of dust and make herself sneeze, she cleaned a spot on an old table with a rag and set the lantern down. Then she brushed the dust off her hands and set to work.

There were heaps of old discarded rubbish up here: broken chairs, old tables, lamps, flatirons, hatboxes, dented pots, chipped porcelain, and a hideous wire angel that Susanna recognized as having been made by Granny

Bondurant. Susanna's mother had described it to her more than once, laughing all the while. While Granny lived, Aunt Winnie had dutifully displayed the monstrosity. Now that the woman was gone, Susanna imagined Winnie had been happy to relinquish the angel to the attic.

As well as discarded treasures, Susanna found boxes of books, leather pouches cracking with age and bulging with old papers, scrapbooks, paintings, tintypes of dead relatives, and all sorts of other things to explore. Although she figured she ought, for the sake of her mission, to begin with the pouches, she decided to look at the tintypes and paintings first.

"Oh, my," she murmured as she held up a picture of this very house. Squinting, she managed to make out the date. "Eighteen thirty. My goodness. I wonder who painted it." She squinted some more, and managed to decipher the name *Mary W. Bondurant* scripted right above the date.

"My word, I wonder who Mary W. Bondurant was." Enlightenment struck with a flash. "Why, I do believe that's my great-great-aunt Mary Furbush! For heaven's sake." Sixty-five years before Susanna had marched upstairs to seek information in this attic, her own ancestor had painted this picture. And the old farmhouse looked just the same today. Amazing.

But she was straying from her purpose. Giving herself a mental scolding, she set aside the painting—she thought she'd carry it downstairs and ask Aunt Winnie if she could take it back to Artesia with her—and decided to look quickly though the tintypes and photographs and then get on to her real work.

"Magdalena Bondurant." Susanna gazed at the old faded picture of a beautiful woman. Even though photography was in its infancy back in the 1850s, the photographer had managed to capture Magdalena's vibrancy and life. She had been a beauty, all right.

Ruing the vanity that made her do it even as curiosity drove her on, Susanna searched her beautiful great-aunt's face to see if any of her characteristics had been passed down to this present generation. She thought she detected a similarity in their eyes. They were shaped the same, at any rate. Susanna didn't think her own eyes held the same glint of mischief and humor. She sighed, wondering if perhaps humor wasn't a worthwhile characteristic after all. She been striving so hard to prove herself to be as good as any man that she'd forgotten it paid, sometimes, to laugh.

Hot on that thought's heels came the unwelcome idea that if anyone could teach her how to appreciate humor, it would probably be Julian Kittrick. He laughed at everything.

"Well, I'll show him this old photograph, anyway. Perhaps if he sees Magdalena, he'll be less apt to want to slander her name."

She set the photograph aside, with the painting. Then she decided she'd wasted enough time, and set to work on the cracked leather pouches.

It was in one of them that Susanna found three more diaries, all written in her great-aunt Magdalena's flowing, flamboyant script.

She let out a squeal that brought Aunt Winnie to the foot of the attic stairs. "What in the name of heaven is going on up there? Are you all right, Susanna?"

Through tears of joy, Susanna called out, "I'm fine, Aunt Winnie. I just found something so exciting."

She wasn't surprised to hear her aunt's sour, "Hmph." Her heart was still thundering with pleasure when Aunt Winnie's footsteps faded away. Very carefully, Susanna packed the three diaries into the old leather pouch. Then she stuck the photograph of Magdalena Bondurant in with them, tucked the painting under her arm along with the pouch, picked up the lantern, and negotiated the stairs.

When she got to her bedroom, she set the diaries on her nightstand, propped the photograph on the bureau where she could see it, removed a painting of Abraham Lincoln from the wall, and tucked it away in her wardrobe. Then she put the painting of the Bondurant farm on the nail formerly reserved for Abraham Lincoln, stripped off her dusty clothes, and washed up.

After she'd done all that, she put on her nightgown, climbed up onto the bed, using the stool provided for the purpose—it was an old-fashioned bed, and a tall one—and picked up the first diary. By the light of her bedside lamp she read far into the night.

The next morning, in spite of how late she'd gone to sleep, Susanna bounced out of bed as if her joints had been replaced by springs. She raced through her morning ablutions, pelted down the stairs, and startled her aunt with another kiss on the cheek.

Without waiting for one of her aunt's usual delicious breakfasts, she snatched a doughnut from the plate piled high with them in the center of the kitchen table and ran for the door. Then, with a thought to her research assistant, she darted back to the plate, hooked two more doughnuts, plopped yet another kiss on her aunt's cheek, and dashed out the door.

"I've got so much to do!" she called out right before the door slammed behind her. She knew she owed Aunt Winnie an explanation. And she'd give her one, too. Later.

First, however, she had to show Julian Kittrick what she'd found.

Julian had spent the last evening drinking in the saloon, as he always did, because he was a newspaperman and that's what newspapermen did. He was, therefore, not entirely pleased to hear a knock at his door a full half hour before he'd asked to be awakened this morning.

He pulled a pillow over his head, hoping it was all a mistake and whoever that misguided soul was would realize it and go away. Whoever it was didn't. The pounding intensified.

"Go away!" he called, and frowned. His voice was as hoarse as a frog's.

Damn. He hated drinking. He hated the taste; he hated the feeling; and most of all, he hated the aftereffects. He never drank much, but last night, hoping to clear his head of visions of what he'd like to do with Susanna Clement, he'd downed more than his usual minimum. This morning he felt all the extras, too. His head ached. His eyes burned as if someone had left them out in the sun too long.

Snarling curses, he flung his legs over the side of the bed, grabbed his robe, and was stuffing his arms into it when he got to the door and flung it open. "What!"

Oh, cripes. It was Susanna Clement. He blinked down at her, wondering if his eyes could be deceiving him. Maybe this was an extension of the dream he'd been having in which he and Susanna had been doing some mighty interesting things. They were things he was pretty sure she didn't know how to do.

"Oh, Mr. Kittrick!" she cried, making him wince and evidently not even noticing his state of dishabille. "Look what I found!"

She thrust a raggedy old book at him, and he had to take a step back or be punched in the stomach with it. He blinked some more. "What's that?"

She breezed past him, leaving a fresh scent in her wake that was greatly at odds with the foul stench of the saloon he'd left too few hours before. Without his consent, his head lifted and he breathed deeply. He felt better afterward, as if Susanna's bright presence had cleansed his insides. Strange, the effect she had on him.

"It's early, Miss Clement. What are you doing here, at my hotel room?" Beginning to wake up, he even found the wit to ask, "Aren't you worried about what people will say?" He wiggled his eyebrows experimentally and discovered his head didn't ache as much as it had a moment before.

"Don't be ridiculous!"

She spun around, and he noticed the flush of excitement on her cheeks. He'd already heard it in her voice. Because he wasn't quite awake enough to guard his tongue, he said, "Well, then, since I'm not ready to get up yet, why don't you join me for a little nap?"

Her smile vanished, and she gaped at him, shocked. He shook his head. Silly girl. What did she expect but indecent suggestions if she was going to be showing up at a man's hotel door like this?

"Just kidding," he croaked. Lord, he needed water. He padded over to the pitcher and poured himself a glass.

"Why aren't you dressed yet?" she demanded of his back. "You don't even have any slippers on."

Julian glanced down at his naked toes. He grunted and drank some more water before he responded.

"I'm not dressed because it's too early to be awake, much less dressed." He turned around, his glass in his hand, and eyed her up and down.

She stood in a beam of light that had dared sneak through his closed curtains. Sunlight outlined her figure, brightened her hair, made her eyes gleam, and kissed the blush in her cheeks, not unlike the way Julian would like to kiss it. In spite of himself, last night's extra drinks, and his determination to live the journalist's life, his mood softened. She was nearly jumping up and down with enthusiasm, and he discovered he wanted to know why. His grin caught him by surprise.

"All right, Miss Clement. Since you've had the temerity to come here and wake me up, I guess I'll have to get dressed."

"Please do, Mr. Kittrick. I've made the most wonderful discovery."

"You have, have you?"

"Yes, indeed, I have."

He thought it was cute the way she seemed to vibrate with excitement. "Do you want to step outside so I can get dressed?" Because his frame of mind was lifting by the second and an impulse to tease her overcame him, he waggled his eyebrows again suggestively and said, "Or would you care to help me?" When he'd done that with his eyebrows before, he'd made her blush.

This time she only frowned in thought. "Don't be silly," she said and turned to look at his room.

So did he. For the first time in his adult life, Julian was glad Father Patrick had taught him to be orderly. Except for yesterday's clothes, which he'd flung over the back of a chair last night, the room was neat as a pin.

She pointed at a screen in the corner. "Why don't you stand behind that screen and dress, Mr. Kittrick? I want to read some things to you. This will be efficient, and we won't waste any time."

"You want to remain in my room while I dress?"

He'd touched her on a sore spot. She stiffened up like a poker, and his insides tickled as if she'd diddled them with a feather. He shook his head, wondering if he'd drunk more than he remembered.

"We are on a mission, Mr. Kittrick. There is nothing unseemly about being zealous about it."

"Tell that to your aunt when she hears about you coming all by your lonesome to my hotel room this morning."

Her cheeks caught fire. Julian had to make a conscious decision whether to stand there and watch them burn, say something else that would make them burn hotter, or turn and select the clothes he would wear today. With a sigh of regret, he turned.

Because he couldn't stand to let the moment pass without one more little jibe, he said, "All right, Miss Clement. But don't be shocked when I take off my robe to bathe. The sink, as you can clearly see, is nowhere near that modesty screen."

He peeked over his shoulder and was delighted to see her blush deepen. She whirled around, clutching that book to her breasts as if it were a life buoy. He'd like to clutch her breasts. He shook his head, wishing these thoughts would leave him alone. He really didn't need a Puritanical virgin and her outraged relatives running him out of town.

He could not, however, fail to appreciate her little

waist. Or the flare of her hips. With another shake of
his head, he decided *to hell with it,* shucked off his robe,
and washed, deciding Miss Clement could be shocked
or not as she wished. He also decided that he didn't
know which reaction he'd prefer in her.

With a towel wrapped around his waist, he went to
the wardrobe, grabbed a clean shirt, another lightweight
summer suit, and walked over to the screen. He snabbled
a fresh collar from the bureau drawer on his way, and
grinned when he saw Susanna, stiff-backed and rigid,
standing still as a statue and staring straight at the curtains he'd so carelessly pulled closed last night. He'd
succeeded in rattling her, anyway.

"You can look now," he said after he was safely
behind the screen. He glanced down at his stiff sex and
wondered what she'd do if he revealed himself to her in
this condition. He wondered if she even knew men's
bodies could do things like this—or what men and
women could do together afterward. Ah, well, some
things were destined to remain mysteries, he reckoned.

"I could have stepped outside while you washed,"
she said in a stifled voice.

All at once, Julian felt a spurt of pure joy. By gad,
he adored this woman! She was the most fun he'd had
in years. He lifted his chin so he could talk over the
screen. "Too late. If you expect to do any more journalistic investigations, Miss Clement, you'd be wise to
anticipate problems of an intimate nature."

She sniffed. "Yes. Well, thank you for pointing out
this one."

He'd like to point out something else to her. With a
chuckle, he stepped into his trousers. He had a difficult
time fastening them in front.

When Julian flung off his robe, Susanna had peeked
over her shoulder and gaped at his broad back and
known she'd made a hideous mistake by not leaving his
room when he suggested it. Too late she'd discovered
that she could be affected by the sight of a man's naked

body in a way she'd never even dreamed was possible. Until now.

Merely watching the play of light on his torso, the way the shadows dipped here and there to create a sculpted effect made her salivate. Good gracious, he was built like one of those statues people put up in museums. She didn't know real men could look like that. She'd always assumed those statues were the product of artistic license. Swallowing hard, she wished she'd never discovered her mistake.

Small wonder people draped sheets around the male statues in museums. They did so to protect the female population from fainting dead away in museum lobbies. If she saw Julian Kittrick face-first, buck naked, she'd probably swoon, too, and she didn't even lace her corset tightly. As it was, her skin was blazing hot, and it felt as though lava had taken to bubbling through her veins. This wasn't fair.

She tried and failed to make herself turn her head and stop goggling at him. He splashed water on his face, some of it trickled down his back, and she almost groaned aloud. She wanted to go over to him and wipe that water away with her bare hands, to feel the muscles delineated under his smooth skin, to turn him around and run her fingers through the hair she could no longer see but knew covered his chest, to press those rounded buttocks and see if they were as hard as they looked. Merciful heavens, her own hips weren't hard like that.

Of course they aren't, you ninny. Men and women are built differently. Susanna knew she was fallen beyond redemption when she wished she could investigate the differences herself. On Julian Kittrick's body. In great, painstaking, intimate detail. With her own two hands.

Good Lord. She'd known since shortly after meeting him that she was going to have to fight a good fight to protect her great-aunt's name from his journalistic talons. She'd had no idea until this very moment that she'd have to fight to protect herself from herself and her own improper urges.

The knowledge made her very crabby. With cheeks afire and a palpitating heart, she turned and stared at the window curtains. She'd like to have flung them open and stared out at the day but, too late, she began to hope that no one had seen her enter this blasted hotel.

Chapter Six

"All set, Miss Clement."

His tone sounded impertinent to Susanna, although her perception might have been tainted by her fevered thoughts. She wondered if he had any inkling of what effect the sight of his naked backside did to her. No, he couldn't have, because he didn't know she'd looked. Thank God.

It was a wicked thing for her to have done, but she couldn't regret it. Although she'd probably die from the unrequited urges the sight of his body had spawned, she'd be forever grateful she'd caught that one glimpse of it, however fleeting. She never thought the masculine form could be so magnificent. Nor that she would be so affected by it. Julian Kittrick was pure perfection. His broad shoulders were breathtaking. She could imagine running her hands along them, feeling the power in the strong muscles of his back. As her fingers continued their journey, they'd caress his tapered waist, slowly her feathery touch would release him, moving downward, eager to cup his firm, smooth . . .

"Miss Clement?"

His voice made her jump. Susanna was afraid to look at him, certain he had read her thoughts.

"Are you warm, Miss Clement? You look rather flushed." His smile was wicked. Drat him!

Flustered, Susanna was at a loss for words. She remembered the doughnuts she'd brought and thrust them, wrapped up in a paper, at him. "Here. I brought you some breakfast."

His twinkle was impossibly devilish. She wished she'd made her tone more gracious.

"Thank you very much, Miss Clement. I can tell how much pleasure doing so has given you." He unwrapped the paper. "Yum. They look good. Did you make these?"

"No, my aunt Winnie did. She's a good cook."

"And has she handed this extremely valuable womanly accomplishment down to her niece?"

She couldn't tell if he was teasing her, but she suspected he was. She hated being a figure of fun to anyone; it was especially galling coming from Julian Kittrick.

"I can cook, yes." She opted not to add that cooking wasn't her forte. She never had paid attention to the culinary arts. She simply didn't care about the domestic duties deemed women's work. But, to her consternation, at this moment she did care. She wanted to be everything this terrible man valued in a female.

Susanna sniffed and told herself she'd get over it. He was a very handsome man. It was natural that she should feel some slight attraction to him. Susanna lived in an enlightened age, and had gone to an enlightened school run by enlightened women. She knew that men weren't the only members of the human race who experienced animal passions from time to time. Miss Amberly had advocated giving oneself up to prayer and meditation until the feelings passed. However, although Susanna valued Miss Amberly more than words could say, she wasn't sure prayer and meditation would work in her case.

"Is there anywhere in this town where I can get some coffee to go with these doughnuts, Miss Clement?"

Grudgingly she said, "I suppose you can come to my aunt and uncle's place and have some coffee. We can go over these diaries there."

"You found more diaries?" he asked as they walked out the door.

She scowled up at him again. "That's why I came to see you this morning, Mr. Kittrick. Yes, I found more diaries. Three of them, as a matter of fact. And they give the most abundant proof I've seen so far that Magdalena Bondurant was involved in a great enterprise. That this enterprise was the Underground Railroad, I have no doubt at all."

"Does she mention it by name?"

This was the tricky part. "Not in so many words. But that's only because she was so discreet. She wasn't about to jeopardize the valuable work she was undertaking."

She didn't appreciate his frown and held her breath while he pondered her answer.

At last he said, "Hmm. I'm afraid you'll still have some work to do if you want to convince me."

That's what she'd feared. "Oh, but Mr. Kittrick, it is so plain in these diaries! Why, she even mentions that storage facility again, and she says the storage facility is . . ." She flipped through pages of the diary she'd brought with her. "Here it is. 'The storage facility is ready to receive its visitors. It is deep in the McKenzie woods, and no one will suspect,' " she read as they walked.

She gazed up at Julian, trying to hide the zeal in her heart. When she saw the expression in his perfectly spectacular blue eyes transform from one of mockery to one of slightly affectionate teasing, she turned away, embarrassed.

"You know," he said after a moment or two, "she might only have been writing about a lovers' trysting place or something."

His words put to flight any thoughts Susanna had about him joining with her belief in her great-aunt's noble intentions. She cried, "No! That's absurd! Magdalena Bondurant was no hussy, whatever you choose to think. She was engaged to marry Danilo!"

Blast! When would she ever learn to guard her tongue? At the moment Susanna wished she'd bitten it rather than having blurted out Magdalena's association with Danilo.

"Who's Danilo?"

Susanna wasn't surprised to encounter Julian's look of inquiry when she dared peek up at him. She licked her lips, trying to decide how much to tell him. "An actor. His real name was Daniel Matteucci, but he preferred Danilo for artistic reasons."

He still seemed bewildered, so she added, "He was also a playwright. They were engaged to be married."

"I didn't know that. How did you find all this out?"

How did she find it out? Why, from Danilo, of course. The ghost. In the cemetery. Blast. Susanna cudgeled her brain for an answer that wouldn't make her sound either insane or idiotic. Before she'd come up with anything, Julian spoke again.

"Is this an old family rumor, Miss Clement?"

She considered lying and saying *yes,* but her conscience wouldn't let her. "No," she said reluctantly. "My family doesn't like to talk about Magdalena. They consider her a skeleton."

He threw back his head and laughed. She glared at him, and hated that he looked so natural and happy and handsome, laughing into the beautiful Maine morning air the way he was doing. It struck her that Julian was beautiful himself, and a pang of envy snagged in her chest.

It wasn't fair that some people had all the looks as well as all the privileges in this world. Add to his masculine beauty his education, his brains, the fact that he seemed totally at ease in the world, and Susanna had to fight hard to keep from hating him.

Having been born a female, in the territory, and into a family with infinitely more love than wealth to offer their children, Susanna resented Julian his status. While she'd had to earn a scholarship to attend college, she'd wager anything that Julian had parents whose names alone had guaranteed him entry. He'd probably gone to one of those fancy East Coast universities, too.

Even if he hadn't been born into wealth—and he gave every indication of having been—he was a man. That alone afforded him a place in the world. Susanna Clement would have to scratch and fight and struggle if she ever expected to dig out a toehold for herself. No, it really wasn't fair. Maybe that was why she felt such a deep kinship with Magdalena Bondurant. Magdalena had all but thumbed her nose at conventional society, but she'd never lost her honor or her integrity or her commitment to righting society's wrongs.

"When you've had your laugh, Mr. Kittrick, perhaps I can answer your question." Her tone was as sour as the crabapple she'd tried to eat last Sunday.

Julian snatched out his handkerchief and wiped his eyes. He still had a wonderful grin on his face when he finally managed to stop laughing.

"Sorry, Miss Clement. You really do make me laugh, you know."

"Yes, I know that quite well by this time, Mr. Kittrick." She detested it, too. "At any rate, I met a gentleman recently who explained Magdalena's relationship with this fellow named Danilo. They were engaged to be married. He was the director of the theatrical company with which she traveled, and he wrote parts in plays for her."

"Interesting. What's the name of this fellow who gave you all this information?"

Drat it all. She should have anticipated this question. "I can't recall at the moment, but I'll look at my notes this evening." Perhaps by that time she'd have thought of a satisfactory answer. She hated having to lie. Maybe Danilo could help her think of some way to put Julian off; she'd pay the cemetery a visit tonight.

"Hmm. Well, don't forget that even if they were engaged, Magdalena Bondurant wouldn't have been the first female in the universe to forget her promises to one man when another one came along."

"She'd never!" Susanna whirled around and slammed her fists onto her hips. "Not everyone in the world suffers from your moral laxity, Mr. Kittrick, and I resent your implication greatly."

She just *hated* seeing that knowing smirk of his appear.

"You're really cute when you're in a miff, you know that, Miss Clement?"

"Oh! You're impossible!" She turned again, and resumed walking. He was the most arrogant, irreverent, *insufferable* man on the face of the earth. That he was fiendishly handsome made it all the worse.

They'd reached the Dexter place by this time, and Julian greeted Aunt Winnie with all the charm he possessed, which was considerable. Before Susanna's aunt had quit blushing, she'd prepared a magnificent breakfast for him. Susanna had the feeling her own plate was an afterthought. At least they'd be well fortified when they tackled the rest of Mr. Sedgewick's papers this morning. And armed with lots more information, too, thanks to her.

They pored over Magdalena's diaries while they ate. Susanna didn't notice that their heads were practically touching over the second of those volumes until she suddenly became aware of a warm breath on her cheek and an unfamiliar heat coursing through her body. She turned her head and discovered she was staring straight into the laughing eyes of Julian Kittrick. She sat up again with a jerk. His grin broadened.

"Scared?" he whispered, teasing her again.

Susanna didn't appreciate his tone one little bit. Yes, she was scared. She wasn't like him, a scoundrel and a practiced flirt. She was an absolute innocent. For the first time in her life, she wished she wasn't.

"Don't be ridiculous," she snapped.

He laughed. What a surprise.

"Would you like more coffee, Mr. Kittrick?"

Susanna looked up to find Aunt Winnie standing at the stove with the coffeepot in her hand and a smile on her face. She wasn't sure if her grin was teasing or a lasting result of Julian Kittrick's charm. In any case, Susanna was grateful for the interruption. In a battle of flirtation with Mr. Kittrick, she was certain to lose.

"Thank you kindly, Mrs. Dexter. I didn't expect to have so lavish a breakfast this morning. I was awakened rather earlier than I'd intended and had to hustle out of my hotel before I'd eaten."

Susanna scowled at him. He laughed again.

After they'd left the Dexter place and headed down the road to Sedgewick's house, Julian decided he'd better go easier on Susanna Clement. Although he respected her in all other matters, particularly in regards to her abilities as a researcher and a writer, she wasn't up to his level when it came to dalliance. It was a downright pity, too. He'd love to teach her a thing or two.

He'd never dallied with virgins, however, and he didn't intend to start now. Hell, if he got too carried away, he'd find himself married, and then there would be hell to pay. He shivered, thinking about the consequences a man's folly could have.

It was beyond his comprehension how parents could abandon their children the way his parents had abandoned him. He had, however, harbored a terror in his bosom for years now that he'd discover the same careless streak in himself. He'd sooner die than subject another innocent child to what he'd gone through, and he didn't want to die. He also didn't trust himself not to repeat his parents' sins.

Father Patrick had tried to tell him that his parents weren't necessarily evil. He'd suggested that perhaps they'd died and hadn't had an opportunity to provide for him. Julian didn't buy it for a second. Father Patrick was a saint. He always believed only the best of everyone.

Julian knew better. People did what they had to do in order to survive in this miserable world. Obviously his parents had considered him an obstacle to their own survival and had dumped him as a consequence. Julian understood things like that because, he presumed, his parents had lived in the same general neighborhood he had.

It was pure luck that he hadn't succumbed to some vile disease or been forced to sell his body to perverts before Father Patrick found him. Julian couldn't remember a time in his early life when he hadn't been on the streets, although since he'd survived until his sixth year—and in a relatively healthy condition—he must at least have been given a fighting chance in the beginning. He couldn't remember by whom. He couldn't recall anything, in fact, before his third or fourth year. He didn't rightly know the date of his own birth, although he'd known his name when Father Patrick had asked him. The date November 30 had stuck in his little head, too, and he'd offered that as his birthday. To this day, he didn't know if that was really his birthday or some other date he'd remembered for some reason unrelated to his nativity.

With a sigh for the perversity of mankind and fate, he shook himself and opted to cease thinking ugly thoughts. Susanna Clement wasn't ugly. She was sprightly and pretty and industrious and about as far removed from the misery of his youth as a body could be. He'd think about her for a while.

He glanced down at her now. Her hair glistened in the morning sunshine. She had very pretty hair. It looked thick and silky, and Julian wished he could test it with his fingers. He'd love to loosen her soft bun and run his fingers along her scalp, to tilt her head back and taste her lips. Alas, he knew he didn't dare. She was still mad as a hornet at him. Besides, he didn't want to start touching her for fear he wouldn't be able to stop.

Her feet beat out a militant tattoo on the leafy path. In spite of his glum musings about his unhappy past, he felt a bubble of mirth in his chest. Thank God that, whoever his parents were, they'd blessed him with a sense of humor. He was pretty sure he'd never have survived without it.

"So, Miss Clement, you march to a right quick step. You contemplating a military career by any chance?"

She stopped dead in the rutted road. "What?" Her hot frown shot straight through him, lodged in his sex, and heated him inside and out. He thrust a hand into his pockets to hide his condition.

Attempting a meek tone, he said, "I'm sorry I riled you earlier, Miss Clement. I'll try to behave myself from now on. Can we be friends?"

She scowled at the hand he held out as if she feared it would smack her. Ha. If she only knew what he really wanted to do with that hand, she'd smack him.

"I don't appreciate being laughed at, Mr. Kittrick. While I may not be as sophisticated in the ways of the world as the females with whom you are accustomed to dealing, I am an intelligent woman with a good education. I'm unused to casual banter and insinuating suggestions." Her scowl was pure defiance. "I can't guarantee to be your friend because I don't trust your motives, but I will be your colleague until this assignment is over. If you will be so kind as to restrain your improper speech, I should very much appreciate it."

That would be completely impossible. Julian didn't tell her so. Instead he said, "I'll do my best, Miss Clement. I'll try."

She sniffed imperiously. "My teacher Miss Amberly used to tell me that one either tried or one did, Mr. Kittrick. I'm sure if you put your mind to it, you'll succeed in curbing your baser nature."

Impossible shot through Julian's mind once more. Since he didn't want her to be mad at him any longer, he said submissively, "Yes, ma'am. Will you please shake my hand now?"

She continued to frown at his hand for a moment. Julian could clearly read mistrust of his motives on her face, and he admired her perspicacity. After what seemed like hours, she took his hand and shook it briskly once. Then she dropped it as if the same sparks that had shot through him at her touch had also affected her.

They finished working at the Sedgewick place in the early afternoon. Julian was pleased with their haul of information so far. Although he wouldn't tell Susanna, because it was too much fun to keep her in doubt, he'd begun to believe that maybe—just maybe—Magdalena Bondurant wasn't the floozy he'd at first assumed her to be.

What bothered him even more than that was his fierce reluctance to part company with Miss Susanna Clement. He wanted to hang out with her, to stroll by the river and through the woods with her. To *oh* and *ah* over bluebirds and chipmunks and chattering squirrels with her. To be with her, wherever she wanted to be.

Obviously he was losing his mind. Because he couldn't seem to help himself, he asked, "What are your plans for the evening, Miss Clement?"

Her eyes were as bright as Christmas candles. They fairly shone when she peered up at him. His chest clenched. So did his fingers. What happened to his lower reaches was too improper to mention.

"I'm going to the cemetery, and I just can't wait until twilight!"

As soon as she'd spoken, she gasped, as if she'd said something she shouldn't have. Which she might well have. The cemetery? "Why in the world are you going to the cemetery? Oh, that's right. You like to sit and meditate at your late great-aunt's empty grave, don't you?"

That was rather sweet of her, actually. Julian, who'd never admired sweetness in his entire life, preferring other attributes in his own females, admired Susanna's absolute devotion to her great-aunt.

"Um, yes. Yes, that's it, all right. I want to ponder all the things we discovered yesterday and today, and to try to make sense of them. Establish a pattern, if you know what I mean."

"Yes, I believe I do. But I still don't understand why you want to do it in a graveyard. Wouldn't it be easier if you could spread things out on a desk and work that way?"

Her little chin lifted, and he grinned. She was as defiant as all hell, and her attitude tickled him. "We all have our own methods of organization, Mr. Kittrick. Mine works for me just as well as yours does for you."

He acknowledged the justice of her statement with a nod. "Right. I'm sure that's true." They'd reached her aunt and uncle's gate. Without wanting to, Julian pushed it open and stood back so Susanna could pass through it before him. She did it with a haughty sweep of her skirts and left a faint scent of flowers in her wake. He inhaled deeply and wished he could take her back to his hotel room and make love to her until the sun set and rose and set again.

Susanna seemed completely unaffected by his own presence. She strode down the walk, tripped up the stairs, and waved him off as if he were a lackey assigned the duty of seeing the queen to her chambers.

He stuffed his hands into his pockets and moped back to his solitary hotel room. There was an entire evening ahead of him. The prospect of drinking it away in the saloon seemed even more dismal today than it usually did.

Susanna tried to keep from running all the way to the Spring Hill Cemetery. She didn't want people to think she was a lunatic, and she didn't want anyone to follow her. She had business to transact with Danilo, and she sure as the devil didn't crave an audience.

She burst through the trees and screeched to a halt beside Magdalena Bondurant's empty grave. She'd been longing to talk with Danilo ever since she'd discovered the other three diaries. In fact, her mouth was open and her words were practically tripping over themselves in their hurry to leave her lips when she realized Danilo wasn't there.

She stopped short and looked around. No ghost.

"Danilo?"

She didn't want to shout for fear of attracting the attention of other visitors to the graveyard. Not that there were any. Thank God. She walked over to Danilo's burial site and bent down, thinking perhaps he was napping in there. That is, if ghosts napped. There was a whole lot about this haunting business that she didn't understand yet, although she aimed to find out.

"Danilo?"

Nothing. Indignation and impatience began sniping at each other in her breast. Blast it, he was supposed to *be* here when she needed him. She frowned and said, more loudly, "Danilo! Danilo, where are you? I have all sorts of things to report to you."

Nothing. Damn and blast. Where was he? How could he desert her this way? She *needed* him! She needed his interpretation of certain passages in Magdalena's diaries; she needed him to help her plot out an ongoing strategy.

How did one go about conjuring a ghost? She hadn't had to do anything at all the first time they'd met; he'd merely appeared out of nowhere and frightened her half to death. She was beginning to feel sorely used when a chill crept over her. Gooseflesh rose on her arms, and she rubbed them, slightly uneasy. She turned around slowly, then whirled back the other way, her nerves crackling.

She cried tartly, "Danilo! Danilo, if you're here, please become visible and quit playing games. This isn't funny!"

"I should say it's not!"

With a sharp screech, Susanna jerked around again—and there he was. Patting at his voluminous red-lined cape and looking cranky, Danilo stood half submerged in the Homstead monument. *"I didn't know you were coming this evening, or I'd have rolled out the red car- pet and been waiting for you. How am I supposed to know when you plan to grace this vile place with your presence? I may be a ghost, but I'm not a mind reader."*

"I beg your pardon." Torn between contrition and anger, Susanna fought with her emotions. "Where were you? How am I supposed to find you if you're not here when I come to report?"

"A simple calling of my name will do, Miss Clement. No need to shriek or holler."

"Hmmm. It seems to me that you should stick pretty close to this spot if you expect me to give you regular summaries of how our work is progressing."

"Well, I like that!" Danilo flung himself down on the monument and turned his head away, pouting fiercely and reminding Susanna of a sulky child. She wondered if all actors were like that, or if it was a ghostly trait. Before she could ask, he turned around again and frowned at her.

"I'll have you know, young lady, that I was on an errand of mercy when you flounced over here expecting me to be at your beck and call. And I was going to all that trouble for a person who doesn't deserve it, too, what's more!"

She blinked at him, and realized he was mightily vexed. Because she both liked and needed him, she de- cided a conciliatory tone would best suit her purpose. "I beg your pardon, Danilo. I didn't mean to be impa- tient. I only feared that you wouldn't appear, and tonight I particularly wanted to talk to you. What was this errand of mercy of yours?"

He lifted his chin and sniffed. *"Your young man—"*

"I don't have a young man!"

His frown deepened. *"Don't interrupt me, if you please, young lady. I wasn't very old when my life was so tragically snuffed out, but I'd be in my seventies now, and I think that advanced an age deserves some re- spect."*

"I beg your pardon." Susanna tried her best to be

penitent. She didn't quite succeed, but she did manage
to adopt an apologetic expression.

He sniffed again and gave her a regal nod. *"Very well.
As I was saying, that young man of yours, Mr. Julian
Kittrick, has some mighty unpleasant notions about his
parents in his head."*

Susanna stared, not having anticipated this particular
wrinkle. "He does?"

*"He does. And since he comes from an even more
unsavory neighborhood in New York City than the one
I was born into, I decided to find out if he has reason
to harbor thoughts of so unkind a nature."*

"He did? You did? I thought he was rich and pam-
pered."

Danilo's eyes widened and his ghostly brows lifted.
*"My dear young lady, that poor boy, however much I
dislike him for being a scandalmonger and a yellow
journalist and an impudent so-and-so, barely survived
his infancy. But for the sake of an earthly benefactor,
he'd surely never have lived to adulthood."*

"But—but what about his parents?"

"Didn't have any."

No parents? Good heavens. "How—how did he live?
You said he had a benefactor."

*"Not until he was six years old. The boy never knew
his parents. He lived with a horde of raggedy urchins
on the streets of New York until a priest rescued him."*

"My goodness. How do you know that?"

Danilo buffed his ghostly fingernails against the lapels
of his ghostly cape. *"I have connections from beyond,
you know."*

"Oh. That's right, I suppose you do."

"Yes." He peered at her slyly. *"I also manage to get
around quite nicely on my own."*

"Of course." Stunned by Danilo's revelation, Susanna sank down onto her aunt's headstone, completely
forgetting how much she'd deplored Julian's doing
much the same thing only a few days earlier. "I didn't

know about Mr. Kittrick's unhappy past. I never even suspected.''

"Well, of course you didn't. He's almost as good an actor as I am." Danilo's frown deepened. *"Well, perhaps he's not that good."*

"No, I'm sure he's not," she said mechanically, and shook her head. "I had no idea."

"People always think they know everything, and half the time they don't know anything at all."

She nodded. "I certainly didn't suspect Mr. Kittrick's background to be one of poverty and struggle. Perhaps you're right about us not knowing anything."

"Of course I'm right."

"Did you find out anything for him?"

"Not enough. But I'll keep trying. I've been observing the two of you work, and I have to say that, however misguided Julian Kittrick is about some things, he at least seems to want to discover the truth about my beloved Magdalena."

"Yes, he does. I'm sure of it."

Danilo heaved a theatrical sigh. *"And even though the truth he longs to discover is one that would ruin my darling's name forever, I shall do my best to set his mind at ease on the matter of his parents. Turnabout being fair play, and all that."*

"That's very kind of you, Danilo. Very magnanimous."

"I know it is."

Susanna thought about what Danilo said about Julian's childhood and suddenly felt guilty for her unfavorable characterization of the newspaperman. "I had no idea, you know. I thought he was so cocky and brash because he grew up rich and wallowing in privilege."

"Not at all, Miss Clement. He's cocky and brash because he had to be in order to survive. He's undoubtedly concealing a good deal of shame underneath that audacious manner of his, too."

She shook her head, feeling devastatingly sad for the poor child Julian Kittrick had once been. "I had no idea in the world. I completely misjudged him.''

''Probably not completely.'' Danilo's voice was extremely dry.

"I mean, I misjudged his background.''

''Yes. Well, everything's not as it seems more often than it is.'' He frowned. *''Or something like that.''*

"I guess so.''

Susanna sat quietly, imagining Julian as a child, wondering what it must have been like for him. She shook herself out of her reverie and looked up to find Danilo folding his cape precisely over his crossed knees. If he weren't transparent, he'd look exactly like Susanna had always pictured a lofty British gentleman. Which, she supposed, was the effect he was aiming for. "Can you appear in the daylight?''

He tilted his head to one side. *''It's very difficult and takes a good deal of energy. Why do you ask?''*

"You said you were watching us.'' All at once, the notion of being spied on made her shiver.

Danilo must have noticed, because his face sprouted a cynical expression. *''Don't worry, Miss Clement. I'm no voyeur. I'm only interested in observing you and that miserable journalist for Magdalena's sake.''*

"I see. But you can appear if you need to?''

''Not without great effort and risking harm to my substance—or what's left of it. Appearing in the daylight saps my strength terribly. Why? Do you want me to materialize in front of that fellow and say 'boo' or something? I don't do parlor tricks.''

Susanna could tell she'd offended him. "I beg your pardon, Danilo. I didn't mean to imply that I wanted you to do anything unsavory or undignified. I've just never been able to ask questions of a ghost before.''

''I suppose there's some justice in your observation, Miss Clement, and I also suppose I don't blame you for asking me such questions.''

"Thank you.'' She felt very humble, but quickly her humility was banished by excitement. "Oh, Danilo! Look what I found in the attic!''

She held out the diaries in both hands. Danilo peered at them with furrowed brows.

"What are those?"

He wafted closer. Susanna realized she no longer harbored even a hint of fear of him.

"They're three more of Magdalena's diaries. And there's lots of information about a Mr. McKenzie. I think he's the one who had the jewels, and she writes about a storage facility on McKenzie land, too. We found references to a cabin—which is probably what Magdalena called the storage facility—and gems and Mr. McKenzie in Mr. Sedgewick's papers as well."

Danilo snorted. *"Sedgewick! So you took my advice and went to visit that villainous old fraud."*

Susanna opened her mouth to agree with him but didn't get the chance.

"What in the name of holy hell is going on here?"

Susanna jumped up and spun around. Danilo rose into the air and hovered like the specter he was.

Julian Kittrick, wild-eyed, stared at the both of them. If Susanna hadn't been so startled by his untimely intrusion, she might have laughed at the expression of shock on his handsome face.

Chapter
Seven

"I don't care what you do or don't believe in, you cheeky twit!"

Danilo was leaning toward Julian in an extremely belligerent fashion. Susanna almost didn't blame him, since Julian had said some awfully cutting things after he'd overcome his initial state of shock, but she also understood Julian's unwillingness to believe in ghosts. Danilo did rather turn one's preconceived notions about how the world worked topsy-turvy.

"This is outrageous! I don't believe in you for a second. You're some kind of figment. A trick. A schoolyard prank."

"How dare you. I'll show you a damned prank!"

With that, Danilo swept Julian's straw hat off of his head and shot up into the top branches of a nearby maple tree. There he sat, twirling Julian's hat in his ghostly fingers and smirking. *"How's that for a figment?"*

"Hey! Give me back my hat!"

"Not until you show some manners."

Although amused by the flustered Julian, Susanna

knew she really should put an end to Danilo's taunting. She grabbed Julian by the coat sleeve and yanked hard. He whirled around.

"What?"

"Stop yelling at Danilo, Mr. Kittrick. I didn't believe it at first, either, but it's true. He's a ghost, and he's here, and so are we, and we're all interested in the same thing. We all want to discover how Magdalena Bondurant disappeared, what she was doing when it happened, who else was involved, and if her disappearance had any connection to those jewels."

His blond hair wild and his face set into a mask of fury, Julian looked down at Susanna—and softened. Susanna could hardly believe her eyes when his face lost its rage, his hard mouth smoothed out, and his high color faded. He even smiled. She nearly fainted dead away on the spot. Merciful heavens, the man was so handsome he was dangerous.

"I beg your pardon, Miss Clement." He raked a hand through his hair, mussing it further. Susanna wished she could do that. She'd love to see if his hair was as silky as it looked. "But please tell me. You can give it up now. This is some kind of joke, isn't it? I mean, I know I've given you a hard time the past few days, and you deserve to get back at me, but you've had your fun. Come on now, tell me. I'll admit it; you did a good job. It's really kind of funny." He gave two strained *ha-ha's,* then stopped and stared down at her. Susanna could feel the pleading in his gaze.

She shook her head. "No, Mr. Kittrick. This isn't a joke. This is Danilo, and he's a ghost. In life, he was an actor and a playwright, and he was engaged to be married to Magdalena Bondurant. He knew her better than anyone else. They were in love." She didn't know why she added that, but it seemed important somehow.

He didn't say anything. She tried again.

"I don't know if you recall when I mentioned Danilo to you?"

He nodded.

"Well, when you asked me who told me about Danilo and Magdalena, I felt stupid for not having provided myself with an answer because I knew you'd never believe me if I told you the truth."

Julian glanced up into the maple tree. Danilo waved.

"I don't believe it." Julian's voice had sunk to a whisper. Susanna hoped that signified a lessening of his doubts.

Then he said, "I'm losing my mind."

"No, you're not."

"You're right. I've already lost my mind."

She smiled, and felt a rush of tenderness for the formerly flippant and still far too handsome newspaper reporter standing before her. She wanted to hug him, and the urge didn't shock her as much as she knew it should. "You haven't lost your mind. You've only had your world turned upside down."

He looked up into the tree again. Danilo was inspecting his fingernails and looking smug. Julian's hat sat at a dashing angle on his transparent black hair.

"I—I . . ." Julian stopped talking and swallowed.

"You're confused?" Susanna offered, trying to help.

He frowned at her. "I guess."

"Being confused is perfectly understandable, Mr. Kittrick. After all, it's not every day one meets a ghost."

After a hesitation that reeked of doubt, Julian repeated, "I guess."

From the branches of the maple tree, Susanna heard Danilo sniff. She tried to decide what the best thing to say might be, but didn't dare deliberate too long for fear Julian's rational mind would erect more barriers to prevent his believing in the corroboration of his eyes and ears. She couldn't in all honesty blame him. After all, how many times did a journalist get to meet up with a ghost when he was sober? Julian seemed almost vulnerable right now. She needed to strike while the iron was hot, as it were.

So she cleared her throat and said, "You really must pay attention to the evidence of your senses, Mr. Kittrick. After all, you can *see* Danilo. You can *hear* him."

Julian peeked up into the branches of the maple tree. Danilo waved again and said, *"Howdy,"* a greeting that seemed to go with the straw hat still sitting on his head. Susanna saw Julian's Adam's apple bob up and down when he swallowed.

"You see? You heard him. There he is. Big as life." Poor phrasing, Susanna decided with a frown.

"Big as life," Julian whispered, repeating her words. "Except that you want me to believe he's dead."

"Well . . ."

"Yes!"

Danilo's shout made Julian cringe. Susanna fought the impulse to throw her arms around him. She wasn't sure it was borne merely of the desire to give solace to a fellow human being in distress; it also might have sprung from less noble feelings having to do solely with Julian Kittrick. Danilo looked angry. If he'd been alive, Susanna was sure he'd have gone red in the face from fury by this time.

"Yes, she wants you to believe I'm dead, because it's the truth! I swear, you'd think a journalist would believe what he sees and hears! I thought that's what you people did for a living, search out evidence. Find proof of the unusual. Or do you prefer to make it all up?"

Danilo's barb evidently struck a raw nerve. Julian said with a growl, "We don't make stuff up! What's the matter with the two of you, anyway? You're always accusing me of making things up!"

Susanna murmured, "Now, now," and smiled at Danilo, who didn't smile back. He looked, in fact, totally huffy. He whipped Julian's straw hat off of his head and sent it sailing through the air above Julian and Susanna. Julian made a quick swipe for it but missed. The hat came to rest on Magdalena Bondurant's headstone. Julian grabbed it off and hugged it to his chest as if it were a lifeline and he a drowning man. Susanna felt a swell of compassion for him and allowed herself to touch his arm lightly.

"I know it's difficult to believe, Mr. Kittrick, but it's true. Danilo is a ghost, and he's here, and he can help us." Sympathy oozed from her voice.

Julian scowled at her. "Don't patronize me."

Her compassion fled, and she snatched her hand back, irritated that she'd succumbed to her sympathetic impulses. "I'm not patronizing you! I'm trying to get you to believe the truth!"

"You're trying to get me to believe in ghosts." Julian sounded extremely annoyed.

"Yes! Yes, I'm trying to get you to believe in ghosts. In Danilo, at least, because he's about the best source we have for information regarding Magdalena Bondurant's life and the time during which she disappeared."

Skepticism radiated from Julian's countenance, and it annoyed Susanna almost beyond tolerance. "Oh, for heaven's sake, I've never met anyone so stubborn in my whole life!"

Evidently Danilo felt the same way. All at once, he soared down from the maple tree, executed two complete swoops around the graveyard, looking more like a crazed bird than anything else, shot as straight and quick as a bullet through three of the taller tomb markers—it looked to Susanna as if he did that on purpose, to prove a point to Julian—and stopped less than an inch from the newspaperman. In fact, parts of him took up the same space Julian did. Danilo shouted *"Boo!"* into Julian's face.

Shocked, Julian staggered back several paces and sat with a plunk on the headstone of someone named Brewer. Susanna pursed her lips, torn between annoyance and laughter. She admired Danilo's dramatic skills in that moment more than she could say. If one *had* to do business with a ghost, she thought she was lucky to have found an entertaining one.

Danilo folded his arms over his chest. *"There!"* he cried, eyeing the result of his startling flight triumphantly. *"Try* that *on for size! You demand proof, I'll*

*give you proof! I'll haunt you until you admit that you
believe in me.''*

Julian sat there, blinking up at the ghost, his straw hat
crunched between the flat of his hand and Brewer's
tombstone. Susanna had never even dared hope to see
him looking this uncertain. Why, he seemed almost human sprawled there, disbelief written all over his fea-
tures. He looked vulnerable. He looked unlike the
cynical newspaperman she'd come to know and—well,
to know, anyway. He looked quite funny, in fact.

Humor won the battle in her breast, and she burst out
laughing. Both men turned to glower at her. She waved
a hand in their direction, helpless with mirth. "I—I—"

"You find this amusing,'' Danilo muttered. It was an
accusation.

She shook her head and tried to formulate a denial,
but she couldn't speak through her burbling hilarity. She
slapped a hand over her mouth too late to stop a wholly
undignified snort from escaping. She felt her face heat
up and was embarrassed at having made such an awful
noise. Danilo glared at her.

Julian blinked several more times, evidently at a loss
as to what to do or say. At last he pushed himself up
from the tombstone.

"All right," he said.

Susanna had to grab her handkerchief from her skirt
pocket and mop her streaming eyes. She still couldn't
speak, although she sensed it was her turn to say something.

Danilo grumbled, *"All right, what?''* His arms were
still crossed over his chest. He looked excessively
grumpy.

Julian cleared his throat. "All right, I . . ." He stopped
speaking and sucked in an enormous breath that puffed
his chest out. "All right, I—believe in you." He looked
as though it was difficult for him to give credence to the
words that had just issued from his lips.

Danilo rolled his eyes. *"Why, how terribly kind of*

you. How beneficent. How generous. How magnanimous."

Susanna wiped her eyes again. "You—you d-do?" Another bout of hilarity claimed her, and she doubled over with it. She didn't mean to because she had a feeling Julian Kittrick didn't appreciate being laughed at any more than did Danilo. But she wasn't really laughing at either of them. Not really. It was the circumstances, not them. Another snort caught her off guard, and she got embarrassed all over again.

"I—I'm s-s-sorry." With a mighty effort, she stopped laughing.

"Right." Skepticism shone from Danilo's ghostly face.

"No, really I am." She got the whole sentence out before she snorted yet a third time.

Julian stood up and dusted off his rear end. He glanced down at Brewer's headstone as if offering it a mental apology. His mien tickled Susanna and almost sent her off into another gale of laughter. She held herself in check only with a terrible struggle.

"All right." She hiccuped and snorted once more. Through the fingers pressed to her mouth she said, "I—I'm sorry."

Danilo tapped his foot. She tried not to look, because the blades of grass thrusting through his transparent foot made her want to laugh again. Oh, dear. She really had to get herself under control; this would never do.

Julian cleared his throat. "Okay, let's say I believe in you. Where do we go from here?"

"I have no idea where you *plan to go,"* Danilo said, huffy. *"I plan to stay right here and listen to what Miss Clement has to say about the diaries she found and the information you unearthed in that vile Mr. Sedgewick's moldy old tomb of a house."*

"Yes," Susanna said without even the flicker of a giggle. She was proud of herself. "Danilo can probably offer all sorts of insights into the papers we found, Mr. Kittrick."

Julian still didn't appear convinced, but Susanna decided she'd be better off not waiting until he believed wholeheartedly. Knowing him, he'd probably come up with some excuse to disbelieve, and then they'd never get anywhere.

After one last dab with her handkerchief that didn't completely wipe away her tears of laughter, she hauled out the first of the three diaries. Before either Danilo or Julian could say another word, she said, "All right. Take a look at this." She tapped the page. "Right here Magdalena makes mention of a place in McKenzie's woods. 'The storage facility is ready,' it says here. And here"— she hauled out her notebook and tapped it—"in this notation I made at Sedgewick's place, it says, 'Damn McKenzie. He's going to let her use the cabin, and I can't make him listen to reason about the gems.' " She looked up at Danilo, her amusement forgotten in the intensity of her interest. "Tell me, Danilo. That cabin in McKenzie's woods was used to hide runaway slaves, wasn't it? And the gems he talked about were going to be sold to help slaves escape. I *know* Magdalena was working with the Underground Railroad. I *know* it!"

Danilo looked disconcerted for a moment. He turned away, then turned back again. Susanna got the impression that the gesture, although somewhat dramatic, was unstudied. Her nerves jumped; her skin itched; excitement ate at her insides like acid. Still Danilo didn't say anything.

She opened her mouth, willing to urge him on, when at last he spoke.

"Yes." His voice was very soft. He sounded not at all like the theatrical ghost Susanna had come to know. He sounded almost as vulnerable as Julian Kittrick had looked a few moments before.

"Yes?" Her own voice was breathy in the still evening air. "Yes? Magdalena Bondurant was working with the Underground Railroad?"

Danilo bowed his head. *"I believe so."*

"And the gems? Were the gems McKenzie's? And

was he willing to sell them to help finance Magdalena's Underground Railroad project?''

Danilo shrugged. *"I don't know about the gems. I heard rumors, but I tried to stay out of it."*

"You tried to stay out of it?"

He nodded and looked sad. *"I didn't want to know what was going on."*

"Why?"

Danilo heaved a big sigh, and Susanna reassessed her conclusion about ghosts breathing. His sigh didn't seem to be merely for effect this time.

"What she was doing was illegal, you know." Danilo stared at the ground peeking through his transparent shoes.

"Yes. Yes, I understand that. But it was a noble enterprise."

"That's what she always said." Danilo did not look as though he necessarily agreed. *"It was still illegal."*

Susanna nodded. "I understand." And she did, too. Not that she'd allow a little thing like a magnanimous work's relative illegality stand in her way any more than Magdalena Bondurant had let it stand in hers.

Danilo's shoulders slumped. *"She asked me to work with her, but I refused."*

"You refused?" Susanna stared at him, surprised.

"It was dangerous, illegal work. I wasn't afraid for myself—or not too much, anyway—but I was terrified for her. She never thought about her own safety, you know. She only thought about the good she might do." He threw out his arms. *"I thought that if I refused to help her, she'd stop it. It was no business for a female to be in! She might have been hurt. Arrested."*

He whirled around, his red-lined cape fluttering around him and reminding Susanna of tales of vampires she'd listened to in college. Vampires were big news these days, but Susanna didn't believe in them. Of course, she'd never believed in ghosts either.

She said softly, "But she refused to quit merely because you wouldn't help her."

The ghost didn't answer for a moment. Her own breathing was ragged. She glanced at Julian, and found him staring at Danilo's back, too. Julian seemed to feel her gaze on him, because he turned his head, and they exchanged a glance. Susanna felt not quite so alone.

At last Danilo swirled around again. *"Yes, she refused to quit! And it killed her!"*

Until she'd met Danilo, Susanna hadn't realized that ghosts could cry. Huge, translucent teardrops coursed down his cheeks. She felt sorry for him, understanding for perhaps the first time how very much he had loved Susanna's great-aunt. However, she didn't entirely go along with his theory.

"You don't know that."

"What?" Danilo seemed annoyed when he hauled out a transparent handkerchief from his transparent cape and wiped the transparent tears away from his transparent cheeks. *"What do you mean? You mean you don't go along with my theory? Do you have a better one?"*

Fascinated by these ghostly activities and sorry she'd annoyed Danilo, Susanna almost lost track of her reasoning. "Well, I mean you don't know that it was her activities with the Underground Railroad that were responsible for her disappearance. I mean, you don't *know* even, really, that she's dead."

She appreciated Danilo's look of outrage and shrugged helplessly. "Well, it's true, Danilo. We don't really *know* anything at all about her disappearance. I mean, you said yourself that you haven't met her spirit in your ghostly realm or anything." She made a sweeping gesture with her arm.

Danilo glowered at her, looking more substantial than he had only moments before. *"No, I haven't, but that doesn't mean anything."*

"It doesn't?"

"No."

"But it might mean that she's not dead, couldn't it?"

The ghost shrugged, making his cape ripple angrily.

"That's right."

Julian's voice surprised them both, and Susanna and Danilo looked at him. He seemed to have recovered his composure.

Danilo said, *"What do* you *know about it? You don't even believe in me."*

"Sure I do," Julian assured him, sounding almost as nonchalant as ever. "But Miss Clement's right. Nobody knows what happened to her. In fact, my own theory is that she took those jewels—and both the diaries and papers in Sedgewick's library indicate there *were* jewels, and that they came from this fellow McKenzie—and skipped town with them. Ran off. Probably went somewhere far away and is still living the good life with the profits from the stolen gems."

His smile was a work of art. If Susanna hadn't been so annoyed with his reasoning, she might have appreciated it. Since she was annoyed, she only huffed in irritation.

Danilo, however, seemed to swell with antagonism and fury. For the first time since she'd met him, Susanna felt real trepidation skitter up her spine.

"What—did—you—say?" Danilo's voice, too, had taken on an unearthly timbre, as if he were speaking from an echoing tomb.

Oh, dear. Susanna wished, for all their sakes, that Julian had kept his cynical opinions to himself in this instance. "He doesn't really mean it, Danilo. Truly he doesn't."

"I do, too!" It was Julian's turn to look outraged.

Danilo stabbed Julian's chest with a finger that slid right through his summer suit coat. Julian stared down at the half finger attached to the transparent hand sticking out of Danilo's jacket. The effect was extremely unusual. Susanna couldn't help staring herself.

"I've taken all I intend to take from you for one evening, you insolent puppy. I know the human animal is a pathetic thing and that journalists, with their mistrust and pessimism and eagerness to believe the worst of others, are more pathetic than most, but I will not *stand*

*still and listen to my beloved Magdalena being slan-
dered by a whippersnapper like* you!''

With that, Danilo swirled his cape. A tremendous
thunderclap rent the air; lightning flashed overhead; and
wind blew like a hurricane, sending Julian's hat and Susanna's hairpins flying. Susanna screamed and covered
her ears. Her skirt whooshed up to her waist, and she
would have been embarrassed except that she was too
shocked. The whole universe—at least the part in which
she and Julian stood—underwent its own brief storm,
complete with alarming atmospheric effects. The whole
thing lasted no more than ten seconds.

When it ended, Susanna realized she'd squeezed her
eyes shut. Her hands still covered her ears. When she
cracked her eyes open, she didn't see Julian. She
whipped her head back and forth, her heart hammering
a frantic *rat-a-tat* in her breast.

''Oh, Lord! You didn't kill him, did you, Danilo?''

No answer greeted her. She turned with a whirl and
realized that Danilo, too, had disappeared. ''Oh, dear.''

Good heavens, how would she account for this? How
did one go about explaining the disappearance of a
newspaper journalist in a strong wind in the Spring Hill
Cemetery? Although she wouldn't know for sure until
she checked, Susanna had a suspicion that Danilo's
ghostly powers had been expended for Julian Kittrick's
sake; that this was a personal hurricane and that it hadn't
extended to the rest of the town.

''Mr. Kittrick?'' She peered everywhere, but saw no
trace of him. Worried, she forgot propriety. ''Julian?''

''Goddamn it, I'm up here. Get me down!''

Susanna was shocked and annoyed by Julian's pro-
fane language for only a moment. As soon as she saw
him, clinging for dear life—and upside down, too—to
the very top branches of the maple tree, offense fled,
and she burst out laughing for the second time that evening.

*   *   *

"Damn it all, it's not funny!"

Susanna glanced out of the corner of her eye at the leaves dripping from Julian's formerly dashing light-weight summer suit. It no longer dashed, but hung limply from his muscled limbs. His hat was ruined be-yond redemption. She giggled again, infuriating him.

"I'm s-s-sorry," she stammered, spoiling the effect with an enormous guffaw.

Limping at her side—he'd lost one of his shoes in his flight—Julian shot her a look that he hoped would si-lence her once and for all. "It's not funny."

"Of c-c-course n-not." She snorted, and tried to smother her laughter by holding her handkerchief over her mouth. It didn't work.

"Damn it all, stop laughing at me!"

Startled, Susanna stopped and stared at him wide-eyed. He supposed he had frightened her. Seeing the wariness in her eyes, Julian almost felt guilty. But then he remembered that she was laughing at his expense, enjoying his humiliation. Julian scowled to remind both Susanna and himself that he was angry.

"I'm s-sorry," she stammered.

"So you've said."

"I p-promise I won't tell anyone else. B-but I'll bet you'll never deny the existence of ghosts again."

He glared at her for a good minute before a reluctant grin spread over his face. He'd been patting dust and leaves from his clothing ever since Susanna had man-aged to guide him down from the maple tree. He'd been sure he'd never make it, and was convinced he was about to join Danilo on the other side, but she'd talked him down at last. He was truly grateful, even if he did feel like a fool.

"I'll never get this suit clean again, that's for sure." He frowned at the stains on his sleeve. Damn. He loved this suit.

Susanna eyed him askance. Thank God she didn't laugh again, although she did have an impish grin on her face. Funny. Until this evening, he wouldn't have

believed her capable of laughing at all. He guessed he'd
been wrong. He couldn't think of too many things fun-
nier than what had happened to him back there in that
rotten graveyard. His grin broadened.

Susanna seemed to relax a bit. "I think there's a new-
fangled dry-process cleaning establishment in Palmyra.
Maybe they can get the stains out for you."

He tore his gaze away from her pretty brown eyes and
scowled at his coat sleeve. "Maybe."

To his surprise, she reached out and pinched the fabric
between her fingers. "It's seersucker. That should clean
up pretty well, although, since it's white, it might stain.
Perhaps if you brought it to my house tomorrow morning, I could rub some soda and water into the worse
stains before you take it to be cleaned."

Nobody had ever offered to do his laundry before.
Julian was touched, but he only squinted at his coat
sleeve as if studying it for a moment before he said,
"Thanks. Maybe I'll do that."

She giggled again. This time he almost didn't resent
it. "You must admit that was a pretty spectacular way
to prove a point," she said.

He said, "I guess," and wished he didn't have to
leave Susanna at her aunt's front door. He wanted to sit
on the porch steps with her, drape his arm around her
shoulder, and smooch until the sun came up.

Now he definitely knew he was losing his mind.

Chapter Eight

Susanna awoke with a scream choked in her throat. The scream couldn't escape, but lodged there and caused an awful rasping sound to permeate the air in her bedroom. The strangled noise sounded like a snake's hiss, and it terrified her almost more than the dream she just had.

Thrashing at the blankets binding her limbs like ropes, she sat up and gasped for air, sucking in lungful after lungful, her body shaking like a leaf and dripping with perspiration. "Oh, my Lord," crawled from her throat, past her trapped scream. "Oh, my sweet Lord in heaven."

She slammed a hand over her thundering heart and realized she was crying. Her face was wet with salty tears that crept into her mouth and tasted of panic and despair. And loneliness. Terrible, awful, unrelenting solitude. She shuddered and hugged herself more tightly.

Good grief. She'd never had such a terrifying nightmare; in it she'd felt so isolated. With a trembling hand she reached over and tried to strike a sulfur match. She needed light like she needed air. It took her several tries, but at last she was able to ignite the wick on her bedside lamp. Then she tipped the clock on her nightstand and squinted at its face.

"Three o'clock," she said out loud. Her voice, although soft and breathy, gave her an iota of comfort.

She'd never been alone before—not like in her dream. She'd never, until now, understood how much a person could crave the sound of a human voice. Even her own.

What had it meant? Abandonment. Loss. Stark, brutal terror.

She couldn't stand to think about it. She needed perspective. To attain it, she had to get up. Exercise. She needed to walk. In her dream she'd been shackled, bound by something awful. And doomed. Even though Susanna had no idea what had happened to her in that awful dream, she had known herself to be utterly, irredeemably beyond the hope of human or divine help.

Her knees felt like rubber when she swung them over the side of her bed. She had to move around, to clear her head of the clinging tentacles of horror. They were cleaving to her conscience like cobwebs clung to rafters in abandoned attics and cellars in old houses.

Where had that thought come from? Rattled, Susanna shook her head hard, trying to shake the cobwebs loose. Perhaps if she walked around her comfortable, familiar, friendly room, looked out the window at the starry night sky, and . . .

She sucked in another deep breath. No. That's right. She wasn't in New Mexico Territory any longer. She was in Palmyra, Maine, and she couldn't see but a very few stars from her bedroom window.

Well, that was all right. The friendly, familiar tree branches would do. A pretty maple tree grew right outside her bedroom window. Susanna loved that tree. She'd never seen a maple tree until she visited Maine. She hoped the leaves would begin to turn before she had to go home again. Fall colors. Her mother had told her all about the fall colors here. Yes. She'd commune with nature in the guise of her maple tree and set her leftover fears at bay that way.

Her hand still shook when she unlatched the window, shoved it open, leaned out, and breathed deeply of the damp, mossy night atmosphere. Crisp air filled lungs that only moments before had felt as though they'd never work again.

Because she didn't want to remember her dream, she concentrated on the properties of Maine air as opposed to that in the territory. She wondered if she'd ever get used to the wonders sufficient rainfall could perform on a landscape. Here everything smelled of moisture and growth. Back home, everything was dust and struggle. It was astonishing to her how green everything was here. Why, there was even moss growing on the sides of trees.

Not, of course, that she could see any of it at this hour of the night. Morning. Whatever it was. Three o'clock. It was three o'clock. She shivered again, not from cold, but from leftover dread.

After several minutes, during which she grabbed at every comforting thought she'd ever had about anything, Susanna had calmed down enough to consider her nightmare. She felt she had to, as if the dream held a desperate message.

She'd never been so frightened. In her dream, she'd been trapped and unable to move, chained up in some room or cellar somewhere. She distinctly recalled the chains and the feeling of being underground. The chains had been heavy and cold and metallic and unyielding, and she'd known with the understanding that comes from absolute certainty that it would do no good to rattle them or to cry for help. She'd been beyond help, and she'd known it.

She'd been trapped somewhere dark, and she'd known that no light would ever reach her again. Despair had filled her. She'd been helpless and hopeless, and she'd known—she'd *known*—beyond the shadow of any doubt that she was doomed. She'd been abandoned there. She'd known, somehow, some way, that no one would ever come to rescue her, that she was alone, and that she was going to die. Horribly. Of starvation and thirst and who knew what else?

"My Lord," she whispered to the black night. "My Lord, where did those awful feelings come from?"

She frowned, and had to acknowledge that they had felt more like memories than new sensations. But she'd never been trapped anywhere; never been held captive. That's what it had felt like. She'd been someone's captive.

Indians. Perhaps her fertile brain had concocted a dream about the awful stories she used to hear about Indian attacks. Indians were said to take captives. In the territory, people whispered dreadful tales about women who'd been kept for years as slaves or worse by various Indian tribes. Maybe her imagination had spun a fanciful dream about Indians and . . .

No. Her dream had nothing to do with Indians; Susanna knew it instinctively. Besides, she had no imagination. Whatever horrible thing she'd been dreaming about had happened here. In Maine. She knew it without knowing how or why.

Her dream had spawned the most morbid sensations she'd ever felt. She couldn't imagine anyone actually enduring that sort of entrapment. In fact, she'd never imagined such a fate at all until she'd dreamed it. How could she have dreamed something beyond her experience or invention? Susanna didn't know, but she had to smooth her hands over her arms to make the creeping sensation go away.

Gentle night breezes were cooling her skin where moments before she'd been sweating in terror. It felt good to be cool. She'd felt all but smothered in bed.

She shuddered and wrapped her arms around her body, hugging herself hard and wishing someone else's arms were performing the service. Someone strong and brave and unafraid—even a little bit cocky. Someone—no. She didn't want to begin thinking those things. Those thoughts were dangerous, and she'd already felt herself to be in too much danger tonight. She needed to forget about danger entirely.

"What a ghastly dream. You've been concentrating too hard on Magdalena Bondurant lately, Susanna Clement. You've begun to spin lurid fancies in your imagination about her possible demise."

She spoke the words aloud crisply, efficiently. She spoke them as an experiment, hoping she'd believe them.

She almost did.

Yet the situation had felt so real. So true, somehow. She'd been trapped. Chained, as if in a dungeon. She shook her head hard and whispered, "No. There aren't any dungeons in Maine. Your brain's somehow got Maine mixed up with English castles and medieval knights and princesses and so forth."

Again, her practical words were only partially successful in banishing the eerie sensation her dream had left inside of her. In spite of herself and her best attempts to relieve nerves still shaky with terror, a suspicion snaked its sneaky way past the barriers she erected against it.

Her dream had been about Magdalena Bondurant, all right, but she knew beyond understanding that it hadn't been anything Susanna's own brain had manufactured. It had been real.

Susanna's thoughts fastened on her great-aunt and she shuddered again. Susanna didn't know what had happened to Magdalena. Nobody did. For the first time since she'd begun her research, however, Susanna hoped Julian Kittrick was more right than she about Magdalena's ultimate fate. If Magdalena had endured in reality what Susanna had just endured in a dream, Susanna didn't want to know it.

"Stop it this instant!" She stamped her foot and felt minimally better. Temper helped. For the first time in her life, Susanna was glad she had one. Anger was certainly better than despair.

Anyway, it was crazy to think she could dream about

someone else's experiences and memories. Even if Magdalena had suffered such a horrible fate, how could the memories of her experience have become embedded in Susanna's mind? It was silly even to consider such a possibility. Silly and foolish. Asinine. Irrational. Inane. Too fanciful for words.

"Absurd." She spoke the word firmly, resolutely, knowing it was true even though she couldn't quite make herself believe it. So she said it again.

"Absurd. Don't be absurd, Susanna Clement. A person can't dream another person's memories."

Another shiver racked her body. She wasn't cold on the outside in spite of the breeze drying her perspiration-soaked nightgown. The icy horror that clawed at Susanna's insides went deeper than her flesh and blood. It invaded her heart and soul and mind, and she had a terrible suspicion it wouldn't let her rest now that it had found her.

It took her what seemed like aeons to calm down enough to brave her bed again. In fact, for a long time she sat in her rocking chair with a quilt wrapped around her, staring into the flickering candle flame, hoping she'd drop off to sleep that way and avoid her bed entirely. She didn't. At about four-thirty she smoothed out the sheets, erasing any hint of the battle she'd fought with them and her blankets. Then, taking elaborate pains to seem casual, she crawled into bed and pulled up the covers. She shut her eyes. She thought gentle thoughts about birds and butterflies and bees, placid skies, green rolling hills and flowers. And Julian Kittrick.

She imagined them having a friendly, happy conversation without rancor or bitter words. Next to the Sebasticook River. They were fishing, even, and enjoying the blissful summer sunshine. She wore a white frock and had a frilly white parasol by her side. She looked quite elegant, really. He was as handsome as ever, and wore his white seersucker suit—the one with the stains it had collected during a particularly interesting haunting.

She sat up, gasping for breath and darting frantic glances around her candlelit room. Blast! *Why* had she remembered haunting?

Three times she was on the edge of sleep when a prickle of nameless dread jerked her awake, her heart pounding, her mouth dry, her brain screaming. Three times she settled back against her pillows again, furious with herself and her nerves.

She never used to be a victim of her nerves. That sort of thing was the property of females unlike Susanna Clement. Susanna had a life of useful work to live and didn't need silly affectations such as nervous vapors and so forth to be considered interesting in this world run by men for men. She was interesting all by herself, because she was *interested*.

At last, too exhausted to fight her demons any longer, Susanna drifted past terror and into sleep. No further dreams troubled her.

"You look like hell. Are you sick?"

Susanna, her face a mask of fury, jerked the seersucker coat out of Julian's arms and he wished he'd phrased his observation with more delicacy. Still, it troubled him to see those dark circles under eyes that looked puffy, the pallor of her skin, the drawn look about her mouth. She'd always appeared so healthy and alert before. Alive. Ready to take on the world. With an internal grin, he acknowledged that she was always ready to take *him* on, at any rate.

Not this morning. This morning she appeared tired. Almost sick.

"I'm fine," she said with a snarl.

"Rough night?" He imbued the two words with sympathy, thinking his own night hadn't been great either.

"I had a little trouble sleeping, is all."

"I'm sorry to hear it." He trailed after her, past her aunt's big black stove speckled with flatirons, the big holey pie safe, the icebox, and into the laundry room. There he watched with interest as she rubbed soda and water into the stains on his coat sleeves. He hoped they'd come out. He loved that seersucker suit. It seemed so—so journalistic to him for some reason. He glanced down at the suit he wore this morning, a light tan gabardine, and decided it wasn't half bad. It was kind of journalistic, too, in its own way. But that seersucker—well, that suit was just right for him and for his job and for the image he'd tried so hard to create and now worked diligently to maintain. It was jaunty. Like him.

That blasted ghost had ruined his hat, and he'd had to buy a new one this morning. Julian, who had been twirling it in his fingers, was pleased to see that this one had the same spiffy shape as the old one. He had an image to uphold, after all.

Julian eyed Susanna as she vigorously rubbed at the stains on his jacket. She looked about as grumpy as a bear, and he felt a compulsion to cheer her up.

"Will you help me look for my shoe today after we're through in the courthouse?" he asked, striving for a light tone.

"Yes."

She was really working his coat over hard. As Julian watched, he was glad she hadn't had the duty of scrubbing the stains off of his own skin last night—although, when he'd been soaking in the bath he'd ordered, he had entertained a pretty enjoyable daydream or two about Susanna Clement and a bar of soap and his own revered skin. If that's the way she wielded cleaning equipment, however, he'd as soon skip it.

"Don't rub any holes in it, please," he said for fun. She turned and glowered at him, and he guessed lack of sleep had chased off the humor she'd displayed yesterday in the graveyard. "Just kidding."

She took a deep breath. "I beg your pardon, Mr. Kittrick. I didn't sleep well at all. I awoke with a dreadful headache, and it has affected my mood this morning. I didn't mean to take out my headache on you."

Her chest expanded as she took another breath, a deep one, and Julian was sure she was going to offer him an expanded version of her overnight activities. Her mouth clanked shut, however, and she didn't. Her brow creased with worry lines, and she resumed her attack on his coat sleeve. He didn't like seeing those lines marring her pretty forehead.

Something was wrong with her. The idea of Susanna Clement being troubled bothered him. He felt an urge to solve her problems for her, which was almost as startling as the compulsion to embrace her that attacked him every time he was in her presence. "Is everything all right, Miss Clement? You seem worried about something. I'd like to help if I can."

She heaved an enormous sigh. "I'm all right." Then she frowned heavily and said, "No, that's not true. I'm not all right."

Julian cocked his head, wondering what he was supposed to do with that contradiction. Before he'd thought of anything scintillating to add to the conversation, she said, "Well, I guess I'm all right now."

He was glad of that. At least he thought he was.

She slammed his coat down on the laundry-room table and turned around, her expression intense. "No, I'm not all right. Something's wrong."

Without even considering if it was a prudent thing to do or not, Julian took her gently by the shoulder and led her to a bench against the far wall. "Why don't you tell me about it, Miss Clement? Maybe I can help."

What he wanted to do was wrap his arms around her, settle her in his lap, and rock her until her eyelids closed over her pretty eyes and she slept. He wanted to hold her and gently care for her. He'd never had feelings like this in his life—at least not so close to the surface and when he was sober—and they scared him. He was a cynical journalist, for the love of Mike. He wasn't supposed to be harboring soft emotions for a female in his hard-hearted breast. Love 'em and leave 'em. That's the way he was supposed to play the game, damn it.

Yet she needed him, and he couldn't seem to help himself. God save him, he cared about Susanna Clement's unhappiness. Wanted to banish it. He was sure he'd recover his rakish infidel character soon. He just needed to tough it out.

Until he did, his compulsion to cuddle Susanna Clement was too strong to allow him rest. He pressed her gently down onto the bench and sat next to her, holding her hand in one of his and gently stroking it with the other. "Here. Sit down here, Miss Clement. Do you need a drink of water?"

She shook her head. "No. Thank you."

"Do you need anything? Anything at all? Laudanum? Do you need some laudanum?"

Her sleepy eyes opened wide. "Laudanum! For heaven's sake, Mr. Kittrick. I had a little trouble sleeping last night. I'm not a drug addict!"

"Of course not," he murmured, thinking he ought to have known better. "But would you like me to fetch you some—some . . ." Good God, what did people take to feel better these days? His own friends drank whiskey, but he was pretty sure she wouldn't like that suggestion any better than she had the laudanum.

She shook her head again. "I'll be all right, thank you."

Her eyes looked like huge dark-rimmed saucers when she peered up at him. The heart he wasn't supposed to have reeled sharply and began to ache.

"Are you sure you don't need anything? It's no trouble, Miss Clement. In fact, it's the least I can do. Your aunt is right in the kitchen. Let me get her to brew you a—a—a posset or something." Whatever the hell a posset was. It sounded medicinal.

Her brows snapped together and she regained control of her hand. "For heaven's sake, stop hovering over me! You're about to drive me insane!"

"I'm not hovering." His hand felt empty. It wanted hers back again.

"You are too!"

Was he hovering? Julian frowned and looked around the laundry room. Well, maybe he'd been hovering a little bit. Still, he was doing it for her, and the behavior was so unlike him that her annoyance with it both angered him and hurt his feelings. A little bit. Newspapermen didn't really have feelings. He was about to tell her so when her next words distracted him.

"I beg your pardon, Mr. Kittrick. That was unkind of me. I know you're only trying to be helpful." She heaved another enormous sigh.

Yes. Julian nodded, glad she understood at last, damn her. That's exactly what he was trying to be, helpful. Slightly mollified, he decided he could be gracious. "Think nothing of it, Miss Clement." By this time he was used to her scrappy ways. He decided he'd be better off not saying so or they'd just get into another fight.

"I really don't need to rest, however. Nor do I need a posset. Thank you."

With Julian frowning after her, she got up from the bench and walked back to the laundry tub. Damn it, she was supposed to rest and tell him her problems, not keep working. Didn't she know anything?

Instead, she picked up his coat again and scrubbed soda and water into another stain as if it were an enemy she were trying to eradicate from her life. Her expression was far too serious for the task at hand. Julian watched her, troubled, unsure what to say. He didn't want to provoke another snub.

He decided to be gentle. When he'd been bored almost to death in Wyoming once, he'd been forced into reading the only thing at hand: a romantical story written by some woman and serialized in a periodical. It had reeked of sentiment, but he guessed females liked that sort of stuff. He decided to create a speech like the ones those sappy guys in the story had spoken. He cleared his throat.

"Please, Miss Clement. It troubles me to see you in such distress. Won't you please share your worries with me? I might not be able to help you, but you know what they say. A burden shared is a burden eased." God save him, he'd said the whole thing without throwing up—

and with a southern accent to boot. He was grateful none
of his *Denver Post* cronies could hear him now; he'd
never live it down.

His efforts weren't wasted, though. Julian was gratified when Susanna slapped his poor abused jacket onto
the laundry table once more and turned around. Her expression was bleak, and he had to fight another urge to
leap up, run over to her, and hug her. Criminy, he was
in real trouble here. Her eyes fairly begged for his sympathy. Little did they know that he was already prepared
to crawl on his hands and knees over hot coals for her.
He settled for rising from the bench and walking over
to her. He stuffed his hands into his pockets so they
wouldn't do anything untoward.

"Oh, Mr. Kittrick, I had the most ghastly dream last
night. It woke me up about three o'clock, and wouldn't
let me get back to sleep. It was terrifying."

He stared down at her. His eyes quit squinting and
opened wide. His heart stopped aching. His tender emotions crashed. He mentally got up from his hands and
knees and figuratively dusted them off, feeling silly
about burning them on those hot coals.

"You had a nightmare? And that's why you look like
hell and are as cranky as a rusted pump handle?"

"I'm not cranky!"

He shrugged. "Well, you're sure not dancing jigs."

She yanked her skirts out of his way—so that she
could walk past him without contaminating them, he
guessed. "Just because I don't feel like dancing jigs
doesn't mean I'm cranky."

He rolled his eyes. "Of course not." He decided not
to argue with her about it. His gaze narrowed as it followed her around the laundry room. She really was in a
state. Before this morning, he'd believed her incapable
of the emotional displays females put on for the benefit
of the men in their lives. He didn't know whether to be
relieved or disappointed to discover Susanna Clement
wasn't so unlike her fellow females as he'd begun to
believe her to be.

She stopped pacing and turned around to glare at him some more. Fine. He was used to it.

"It wasn't a mere nightmare, either."

All right. That cleared everything right up. Now what was he supposed to say? Was he supposed to *ooh* and *ah* over the severity of Susanna Clement's nightmares as compared to those of less sensitive females? What did one do in cases like these? Julian didn't know, so he remained silent. He did shrug his shoulders. The gesture wasn't meant to convey that he didn't care, but to invite further disclosures. He guessed she'd misinterpreted it when her eyebrows dipped ominously and her face took on an expression with which he was familiar.

Holding his hands out in a beseeching gesture, he said hurriedly, "I didn't mean it the way you're taking it."

"How do you know how I'm taking anything?" She braced her fists on her hips and assumed a fighting stance.

He sighed heavily. "I'm sorry, Miss Clement. I'm trying to understand this dream of yours so I can help you if I can. I didn't intend to demean the severity of your nightm—of whatever it was you had that kept you awake."

She dropped her arms to her sides, much to Julian's relief, and turned away from him again. "It was awful."

Her voice quivered, astonishing Julian. Good God, she wasn't going to cry, was she?

No. Thank heavens. She was too peppery for that. He saw her shoulders square as she cleared her throat.

"In this dream—or whatever it was—I was trapped. Chained up somewhere. In real chains."

She glanced over her shoulder. Evidently she needed him to understand about the chains, so he nodded to show that he did. Satisfied, she went on. "I mean literal chains, Mr. Kittrick. It wasn't just like in one of those dreams where you can't move very well. I was chained up in irons. I don't know where I was, but I knew I was doomed to die there." She shuddered, turned away from him, and hugged herself.

Julian tried not to notice. He tipped his head to one side. "How did you know you were destined to die?"

"I don't know. I just knew it. Somehow I understood that I had been abandoned by someone. Someone I loved. Someone whose desertion mattered. It felt like a betrayal."

Her shoulders began to shake slightly, and Julian decided *to hell with it*. He went up to her and rested his hands lightly on them, smoothing them up and down her arms, trying to offer her what comfort he could. Evidently it worked, because she stopped shaking and sucked in another deep breath.

"It was awful."

"Sounds like it."

Agitated, she whirled around again and stared up into his face. Her expression was intense, as if she needed him to believe her. He tried his hardest.

"I mean it, Mr. Kittrick. It was awful. I knew I had been abandoned in that dark place, chained to the wall with rats and mice and spiders all around me, and I was unable to get free. And I knew—I *knew*—that the only person in the world who cared about me wasn't going to rescue me."

"How did you know all that stuff?"

She stared at him for a moment before whispering, "I don't know."

All right. Julian licked his lips. He was beginning to have trouble concentrating on what she was saying because her eyes were so beautiful, and her expression so eloquent, and her shoulders so small, and her skin so soft, they were all distracting him. "And, um, you say this wasn't a nightmare? *Only* a nightmare," he clarified, not wanting to get on her snippy side.

She shook her head. "No. It was more like memories."

"Memories? When have you been locked up like that?"

"That's just it, Mr. Kittrick." She tried to pull away, but he held her fast with his big hands. "I've never had an experience anything akin to that. Even when I was arrested in college, they put us all in a big room together. And they certainly didn't chain us to the walls.''

He blinked, and decided to ask later. He didn't want to distract her now. "I see.''

This time she licked her lips. Julian stared at her pink tongue avidly, wanting to taste it. Wanting to taste her. Lordy, he had it bad. She took a deep breath. Her breasts brushed his chest, and he almost died then and there.

"I came to a conclusion, Mr. Kittrick.''

He scrambled to remember what they'd been talking about. "You did?''

"Yes. I think those memories aren't mine at all. I think they're Magdalena Bondurant's and that they're what she went through at the end of her life.''

Striving manfully to keep his attention away from Susanna's full breasts and onto the subject, Julian said, "But we don't even know she's dead.''

"I do now.''

"You do?''

"Yes. Those were her memories, and somehow or other they entered my head last night while I was sleeping. She's trying to communicate with me somehow.''

Thoughts of seduction flew right out of Julian's head. "That's crazy.''

This time she jerked out of his grip easily and stormed away from him. "It's not crazy. It's the truth! Blast you, Julian Kittrick, why are you so reluctant to believe the truth?''

Annoyed, Julian snapped, "What truth? First you want me to believe in ghosts, and now you want me to believe some dead lady is sending her memories across time and space to lodge in your brain and keep you up nights. That's not truth, Miss Clement. It's lunacy.''

"Oh, you make me so mad!''

She stamped that little foot of hers, making Julian wince. The floor of the laundry room was made of stone. It was rough, and her slippers were thin.

Furious, she stomped over to him and stabbed him in

the chest with her forefinger. "You just don't want to believe anything unless it fits into the tidy little package your brain has made of the world, do you?"

"What tidy little package? The world works in specific ways documented by men of science and philosophy, Miss Clement. Ghosts and spiritual manifestations aren't part of it, no matter how many nightmares you have."

"It wasn't a nightmare, blast you!"

To shut her up, Julian grabbed and kissed her.

Chapter Nine

He hadn't meant to do it. It was a foolish thing to do. Stupid. Dangerous.

Delicious. His lips skimmed hers gently at first. His heart registered delight when he heard her gasp. He didn't know if she gasped in terror, fury, or pleasure, but he aimed to make sure the latter sensation flourished in her as it did in him. Her hands gripped his shoulders convulsively for several seconds, then stilled. Julian felt a lick of pure triumph when they slid around his back.

He groaned. He hadn't meant to, but when he felt her breasts, the lushness of which he'd been admiring since the day they met, flatten against his chest, his groan escaped without his awareness. She was a tidy package, Miss Susanna Clement. And this was the most pleasant way to keep her quiet that he'd discovered so far.

She tasted like fresh yeasty bread and cinnamon, with a little strong coffee thrown in to keep her from being cloyingly sweet. He grinned inside as the metaphor struck him. How perfect for her.

Her lips were soft and pliant, and he plied them open

with the ease of long practice. His tongue slid between them and he heard her gasp again. Her hands tightened on his back, and she pulled him closer. He maneuvered her body between his thighs so that he could feel her pelvis against his arousal. He ached to feel her naked against him, to see the perfections of the body he could only imagine through those layers of fabric.

She felt like heaven in his arms. And she was quiet. Blissfully quiet. Meltingly quiet. Responsive. Delightful.

Until she pushed herself away from him.

He blinked down at her, feeling bereft. "Wait."

She didn't wait. She backed away, her bosom heaving. Her hand flew up to her mouth and she pressed the back of it against lips still moist from his kiss. He held out a hand, wishing she would take it and return to him.

She didn't. Instead, she looked at his outstretched hand as if it were a loathsome, warty toad and shouted, "What did you do that for?" Swiping furiously at her lips, which moments before Julian could have sworn had been devouring his mouth as his had been devouring hers, she swung around and said, "Ooh! I can't believe you did that! And in my own aunt's laundry room!"

He couldn't believe he'd done it either, actually. And she was right about the locale. It was no good seducing a female in her own aunt's laundry room. Tactical error, that. No matter how good it had felt. How right. How perfectly perfect. Still, a true seducer would have selected more congenial, less dangerous surroundings.

He tugged his coat to order and hoped it was long enough to hide the evidence of his arousal. An apology flirted with his tongue, but he decided not to give it to her—mostly because he wasn't sorry. Damn it, kissing her had been the best thing about his trip to Maine so far. And she'd enjoyed it, too, for a while. Frankly, he resented her attitude.

"Don't get persnickety with me, Miss Clement. You weren't an unwilling partner, you know."

Her eyes were glorious when she spun around again, and they glowed with righteous wrath. So did her cheeks. It was all he could do to keep from grabbing and kissing her again. He shoved his hands back into his pockets and spared a moment to be grateful to the inventor of pockets. Sure, pockets were good for storing things, but they were also really, really handy to tuck one's hands into when one needed to get them out of harm's way.

"How dare you?" Her voice throbbed with fury.

He shrugged, calling up the images of every devil-may-care newspaper reporter he'd ever hero-worshiped in his life. "Oh, come now, Miss Clement. It was just a kiss."

She gasped in outrage. He was pretty outraged himself. Just a kiss, his hind leg. That had been the most magnificent coming together of two sets of lips he'd ever experienced. Since he perceived the truth did him no credit, he kept it to himself and only shrugged again. "Don't make too much of it, my dear."

"My dear? My *dear*? Why, you callous, unspeakable cad. You lecherous, cavalier, irreverent rogue! You—"

Irritated, he cut her off. "Yes, yes, yes. I'm all those things and more. I'm a wastrel and a scoundrel and a no-good, pitiless, ruthless, coldhearted villain."

Her chest heaved. Julian tried not to stare at her bosom. He also tried not to ache to have her back in his arms again. His shoulders hunched up so far they almost touched his ears. Damn it, what was the matter with him, anyway?

"Yes," she said furiously. "Yes, you're all of those things."

Her words stung. He succumbed to the pressure to hurt her back. "Right. While you, on the other hand, are an innocent maiden, sheltered from the world and unused to the callous, hard-hearted likes of me."

He could tell she didn't like his description of her. He'd learned by this time that she chose to consider herself a woman of the world, no matter how little of the world she'd actually seen.

"I'm not used to unprincipled newspaper reporters, at any rate," she muttered.

Her cheeks were as bright a pink as Julian had ever seen. He could tell how embarrassed she was, and wished he didn't feel so damned guilty about having caused her such discomfort. He lifted his chin, feeling decidedly warm himself, although his heat had nothing to do with embarrassment and all too much to do with sexual excitement.

"Let's just forget about it, shall we? We have a lot of work to do." As if he could ever forget the way she'd felt in his arms. He'd have laughed cynically to give himself more of an air of nonchalance, except that his throat was thick, and he no longer felt the least bit cynical.

She took a huge breath that thrust her bosom at him. He closed his eyes and shook his head, wishing she had even a trace of an idea what she looked like to him when she did that. She looked like his most erotic fantasies come to life. Criminy, she had a beautiful body.

"Can you promise me this won't happen again?"

No. He couldn't promise her any such thing. He didn't suppose she had to know it. He cleared his throat. "Yeah. It won't happen again."

After a several-second pause, during which he held his breath and might actually have prayed—he couldn't remember afterward—she gave him a curt nod. "All right then." She didn't seem pleased with herself for capitulating, and added, "This work is too important to allow an indiscretion to ruin it."

He nodded, thinking *indiscretion* was an appropriate word. He'd aim for a more secluded spot next time, and maybe finish what he'd started then. He was pretty sure he wasn't going to be able to get Susanna Clement out of his system until he knew what it was he was missing. The awful thought that this is how men got trapped into marriage paid his brain a brief visit, but was so appalling he banished it.

Evidently not trusting him—and she had no idea how

right she was to doubt him—she cocked her head, squinted at him, and asked cautiously, "Do you agree, Mr. Kittrick? If you don't agree, I suppose we can work independently of each other."

He quelled his panic, and was pleased that his voice betrayed none of his inner turmoil when he answered her. "I think we'd be foolish to go our separate ways at this point in time, Miss Clement. After all, even your ghost believes us to be working together now."

She frowned. "That's right. He might get worried if we split up."

"Exactly. It would be foolish to dissolve our partnership now."

"Exactly."

Partnership. Until this minute, Julian hadn't considered all the ramifications of that word. It had always seemed an innocuous word to him, devoid of sexual implications. No longer. At the moment, the kind of partnership he wanted to undertake with Susanna Clement would have sent her screaming from the room if he'd divulged it to her.

"All right." She still seemed uneasy. "So we'll forget the past several minutes and continue on as we were yesterday."

Impossible. "Right. Exactly. We'll forget 'em."

She nodded once, briskly, and didn't move. Julian sighed, and knew it was his turn now. "You're safe with me, Miss Clement. I won't bother you again."

"You promise?"

"I promise." The next time wouldn't be a bother— and Julian planned to secure Susanna's full cooperation beforehand.

She nodded again. "Well then, let me finish with your jacket. We can drop it off at the dry-process cleaners before we head out to the courtroom."

Julian breathed a sigh of relief. Thank God they'd smoothed over that one. "Good. Thank you, Miss Clement. I really appreciate your trying to save my jacket."

His relief when she giggled couldn't be measured.

*   *   *

That evening, Julian braced himself for their trip to the Spring Hill Cemetery. Susanna's mistrust of him and his motives was about to send him over the edge.

"I promise I won't do anything to annoy Danilo, Miss Clement." He spoke through gritted teeth, and knew he was being irrational. After all, he supposed he might have behaved badly yesterday with that damned ghost. But honestly, what did she expect? He was a reporter, for the love of Mike. Reporters didn't believe in ghosts. At least he *hadn't* believed in ghosts. Until yesterday.

Even today, Julian's mind was unsettled, and he was undecided on the issue. Of course, there was the evidence of his jacket. And he certainly hadn't imagined being suspended in that maple tree, clinging like a monkey to the branches and staring at the hard, rocky, deadly ground sixty feet below him. Shoot, that had been frightening.

Still and all . . . he might have dreamed the hanging-suspended part, but he couldn't so easily explain away those stains.

But honestly. Danilo, the Gypsy King? He snorted with contempt, then wished he hadn't when Susanna turned to look up at him.

"Is something wrong, Mr. Kittrick?"

He managed a careless smile. "No. Nothing." Nothing much, anyway. If he could discount his burgeoning insanity. The thought didn't sit well with him, and his smile died as quickly as it had been born. There had to be some other explanation for the phenomenon of Danilo.

They had reached the graveyard by this time. Julian experienced a strange reluctance to tromp through the mossy undergrowth toward Magdalena Bondurant's grave. He was being illogical. There was nothing to be afraid of. Hell, *Susanna* wasn't afraid; it would be unmanly of him to shrink back in the face of her bravado.

Aw, hell. He hated this.

In spite of his most fervent lectures to himself about

bravery, courage, and his duty as a man and a journalist, Julian found himself hanging back slightly as they approached their destination. He paused to read headstones along the way, pretending curiosity.

"They don't go in for humor in death like they do back home," he observed, trying to sound casual.

"What do you mean?" Susanna stopped and turned to look at him.

"Well, for example, back home they're liable to carve stuff like, 'Here lies Frederick Bluth, hung in his youth for a crime uncouth. 'Twas a mournful day when they learned the truth.' "

Her big brown eyes blinked as she assimilated the message etched into poor Frederick Bluth's tombstone. "How awful," she murmured.

Julian shrugged. "Yeah. I guess so."

"Well, you don't have to worry about that sort of uncivilized practice here," a voice sang out behind him.

Julian's heart nearly jumped out of his skin, and his knees almost buckled. He managed to keep from hollering in terror only because his throat had closed up on him.

Susanna cried delightedly, "Danilo! I'm so happy to see you!"

That made one of them. Trying to hide his trembling, Julian turned and saw that Danilo was smirking at him from where he sat on another headstone, his knees crossed, his cape billowing around him. There was no breeze tonight. The effect must be caused by some ghostly atmospheric oddity that Julian preferred not to contemplate at the moment. Damn it, he hated being scared! Especially since Danilo seemed all too well aware of his fear.

"I don't like being sneaked up on," he said with as much dignity as he could summon.

It wasn't much, and Danilo knew it. His smirk broadened, and he buffed his fingernails against his cape. *"What a pity."*

Susanna seemed unaware of the hostility bubbling between the two men. "Oh, Danilo, the most awful thing happened!"

The ghost ceased taunting Julian. *"What?"*

"I dreamed about what happened to Magdalena Bondurant."

It seemed to Julian that Danilo actually paled, although how a ghost could do such a thing eluded him.

"What do you mean?" Danilo asked in a voice as ghostly as he was.

"I had a horrible dream last night—only it wasn't really a dream. It was more like memories. In them, I was trapped. I was being held a captive and chained up somewhere." She shuddered. "It was awful."

Danilo looked stricken. *"Is that what happened to Magdalena? Oh, my sweet heaven."*

Beginning to recover his composure, Julian took note of Danilo's expression, and curiosity compelled him to say, "You mean you really don't know what happened to her?"

"Well, of course I don't know what happened to her! Why else would I be seeking help from you people?" Danilo waved his hand as if to indicate how beneath him he considered the two of them. *"What do you take me for, anyway?"*

Julian elected not to answer that question, but to pursue this conversation along journalistic lines. "So you never had any inkling of Magdalena's ultimate fate."

"None."

"Well, I know how she met her end," Susanna declared with another shudder. "And it was vile."

Danilo seemed to shrink into himself. His cape no longer fluttered. He moved over to Magdalena's headstone and stared down at it, his expression morose. For an instant, even Julian felt almost sorry for him. *"I feared as much,"* the ghost whispered. *"It was Sedgewick. I know it."*

"You mean Mr. Sedgewick killed her?" Susanna's eyes opened up as wide as dinner plates. Julian was enchanted.

The ghost shrugged. *"He might as well have. That's how it ended, it seems."*

"I don't understand."

Neither did Julian. He was beginning to feel a little irritated, as a matter of fact. He hated all this beating about the bush that Danilo seemed to love so well. Drama, schmama. Julian wanted facts. He *craved* facts. "Listen," he said, "all this is very interesting and theatrical and all that, but what we need is some solid evidence of what went on around here thirty-eight years ago. Dreams and so forth are fine and dandy, but where in the name of God would somebody chain a woman up here in the civilized state of Maine? And *why* would a man do such a thing, for that matter? None of this makes any sense."

Susanna and Danilo both glowered at him. Exasperated, Julian shot a glance up into the tree branches. "So sorry to burst your bubbles, but let's be sensible about this, shall we? I know that might be a stretch for the two of you."

"How dare you!" Susanna seemed to grow several inches as she stiffened with indignation.

Julian didn't care. His own indignation had managed to banish his terror, and he used it to advantage. "Don't get huffy with me, Miss Clement. You expect me to write an article about how wonderful your great-aunt was, but I'll be damned if I'll inflict some romantic balderdash about a female chained in a castle dungeon on the readers of the *Denver Post*. They'd laugh me out of town! I need facts. Solid, immutable facts. They won't accept your dream as proof, my dear, no matter how bad it was."

She was puffing up like an adder. Julian enjoyed the effect of her fury on her bodice, even if he was irked with her.

"It wasn't a dream!"

"Yeah, you've said that before."

"Just a minute, children. Try not to kill each other until we've gotten to the bottom of this, if you will."

Danilo's wry voice cut through the tension between Julian and Susanna like a knife. Both of them turned to glare at him. He looked merely supercilious. *"I hate to admit it,"* he said when he had their attention, *"but Mr. Kittrick is right."*

Susanna seemed to deflate. "Blast!"

It was Julian's turn to smirk. "Told you so."

Danilo glared at him. *"No matter how misguided and wrongheaded he is."*

"Hey! I am not—"

Holding up his hand in an imperious gesture, Danilo cut Julian's protest short. *"Don't interrupt me, young man."* He skewered Julian with a sharp glance, as if he'd just remembered something. *"By the way, it might interest you to know that your parents didn't abandon you on the streets of New York willy-nilly. They died of the cholera, and tried with their last breath to secure your future. The illness got to them first. Your mother has been miserable about it ever since. She's pleased to know you survived."* Danilo sniffed. *"I didn't tell her you've taken to such an unworthy occupation as yellow journalism."*

Julian's mouth dropped open and his brain turned off. He couldn't think. He couldn't believe the words he'd just heard.

Evidently that was the exact effect Danilo had been hoping to achieve when he dropped his little tidbit into the conversation. He turned his back on Julian and faced Susanna.

Julian shook his head hard, trying to assimilate the information Danilo had given him. It wouldn't be assimilated. "Wait!"

Danilo turned and frowned at him. Julian ignored his sour mien.

"Wait," he said again, less sharply. "Do you mean to tell me you've communicated with my parents?"

He glanced at Susanna and found her watching him closely, a soft expression on her face. He couldn't tolerate compassion at the moment, and resolutely turned away from her. He was unsettled enough already and was fearful lest he burst into tears and disgrace himself and his profession. Her sympathy might just make the dam overflow.

"Tell me what you mean," he said to the ghost. Danilo stiffened, and he added, "Please?" God, he sounded pathetic. He couldn't help it.

Smirking again—Danilo seemed to reserve his smirks for Julian—the ghost said, *"Yes, Mr. Kittrick. Not only did I speak to your parents, but I sought them out solely for your benefit. Even though you don't deserve my consideration because you're hoping to discover scandal and disgrace about the woman I love, I wanted you to know that I appreciate you looking into Magdalena's fate."*

"What—what were their names? Who were they? When did they die?"

Something else struck him suddenly. He swallowed the lump in his throat and asked, his voice shaky, "When is my real birthday? Did they tell you?" It had always seemed disgraceful to him that he didn't even know the date of his own birth. He'd covered it up, but not knowing had always hurt. A person's birthday was such a personal thing, and it was something most folks didn't even have to think about. Not Julian Kittrick, who until this moment had believed he'd been abandoned on the streets of New York by the two people who should have done their best to see to his welfare. He couldn't quite comprehend the fullness of Danilo's revelation.

He had to swallow again when Danilo gave him a considering look that lasted much too long for Julian's peace of mind. After several moments the ghost said, *"I'll ask them about your birthday."*

It was all Julian could do to get out the one word. "Thanks."

"And their names were Emmett and Kathleen Kittrick."

Julian nodded numbly. The only thing he'd remembered about his birth family during his entire thirty-two years on earth were his first and last names. Sometimes he'd doubted even that, but had clung to it doggedly as the only relic left to him by his parents. He wondered if they'd given him a middle name, but his heart was too heavy to ask.

"Can't Mr. Kittrick's parents appear to him?"

Julian had forgotten all about Susanna, which surprised him when he pondered it later. She'd been all he could think about for days now. Her voice, which was gentle and thick with emotion, caught him off guard, though, and he jerked toward her. She'd been wiping her eyes with her hankie, but stuffed it into her skirt pocket when Julian turned.

"Appearing to living people isn't as easy as I've made it out to be," Danilo informed them as if he were lecturing a class. *"The circumstances have to be perfect."*

"They do?" Susanna sniffed loudly and looked embarrassed when she had to whip out her hankie again to wipe her nose.

"What constitutes perfect circumstances?" Julian was glad to get off the topic of his own abysmal infancy for a moment, even though he was fairly bursting to learn more about it.

"For one thing, if a person dies with all or most of his personal life's problems in order, he seldom takes to haunting."

"Why not?" Julian noticed that Susanna didn't thrust her handkerchief back into her pocket, but clung to it, evidently fearing she might still need it. He hoped she was wrong.

"If a person has no unresolved issues on this mortal coil, why should he want to stick around down here? Believe me, the afterlife affords more beauty and peace than this rotten place." Danilo glanced around with a look of disgust on his transparent face.

Julian had to clear his throat before his voice would work. "And my parents didn't have unresolved issues down here?" He wanted to ask what he was if not an unresolved issue, but it hurt too much and he didn't.

"That's only one of the circumstances required, Mr. Kittrick. Your parents died in New York, not here in Palmyra. They also died of illness and knew their fate was coming. They were a good, loving couple, from everything I've been able to dig up about them, in spite of the fact that they came from Ireland—"

"Ireland," Julian whispered, interrupting Danilo, who didn't appreciate it. He was a mere generation away from Ireland. Imagine that. He'd had no idea.

The ghost gave him a hot scowl before resuming his narrative. *"Yes. You're Irish. Didn't surprise me a bit."*

"I didn't know Kittrick was an Irish name," murmured Susanna.

"I didn't either, but he acts Irish."

Julian would have taken exception if he weren't still so stunned. "Please go on, Danilo. What other conditions need to prevail for ghosts to appear in public?"

"Face it, Mr. Kittrick, a contented spirit probably isn't going to want to wander the earth for decades or centuries after it should be enjoying its retirement."

"So you weren't contented, Danilo? I'm very sorry to hear it." Susanna had to dab at her eyes again. Until now, Julian hadn't pegged her for a weepy woman.

"Hmph. Of course I wasn't contented. For one thing, my life was snuffed out by a fiend in a vicious act of brutality—"

"Good heavens!"

"Please," Danilo commanded, frowning heavily at Susanna. *"Don't interrupt me."*

"I beg your pardon."

Julian had also never heard her sound so contrite.

"Ahem. As I was saying, my life was brutally taken, cut short in the flower of its youth, by a callous and wretched man." He held up a hand to stop Susanna from speaking. She'd opened her mouth, but shut it again when she saw he didn't care to be interrupted. *"Also, I had been worrying about Magdalena for years. I didn't know what she was up to, although, as I've already told*

you, I suspected her involvement with this wretched Underground Railroad—"

That was more than Susanna could take and remain silent. "It wasn't wretched!"

Julian found her passion for this cause of her great-aunt's amusing. Apparently Danilo did not. He scowled again.

"If you insist upon interrupting me every time I try to explain myself, Miss Clement, I shan't continue. You asked the question, after all. I'm trying to give you an answer."

"I beg your pardon."

"At any rate, we now have a combination of circumstances, as you can see. I was worried when I died, and I died a sudden and violent death. My spirit, therefore, did not rest easily in the afterlife."

"Mercy," Susanna murmured.

Danilo's ghostly eyebrows dipped ominously. *"There's more,"* he said in a severe tone.

Susanna clamped her mouth shut. For the first time since he'd heard about his parents, Julian grinned.

"Those two conditions alone might have made it possible for me to appear to living human beings, but they wouldn't have made it worth my while. However, when I heard the two of you arguing in the cemetery the other day, and I realized that you, young lady, were as eager as I to discover what happened to my beloved Magdalena, then I knew it was time to appear and offer my support to your honorable cause." Danilo lifted his chin and assumed a noble pose.

Julian rolled his eyes but said nothing.

Susanna digested Danilo's story for a moment or two, her brows knit in thought. Then she cocked her head to one side. "What I don't understand is why Magdalena herself didn't appear to us. I mean, surely she must be as eager as we are to clear her name and—and—settle her spirit and so forth."

Danilo's expression changed so suddenly that Julian gave a start of surprise. From the self-assured, conceited actor Danilo, the Gypsy King, he transformed in the blink of an eye to an anguished lover.

"That's just it," he cried. *"Wherever she is, she can't get out. It's the only explanation. After hearing about your overnight experience, Miss Clement, I know—I know—that wherever she is, she's still trapped. Spirits can be shackled, you know. They can be frozen in time and space and held captive if the forces surrounding them are strong enough."*

Julian and Susanna chorused together, "They can?"

Danilo nodded. *"They can. And I greatly fear that Magdalena's spirit is being held captive."*

This didn't make sense to Julian. "But what kind of force could have trapped her spirit? I mean, it would have to be a pretty powerful one, wouldn't it?"

The ghost whirled around, his cape billowing. *"Evil!"* he cried. *"It's the power of evil that's holding her. And the perpetrator is none other than that devilish miser Philip Sedgewick!"*

Julian and Susanna stared at each other, shocked, for a moment before Susanna murmured, "My goodness."

Chapter Ten

"Sedgewick? You mean the ancestor of the Sedgewick whose papers we just went through?" Susanna felt a creeping sensation in her chest. She didn't like thinking that the current Mr. Sedgewick—who was miserly and mean-spirited in his own right—might be a descendant of an even worse one.

Danilo bowed. *"The same."*

"How do you know that?"

Susanna frowned at Julian to let him know he shouldn't use that tone with Danilo. He merely shrugged, and she wanted to punch him.

"I know," said Danilo, who had taken exception to Julian's tone of voice just as Susanna knew he would, *"because Sedgewick is the fiend who murdered me."*

Susanna's own gasp of astonishment again joined Julian's in a chorus. Danilo watched their reactions, obviously feeling smug at having dropped such a bombshell on them.

And then he vanished.

Susanna was left blinking into the patch of moonlight

that had lately held what she'd begun to think of as her own personal ghost.

Julian muttered, "Damn, I wish he wouldn't do that."

"It's just his way," Susanna whispered, more shaken than she wanted to admit. She'd already blubbered like a baby this evening. She didn't want Julian to think she was a weak-willed, simpleminded female who went into spasms of nervous agitation and cried every time anything the least bit out of the ordinary happened. Not that ghosts weren't more than the *least* bit out of the ordinary. She gave herself a good mental shake and told herself to get a grip on her sensibilities.

"I still wish he wouldn't do it. I had more questions for him."

"About his—murder?" Susanna didn't even like to say the word, much less think of it in connection with a friend of hers. It surprised her to realize she'd begun to consider Danilo a friend.

"Well, that, too." Julian scuffed the toe of his shoe in the dirt.

He seemed disconcerted, and Susanna remembered he had an even greater stake in all of their researches than she did. Compassion filled her suddenly, and she reached out to him before she realized what she was doing. "Of course," she said tenderly. "You need to learn more about your parents, too, don't you?"

His black frown took her aback, and she withdrew the hand she'd placed on his coat sleeve. She ought to have known better than to have felt the least bit of sympathy for *him*.

"Yeah. I'd like to know more about them," he said, sounding like a sullen child.

In spite of herself, Susanna's insides softened. Poor Julian. Reared on the mean streets of New York City— Susanna had read about them. The ghastly accounts of the New York slums by the social reformer Jacob Riis had seemed incredible to her until she'd seen the photographs that backed up his observations. It made her feel sick to her stomach to consider the poor little child

Julian had once been surviving in those surroundings. No wonder he was hard and cynical. The true wonder was that he'd survived at all.

"And you want to know when your birthday is, too."

"Yeah. That, too."

"Perfectly understandable." She made her voice firm and matter-of-fact and tried to hide the tears that wanted to spill down her cheeks. To keep herself from crying and humiliating Julian completely, she made a joke. "After all, how can you know how to behave if you don't know what influences are at work on the people born under your astrological sign on any given day?"

It worked. He turned to frown at her. "Are you serious? Don't tell me you actually believe that hogwash."

He looked so incensed that Susanna laughed, grateful to have the delicate mood banished. After a couple of seconds he realized she'd been teasing, and his fierce expression relaxed. "Dammit, Susanna, don't say things like that. I think you mean them."

Her casual use of her given name startled her. She hadn't given him permission to call her Susanna. Yet she liked the way he said it. A lot.

Because she didn't want to make something out of nothing, or even worse, make nothing out of something, she decided to ignore it entirely. She licked her lips and thought furiously for a second before she hit upon a diversion.

"You know, Mr. Kittrick, I think it would behoove us to find this cabin on the old McKenzie lands. Both Magdalena and Sedgewick wrote about it. I have a feeling it's important."

He seemed willing to accept this new tack. "You think so?"

"Yes. For one thing, I'd wager anything that it's where Magdalena planned to hide runaway slaves. I'm sure it's what she called the storage facility. For another thing, nobody seems to know anything about it. It stands to reason that if it was hidden then, it's still hidden today, and if it's been hidden all these years, it might well be where the jewels are stashed.''

"If she didn't run off with them."

"Don't start that again, if you please."

He eyed her slantwise, and she realized he'd deliberately tried to get a rise out of her.

Merciful heavens, was she that easy to bait? Apparently she was. She harumphed indignantly. Julian laughed. Susanna wondered how things, which only moments before had seemed so different and charitable, could have reverted to their same old annoying familiarity in so short a time.

"No! Please, no! Oh, no!"

"Susanna! Susanna, wake up, dear! Oh, heavenly days, what's the matter?"

Screaming in terror, Susanna awoke to discover Aunt Winnie holding her tightly and rocking her back and forth. Susanna's heart was hammering like a piston. Horror consumed her, and she felt a sinking, hopeless panic crawling up her spine. She'd lost the only thing in the world that had ever mattered to her. She didn't know what it was, but she knew it was lost to her forever and that she was doomed because of it.

"Good heavens, Susanna, what a dreadful nightmare you've been having. Why, you nearly frightened your uncle and me to death when you started shouting."

Feeling frantic, Susanna grabbed for reality with every ounce of her mental strength. Quivering like a jellied aspic, she clutched spasmodically at her aunt's bathrobe and willed herself to calm down. It had been another dream. That's all. Only another dream.

She didn't believe it.

Nevertheless, she forced herself to stop trembling. She took a huge breath, and then another. After what seemed like days, but could only have been a second or two, she managed to say in a shaky voice, "I'm so sorry, Aunt Winnie. I had a horrible dream."

"I should say so!" Her aunt laughed. Her voice

sounded shaky, too. "Maybe it's all this digging into old, moldy history that's getting to you, Susanna. Maybe that young man of yours ought to take you to Simpson's for an ice-cream soda or something and help you forget what's best forgotten."

Not on her life. Too rattled to say so—and, anyway, she knew her aunt would never understand—Susanna attempted a chuckle. She managed to unclench her fingers from Aunt Winnie's robe and immediately felt abandoned. Although she didn't want to give Aunt Winnie any more ammunition to fuel her beliefs, Susanna wrapped her arms around herself and hugged hard. Oh, how she wished Julian Kittrick were here! Julian, for all his faults, was the only living being in the world who knew what demons tormented her.

After taking another deep breath Susanna said, "You're probably right, Aunt Winnie. All work and no play, and all that."

"Exactly." Winnie gave Susanna a brisk pat on the shoulder.

Susanna could tell her aunt was glad things seemed to be returning to normal. If only she knew! But no. Susanna didn't want anyone to know. Not yet. Not until it was all over, and she and Julian had discovered the truth, and Danilo's spirit could rest in peace. And Magdalena's, too, if possible.

"Are you all right now, dear? Do you need a glass of water or a cup of hot cocoa or anything?"

"No, thank you, Aunt Winnie. I'm fine now. It was just an awful nightmare, is all. I'll be fine."

"Well, if you're sure." Winnie sounded doubtful.

Susanna smiled at her, almost cracking her cheeks with the strain. "I'm sure, Aunt Winnie. Thank you."

Her aunt bustled off. Susanna got up from her bed on wobbly legs and sank into the rocking chair she'd set beside her window. It took a good deal of effort to reach out and push the window open, both because her hands were shaking and because she felt completely drained. Energyless. Inert.

"Sweet heaven," she whispered to the maple leaves. "That was simply awful."

She wanted Julian with her right now. She wanted him to know exactly what had happened tonight. More than that—worse than that—she wanted him to hold her; to hold her tight, to cradle her body against his and give her strength. She wanted him to kiss her again, to make her forget all about the past hour or so.

She sank her face into her hands and wondered if there was something about Magdalena's life that was corrupting her own character. She shouldn't be wanting any man to hold her, much less the cocky and rakish Julian Kittrick. But she did.

Lifting her head, she decided to berate herself later about her lack of moral principles. Right now, before she forgot them, she should write down these latest— what? Dreams? She still didn't believe they were dreams. She felt so weak, though, she wasn't sure she could rise to fetch a pencil and paper.

Pressing her hand to her still-thundering heart, she took and released several big, calming breaths. Miss Amberly had advocated deep, meditative breathing as a method of relaxation and mental renewal. Susanna had never had occasion to test Miss Amberly's theory before this minute. Tonight she prayed her former teacher was right.

After several tense moments Susanna decided Miss Amberly's credit remained intact. Her heartbeat slowed, her nerves stopped jangling, her skin became less clammy, her jaw unclenched, and her hands lost their clawlike quality and began resting naturally on the arms of her rocker rather than clutching them in a death grip. After several more moments Susanna felt steady enough to go to her desk and pick up a pencil and her notebook. Sitting down in her rocking chair again, she began to document this latest phenomenon.

"Good God, you look even worse this morning than you did yesterday."

Susanna stopped in her tracks and debated the various merits of bursting into tears or scratching Julian's eyes out. After a struggle with her better nature, she did neither. Bowing to Miss Amberly's wisdom, she breathed in and released three or four deep, calming breaths.

Then she shrieked, *"You can go straight to perdition, Julian Kittrick!"*

Shocked, he jerked backward. Pressing her advantage, Susanna stalked him, holding her notes out before her. "How *dare* you greet me that way? How *dare* you tell me I look poorly? If you'd been through what I've been through, you wouldn't *dare* treat me this way!"

"Treat you what way?"

He sounded almost intimidated. Susanna wished she'd thought to screech at him sooner. "You wouldn't treat me callously! You wouldn't be rude and unkind and—and—and you wouldn't be such a damned *man*!"

She'd never uttered a curse word aloud in her life, and she could hardly believe she'd done so now. If she weren't so exhausted and unnerved by her overnight adventures she never would have lost her self-control so completely. Furious, ashamed, and totally dismayed both with herself and with Julian, Susanna put a hand to her eyes and bowed her head.

Julian cleared his throat. "I beg your pardon. I didn't mean to be rude. I—I was shocked to see you looking so tired and worn out. I was afraid you were sick or something."

"I'm not sick." She spoke into her hand, and the words were muffled.

"I'm glad of that."

She lifted her head. Her first and third fingers parted, and she squinted at him through them. He shrugged helplessly. Susanna was reminded of her aunt Winnie telling her about how useless Uncle Cyrus was in a crisis, and she contemplated forgiving Julian for being a man.

He held out a hand to her. It appeared to be a gesture

of conciliation. "Please forgive me, Susanna. I'd never be mean to you on purpose."

Removing her hand from her face, Susanna squinted at him some more, not ready to forgive him yet. He didn't move his hand, but held it in front of her, palm up, as if he expected her to put her own hand in his. She didn't. Deciding instead to put him to use because she didn't feel like accepting his apology yet, she slapped her notes into his open palm.

"Ow!" His beautiful blue eyes accused her.

She didn't care. "Read that." Ignoring all of her mother and Miss Amberly's endless lessons in good manners, she pointed at the notes with a steady forefinger. "And then perhaps I'll speak to you again."

He looked at the notes, then at her. "Well . . . all right."

So, while Susanna scowled murderously and contemplated the serious lack of equity that prevailed in the universe between the sexes and how, if she had the running of things, women would wield the power and men would wash the blasted stains out of their own blasted white jackets, Julian read her notes.

After several minutes, during which Susanna tapped her foot and he remained silent, he grunted and pointed at a passage. "What do you mean here? 'If I could only draw the wire out of my hoop, perhaps I could unlock the manacles'?" He looked up and eyed her keenly. "What hoop? What wire? What the hell are you talking about here?"

Forgetting her own recent lapse into profanity, Susanna said hotly, "Don't you dare swear at me, Julian Kittrick."

He made a visual inspection of Susanna's skirt, which embarrassed her. Then he scowled, too. "Well, I don't see any hoop. I'm only trying to understand what you mean here, for heaven's sake. I'm not trying to pick a fight."

"Hmph!" Susanna was fairly spoiling for a fight herself.

"Do you mean those bustle things ladies wear?"

"No, I do *not* mean those *bustle things.* I wrote 'hoop,' and I meant hoop. I distinctly remember being dressed in a gown with a huge hoopskirt. That's what ladies wore forty years ago, in case you didn't know it."

"Oh." His scowl intensified. "I didn't know that."

Susanna sniffed.

"But why would you be wearing a hoop in your dream?

"Oh, for heaven's sake!" She snatched her notebook out of his hand. He snatched it back. Irate, she turned and stomped to the Homstead tombstone. They'd agreed to meet in the cemetery this morning for privacy's sake. Susanna didn't want anyone else to know what they were doing. It was all too personal—and it was becoming far too frightening—to allow anyone else in on it.

"Listen, Susanna, I know you're in a bad mood. And I'm sorry you had a rough night. But please, just tell me what you mean."

She whirled around again. "When did I give you permission to call me by my Christian name, Mr. Julian Kittrick? Hmmm?"

He sighed, exasperated. "You didn't, I guess."

"Exactly!" Somehow she didn't feel as triumphant as she thought she should.

"But, what the hell. You can call me Julian. In fact, I wish you would. I mean, we're business associates, after all."

There was something wrong with his reasoning, but Susanna, weary and in a really, really bad mood, couldn't think of what it was to save her life. She chose instead to answer his question. "*I* wasn't the one dreaming, *Julian.*" She spoke his given name deliberately, trying to sound sarcastic. She was annoyed by how pleasant it felt on her tongue.

She didn't appreciate his knowing smile, either, so she turned away from it when she continued her explanation. "Somehow or other, I've managed to tap into Magdalena Bondurant's memories. Or her soul. Or something.

Or maybe her spirit is calling out to me. I don't know. All I do know—and I'm sure of it—is that the memories of what she went through at the end of her life have become embedded in my own mind, and they seem to be pouring forth while I sleep. It's—it's as if she has no other outlet and has chosen me to tell her story. Or something.''

She shivered and hugged herself, fighting tears. She swallowed them resolutely, determined to give Julian no excuse not to believe her. ''It's the only explanation. I know it's the truth. It's hellishly uncomfortable, too, I can tell you.''

Julian said nothing for a moment. Susanna turned to see what was taking him so long. He looked skeptical, and she was furious at him. She refused to give him an excuse to disbelieve her by crying or screaming. She only stared at him, adamant.

At last he said, ''Listen, I don't want to start an argument or anything, but, well, that sounds just plain crazy.''

''It's not crazy! I don't care what it sounds like! It's the truth. I wasn't even me when I was having those thoughts. I was some lady locked up somewhere in the dark, in iron manacles, and wishing I could get a hand free so that I could work the wire out of my hoopskirt and unlock the shackles. It's as clear as day!''

''It's as clear as mud.''

Susanna gasped in indignation, but before she could shower him with invective, Julian raised his hand. ''All right, all right. Don't get mad at me yet. Let me finish reading this, and then we'll talk about it.''

''I don't want to talk to you!''

''I'm sure you don't, but we're in this together, so you'll have to.''

She hated that he was right. She flounced over to Magdalena's headstone, crossed her arms over her chest, and sat in a huff. She tapped her foot while Julian finished reading about her overnight experiences. If *he* were being haunted by Magdalena Bondurant's spirit, he wouldn't be so quick to disparage her notes. He'd be as worn out and frightened as she was.

Julian looked thoughtful when he was through. Susanna continued to glare at him, but she'd be boiled in oil before she'd say another word and risk his scorn. Let him speak first; then she'd know how to react.

"Maybe you're right."

She gaped at him, astonished. "What?"

"I said, 'maybe you're right.' I mean, it's crazy, but everything else about this investigation is crazy, too. And after what Danilo said about spirits being trapped and all, well . . ." He shrugged. "I don't know. Maybe you're right."

"I am."

He eyed her over her notes, a frown knitting his brow. "Maybe."

She decided not to bicker. Instead she took one of Magdalena's diaries out of her skirt pocket and opened it to the place she'd marked. "See here, Julian." She tried to speak his name casually, but it felt foreign on her tongue. And sweet, like the Turkish delight Miss Amberly had let her taste once. "This diary is dated a full year prior to the one I showed you the first time. I think she'd just begun to work with the Underground Railroad when she wrote it. Before I went to bed last night, I read it through, and I marked a passage that might possibly be directions to the cabin."

"Directions to the cabin? Where?" He walked over and peered down at the book in her hands.

"Here, in this passage. I think it's in a kind of code, as if Magdalena didn't want to be specific even in her most personal notations for fear of discovery." She looked up at him. "You may have observed that she never once refers to the place as a cabin, but to a storage facility. It's Sedgewick who called it a cabin."

His frown conveyed his doubt, but Susanna forged on in spite of him. "Listen to this: 'To the north of the well next to Mr. McKenzie's barn, a tumbledown wall marks the old McKenzie family plot.' " She looked up again, hopefully. "Aunt Winnie said a lot of families used to bury their kin on their own property in Colonial days."

"Hmmm."

"And did you take note of the wording? Doesn't it sound stilted to you? I mean, she wasn't generally that—that formal in her personal diary. Doesn't it sound like what she'd written might be directions or something, as if she'd documented them because she didn't want to forget, yet didn't want anyone to know what they were directions to, if they happened to find her diary?"

"Well . . ." Julian grimaced. "No."

"Hmph. Well, it does to me." Susanna decided to ignore his incredulity and plowed onward. "Here's some more. Maybe this will convince you: 'If one turns left at the headstone of Leola McKenzie—born 1756, died 1820' . . . Isn't that something? Imagine, people living here back then. They wouldn't have any of the conveniences we have today. Life must have been so hard."

Julian grunted.

Faintly annoyed that he wasn't as thrilled by the dates as she, she resumed reading. " 'If one turns left at the headstone of Leola McKenzie'—and then she gives the dates—'and follows the bramble bushes into the woods'—I think those are some kind of berry bushes—'one discovers a large maple tree suitable for tapping. The path is negligible, but it is there, and it leads to the storage facility.' There!"

Susanna poked the page in triumph. "Did you hear that? She refers to 'the storage facility' again. I'm *sure* that's the cabin."

"Why are you sure it's the cabin?"

"What else could it be?"

"I don't know, but why are you so sure it is?"

She frowned. "Well, why shouldn't it be?"

"But didn't she just call it a cabin before?"

"No, no, no! You weren't paying attention to me! How typical. *She* never called it a cabin. It was *Sedgewick* who called it the cabin. Magdalena always referred to it as a storage facility."

He shook his head, and his doubt chafed her already jumpy nerves. "Well, what else could she be talking about?"

"Anything. She might be referring to anything at all."

"Like what?"

"I don't know. An icehouse. A chicken coop. Anything."

"She wouldn't call an icehouse or a chicken coop a storage facility; she'd call it an icehouse or a chicken coop. For heaven's sake, *think*!"

"I am thinking!"

Susanna stood in a huff. "Well, *I* plan to see if I can't find this storage facility of hers, and then we'll know, won't we?"

"Maybe. Maybe not. If it's there, it's probably fallen to ruins, and there won't be anything left to tell us one way or the other."

"Oh, you're simply impossible!"

He frowned at her, his hands stuffed into his trousers pockets. "Maybe. I'm going with you, though. I don't want you wandering around in the woods by yourself."

"I don't need your help."

"The hell you don't."

"I *don't*! Besides, I'd rather not have you along if you're going to doubt everything before we give it a chance."

"We're in this together, remember?"

"Don't worry." She eyed him with contempt. "I'll tell you what I find. I won't keep it a secret."

"I'm not worried about that, Susanna. I trust you." His grin stole her breath away. She pretended not to notice. "But I don't want you wandering around in those woods alone. There might be—things—in them."

"What kinds of things?"

He shrugged. "I don't know. Bears. Cougars." He threw out his arms. "Ghosts."

Ghosts. Merciful heavens, what if he was right? That's all she needed, was to meet up with the kind of spirit that had been haunting her nights, only in the daytime. The idea made her go cold inside. "Oh, very well," she said ungraciously.

The grin he gave her this time was as breathtaking as his other one had been. She tried to hide her reaction to it by flipping through the diary, pretending to look for another passage.

"So, do you know where this McKenzie character lives? Or are we going to have to do another search through the Palmyra courthouse records? They're going to get sick of us pretty soon."

She looked up from the book, not trusting the teasing quality of his voice. He was still grinning, and she still reacted to his grin in a way she wished she wouldn't. Commanding herself to recall Miss Amberly's advice about men being devils sent to earth to seduce and torment innocent woman, she sucked in a breath. "I asked Aunt Winnie this morning at breakfast if she knew anyone named McKenzie. She said the last McKenzie died twenty years ago, but she told me where his farm used to be."

"Good."

He smiled his approval. She was beginning to feel light-headed from all the deep breathing she was doing as she attempted to counteract Julian's effect on her. Good heavens, this would never do. Her reaction to him was scandalous. Miss Amberly would be horrified with her. She swallowed nervously and decided deep breathing worked better when she was alone in her rocking chair and couldn't fall over if she hyperventilated. "Yes, well, I think I can find the old McKenzie farmhouse, if you want to follow me."

"Gladly."

So Susanna led the way through the woods and up the road, to the dilapidated old barn Aunt Winnie told her to look for. Aunt Winnie, bless her heart, believed Susanna was going to look for botanical samples to take back to New Mexico Territory with her. Susanna had given up trying to interest her aunt in Magdalena Bondurant.

"She said this barn belonged to the McKenzies. There's supposed to be the remains of a house here, too, but it burned down twenty years or more ago, and Aunt Winnie says it's probably all grown over by this time."

Julian eyed the barn with disfavor. "It's leaning."

"You'd lean, too, if you'd been around for two hundred years and nobody'd bothered to repair you," Susanna said more caustically than she meant to.

She was just jittery. She couldn't account for the disturbing effect these surroundings had on her nervous system. At first she thought her unsteady senses might have something to do with being alone in Julian Kittrick's company. This sensation wasn't pleasant, however, and she'd discarded the theory because, however much she deplored it as a product of a weak character, she didn't find being alone with Julian unpleasant at all. Far from it. Not even when she was so mad at him that she wanted to beat him about the head and shoulders.

No. Something else was making her skin crawl, and she didn't know what it was. Perhaps she was only excited because they might be nearing the solution to their mystery. She tried that theory on for size while they skirted the barn, picking their way through dense undergrowth, but it didn't fit either.

"Bother," she said, irked.

"Need a hand, Susanna?"

Susanna looked up, startled, and discovered Julian holding out his hand to help her. She declined, primarily because she feared his hand would feel too good holding hers. "Thank you, no. I'm fine, really."

"Well, I'm here if you need me."

She glanced at him and saw a look of concern on his face. "Thank you. I'm just feeling a bit unsettled about all of this, is all."

"Yeah, it's creepy around here, isn't it?"

She stopped and stared at him. "You mean you feel it, too?" That made her feel better for some reason.

"The place gives me the willies."

"Me, too."

"But since we're here, we might as well search for this storage facility of Magdalena's. What are the directions again?"

"I've got the passage marked." Susanna drew the book out of her pocket and turned to the page where she'd stuck her mother's embroidered bookmark. "Here it is: 'To the north of the well next to Mr. McKenzie's barn . . .' "

"We'd better watch our steps, then. Don't want to fall into an unmarked well and break a leg. Or worse." He gave his shoulders a nervous twitch.

She shuddered at the thought. "Good point. Anyway, it goes on, 'a tumbledown wall marks the old McKenzie family plot. If one turns left at the headstone of Leola McKenzie—born 1756, died 1820—and follows the bramble bushes into the woods, one discovers a large maple tree suitable for tapping. The path is negligible, but it is there, and it leads to the storage facility.' " She looked around, frowning. "I guess that means there must be a well and a wall around here somewhere."

Julian glanced around, too. "It'll take some luck to find them. What a mess this place is."

"A lot can happen in twenty years, I guess."

"I guess."

They spent twenty-five minutes searching through the encroaching shrubbery. Susanna was beginning to wonder if perhaps there wasn't another McKenzie family in Palmyra when Julian cried out, "Here! Over here! This looks like the remains of an old stone wall. And look here. It's a boarded-over well. Thank God for that, anyway."

She hurried to where he was bending over, pulling bushes away from a pile of old stones.

"Damn, this suit will never be the same again. You might have another cleaning job on your hands tomorrow."

"I don't mind," she murmured, and was surprised to discover it was the truth.

His chuckle should have annoyed her, but it didn't.

Susanna chalked it up to the strange feeling of unease still troubling her. "I think you're right. That does look as if it might be an old wall."

Julian dusted off his hands. "Okay, so we've found the well and the wall. What do we do now?"

"We need to find Leola McKenzie's headstone."

"Great."

Julian eyed the patch of property that might once have been the McKenzie family plot. So did Susanna, and her heart sank. "Um, I don't see any headstones. Do you?"

"Of course not." He sounded cross.

Thinking hard, Susanna studied their surroundings, considering the effects several years of rain and sun and ample vegetation might have on a graveyard. She decided that the stones must now be covered with moss and vines and started looking for lumps of greenery rather than stones—and saw several. Feeling optimistic, she headed for the first of these and pulled a handful of vines away. "I wish I'd thought to bring some gardening gloves with me. I didn't know we'd be doing . . ." Her muttered complaint faded away, and she sucked in a victorious breath. "I found it!"

She heard Julian run up behind her and stop. "Well, I'll be damned."

Susanna refrained from reprimanding him about his language. Instead, she looked over her shoulder, thrilled that it should have been she and her own superior reasoning powers that had overcome this latest obstacle to their search. She felt her cheeks warm when she saw Julian's approving smile.

"Well done, Susanna."

"Thank you."

He helped her uncover the rest of the headstone. The carving on it could hardly be read, but the stone wasn't that of Leola McKenzie. Now that they knew what they were looking for, however, the remainder of their search proved simple, except for scratches from the brambles. After another several minutes they found the headstone they needed.

Julian stood and stretched the kinks out of his back. "All right. Now what are we supposed to look for?"

Susanna referred to the diary. "We're supposed to find a maple tree to the left of it."

They both looked to the left.

"Damnation!"

An entire grove of maple trees greeted their eyes.

Chapter
Eleven

They made their way through the overgrown field, maneuvering over fallen logs and through thorny patches. Susanna struggled as she tried to negotiate the dried branches that clawed at her long skirt.

Julian thought about offering his hand, but he knew how touchy she was. He admired the hell out of her, though. Imagine her thinking to look for overgrown lumps rather than headstones. It would take more than lumpy headstones this time, though. All those maple trees looked alike, and he didn't care who was doing the looking. "I don't know how you're going to decide which tree is the one that marks the path."

She was out of breath by the time she caught up with him. "Let me think about it."

"Fine. You think about it."

She flung herself down on a big rock and frowned at him. "You needn't sound so pessimistic. I'm sure there's a reasonable approach to this, if we can only think of it."

"I'm willing to listen." He sat on a fallen log and

threw out an arm as if offering her free rein. "Think away."

She reacted exactly as he knew she would, getting all indignant and huffy, and he grinned inside. He was becoming a real expert at riling her. After having known her for only a few days, he could get her all puffed up in only a couple of words or a gesture or two. It was fun teasing her. It would be more fun to do other things with her, but Julian didn't quite dare try.

He sighed heavily and wished he knew the first thing about courting proper ladies. Father Patrick had taught him tons of stuff about morals and character and integrity, and how to get on in life off the streets, but the good father didn't know beans about courting females. Stood to reason he wouldn't, having taken a vow of celibacy and all.

Julian had taken no such vow, however, and he didn't plan to. Celibacy was something he didn't fancy in the least. He'd never had trouble finding ladies to oblige him in his quest to avoid it, either. He didn't want a quick tumble with Susanna Clement, though. The truth bothered him a little bit. He'd never contemplated a permanent relationship with a female before he took this trip to Palmyra.

Not that he was thinking about one now. Or not very much, anyway. He scowled and yanked up a piece of dry grass to chew on, misliking the path down which his thoughts seemed to be leading him.

Damn it all, he was a cheeky, devil-may-care journalist. Cheeky, devil-may-care journalists didn't crave permanence in relationships with women. They played around. They loved 'em and left 'em. They didn't succumb to the lure of domesticity no matter how much their hearts cried out for things they'd never had, such as homes and families and one perfect—or near-perfect—woman to share them with.

Julian shook his head, more annoyed with himself than he'd ever been. "Damn!"

"For heaven's sake, stop being so impatient! I'm thinking about it."

He squinted at Susanna, wondering what the hell she was talking about. Then he remembered. The maple trees. He glanced at them and looked away again, feeling defeated. There were so many of them. They'd never find the one in the diary.

"I have it!"

Her voice startled him so badly, he dropped his stalk of grass. "You have what?"

"I know which tree to look for."

He glanced at the maples again and then at her. "You do?"

"Of course. It's simple!" She surged up from her rock, energized.

Feeling far from energized himself, Julian stood anyway. She dashed into the stand of trees and he followed, puzzled, hoping she was right, sure she was wrong. He lost her among the trees almost at once and didn't like it. This part of the woods was dense and dark, and he didn't like her to be out of his sight.

Suddenly he heard her cry, "Aha! I was right!"

"You were?" It took him a few seconds, but he found her. She was all but hugging a huge old maple tree.

"I was! Look here! This tree is *aeons* older than the other ones! I knew that if I looked in the direction the diary pointed, I could find one that had been tapped for syrup. See? Way up there? It's an old tap! And see here? The bark even has initials carved in it from fifty years ago!" She pointed up into the branches.

Julian tilted his head back, shaded his eyes, and squinted. "Well, I'll be damned."

"I know."

He chuckled. "All right, Miss Wonderful, where are the alleged bramble bushes we're supposed to follow into the woods to guide our path?"

She pointed with even more enthusiasm, and Julian realized she'd tugged some sticky bushes back. Sure enough, there seemed to be a narrow beaten track, obscured from sight until Susanna uncovered it, leading into the woods behind the stand of maples.

"Well, how about that."

"Pretty clever, aren't I? Even *you* must admit it now." Susanna beamed at him, her hands crossed over her bosom, her expression one of perfect triumph.

"Pretty damned smart," he said, enjoying the spectacle of her in all her gloating glory. "I admit it."

"Ha!"

She was too smug. Too damned cute. Too blasted *right.* And absolutely adorable. Julian couldn't help himself. He reached out, drew her into a bear hug, and kissed her tempting lips.

Susanna didn't know how long she allowed Julian's kiss to continue—or when she started kissing him back. She almost didn't care. At last, though, her sense of mission overcame the deliciousness of being in Julian's arms—and where were they last night when she needed them?—and she tried to draw away from him.

"No," she whimpered, pressing on his shoulders.

"Yes," he whimpered back, trying to draw her more closely to his chest.

"No!" she cried more firmly.

He sighed deeply and looked down into her eyes. His glowed like hot coals. Hot blue coals. It was all she could do not to give into their entreaty.

"We—we have a duty to perform," she stammered.

He sighed again.

"We must forge onward and discover the truth."

He nodded. Then he shook his head and said, "Aw, Susanna, I can't help it," and bent to kiss her again. She resisted feebly, but it was enough. With another heart-wrenching sigh, he let her go. "You're right, of course."

She tugged her shirtwaist, which had become twisted in the exchange. She couldn't think of a thing to say now, but her lips felt swollen, her cheeks were hot, and her body was singing. She was sure these were signs of a fallen nature.

"I'm sorry, Susanna. I didn't mean to be so crude."

Her hands stilled on her skirt and she stared up at him, sure those words couldn't have come out of his mouth. An apology? From Julian Kittrick? What was the world coming to?

Besides, she didn't deserve it. She'd been as much a participant in that kiss as he, more's the pity. With one final tug to make sure her bodice behaved itself, she said, "We shan't speak of it again, if you please." Good heavens, she sounded like a complete prig. Well, she thought sourly, better a prig than a wanton.

Julian said meekly, "All right. Er, do you want to lead the way?"

She eyed him closely. He'd never given her any reason to believe he was meek before now; she didn't entirely trust him. Yet he looked docile enough. And Susanna was certain he wouldn't attack her from behind. After that torrid kiss, he knew good and well he didn't have to. How aggravating.

"Certainly. I'll be happy to lead the way."

He held his arm out, gesturing her to precede him, so she did.

The going was rough at first, and Susanna was almost glad of it because it kept her attention from wandering to Julian and that kiss. She hadn't understood kisses could be so all-consuming. Why, she hadn't been able to think of a single thing except the sensations going on in her body. She was sure bodies weren't supposed to feel like that, at least not female bodies. For heaven's sake, it was the female's responsibility to hold the male and his lustful urges in check. If females succumbed to lustful urges, too, the world was done for.

Annoyed, she realized her mind was wandering. Making a concerted effort, she concentrated on keeping track of the path. It was hard to find, since apparently no one had trod on it for decades. It was as if they were breaking new ground, exploring new territory.

That's what Julian's kiss had felt like. It had felt as though Susanna's body had been asleep until his touch awakened it. Sort of like Sleeping Beauty. Or—since they were back East—Rip Van Winkle, although that story wasn't anywhere near as appealing. Oh, but what an awakening! Susanna wasn't sure she was glad to know what she'd been missing all those years.

Discovering that her thoughts had strayed yet again, she uttered a sharp, "Blast!"

"What's wrong?"

Julian was right there, at her shoulder. Susanna was glad of it. The woods were dark and quite spooky, and Julian was a tall, solid, safe presence—well, sort of safe, anyway.

"I'm all right," she lied. "I was just thinking how— how thick the undergrowth is along this path."

"Oh."

They kept walking. The deeper into the woods they walked, the clearer the path became. The sensation of unease that had been niggling at Susanna did not abate. In fact, it intensified until she felt the short hairs on the back of her neck rise and her skin prickle. She was glad when Julian began walking at her side instead of behind her. She was *really* glad when she felt his hand pick up hers, and she shot him a quick smile. He smiled back.

"This place is giving me the creeps."

"You feel it, too?" She didn't feel so foolish knowing that Julian was affected by it as well.

"Yeah, I feel it. It reminds me of all the ghost stories I used to read. Only I used to read them in a nice, snug room with a fire blazing and Father Patrick close by."

She shivered and glanced around. The trees seemed taller here, and they grew close together. She could hardly see a space between them, and if there was space between them, bushes had grown up taller than she was. She had the brief, unsettling thought that there was no escape. One either went forward or one turned around and went back, but there was no sidestepping here. One couldn't walk a yard in either direction to either side of the path.

Of course, she supposed one could climb one of the

trees. She glanced up, and realized most of the lowest tree branches thrust out across the path quite far above her head. She'd be hard-pressed to grab on to one of them and swing herself up if she needed to. Not that she'd need to. She was being foolish. There was nothing in these woods but—well, woods.

If she were alone, she'd be singing to keep herself company. There was something about a jolly song that made things seem less sinister. Sinister? Good grief, she was allowing her imagination to run away with her.

She remembered that she didn't have an imagination, and frowned, irritated.

"You all right, Susanna?"

Glancing up, she found Julian looking down at her, concerned. How sweet.

"I'm fine, thank you. Just a little—edgy, I guess."

"Yeah. Me, too. You didn't look too good. I wondered if you were all right."

"I don't look too good? What does that mean?" His comment irked her. Her perverse nature wanted Julian to think she was beautiful, like Billy Poe did. Even Billy Poe, backwater hick that he was, would never tell her she didn't look good.

Julian apparently understood. He grinned briefly and said, "I didn't mean you aren't pretty, Susanna, I meant that you look pulled. Strained. Like you did this morning after your nightmare. Or whatever it was."

"Oh. I see." Drat. She wished he hadn't brought up those awful dreams. Now that he had, Susanna felt stirrings of the same nameless dread that had troubled her the past two nights. Perhaps it was her—no. That's right. She didn't have an imagination, did she? Blast.

Feeling foolish, she said, "Perhaps we should sing something. Maybe that would take our minds off—this." Her gaze swept the dense woods again, and they seemed even darker and more forbidding now than they had only moments before. She shuddered and did not object when Julian put his arm around her shoulder.

"Good idea," he said. "How about 'Camptown Races'? That's a lively tune."

Susanna didn't approve of racehorse gambling or betting or of the people who wasted their family's bread money at the track. Nevertheless, deciding there was such a thing as too much repression, she lifted her voice and sang—slightly off-key, unfortunately—with Julian. His voice was as handsome as he was, a rich baritone that never hit a note sharp or flat.

Under other circumstances, Susanna might have envied him his tunefulness. Today she only appreciated it because, as ridiculous as it sounded, singing did help. In fact, they walked along the path, hand in hand, singing at the top of their lungs and, she presumed, scaring the birds away for a good half hour. A squirrel scolded them from a tree branch and made her smile, but they didn't see another living thing.

Once or twice Susanna looked behind her to make sure the path was still there. It was. She silently thanked her stars for that. She didn't feel like singing any longer. There was something too oppressive about this ancient forest, these old trees, the silence surrounding them.

"Put my money on the bobtailed nag," sang Julian. "Somebody bet on the bay." Then he stopped singing, too. She felt his hand tighten around hers. "This is really sort of ghostly," he said softly.

"Yes," she agreed. "It is."

"I don't like it."

"Neither do I."

They walked a little farther without speaking, holding hands, reminding Susanna of Hansel and Gretel. She eyed the woods. They no longer seemed lovely to her. They were grotesque, malevolent, gloomy. Tree branches tangled over their heads and hid the sky. It was dark, and she hated it. What she wouldn't give for some of New Mexico Territory's vast, open spaces right this minute.

And then suddenly they walked out of the trees and into a clearing—and saw the cabin.

"Oh!" The one syllable seemed to hang in the air around them, as if the atmosphere didn't know how to absorb it. Because the effect was so uncanny, she spoke again, deliberately. "There it is."

"Yes," said Julian. "There it is."

They both stopped and stared at the dilapidated structure. Although it was in the middle of a clearing, it seemed to be shrouded in shadows. Julian looked up into the sky. Dark clouds hid the sun and cast an ominous darkness on the scene. He muttered a soft "Damn."

Susanna licked her lips and cleared her throat. "I, um, suppose we should investigate it."

"I suppose we should."

Neither one of them took a step forward.

There was something wrong with this place. Julian, who no more believed in evil spirits than he did in the tooth fairy, felt something here was out of kilter with the rest of the universe. Something evil. He was uncomfortable even thinking the word, but there it was.

He eyed the sky again, wishing the sun would come back out. He looked at his watch.

Damn. It was getting on toward sunset. He didn't want to be here after dark. More than that, he didn't want Susanna to be here then. She was susceptible to whatever weirdness hung about this place, and he was worried about her. So far she'd only had those blasted dreams in her own safe bed. He didn't even want to think about what she might experience here, in a place that felt so evil.

The cabin looked like a two-room affair, and it leaned over farther than the McKenzies' barn had. Julian didn't detect signs that the cabin had ever been painted, but if it had been, it was so long ago that not even peels of paint remained. The roof had caved in in spots, the door sagged on its hinges, and the windows gaped at them like malignant black eyes. He didn't see any glass in them; they'd been boarded over sometime in their history.

"There's something wicked about that cabin," Susanna whispered at his side.

She felt it, too, did she? It didn't surprise him. She was sensitive that way. He put his arm around her shoulder and was glad she didn't resist.

Giving her a hug that he hoped was reassuring, he said, "Listen, Susanna, why don't you wait here while I take a gander inside that place. It looks like it might fall down any minute, and I don't want you to get hurt or anything." It sounded feeble. He was sure she wouldn't go for it.

She didn't. "Not for all the money in the world, Julian Kittrick! I've come this far and I'll not give up now. I have as much right to see what's inside that cabin as you do."

Exasperated, he said, "I'm not thinking about your rights, damn it, I'm thinking about your safety."

He felt her shoulders shiver under his arm. She was so small, really, so delicate. He didn't want her exposed to whatever was inside that building.

"I'd feel safer there than out here all by myself. And I don't like the idea of you going in there alone, either. What about your safety?"

He didn't much like the idea of going in there alone himself. He looked down to find her beautiful brown eyes staring up at him, and he fancied they were cloudy with troubling thoughts. He didn't like that, either. He feared that if the outside of that blasted cabin reflected the inside, it just might scare the bejesus out of her. Shoot, she might even go into hysterics on him, and then what would he do? On the other hand, she could get hysterical if he left her alone out here, too. Damn.

Well, he guessed he had to select the lesser of the two evils. "All right, then. Let's brave it together."

Her smile made swallowing his scruples about her state of mind worthwhile. He gave her a big hug and, arm still around her, led the way to the cabin door.

*   *   *

"Criminy, it's as if somebody dropped it here from the sky and no human's ever entered it before."

"It's really a mess, isn't it?" Susanna's nose wrinkled with distaste

"Well, at least it's easy to get into."

Julian wasn't so sure that was a good thing.

It was Susanna who pushed the door open. Jarring the old boards precipitated a small avalanche of dust and a shrieking chorus of squeaks from the old rusty hinges.

"Oh, my," Susanna whispered.

Julian looked at her sharply. He didn't like the tone of her voice. Then he shook his head and told himself to relax. He was reading too much into everything. It was that benighted ghost, he guessed. Before he met Danilo, he'd never been afraid of anything in his life. For the love of God, he grew up in circumstances that made dilapidated cabins in the middle of spooky woods look like paradise.

Keeping that thought in mind, he boldly stepped forward—and almost fell through a rotten patch in the floor. "Damn!"

Susanna held on to his arm, bless her, so he didn't fall down. He extricated his foot from the newly created hole and dusted off his pants. He glared around the room. There was very little furniture: only a few broken chairs and a table listing in a corner.

"Oh, look. There's a closet."

"Be careful. It might be rigged."

She looked up at him. " 'Rigged'?"

"You know. Some blasted ghost might have rigged up a bucket of water, and as soon as you open the door it will all pour out and soak us both."

Although he spoke with more annoyance than humor, he was pleased when she offered up a small—a very small—giggle. "I'll be careful."

"I'll help." He didn't want her more than an arm's distance away from him in this creepy place.

When they opened the closet, the door sounded like six hundred rusty nails scraping against the hull of a metal boat. Julian shook his head, beginning to feel a little bit as if he were in a carnival's haunted house. There was just too much atmosphere to be real in this place. He wondered if someone might be playing an elaborate joke on them, but he couldn't imagine who it would be. Danilo, maybe, although Julian doubted it.

"Look!"

Susanna ducked under his arm and into the closet, and his heart lurched in his chest. "Don't do that!"

She had knelt on the floor and looked up at him. "Don't do what? Look! It's a chest!"

Julian blinked at the dusty chest in Susanna's hands as she rose from her knees. "By George, it is."

"Let's open it and look inside."

He followed her over to the table, where she set the chest down. It was locked with an old-fashioned padlock. There was, of course, no key anywhere in evidence.

"Drat!" Susanna scowled at the chest.

"I'll shoot it off." Julian withdrew the small gun from the back of his trousers.

"I didn't know you carried a gun."

She looked faintly scandalized. Julian rolled his eyes but didn't respond. "Stand back."

He shot the lock off the chest. The report sounded like cannon fire in the confines of the cabin, and the dust the bullet kicked up after it did its work on the lock made them both sneeze. It also thickened the atmosphere oddly. Julian frowned at the haze in the room but didn't dwell on it. He wanted to look inside that chest and then get the hell out of there. The place was giving him the creeps and the shivers.

"Oh, my goodness, will you look at that!"

He turned back to find Susanna bent over the chest. She lifted a stack of yellowed papers out of it, her eyes shining like stars. Lordy, she was pretty.

"I think we just struck pay dirt!"

"I hope you're right." He stuffed his gun back into

his trouser band. "Here. Give me a stack, and we can look through them. Pull up a chair."

"Ick." Susanna dusted off the seat of her chair before she sat. Although he laughed at her, Julian did likewise.

He began reading the first paper. It didn't say much. It seemed to be an account of the sale of sheep in Mississippi. He frowned, wondering what it was doing in the chest, when a soft moan made his head jerk up.

"Good God! What's the matter?" He shot up from his chair and grabbed Susanna by the shoulders. Her eyes had a glazed-over look, and she didn't answer him. She moaned again.

Muttering to himself, he stuffed the papers back into the chest and tucked it under his arm. Then, with the intention of picking Susanna up, he grabbed her again. She was stiff as a board. "Sweet Jesus." Putting his other arm around her waist in a strong grip, he wrestled her to the door—and discovered that somehow, in the few minutes they'd been inside the cabin, the door had been bolted.

He shot a wild look around the cabin. Except for some kind of thick fog that seemed to have pervaded the air, he didn't see a thing. It was cold all at once, though. Icy cold. As cold as the grave.

"Damn it all to hell and back again!"

Furious, still holding on to Susanna and the chest, Julian aimed a vicious kick at the door. The rotten wood collapsed under the blow, and the door gaped open. Gasping for air that didn't reek of malice, he stumbled outside and raced for the path back to town, dragging Susanna with him. He didn't know how far he ran before he no longer felt smothered by that awful atmosphere, but the cabin wasn't in sight when he collapsed onto a patch of soft summer grass, cradling Susanna in his arms. She wasn't there. He held her body, but her spirit was gone; he could sense it as plainly as if somebody had told him so.

Frantic, he called to her. "Susanna! Susanna! Come back to me. God, darling, come back to me!"

He held her tightly against his chest and rocked her, frightened out of his wits. It seemed as though hours passed before he felt a shudder pass through her. "Susanna? Susanna? Are you there? Please, darling, please come back to me." He realized tears streaked his face.

"You—you called me 'darling.' "

The words were so soft and wobbled so badly, Julian could hardly hear them. Then he stared down at her, stunned by their import. By God, he guessed he had called her 'darling.'

But she was back! He crushed her to his chest, both elated at her return and mortified to discover he'd been crying. He wiped a sleeve across his cheeks and pretended he wasn't.

"Good Lord! You scared the hell out of me, Susanna! What happened to you back there?" He chose not to address the "darling" issue.

Since he'd pressed her face into the front of his coat, she couldn't answer. She didn't seem to mind the inconsistency between his words and his actions, though, but clung to him as if he were her salvation. Which he was willing to be, God save him. From the moment he'd seen her under whatever pernicious influence was in that foul cabin, Julian had discovered within himself a new and unexpected objective in his life: to protect and cherish Miss Susanna Clement. What an extraordinary thought! What an incredible dilemma for a formerly blasé, unflappable journalist to be in.

He trusted that his state of agitation at the moment was causing it and that he'd recover soon. In the meantime he couldn't seem to let her go. In fact, he discovered he had to bury his head in her soft hair and breathe in the flowery scent of her until his heart stopped hammering and his eyes quit burning.

After he didn't know how many more minutes, he felt calm enough to lift his head. It was getting duskier and duskier in the deep woods. The sun must be setting by this time, and he knew they should get out of there. He *really* didn't fancy being stuck in this place after dark.

He took one more deep breath. "Damn it, Susanna, you scared the tar out of me back there."

"I'm sorry."

She sounded shaken and anxious and almost shy. The tone was so unlike her that Julian's heart swooped again in fright. He clutched her shoulders and searched her face. Pale. Sickly. Dark circles under the eyes. Tear-streaked cheeks. Brown eyes wide with leftover shock.

He couldn't stand it. "Oh, God, Susanna, don't ever do that to me again." And he hugged her against him once more, almost crushing her in his fervor.

She pressed her hands against him. He could feel her feebly shoving at his shoulders. He didn't want to, but he relaxed his grip slightly. "Can you walk, Susanna? We have to get out of this place before dark."

"Don't ever do *what* to you again?"

What was she talking about? He took another good look at her—and grinned. She was mad at him! Glory be, she was mad at him!

Thank God.

Chapter Twelve

"As if I have any control over whatever was in that place!" Fuming, Susanna struggled along the darkening path. She was still more upset than she wanted to admit. But Julian's words—and the tight grip he kept on her hand—kept her from faltering. She was so angry with him at the moment that she'd have gladly left him to fend for himself if she didn't need him so badly. Her need galled her.

"I'm sorry," he said for about the fiftieth time.

"How dare you accuse me of deliberately being— being—muddled. Or whatever it was that happened."

"I wasn't accusing you of deliberately being mud- dled, Susanna."

The long-suffering patience she heard in his voice in- furiated her. He had no business being long-suffering with her. *She* was the one who'd been—muddled. Or whatever. She shivered, remembering.

After what seemed like forever, perhaps because he refused to argue with her no matter how hard she tried to draw him out, they stumbled out of the woods and saw the McKenzie barn leaning crazily in the fading sunlight.

"Thank God," Julian said. He sounded fervent.

"Thank God," Susanna said. She sounded exhausted, because she was.

She allowed Julian to drag her clear of the McKenzie property before she dug in her heels. "I have to rest, Julian." She sat down on a log beside the roadway. Her heart was thundering with an irregular beat that alarmed her, although she didn't want to say so to Julian.

"Don't you want to get to the cemetery first? Or to your house? Somewhere that's—comforting? Familiar?"

"I'm too tired to move another inch. Just give me a few minutes, will you?" She hated it that her voice sounded querulous. She detested whiners. But she was so tired.

"Here. Let me carry you. You can hold on to the chest."

"Don't be ridiculous!" She glared up at him, but his expression was too tender, and she had to glance away again in a hurry. Blast! That's all she needed to complete her humiliation, to have Julian Kittrick be kind to her. To look at her as if he were humoring a lunatic.

Her eyes filled with sudden tears, and she had to blink furiously to keep them from falling. To her chagrin, Julian sank down at her side and picked up her hands. "What is it, Susanna? You can tell me."

"Stop it!" She tried to draw her hands out of his, but he clung like a barnacle, and she was too weak. "I'm not an invalid!" Even as she said the words, her weakness cried out to her that she was lying. Good grief, she'd never felt so unwell in her life. Even when she'd had the influenza, she'd not felt this light-headed and feeble.

"No, you're not an invalid," Julian agreed, his patient tone making Susanna want to pummel him—after she'd stopped weeping with self-pity. "You've just been through a harrowing experience and need to rest. Sleep and good food and probably lots of water or something. But we have to get you out of these woods, Susanna. There's something wrong here. We have to get you somewhere safe.''

She glowered up at him. ''What do you mean by that?''

He flung out his arms in a dramatic gesture that would have looked more at home on Danilo. ''I don't even know what I mean! All I know is that something happened to you back there—''

Susanna shuddered.

''—and I'll be damned if I'll let whatever it was that got to you there get at you again. I want you away from that cabin, and away from this part of the woods before the sun sets.''

She peered over her shoulder. The forest looked like a solid wall of trees from where she sat—a tall, looming, unfriendly wall. She heaved a big sigh. ''Oh, all right.''

When she tried to stand up, her knees gave out. Julian caught her before she hit the dirt.

''Damn,'' he muttered. ''You're weak as a kitten.''

''Am not,'' she insisted in the face of the truth.

''Right.''

He thrust the chest into her hands. ''Here. Hold this.'' She did, because the command startled her. Before she'd gotten her thoughts unscrambled, and in spite of what must have been his own weariness, Julian swept her off her feet.

''What are you doing?''

''Stop hollering. I'm carrying you. What does it look like I'm doing?''

She'd already flung her unencumbered arm around his neck for balance. Now, as his long, manly strides carried her farther away from the scene of her terror, the thought of resisting this latest indignity waged a puny battle with the relief of being cared for—and lost. With a sigh, Susanna gave up the struggle, hugged the chest in the crook of her arm, laid her cheek against Julian's shoulder, and closed her eyes.

* * *

"Good God, man, what have you done to Miss Clement?"

Susanna's eyes popped open. She realized she'd gone to sleep in Julian's arms and that he'd carried her all the way to the Spring Hill Cemetery. She saw Danilo hovering over them both like a real ghost, his black cape fluttering in the wind around him.

"I didn't do a damned thing to her." Julian sounded very cross and very out of breath.

Susanna, who appreciated him more than she'd ever let on, said, "He didn't do anything to me, Danilo."

Danilo fluttered to earth. He didn't appear to be satisfied by her skimpy reassurance. *"Well, then, what happened? Did you go to that place?"*

"That's what happened to her." After settling Susanna down gently on the Homstead tombstone, Julian shook out his arms and sat beside her. He ripped his hat from his head and wiped his brow. He was breathing hard, and perspiration dewed his forehead.

Susanna felt guilty for having been a burden to him, but when she opened her mouth to say so, tears clogged her throat. Oh, dear, she'd never been so weak that she couldn't use her voice. This was terrible. Before she got her emotions under control, Julian picked up her hand. Surprised, she glanced up at him, and almost burst into tears again.

He looked more worried than she'd have suspected he could look even a day or two before. She'd believed him to be shallow and cold, hard-hearted and insensitive. How wrong she'd been.

"Are you better now?"

His voice was soft, and it quavered slightly. Susanna couldn't tell if the quaver was due to emotion or weariness. It didn't matter. He cared about her. That's the only thing she knew for certain. He cared about her.

With another sigh, she sank against his side. It felt like heaven when his arm went around her. "I think so."

"Better from what? What happened? For the love of

God, tell *me! I've been in a panic worrying about the two of you!''*

Julian seemed to have to tear his gaze away from Susanna's. The look he gave Danilo was so hot, Susanna felt it herself.

''Why the hell didn't you warn us, dammit? Why in hell did you send us off to search for that cabin if you knew what was inside it?''

This time when Julian's voice shook, Susanna could tell it was with rage. She squeezed his arm. ''Don't scold Danilo, Julian. I don't think he knew.''

''Knew what?''

Now Danilo's voice shook. Susanna peered up at him and discovered that he seemed even more transparent than he usually did. It was as if he'd paled with terror or something. Well, good. She didn't want to be the only one. Although she didn't want to leave the shelter of Julian's large, strong body, she decided it was time for her to get her wits together. With a gusty sigh, she sat up straight.

''Hey!'' Julian sounded annoyed and tried to grab her back again.

She smiled at him, feeling dreadfully tender. Oh, my, she'd so totally misjudged him. She wanted to tell him so. That would have to wait, however. Right now they had one mystery to discuss and another one to solve. In spite of her state of fatigue and lingering panic, Susanna sensed that they were on the edge of discovery.

''There's something in that cabin, Danilo. Do you know what it is?''

The ghost turned away. Susanna got the impression he was laboring under some heavy emotion. She scarcely heard his, *''No. No, I don't know what it is. I didn't even know the cabin was there, really.''*

''Bullshit,'' said Julian.

''Julian!''

He glared at her. ''He's lying to us, Susanna. He knows good and well what was back there. And it got you, dammit! You almost lost yourself to whatever it was.'' He squinted at her. ''Can you tell what it was? Was it that same spirit thing that's haunted your dreams lately?''

She thought hard. She didn't really want to remember, because the experience had been horrifying, yet she knew she had to if they ever expected to discover the truth. ''Maybe.''

''Maybe? That's a big help.''

She scowled at Julian. ''Well, I can't help it! You don't know what it was like, for heaven's sake!''

He stared at her hard for perhaps ten seconds; then, much to her surprise, he sank his head in his hands. His shoulders shook. ''No,'' he said. ''I could only watch, helpless. God, it was awful.''

''Oh, Julian.'' She wrapped her arms around him and rested her cheek against his shoulder. The tenderness she felt for him in that moment almost overwhelmed her. ''Thank you for rescuing me.''

''You're welcome.''

Danilo, meanwhile, seemed to have recovered himself. He was back to his full ghostly glory when he spoke again, tartly. *''This is all very touching, but unless you tell me what happened back there, I can't very well help you, can I? Am I to assume that some spirit or unearthly presence took possession of you, Miss Clement?''*

''Took possession of me?'' A strong shudder racked her. ''Yes. Yes, I guess that's what happened. I was possessed.'' For a second or two after the truth hit the air, Julian's arm around her felt like her only link with reality. With sanity.

Danilo said, *''Hmmm.''*

''Shoot, it was awful. I was looking through this chest, and all of a sudden I heard this ghastly moan. It was coming from Susanna. She sounded like she was dying or something, but her eyes were staring off into space at nothing. She looked like—like—I don't know. Like nothing I've ever seen before.''

''I wasn't me,'' Susanna said softly. ''Some other person's spirit had—taken me over. Or something. It was awful,'' she ended, echoing Julian. ''Simply awful.''

''Who was it? Could you tell? Was it Magdalena?''

She looked up and found Danilo staring at her eagerly and looking more substantial than she'd ever seen him. He had his hands clasped in front of him, imitating an attitude of supplication. He looked almost desperate. She didn't want to lie to him or give him false information. Since she'd never been taken over by a ghostly spirit before, however, she felt she had to be very careful in her answer.

''Um, let me see.'' She shut her eyes. Even though the experience was one she never wanted to relive again, she tried to recall what it had felt like to have been— subsumed by another's soul. She couldn't think of another way to describe it.

She felt Julian, who had remained seated beside her, put his arm around her again, and she gave him a brief smile of thanks. She appreciated his support. Then she shut her eyes again and went back to remembering.

''I was trapped. Held captive. I—let me think. I remember that I kept expecting someone to come for me. To rescue me.'' Blackness swept through her for a moment, and she stiffened, afraid it was happening again. Fortunately, the darkness didn't stop and take hold. Julian's arm tightened. She didn't open her eyes, but she felt the tears piling up and couldn't do anything to stop them.

''But something happened. Something awful. Something so bad I can't even give words to it because . . .'' The tears started leaking out from between her tightly closed eyelids, but Susanna didn't stop. Something important had happened to her—had happened to Magdalena—and she'd been given the memories of it, if she could only call them up again.

Suddenly she knew utter despair. ''I don't know what happened. Not for sure. But I know all hope is gone. Oh, Lord! Oh, my heavens, it's awful! That poor woman! What she went through! No one should have to die like that.''

She put her face in her hands and sobbed. Julian threw his other arm around her and drew her close to his chest. He glanced up to find Danilo staring down at the two of them and shaking his head.

"No," the ghost whispered. *"How could she have known?"*

"Known what?" Julian barked. "Damn it, Danilo, if you know something, tell it now. Can't you see that Susanna is at the end of her rope here?"

But Danilo seemed to be at the end of some rope of his own. His head kept shaking back and forth, as if denying the truth of something too terrible for a mortal—or a ghostly—soul to bear. *"No,"* he repeated. *"She couldn't have known. It's impossible. There's no way."*

Julian was getting mighty fed up with all of this. It wasn't bad enough that he had begun to care about this woman he held in his arms. No. Then she had to go and get herself possessed by some evil demon. And if that wasn't enough, the ghost who was supposed to be helping them suddenly went 'round the bend. It was all too much for him to bear.

"Damn it, will you please either tell me what the hell you're talking about or get the hell out of here, Danilo? Poor Susanna's had enough enigmas to handle for one day, and so have I."

For several more seconds, to the accompaniment of Susanna's tears of grief, Danilo stared at them, shaking his head. Julian thought it might be his own overwrought emotions that made the ghost seem to take on a sepulchral, luminescent green color. Then, without even a dramatic puff of smoke to mark his passage out of this mortal plane, Danilo vanished.

Julian muttered "Thank God" and returned his entire attention to Susanna.

"Come on, Susanna, it's all right. It will be all right. Danilo's gone now, and whatever was there in that cabin can't get to you here." He hoped fervently that he was right.

Gradually Susanna's tears subsided. She hiccuped pathetically, the sound tearing at Julian's heart. He hated that. His heart used to be such an impervious article. Cold as ice and hard as a rock. Not any longer. Now it sat in his chest, mushy and soft, aching with fear for Susanna and, God save him, love.

How had he come to this in so short a time? It didn't seem fair somehow.

"Do—do you have a handkerchief, Julian? Mine's all wet."

He hauled out his handkerchief and wiped her streaked cheeks with it. "Are you better now, Susanna? Do you need more time? Do you want to talk about it?"

Lifting her hand to his, she eased the handkerchief out of his fingers and finished the job he'd started before she answered him. Since his hand was free, Julian used it to brush her hair back from her poor, blotchy face. He was more gentle than he could ever remember being about anything.

A full moon had come out by this time. He glanced up and saw it beaming down on them like a giant, smiling, silver face. He didn't want to think about the moon as having human properties. Yet there were shadows on the moon's surface, mysterious shadows hinting of its unknown, unknowable peculiarities. They gave Julian the willies.

"Sheesh," he muttered, disgusted with himself. "Now even the moon's giving me fits."

"You, too?"

He peered down to find Susanna staring up at him. "I've been staring at the moon through the maple leaves these past couple of nights when I had those awful— experiences—and thinking it looked like it was hiding something from us. Something important."

"Yeah, well, I think the moon's got its own problems and we ought to stick to ours." He gave her shoulders a brief squeeze. "You better now?"

She nodded.

"Do you want me to see you home? You must be exhausted. Or do you need to talk about anything first?"

She took a deep breath. Julian got the impression she was trying to give herself courage, and his poor, abused heart pulsed painfully.

"We need to talk about that cabin."

"Now?"

"I think so." Another deep breath. "Because the answer lies there. After what I've been through today, I know it."

"Maybe so, but I think we're going to have to find another way to dig it up, because I'm not letting you go back there again."

Her eyes began to narrow. Julian braced himself.

"You have no right to say what I may and may not do, Julian."

"Yes, I know that, but use your common sense for once, can't you? You damned near lost your mind to that cabin today, and it's not worth the risk to go there again."

"There's no other way. I know it."

"How can you know that?"

"I'm the one who had the experience, remember?"

He shuddered. "How can I ever forget? I thought you were gone forever."

She looked down and twisted his handkerchief in her hands. "I'm sorry."

"Not your fault." The words came out strained. He wanted to draw her back into his arms and kiss her. Make love to her. To forget everything in passion.

"But it doesn't matter. We still need to go back there."

"Damn it, Susanna, you're out of your mind!"

"No, I'm not. The answer is there. And there's only one way to find it, and that's to search for it. There. In the cabin."

"That's crazy!" Frustrated, Julian surged to his feet and began to pace in front of her. "There's got to be another way to find out what happened to Magdalena and those blasted jewels."

"There isn't."

"How do you know that?"

"I just know."

He flung his arms out, threw his head back and cried to the moon, "Lord, won't *somebody* come to this woman's aid? Won't *somebody* give her some sense? Please?"

"Oh, stop that."

He looked down to find her scowling up at him. His handkerchief was a goner; he could tell she'd twisted it beyond redemption. He didn't care about that. "Listen, Susanna, whatever is in that cabin got you today. It *got* you. Remember?"

"I remember. How can I ever forget?"

It hurt him to see her shoulders hunch over and her face pinch up. But, damn it all, she was being deliberately obtuse about this whole business.

"So you want to blithely run back in there and let it get you again? Is that what you want?"

"No!" She leaped to her feet, too. "Of course that's not what I want. If I had a choice, I'd never go near that awful place again. But there is no other choice! I know it. If there were another option, Danilo would have found Magdalena by this time. Don't you see? She's trapped. Her soul is trapped! She can't get out, and I want to release her. To allow her to spend eternity in peace. Can't you understand that?"

He glowered at her for several seconds, his guts churning with all sorts of contradictory emotions. At last he said, "Yes, I suppose I can understand that you want to free your great-aunt's soul from whatever purgatory it's in. But it's not worth it if it's going to cost you your own sanity, dammit!"

She looked down at what used to be a fairly respectable member of the handkerchief family and was now a wrung-out rag. "It doesn't necessarily mean my sanity, Julian."

"Not necessarily? *Not necessarily!*" He grabbed her by the shoulders and shook her. "Dammit, Susanna, I almost lost you today! Dammit, I just found you! I'm not going to risk losing you!''

Her eyes were as big as the moon, only coppery and bright and oddly hopeful. "Wh—what do you mean?''

"What do I *mean*?'' Julian shouted, horrified that he'd allowed his feelings to escape the rigid confines to which he'd relegated them. "What do you think I mean?''

"I don't know.''

"You don't know? You don't *know*? Dammit, Susanna, I . . .'' He couldn't say the word. Instead, he said, "Oh, hell!'' and drew her into a crushing embrace. His lips captured hers before she could do more than open them. Good, saved him time.

His tongue swept into her mouth. He'd startled her; he could tell. He didn't care. Dammit, he loved this woman. He wasn't about to let her get away from him.

The Homstead tombstone was a large flat one, and suitable for any number of purposes. Julian used it for one of them by sinking down onto it and bringing Susanna with him. He managed to shuck off his coat and settle her back on it without losing much momentum. She seemed too stunned to protest, which was fine with him.

"I won't let you go,'' he murmured into her silky hair. "I won't do it. You can argue forever, but I won't do it.''

She didn't seem to be arguing. His hands slid up her bodice to her bosom, and she gasped, but she didn't argue. Her breasts were works of art. Julian wished he could see them *au naturel,* without all the stays and boning interfering with his investigation. One of these days. He promised himself that. And Susanna. He promised her, too, although he didn't do so aloud.

Her lips were like wine: intoxicating, heady, sweet. Her body arched beneath his exploring hands, and a surge of pure joy raced through him. Yes! He'd known she was passionate. He wanted to guide her passions, to educate them, to teach them to respond to his touch. Only his touch.

"Aw, Susanna, you're so beautiful."

Her eyes popped open, as if she was surprised at his assessment of her charms. Silly girl. He kissed her again, hard. Her eyelids fluttered shut, and she sighed. Her sigh turned into a hiss of pleasure when his lips traveled to one of her succulent breasts. Even through layers of fabric, he could feel the nipple harden beneath the assault of his teeth and tongue. She was made to be loved. Underneath her prickly disposition, she was as responsive and delicious as a woman had any right to be. Her very tartness gave her zest. Nothing disagreeably sweet about Susanna Clement.

He was about to burst from his trousers when he pressed Susanna's legs apart and rubbed himself against her thigh. Criminy, he was going to explode. His hand began to explore her leg, but there was too much cloth in his way—drawers, stockings. Shoot, women wore a lot of clothes. Julian was about to dispense with preliminaries and head straight for the hole he knew was in her drawers—because he was intimately acquainted with ladies' underthings—when he came to his senses. Or rather, his conscience nudged his senses aside.

Good grief, he was on the verge of deflowering Susanna Clement on top of a tombstone in a cemetery!

With a groan, he rolled onto his back. He put a hand over his eyes and pressed hard, trying to force his wits back into working order. His arousal was going to kill him. But he couldn't do it. Not here. Not to Susanna. Not to the woman he—oh, God save him!

Her little hand on his cheek made him groan again. "Julian? Julian, are you all right?" Her voice was tiny.

He grunted, "No."

A short silence ensued.

"Um, is there anything I can do for you?"

Was there anything she could do for him? Julian moaned. He knew she deserved better than this from him. He'd behaved like a rutting pig. He should be ashamed of himself. Unfortunately, he wasn't.

He turned his head and opened one eye so he could see her. He was afraid to open both of them for fear the full glory of her would weaken his resolve. And why his generally well-hidden sense of propriety should rear its ugly head at this inconvenient time, he had no idea. He licked his lips.

"I want to make love to you, Susanna." He sounded like a hoarse bullfrog.

"You do?" She sounded like a fluttering sparrow. A happy fluttering sparrow. Well, good. He was glad one of them was happy.

"Yes. I do."

She glanced down at the hand that was resting on his shoulder. It looked like a coy gesture, but Julian knew better. Susanna Clement would commit murder before she played coy. Maybe that was one of the reasons he—liked her so well.

"Oh."

"But that wouldn't be fair to you."

"Oh."

Dammit, she sounded disappointed. Julian knew he'd better not dwell on it, or he'd be a goner. And so would she. He decided to voice the reasons that were struggling in his brain against his ignoble instincts. "You deserve better than a tombstone in the Spring Hill Cemetery, Susanna. Your first time should be on satin sheets in the bridal suite of some fancy hotel somewhere."

"It should?" She looked astonished. "But why? I've never even seen a fancy hotel. They don't have any in Artesia."

"Oh, my Lord." He groaned again, and covered his eyes with his hand once more.

A minute or an hour passed—Julian couldn't keep track of time. He couldn't keep track of anything except Susanna's warm hand on his shoulder, and her breathing, which had gone deep and relaxed and smooth. Shoot. He wished he could get his own breathing under control. Suddenly Susanna's voice broke the silence.

"I—I think I'd like you to make love to me, Julian."

"What?"

Her words galvanized Julian. He rolled off the tombstone and onto his feet as if she'd jolted him with an electric current.

She looked faintly annoyed. "Well, I would."

He ran a hand through his hair, wondering if his fevered brain was making him hear things he wanted to hear. "Susanna, you can't go around saying things like that to a man!"

Her brow furrowed. "I *don't* go around saying things like that to just any old man, Julian Kittrick. How dare you imply that I do!"

"I didn't mean that. I meant—" Oh, Lord, what had he meant? He didn't want to hear that she wanted to make love to him. Yet he did. But he shouldn't. But he really, really wanted her. No. He needed her.

Damn. He thrust a hand through his hair again and wished his emotions would stop running rampant over his self-control and cool themselves down. This was terrible.

"Listen, Susanna. We'd better talk about this later. I—I can't vouch for what I'd do if we try to talk about it tonight. Let me take you home. You need your rest." She should need rest, anyway.

"Well, all right, but I think you're being beastly, Julian Kittrick, and I don't appreciate it."

Beastly! She thought he was being beastly! This is what he got for his self-restraint? He heaved a heartfelt sigh. He knew he wasn't going to be sleeping tonight. He was going to be on fire all night long—and all thanks to his being a beast. Maybe he shouldn't have stopped. Maybe he should have taken her right here in the blasted graveyard. He glanced down at her pale face, still ragged with the ordeal she'd gone through today, and knew he'd been right to stop.

He held out a hand. "Fine. Don't appreciate it. Call me a beast. Swear at me if it'll make you feel any better, but I'm not going to add to your problems by doing something I know you'll regret later.''

She tried to walk away from him in a huff, but he wouldn't let her. He grabbed his coat off the tombstone, and she had to walk home in a huff with him by her side. He tried to kiss her before she scampered up the steps to the front door to her aunt's house, but she dodged him, and he couldn't. He did manage to snatch the chest from her hands before she eluded him. He didn't want her troubling herself about that problem any more this evening.

Her aunt appeared at the door. "Susanna, we've been worried about you. Where have you been?" She shot an accusatory glance at Julian. Great. That's what he needed, irate relatives, when he hadn't done a thing. Well, he hadn't done too much, at any rate.

"We got lost in the woods," he said. "Susanna had a pretty bad scare."

"A scare?" Winnie's face registered alarm.

"Yeah." He ran a hand through his hair again, and only then realized he'd lost his new hat somewhere. Wonderful. What a terrific day this had been. "You'd better let her tell you about it."

He saw Susanna glaring at him from behind her aunt, but he'd run through his small store of nobility by this time. Let her think of something to tell her aunt. He was going to his silent, lonely hotel room and try to sleep. First he was going to stop by the saloon and talk to some real, live human beings for a while and drink a little bit. Drinking wasn't Julian's favorite occupation, but occasionally it served a purpose.

As he stumped off down the road, feeling sorry for himself, he heard Susanna begin to spin a yarn for her aunt.

"Oh, Aunt Winnie, it was awful. First we came across this adorable little bear cub, and then we realized we'd come between the cub and its mother. Well, I can tell you, we had to run for our very . . ."

For a female with no imagination, she did all right, Julian thought, and he grinned in spite of his grump.

Chapter Thirteen

Susanna hated to admit it, but after she'd calmed down and soothed Aunt Winnie's worries, she was glad she hadn't succumbed to the lure of Julian's sensual caresses there in the graveyard. Good heavens, she was enough of a mess as it was. It had taken a half hour to get herself tidied up enough from her venture into the woods this afternoon to join her aunt and uncle for a late supper.

What an adventure! She wondered if she'd ever be able to look back on it with any degree of detachment. She doubted it.

It had taken her a good long while to lay her aunt's suspicions to rest. Aunt Winnie evidently believed she and Julian had been doing exactly what they'd been doing—behaving improperly. Uncle Cyrus paid no attention to their conversation, being too involved with his corn chowder to venture an opinion. He smiled at Susanna every now and then, though, as if to give her encouragement. She'd appreciated it.

Now, as she wiped the supper dishes dry, she peered at Aunt Winnie, who was stirring a pot of soup stock on the stove. "I'm truly sorry, Aunt Winnie. We really didn't mean to be gone so long."

"Well, all I can say is that it's a good thing that man's got some moral principles or you could be ruined, and then what would your parents say? Your uncle and I are responsible for you while you're a guest in our house, don't forget."

Susanna blinked at her aunt. Julian Kittrick a man with moral principles? What a novel idea. After what had transpired on that wretched tombstone, she guessed he was, actually. Blast him!

She gave her aunt a halfhearted smile. "Yes. I won't forget, Aunt. I really am sorry."

"I don't like you wandering around in those woods, though, Susanna, especially out there where the Mc-Kenzies used to live. They're deep and thick and over-grown, and there are animals in them, as you found out today."

"I understand, Aunt Winnie." At the mere mention of what was in those woods, gooseflesh rose on Susanna's arms. If animals were all those woods contained, she'd be very happy.

"There are wildcats in that forest. You can hear them screaming sometimes at night. And don't ever try to make friends with bear cubs. People who aren't from around here do that all the time, and it only leads to grief."

"I can imagine." Screaming wildcats, eh? Susanna wondered if some of the screams people heard had a less earthly source. She shivered and finished her chore.

She went to her bedroom shortly after she'd dried the dishes, and changed into her nightgown. Then she opened her window, sat in the rocker, folded her arms on the windowsill, and peered into the deepening night. The moon had traveled across the sky and had managed to get itself lost in the maple leaves. Drat. She had wanted to stare at it a while longer tonight.

She was exhausted, but her nerves still tingled. She wasn't sure what caused them to tingle: whether it was the awful things that had happened to her in the cabin, or the wonderful ones in the cemetery with Julian.

"Bother. I wish I had that chest." She wanted to go through it, to see what the papers it contained were all about. But she couldn't, because Julian had managed to take it away from her, the—the beast.

She pressed her fingers to her lips, remembering his attack on her. Oh, blast, how she wished he hadn't stopped.

But she mustn't think about that. She must think about the chest and the secrets it held. If Julian Kittrick went through it alone, tonight, without her, she'd beat him with a stick.

She sprang up from her chair, sending it rocking back and forth furiously. Clenching her hands, she tried to school her chaotic emotions into anger and direct them at Julian. She didn't succeed.

"He won't go through it alone," she said after releasing a long sigh. And she knew the words were the truth. For all her confused feelings about him, she was sure Julian would save the chest until they could uncover its secrets together. Perhaps she did believe in his integrity—to a degree.

"Tomorrow," she promised herself. Tomorrow she and Julian, and maybe Danilo, if he'd come back—and what had ailed him this evening, she didn't know—would sort through the papers in that chest and see if they could tell them anything. Then they had to decide when to return to the cabin and what to do when they got there. Susanna knew their answers lay in that haunted place, but she didn't aim to venture into it without a firmly laid out plan. She didn't fancy having her body subsumed by that spirit again, whatever it was.

Rubbing her hands over arms that had suddenly sprouted bumps, she knew she didn't want to go back to that place at all, ever. "But there's no choice," she whispered.

She wondered if Magdalena Bondurant's spirit was hovering somewhere close by, or if it could only communicate with her while she was asleep. She had a feeling that the latter case prevailed, because she knew in her heart that Magdalena was bound by some awful curse and that it was Susanna's job—or her fate—to set her free. Just in case her great-aunt's soul was more mobile than she suspected it was, she whispered, "Please tell me what to do." Then she felt foolish, as if she were succumbing to some senseless mania.

"But I didn't imagine it," she reminded herself stoutly. "It happened."

Many things had happened lately—perhaps too many—that Susanna would never have credited even a month ago. For one thing, she'd never believed in ghosts before. Or haunted shacks. Or demonic possession, if that's what it was. Or falling in love.

She hugged herself tightly and smiled into the maple leaves outside her bedroom window.

Please help me. It's been so long. You're close, so close. For so long I've been trapped here. Helpless. Chained. Please help me. Please help me. You're the only one who can set my spirit free.

Susanna sat up in bed, gasping for breath, grappling with her blankets, her heart clamoring in her chest like an alarm bell.

She pressed a hand to her eyes and bowed her head. She wished she'd stop having these awful—whatever they were. Nightmares, she guessed, although they weren't really nightmares. She knew they were somehow connected with Magdalena Bondurant's memories.

They were dreadful, though, and interfered with her sleep and peace of mind, and she'd be ever so glad when they stopped.

"They won't stop until Magdalena's soul is free."

The voice that said the words was hers, but the understanding behind them wasn't. Susanna darted a wild glance around the room. She was alone. Of course.

Nothing but the odd, agitated, invisible spirit hanging around to disturb her rest.

"Drat it, let me sleep, will you?" She glared at the nothingness in her room, feeling sorely put-upon and not a little angry with whatever was bothering her. "All this haunting is wearing me down. If I'm too tired, I won't be good for anything, and I know I'm going to be in for some rough times when we go back to that blasted cabin. If you want me to help you, let me get a good night's sleep, for pity's sake!"

It took a while for her nerves to settle down enough for her to try to sleep again. She wasn't sure if it was the mild scolding she'd given the restless spirit hovering nearby or what, but she slept the remainder of the night through in peace.

Julian came to call at the Dexter house at ten o'clock the following morning. He'd waited until then, hoping that Susanna would be given an opportunity to sleep late. He knew she needed rest. She'd been through hell these past few days and nights. He hoped her rest had been undisturbed. It must be awful to have nightmares like the ones she'd been having lately.

He found her pacing back and forth like a caged animal on the porch when he walked up, and he guessed he'd waited a little too long. He carried the chest with him. The sight of her, her brow beetled in anger, and her lips pursed into a moue of frustration, lit him up inside. He considered that a bad omen for his future peace of mind and freedom.

"Where were you?" she demanded as soon as he opened the gate.

"At the hotel. I was attempting to give you time to rest." He tried to frown at her as she was frowning at him, but he couldn't do it. He was so happy to see her, he wanted to dance down the path.

"Thank you." She glared at him.

"Are, uh, you feeling better this morning, Susanna?"

"Yes, thank you." Her tone told him to go straight

to hell and not bother to wave good-bye. He ignored it.

"You're certainly looking better today than you have the past couple of days." That had been a mistake, as her expression told him at once. "I mean, you look more rested."

She took a deep breath, and for a second Julian didn't know whether she was going to use it to thank him or hurl insults at him. She thanked him, and he was glad.

"Did you get a good night's sleep for once?"

"Yes. Thank you."

This last thank you came out through gritted teeth. Julian decided to change his tack. He held the chest out as a peace offering. "Want to go through this with me?"

"Well, of course I want to go through that with you! Why do you think I've been waiting here for you for the past two hours?"

He peered at her, wondering why she was in such a snit this morning. Then he took note of the faint flush on her cheeks and the darting quality of her eyes, and he realized that she was embarrassed about last night's passionate episode. Evidently she was snapping at him to make up for her own chagrin. He felt better then, and some of his old nonchalance returned to keep his other, less familiar and more troubling, emotions company. He grinned at her.

"Got any coffee? You really are looking healthier this morning, you know."

She glowered at him as if she were trying to discern the hidden meaning behind his words. "Thank you. I slept almost undisturbed, except for one interlude that didn't last long. There's coffee. Come in, and I'll get you a cup."

"Thanks." He bounded up the steps, feeling much better than he had moments before. There was something about being pecked at by Susanna Clement that energized him. He didn't understand it.

"Good morning, Mr. Kittrick." Aunt Winnie blushed at him from the pie dough she was rolling out. He was pleased to see her cheeks bloom with color because they indicated to him that, Susanna notwithstanding, he hadn't lost his touch with the ladies.

"Good morning, Mrs. Dexter. Beautiful day."

"It certainly is, Mr. Kittrick."

"Hmph."

Julian grinned at Susanna, who was holding out a mug of coffee to him and looking like she wanted to pour its contents over his head. "You know, Susanna, I think you've lived in the territory too long. You've taken on the disposition of a prickly pear."

Aunt Winnie laughed boisterously. Susanna scowled. Julian winked at her.

They left the Dexter house, aiming for the public library, but not before Aunt Winnie had fed Julian a hearty breakfast. He had argued in vain that he'd already eaten, but Aunt Winnie wouldn't be deterred. He didn't mind. Her fussing made him long for something he'd never experienced. He enjoyed having a motherly type of woman fluttering over him and feeding him apple fritters. He'd always regretted not knowing his own mother. He'd also always believed that she'd deserted him, and he felt a vague regret for his misconception now. But how could he have known?

Everything that Danilo had found out about his parents only served to confuse him. Julian had been so sure he'd known what had happened. Hell, he'd figured it out even before Father Patrick found him: His parents' lives had been hard, and they'd discarded their son as a means of lightening their burdens.

He'd taken a cynical pride in having risen above his origins—with the help of a kind man, of course. But now Danilo had thrown all his preconceived notions out the window, and Julian felt mixed up. He wanted to know more about his parents, but the hard shell he'd built up over the years prevented him from begging the ghost for information.

He wished he could meet them, even in ghostly form. He'd like to at least see what they looked liked. Used to look like. He frowned, wishing he could stop thinking about his parents and concentrate instead on the problem of Magdalena Bondurant's disappearance and what it meant to Susanna.

Susanna was in deep trouble, or might be, and he aimed to do everything he could do to keep her safe. He hadn't yet sorted out his feelings about her or what, if anything, he aimed to do about them, but he knew he would try his best to keep her safe. He'd protect her with his life, in fact, if he had to.

He guessed his feelings were pretty well engaged when that knowledge occurred to him. With a sigh, he shifted the chest he was holding under his arm. The thing wasn't heavy, but it was awkward to carry.

"That was mean, what you said about the prickly pear, Julian Kittrick."

"I didn't really mean it." He smiled down at her as she strode by his side. When he was certain she was looking at him, he winked and added, "Much."

At once her aspect turned stormy, just as he knew it would. He really loved needling her; she was such fun to rile. Also, it kept him from doing other things to her, things that might lead to more permanent consequences than a few minutes of temper. He sighed, half regretting his restraint of the night before.

"At least I'm not an irreverent lecher," she said indignantly.

Lecher, was he? As he watched the sun shine on her beautiful hair and took in the full magnificence of her, all indignation and firm stride and intelligence, Julian wished he was. If he were really a lecher, he'd be able to take advantage of her with impunity. Unfortunately, the lessons Father Patrick taught him were too firmly ingrained in him by this time.

"No, you're not, are you?"

She honored him with one of her *hmph*s. They had reached the library by this time, so he held the door for her—behavior quite unlike the sort any self-respecting lecher would produce—and they headed for a quiet table in the corner.

There they deposited the chest, sat in chairs beside each other, and divided the chest's contents between them. Julian was soon riveted by what they revealed.

By damn, Magdalena Bondurant had been every ounce the heroine Susanna wanted him to believe she'd been. By this point in his investigation, Julian wasn't awfully surprised to have Susanna's suspicions confirmed. He'd expect nothing less of an antecedent of the upright Miss Susanna Clement.

"This is correspondence from a woman in Mississippi!" Susanna whispered, her excitement palpable. "And it's definitely referring to helping escaped slaves get to Canada."

"Yeah. Here's another letter, probably from the same woman."

She peered at the paper in front of him eagerly. "Is it from a Mrs. Horace P. Fletcher?"

"I think so. In this one she signs her name Sally Fletcher. I imagine it's the same woman."

"What's the date on your letter?"

He squinted at the faded ink on the yellowing paper. "March twelfth, 1857."

"This one dates from a year earlier. I expect they'd gotten to be on a first-name basis with each other by the time Mrs. Fletcher wrote your letter."

"I suppose so. She's talking here about helping two slaves escape. There's no beating around the bush here. She outright says it."

"Here, too. I expect this correspondence was carried out in the strictest confidence, and was delivered by some means known only to the Underground Railroad operatives. They wouldn't entrust this sort of thing to the post."

"I expect you're right."

"I *told* you so!" Triumph rang in her voice.

Julian grinned in spite of having just had his own theories blown to bits. "Yes, you did."

"And Magdalena must have kept this correspondence in that shack in the woods because she knew it would be safe there. I bet Mr. McKenzie was in on the whole thing."

"You're undoubtedly right. They were using a place on his property as a hideout, apparently with his knowledge and consent, and he supplied the jewels."

"Yes." Susanna's brows knit. "That's another mystery I'll bet we'll find the solution to in that cabin—what happened to the jewels."

He still didn't like the idea of her going back to that cabin. He didn't tell her so, because he didn't want an argument on his hands before it became absolutely necessary. He thought of something else and blurted it out before he could stop himself.

"You know, Susanna, this correspondence proves your great-aunt was involved in the Underground Railroad, but it still doesn't prove she didn't weaken at the last minute and run off with those gems."

"She *didn't*!"

"Shhhh," came a dictatorial hiss from the librarian's desk at the front of the room. Susanna and Julian looked up to find the librarian frowning at them.

"She didn't," Susanna said more quietly but with no less vehemence. "Why would a woman who was willing to risk her life and reputation—her liberty for heaven's sake—in a fight for the freedom of runaway slaves have a complete character breakdown and turn thief at the very moment she was most needed?"

"Well now," Julian said judiciously, wishing he'd kept his thoughts to himself, "we don't know how long she'd been working with the Underground Railroad. Maybe she'd been doing it for only a short while, or maybe she'd been an operative for years and years. Maybe she was tired of it all. After all, clandestine activities, even for good causes, can become extremely stressful on a person's nerves after a while."

"How would *you* know?" Susanna demanded, clearly conveying by her tone that she considered him a stranger to nobility and the pursuit of good causes.

Julian was used to it. "I've been told so by experts," he said wryly.

"Hmph."

"Tell you what, Susanna: If we find those jewels, I'll split them with you."

Her indignation was wonderful to behold. It was all Julian could do to keep his grin at bay. She puffed up like yeast dough on a warm day, and her cheeks blossomed with two fiery banners of anger. Her shoulders squared, her chin went up, her lips firmed, her eyes snapped. She was magnificent. Simply magnificent. He wondered how he'd gone so many years without someone like Susanna Clement in his life. Not that there was another one like her. He was pretty sure they broke the mold as soon as she slipped the chute. Which was probably just as well, or the male population of the world was done for.

"If we are fortunate enough to discover the whereabouts of those jewels, Mr. Julian Kittrick, they should go to a worthwhile cause. A charity or something. They were intended for use in a noble enterprise, and they should be used to benefit another equally noble one. One of which Magdalena would approve."

"Well shoot, Susanna, I'm the worthiest cause I can think of."

"Oh, you—"

"Shhhh."

In a huff, Susanna gathered all the papers together. "Let's continue this discussion elsewhere." She shot a fulminating glance at the librarian. "Someplace where people aren't always listening in and interfering."

Since Julian felt a little guilty about causing the poor librarian grief, he tipped his hat and mouthed an apology as he followed Susanna out of the library. The librarian gave him a frosty scowl, and he figured his charm was running two thirds against him today. The only woman he'd met all day who didn't evidently find him more loathsome than pond scum was Winnie Dexter.

Susanna was chugging along like an engine, her fury propelling her.

"Hey, wait up," he said as he trotted to catch up with her.

"I can't believe you!" she said in reply. "You have no morals, no character. Don't you believe in anything at all?"

He shrugged, somewhat taken aback by her belligerence. "Not much, I guess." At once he mentally apologized to Father Patrick.

"Ooooh! You're simply impossible. I can't understand how I could have lowered myself to kiss you yesterday!"

He managed to laugh—and even to make his laugh sound nonchalant—as her words stung like nettles. "I expect we all do things we regret from time to time." It was the best riposte he could come up with under the circumstances, and he knew it fell far short of ideal.

She gave him another hmph.

"I'm going home to organize my thoughts. I want to visit the cemetery tonight and discuss all this with Danilo." She turned abruptly, and Julian almost ran her over. "Do you plan to join me there?"

He was irked that she'd even ask him. "Of course I plan to come with you. What do you take me for, anyway?"

She tossed her head. "I prefer not to say."

"Dammit, will you get off your high horse? We're in this thing together."

"Hmph."

"Stop hmphing at me, dammit! Just because you're embarrassed about having discovered you're a human female, don't take it out on me."

She stopped in her tracks again and turned. Her face had gone deadly pale. Julian wished he'd kept his snide comment to himself.

"And what, pray, do you mean by that?"

He flung out a hand, feeling frustrated and almost desperate. "Hell, Susanna, it's human for a man to feel desire for a woman, and it's also human the other way around. Don't believe what the moralists tell you. Women have passions, too. In fact, I'd venture to bet you have more than most.''

"I'm not upset because of that."

She bit the words out sharply, and he didn't believe her. "Hogwash. You're just in a state because of what we did last night. I'm only trying to tell you that you needn't feel guilty about it, is all.''

"You mistake me, Julian Kittrick. I'm not upset that I demonstrated that I am a woman of strong passions last night. I've known it for a long time now. I'm upset because I allowed myself to become passionate about you, a man who seems to have no values. A man who laughs at profound things and who derides truly noble acts and enterprises. A hedonist, a cynic, a nihilist, a person who tears down what others try to build up.''

Her assessment of his character struck him like an arrow to the heart. It wounded him. It was also the truth, or the truth as he'd tried to portray himself. It was the truth he'd devised and built on the assumptions he'd made about his own life—assumptions that had now turned out to be false. Damn, it hurt to have this creation of his—himself—cut down by her. And in such a few terse words. Even as he stood before her, bleeding inside, he admired her succinct summation of the success he'd made of himself. She didn't waste time on obfuscation. Cut to the quick, she did.

He slapped his hat—his new hat, purchased this morning to replace the one he'd lost in the woods as he tried to save Susanna Clement from demons—against his trouser leg in a gesture of supreme frustration. "Fine. I'll meet you in the cemetery this evening at dusk.''

And he turned away from her. He strode down the road, trying to decide whether to bellow his rage to the skies or weep in regret and bewilderment.

Susanna felt guilty for having used her tongue so harshly on Julian. As she walked to the cemetery, her feet dragging, she wondered why she'd felt it necessary to say all those mean things to him. He'd been her savior, her rescuer, he'd demonstrated his integrity over and over again, and yet she'd all but annihilated him this morning.

Yet as she hugged her shawl to her bosom—she didn't want him to get any ideas and wanted to conceal her feminine assets—she knew she'd spoken only the truth, even if she had expressed herself rather harshly. Perhaps that was why she felt so gloomy now. She'd been hoping that underneath Julian's veneer of cynicism there lay a heart of gold.

"Ha! That only happens in stories, Susanna Clement."

Hoping no one had heard her talking to herself, she hastily glanced around. She was relieved to find herself alone on the road.

She was ashamed of herself, the more so because Julian had been right. She'd been in a state engendered by acute embarrassment. And she hadn't been honest enough to admit it to herself, or to him. The fact that she had been right, too, and that he wasn't worth wasting herself on, only made it worse.

Julian was a care-for-nobody, a skeptic, a critical, hardened man of the world with no ethics or values, and with a character formed by a hard childhood lived on the streets of New York City. She and he had nothing in common. There was nowhere for them to meet and come to a mutual understanding. Of the two of them, moreover, she was the only one who *wanted* a mutual understanding. She'd been deceiving herself, and she was a fool.

Blast! She hated this. She generally wasn't self-deceptive.

She felt almost humble when she skirted the outlying headstones and headed for their regular meeting place. When she saw the Homstead tombstone, her whole body flushed with renewed embarrassment. She was doubly glad she'd taken a shawl with her, because it gave her something to fiddle with.

Julian sat on the monument, his chin in his hands, looking unhappy. He glanced up when he heard her. "Danilo isn't here yet," he said by way of greeting. "At least he hasn't condescended to appear to me."

An apology for her angry words earlier in the day hovered on the tip of her tongue, but Susanna succumbed to cowardice and didn't utter it. He'd have every right to fling an apology in her face, and she didn't think she could bear that. Instead she said, "He told me once to call to him, and he'd appear if he was nearby."

"You'd better do it then. I don't think he likes me very much." He snorted quietly. "Seems to be a universal sentiment today."

Her conscience smote her. Still, she couldn't find it in herself to say the words. What kind of integrity did *she* have? she wondered bitterly. Deciding to castigate herself later—or perhaps drum up the courage to give Julian the apology he deserved—Susanna called softly, "Danilo! Danilo, are you here?"

For about thirty seconds there were no sounds to be heard except those of the wind in the trees. Susanna was on the verge of trying again when a grumpy voice called out, *"It's about time you got here!"*

She jumped and swirled around. Julian rose from the Homstead tombstone. Danilo sat, as if he'd been there for hours, on Magdalcna Bondurant's headstone, his legs crossed, his feet, shod in transparent patent leather boots, dangling.

He'd obviously recovered from whatever black mood had ailed him last night.

Chapter Fourteen

"Young man," said Danilo before either of them could say a word, *"your birthday is August eleventh. In the year 1863, in case you weren't sure about the exact year."* He brushed a speck of dust off of his transparent black silk lapel, as if he had nothing else in the world to do but hold conversations in cemeteries after dark with young ladies and gentlemen.

Julian and Susanna gaped at him, a reaction he'd both anticipated and now relished, to judge by the satisfied expression on his face. Julian swallowed. He was trying to get his mouth and tongue coordinated enough to ask more about his parents when Danilo spoke again.

"Emmett and Kathleen Kittrick were their names, my dear sir, as I told you before. She was a wee lass of twenty when you were born, and barely twenty-three when she went to her reward. She's quite a pretty little thing. I devoutly pray that the knowledge of your survival and success, even in so vile a profession as journalism, will allow her to get the rest she deserves. Your father, Emmett, while an uneducated, bullying sort of

219

fellow''—here Danilo frowned, as if he didn't approve of Emmett Kittrick—*"has been worried about you, too."*

An aching lump had grown in Julian's throat. He couldn't have asked a question now if his mouth and tongue were as coordinated as an acrobatic troupe.

"I'm so glad you've been able to communicate with them, Danilo."

That was Susanna, and Julian could only be grateful to her. He nodded. It was the least he could do and also, at the moment, the most.

"Um, do they remain unable to travel? They couldn't, er, get out here to see Mr. Kittrick for themselves, even though they now know where he is?"

"As I've tried to explain to you before, the powers of the spirit world aren't infinite, Miss Clement. The circumstances have to be right. Even if the circumstances are positively ideal, most of us can't travel at all, much less flit all over the world, like Mr. Dickens's fanciful creations."

Dickens. Julian wondered suddenly if *A Christmas Carol* had been published before Danilo's death and, if not, how he could have known about it.

As if reading his mind, Danilo said scornfully, *"Mr. Dickens's work was published in 1843, my boy. And even if it hadn't been, I keep abreast of these things, you know. One's passions don't necessarily die with one's body."*

"Oh." Julian finally shoved past the lump in his throat. "No. I didn't know that."

"Well, there's a lot you don't know, isn't there?"

Julian nodded, too numb to take exception. "My birthday's August eleventh? Where did I get November thirtieth?" His voice sounded like he'd borrowed it from someone else.

"I have no idea." Danilo frowned as if Julian had asked him to do something illegal.

"There's no need to be unpleasant about this, Danilo. I'm sure this information comes as a great surprise—

and probably a stunning blow—to Mr. Kittrick."

Both Danilo and Julian turned to peer at Susanna, Julian blinking furiously because he was afraid he was going to cry. What a day, what a day. First Danilo offered him more information about his parents—and about himself, for the love of heaven—than he'd ever known, and then Susanna, who had only that morning vilified him to the skies, was defending him. He wasn't used to having other people take up the cudgels of right on his behalf. Nor was he used to having his sensitive feelings, which were generally so neatly camouflaged that no one even knew they were there, yanked around in this outrageous way.

Susanna peeked at him as if she knew exactly the sort of inner turmoil he was going through. "It stands to reason," she continued as if he or Danilo had offered her an argument. "I mean, how would you like it if you didn't even know your own birthday because you'd been forced to scrabble for a living when you were little bigger than a baby? The whole situation is tragic. It shouldn't be allowed to exist in this great nation of ours, where so much wealth exists. It's a crime and a national disgrace! Why, the entire country ought to be required to look at Jacob Riis's photographs!"

She pounded on a nearby tombstone with her fist and seemed to be getting really worked up. All because of him. Julian's heart flip-flopped inside his chest. Damn, he hated having all these feelings churning around inside him. They never used to bother him. It was only after he'd made this trip to Palmyra, Maine, of all places, that they'd been stirred up.

Danilo sniffed disdainfully. *"Yes, that may be. However, please allow me to convey to Mr. Kittrick the last of the information I have for him, if you will."*

Susanna had drawn another breath, Julian presumed to continue her sermon about poverty and wealth in the United States and its territories, but she released it at Danilo's command. She nodded and gave a brief, "Please do."

After another sniff, Danilo said, *"Mr. and Mrs. Kittrick wished me to convey their deepest love to you."* He sounded as if it might have killed him to give Julian the message if he weren't already dead. *"They also wanted you to know how proud of you they are. Your father indeed seemed particularly pleased that you've chosen to work as a journalist. He had hoped you'd go in for politics, but said a journalist would have been his second choice for you."* His contemptuous expression and supercilious tone of voice ably conveyed his aversion to both professions.

"They did?" Julian's own voice was so small it squeaked.

Danilo nodded. *"They did."*

"Thank you." Julian hadn't felt this humble since he was begging for food on the streets of New York. He'd never sounded humble, even then, having adopted a cocky attitude in his infancy. It was the only way he'd managed to survive. He didn't feel cocky now. He wanted to sit in a corner and bawl.

"You're welcome." Danilo crossed his arms over his chest and looked even more self-satisfied than usual.

"It was very kind of you to get this information for Mr. Kittrick, Danilo," Susanna said. "I don't suppose there's any way for him to see his parents, is there? I mean, they couldn't just appear to him for a minute or something?"

Julian appreciated her asking the ghost that. He couldn't do it himself because he was too overwhelmed.

"As to that, I couldn't say. These things are tricky—as I keep reminding you."

"What I don't understand," said Susanna, "is how you can move about so freely when other ghosts can't."

He turned away from them, then whirled again with a flourishing sweep of his cape. *"In life, my stage was the world. Or at least the eastern seaboard. In death, I find myself able to travel the same circuit."* He shrugged. *"Evidently your parents were confined to New York City."*

"Oh. That makes sense." Susanna frowned heavily. "In a way."

None of this made a particle of sense to Julian. He didn't say so.

Danilo gave his cape another swirl, obviously finding the gesture a satisfying one. His cape billowed around him quite effectively. He looked up, his transparent eyes having opened wide as if he'd just remembered something else. *"Oh, one other thing. I almost forgot to tell you that your middle name is Edgar, supposedly in honor of your mother's father. And they were from Dublin. Came here in 1864."*

His middle name. "Edgar," he said numbly. "Dublin." He'd been born in Ireland. Well, for heaven's sake.

"Yes. And you have an uncle still living in New York City. A fellow named Cullen Kittrick, your father's brother. Evidently he came to the States shortly after your mother and father passed on. He searched for you, but you proved elusive. You might want to look him up. He's a grocer in the Bronx."

"I have an uncle?" His voice had gone completely now; he could only whisper.

"Yes. If he'd found you, you'd undoubtedly be selling cabbages to boisterous people with ghastly accents right now, instead of plying your present trade." Danilo frowned. *"Don't know which fate is worse, frankly."*

"I have an uncle." Julian could hardly take it all in.

"Cullen Kittrick. Grocer. The Bronx. Don't forget, because I shan't repeat myself."

"I won't forget." Julian had planned to visit Father Patrick before he returned to Denver. He guessed he'd look up Cullen Kittrick as well. Uncle Cullen. He had a relative in the world. Just like that. He shook his head, fighting the urge to dash off to New York City and Cullen Kittrick right this minute. Uncle Cullen, by damn.

Again Danilo might have read his mind. *"Before you hurry off to meet this uncle of yours, Mr. Kittrick, don't forget that you have unfinished business here, in Palmyra, Maine."*

"I won't forget," he said again, this time referring to another matter entirely.

"That's right," said Susanna. She surveyed Julian critically, as if questioning his fitness to continue their investigations this evening. Julian drew himself up straight and endeavored to gather his scattered faculties together. They'd never been so ruthlessly walloped before. "I'm fine," he said, hoping he was. "I'll be fine," he amended, in case he wasn't.

Her brows remained drawn. "Well, I hope so. I suppose we can postpone this discussion until tomorrow if you're too upset to go into it now."

"I'm not upset." Peeved, he tried to shake off the last of his unsettled feelings. They wouldn't be shaken off, so he tried to ignore them instead, telling himself he'd allow himself to wallow later.

"Are you sure?"

Her scrutiny bothered him. It was as if she didn't trust him. "Yes, I'm sure. For Pete's sake, I'm a professional. I have to work in spite of these little upsets." Little upsets. He could hardly believe that euphemism had come from his own lips to describe the incredible revelations Danilo had just flung at him.

"Well, all right. But I don't want to have to do this all over again, you know."

Julian snapped, "We won't have to do it again."

She gave him another hard look and Julian decided that, while in some ways his life had just been torn apart and sewn up again in a wholly different pattern, in other ways it hadn't changed at all. "Very well, then. Let's give Danilo a summary of what we found in that chest."

The very air around them seemed to thicken and turn somber. Glancing at the ghost, Julian discovered that he'd sunk down on Magdalena's headstone, as if Susanna's words had deflated him.

In her efficient way, Susanna flipped through the notebook she'd brought until she found her latest set of notes. "All right. Now then, that chest contained the clearest proof we've found yet that Magdalena was involved in the activities of the Underground Railroad. It's a certainty now. In June of 1857, in fact, she was expecting two slaves to be smuggled up from Mississippi, and she planned to hide them in Mr. McKenzie's cabin until they could finish the very last leg of their journey into Canada and ultimate freedom.''

"McKenzie," Danilo murmured softly. *"He* was *in on it, wasn't he?"*

"Yes. I'm sure of it.''

The ghost nodded. *"I always suspected as much."*

"What I don't understand,'' Susanna said, frowning, "is what part Sedgewick played in all this.''

"He murdered me," Danilo said starkly.

Both Julian and Susanna stared at him for several seconds. Julian didn't know what to say to this repetition of Danilo's proclamation that he'd been murdered by Sedgewick. Susanna recovered her voice first.

"Yes, you've said as much before. Er, are you willing to tell us more?''

Danilo shuddered. This time it didn't look so much like a dramatic gesture as an honest shudder. *"I—I don't know. It's difficult for me to speak of it."*

"I'm sure it must be.''

Susanna's voice was very soothing. Julian was almost surprised that she, who could tear bloody strips out of his own personal hide without half trying, could sound so supportive when she wanted to.

"Do you think your demise might be relevant to Magdalena's disappearance, Danilo?''

Now she sounded diplomatic. In spite of the sordidness of the subject matter, Julian grinned. A woman of many parts, Susanna Clement. He admired that in her.

The ghost hesitated for a moment before nodding. *"That's what I fear,"* he said softly, mournfully.

"Why do you fear that it's relevant?''

Danilo turned his back on them and sat sideways on the tombstone. His shoulders slumped. *"I fear it was my death that prevented Magdalena from being rescued from her imprisonment those many years ago."*

"My goodness."

Julian cocked his head to one side. "Why do you think that? Were you trying to find her or something? Did you know where she was?"

A defeated shrug met Julian's question. *"I don't know. I don't know. I should have followed her that last night and insisted she tell me what she was doing. I know I should have. I wanted to know what she was up to because I was so worried about her, yet I didn't insist, and then she was gone. I sensed that something critical was about to happen, you see. Something big. I didn't know about the escaped slaves, but I knew she had been particularly excited—almost feverish—for days, and I also knew—even though I tried to pretend I didn't—that she was involved in the Underground Railroad."*

"Hmmm." Susanna tapped her pencil against her cheek.

"It's my fault she's dead. I know it."

The pencil ceased tapping, and Susanna glanced at Danilo. So did Julian. Even though his relationship with the ghost had been strained from the first, Julian was sorry to see crystalline tears gathering in his translucent eyes. The poor old guy had really loved Magdalena Bondurant. Still did, even after death. Julian was beginning to understand those kinds of feelings.

"So you do think she's dead?" Julian asked.

The ghost nodded unhappily. *"I've felt it for years, but haven't been able to find her on this plane, and I've searched for decades."*

Interesting. What did it mean? Maybe there was more to those overnight terrors Susanna'd been having than he'd previously believed. Maybe she really was picking up some stray thoughts or memories generated by Magdalena Bondurant. She'd said she'd felt trapped. Sounded pretty awful to Julian, who shivered in the cooling breezes of evening. Susanna spoke next.

"Why do you say it was your fault that she's dead, Danilo?"

He flung out his arms, sending his cape flying out to

his sides like bat wings. *"She tried to get me to help her! I refused to get involved. I was afraid.* Afraid!" His glance slid wildly between Susanna to Julian. *"I've always been a coward. Always. After years of begging, I finally exacted a promise from her. She agreed that she would marry me at last. Finally! We'd loved each other for years, but she wouldn't marry me because, she said, she didn't want to lose her freedom. But she'd finally agreed to be mine. She wouldn't do it, though, until she'd finished one last job."*

As Danilo put his hands to his face and sobbed miserably, Julian and Susanna exchanged a glance. Although emotional displays weren't unusual from Danilo, somehow this one seemed genuine. Julian felt bad for him. So, he could clearly perceive, did Susanna.

"And that villain!"

The two onlookers' heads swiveled toward Danilo again. He'd lifted his eyes to the heavens in an attitude bespeaking his rage and anguish. He even shook his fist in the air, as if he were shaking it at God. Julian hoped he wouldn't get hysterical and disappear before he finished his story.

After clearing her throat, Susanna asked, "What villain?"

"Sedgewick?" Julian suggested.

Danilo's head lowered again. So did his hands. *"Sedgewick,"* he said in a voice of loathing.

At last they seemed to be getting somewhere. At least maybe they could tie all the loose ends together if they could keep Danilo talking. "All right. Can you tell us exactly how Sedgewick figures into all this, please?" Julian tried to keep his voice pitched to a soothing timbre.

"I followed him. Him! *Instead of joining with my darling in her noble enterprise, what did I do? I waited until she'd been missing for two days, and then I tried to find her by following* him. *Oh, woe! Oh, alas!"*

Uh-oh. Julian didn't like the sound of this. Once Danilo started woeing and alasing, anything was liable to happen, and it usually involved his disappearance. To keep the ghost on track, he asked sensibly, "Where did you follow him?"

"More to the point," Susanna added, "why did you follow him?"

Although Julian didn't appreciate her stealing his thunder, he did approve of her conciseness.

Danilo drew his cape around his shoulders, as if trying to warm himself. It seemed an odd thing for a ghost, who couldn't possibly feel heat or cold, to do. On the other hand, maybe he could feel temperatures. Julian decided to ask later. Then he scolded himself for allowing his mind to wander. He really must have been rattled by the information about his parents; he'd never allowed his mind to wander before.

"Magdalena had gone missing two days before. She had slipped away after the Saturday night performance. In the provinces, you know, they didn't used to allow plays to be staged on Sundays, so we did our last weekly performance on Saturday night and were dark on Sunday."

The provinces. What the hell were the—oh. Julian grinned when he realized that Danilo had at last hit upon something the two of them could agree on. Palmyra, Maine, wasn't exactly a cultural mecca.

Danilo continued. *"I wondered where she was, although I didn't begin to worry until Monday afternoon came, and she didn't arrive at the theater to rehearse. Often she spent Sundays with her relations. They didn't approve of her profession, you know, and she tried to conciliate them by attending church with them and generally showing them that she wasn't a wicked, fallen woman."* He scowled hideously. It was the first time he'd ever appeared truly ghoulish to Julian.

"I went to her house—the same house your aunt and uncle live in today, Miss Clement—and asked if she wasn't coming to the theater. Her mother was surprised to see me, since she'd assumed Magdalena had stayed

the prior two nights with Glynis Wilkinson, a friend and fellow actress with the company."

"My goodness," whispered Susanna when Danilo paused. Julian had a feeling she'd done so to encourage the ghost to continue his narrative, and Julian approved. She was using a time-honored journalistic technique, if she only knew it. Show the interviewee that you were interested in his story by murmuring encouraging noises from time to time, and you could keep most folks blabbing on for damned near ever.

Danilo nodded, his aspect gloomier than ever. *"I knew, of course, that Glynis hadn't seen Magdalena since Saturday night, because I'd asked her."* He commenced staring off into the forest beyond the graveyard, a bitter frown on his face.

Susanna gently cleared her throat and asked, "Then what did you do, Danilo?"

The ghost shrugged. *"When she didn't show up for the performance, I had the understudy take her part. We were doing* The Gypsy King *that night, my own work, and the play from which I have derived my name for all eternity."*

A sense of drama was so ingrained in Danilo that he actually took a bow from his seat on the tombstone. Julian fought his grin. He was pretty sure neither Danilo himself nor Susanna would find any humor in this present situation. He didn't either, really, but he could appreciate a good show when he saw one.

Susanna muttered another of her my goodnesses, which seemed to spur Danilo on. *"After the performance, I saw Sedgewick skulking about."*

"Skulking? Where was he skulking?"

"Outside the theater. He was too cheap to buy a ticket, you know, but often dallied outside the theater, hoping to snag an unused ticket from a theatergoer."

"Did that happen often?"

Danilo blinked at Julian as if the question had surprised him.

Julian lifted his shoulders in a self-deprecatory gesture. "I mean, it seems to me that if a person bought a ticket, he'd want to use it. Just curious, is all."

"Sometimes a patron would buy more tickets than he needed for his own use, thinking to invite a friend or something. If the friend wasn't able to attend, the person might try to resell the unused ticket, or give it away. Sedgewick always tried to find the giveaways, of course."

"I see." Julian nodded.

"That night, though, he didn't show up until after the performance was over. I, needless to say, was seething with anguish over my darling Magdalena. What could have happened to her? Where was she? No one had seen her. It wasn't like her to miss a performance. Even when she was sick, she tried to perform. She was a true artist. I was outside, wondering where to begin looking for her when I saw the devil."

"Where was he?" Susanna asked. "I mean, was he just standing outside the theater?"

"No. He was talking to Glynis." His frown deepened.

"Um, did he generally talk to the cast?"

Danilo gave Julian an exasperated glare. *"Of course he didn't generally talk to the cast. The man was a Philistine, and we all knew it! He had no appreciation of the arts. He worshiped gold. Filthy lucre. He collected art and beauty not for its own sake, but because it could garner him wealth or envy. He only courted Magdalena because she was beautiful and vibrant. He wanted her because he wanted other men to envy him, to want what he had. But she wouldn't have anything to do with him. She had seen through his outer trappings and discerned the withered husk at his core. Magdalena was a goddess come to earth."*

"Interesting. Do you think Sedgewick knew she'd agreed to marry you?"

"I don't know. If so, it might have sent him over the edge into even baser villainy than he'd indulged in before."

Julian squinted, not quite understanding. "Wait a

minute. Was this guy merely a nasty bit of goods and a miser, or was he genuinely evil? I mean, was he a criminal or something? Before he killed you, I mean.''

For his pains, he got another hot scowl from Danilo and an even hotter one from Susanna. Julian shrugged, feeling helpless. ''Just wondering.''

''The man would use any means, fair or foul, to achieve his ends. He ruined people in Palmyra for no better reason than that he felt his honor—honor, ha! — had been impugned.''

''My goodness. He sounds like a perfectly vile person.''

''He was. He was also engaged in trade with southern cotton growers, fabricmakers, and merchants, so he was profiting from the results of slavery in direct ways. It was to his advantage to see that the Underground Railroad did not continue its good work.''

''My goodness,'' Susanna whispered again. She sounded both surprised and dismayed.

Julian shared her sentiments. They seemed to be getting into some very deep, very murky, waters here. He'd had no idea when he set out to get this story that it would lead him into such interesting territory. ''So what happened then? How long did he talk to Glynis?''

''Not long. Glynis didn't like him any more than the rest of us did. She came over to me afterward because she was troubled by some things he'd said to her.''

''Like what?'' Susanna was sitting on the edge of her own tombstone, that of Mr. Brewer, by this time. Every time Danilo spoke, she scribbled furiously in her notebook, trying to capture his words verbatim.

''She said he'd seemed nervous, shifty—which to my mind was nothing out of the ordinary. Then she said he'd asked questions about the belongings Magdalena kept in the dressing room.''

''Her belongings?'' Julian saw Susanna's eyebrows lift in surprise as she asked the question.

Danilo nodded. *''Yes. That in itself was odd. What*

seemed odder to Glynis was that he didn't say a word about Magdalena herself.''

Julian chewed that over for a second. "Oh. You mean that, while the rest of you were wondering where she was, he didn't even seem to notice she was gone?"

"Exactly. And I believe now, as I believed then, that his lack of interest in her whereabouts was explained by the fact that he knew very well where she was. And he knew where she was, because it had been he, *when he realized he'd never get her by fair means, who had kidnapped her.''*

Susanna gave out with another, "My goodness."

Julian scratched his head. "So what did you do then?"

"What did I *do? I watched him. He approached other members of the theatrical troupe. None of them wanted anything to do with him, of course, because the man was a known cheapskate.''* Danilo buffed his fingernails against his cape and scowled down at the result. *"Some of our patrons delighted in offering refreshment to the players after a particularly good performance. That night, even without Magdalena, we had performed well. I, in my role as Danilo, the Gypsy King, was particularly effective, undoubtedly because of my worry over Magdalena. My usually fine performance was only enhanced by my genuine anguish.''*

"Of course. Makes sense." It occurred to Julian to be grateful he hadn't gone into the theater. His life had been hard enough with reality as his only obstacle to overcome and with only one role to create—himself. If he'd had to pamper his muse, change skins like a chameleon, produce emotions out of thin air while suppressing genuine ones, he'd probably have ended up in a lunatic asylum long before now.

"What happened after he stopped talking to people? Did he talk to you?"

"Ha! Never! Mr. Sedgewick and I had not been on speaking terms for months.''

"I see."

It looked to Julian as if Susanna wanted to ask why, but wasn't sure she should. He took the problem out of her hands. "Why weren't you on speaking terms? Because of Magdalena?"

"Magdalena, certainly. There were other reasons. Sedgewick had tried to close my theater."

"The cad!"

Julian couldn't help it. He had to smile at Susanna's indignant exclamation. Fortunately, Danilo wasn't paying attention to him.

"Indeed. He was a cad among cads. The theater, you see, was on McKenzie property. Sedgewick tried to declare the property was actually his. He even filed a lawsuit and went to court, but the judge ruled against him. Not only did the records in the courthouse archives not bear out his claim, but I, in what I believe to be one of my more stirring performances, pled for our cause with the court in front of a jury. I was wonderful."

Julian could picture it in his mind's eye, and he smiled again.

"That was good of you," Susanna murmured. The little diplomat. Julian thought *she* was wonderful.

Danilo gave another small bow. *"At any rate, Sedgewick lost, and he'd hated me ever since. The feeling was mutual, believe me. But I watched him that night. I had a niggling feeling in my heart that he knew something about Magdalena and her disappearance. Even before speaking with Glynis, I knew he'd had something to do with it. I just had a* feeling."

"So what did you do?"

"What did I do?" Danilo looked first at Susanna and then at Julian. *"I followed the dastardly villain."*

Ah, they were back to that again. Julian had a feeling they were narrowing in on the point of this evening's show. There were times, and this was one of them, when Julian wished Danilo had been an accountant in life instead of an actor. Accountants were only interested in the bottom line. "Where did he lead you?"

"Into the woods."

"Where into the woods?"

"Deep into McKenzie land."

A chill shot through Julian. "He didn't lead you to that damned cabin, did he?"

Danilo seemed to stare straight through Julian. In fact, Julian could almost feel his piercing gaze drilling into him. *"I think so,"* the ghost whispered. *"I think we were almost at that cabin when it all happened."*

Susanna sucked in a breath. "Oh, Danilo! Tell us everything!"

So, after another dramatic pause, he did.

Chapter Fifteen

"He suspected someone was following him."

Danilo's voice was low, funereal. Susanna thought it was thrillingly appropriate to the place they were in and the gravity of the story he was telling.

"He kept turning and peering behind him, those squinting eyes of his darting here and there. He was a miserable fellow, a paltry excuse for a man. His shoulders hunched forward, as if he didn't want to share the air around him with anyone else, but wanted to hug it to himself. His nose was long and sharp and quivered like a rat's when he was talking, and his eyes were beady." The ghost paused, staring off into space as if he were remembering.

Susanna listened with her whole being, her nerves tingling with suspense.

"The forest is thick there, where we followed the path running past the McKenzie family plot, and it was nighttime. Nearly midnight. In spots I could barely see to put one foot in front of the other, but I kept following him. I paused from time to time and strained to hear him in

front of me. I didn't want him to veer off onto a path I couldn't see or something and lose his trail that way."

Susanna felt the hairs on her neck rise. A chilling memory assailed her, of how it had felt when she and Julian had trod that same path into the woods. She remembered it well, too well.

"I don't know where I was when I paused for the last time, but I could no longer hear Sedgewick's footsteps ahead of me. I didn't know what to do. Should I return to the theater or continue onward? I didn't know where I was, or if I'd ever be able to find my way back. Something pulled me onward, though. To this day I believe it was Magdalena, whose spirit was calling to mine." His head drooped until his chin nearly rested on his chest. In a whisper, he went on, *"She might have been dead even then."*

"My goodness."

Darkness had thickened around them by this time. As a rule, Susanna didn't feel frightened in the Spring Hill Cemetery. Danilo was her friend; she didn't fear ghostly interference. But tonight, with Danilo spinning his lurid tale, she wished she were sitting on the Homstead tombstone, next to Julian, held safely in his arms. She'd not go to him, though. She'd made enough of a fool of herself with him already.

She couldn't help but be grateful when he got up and walked over to join her, however. She even smiled at him before she remembered she was supposed to be striving for detachment in their relationship. Relationship? What relationship?

Well, never mind. Lifting her chin, she edged farther forward on the stone marking Mr. Brewer's last resting place. Julian's presence comforted her, though. She couldn't deny it. Her shawl drooped from her shoulders, and she let it fall. The weather was too hot for it, in any case.

Julian sighed, and she wondered if he was regretting his outrageous attack on her person the night before. More likely, he was regretting that she hadn't suc-

cumbed to his vicious lures. She tried to stop her conscience from berating her and telling her that his lures
hadn't been vicious, but delicious, and that she'd been
as much a party to the action as he.

To divert her mind from its fruitless ambulations, she
urged, ''Pray continue, Danilo.''

*''I don't know how long I stood there, trying to hear
something; it felt like hours. But it was silent as the tomb
in that forest.''* Susanna shivered involuntarily at Danilo's descriptive phrase.

*''After I determined that I'd lost his trail, I stood there
another long while, trying to determine what to do. At
last I decided to continue walking. Where I stood, I
could tell that I was still on a path, because it was free
of bushes and debris and beaten down. If I was on a
path, it must lead somewhere. I didn't dare turn off the
path, and I didn't want to return to the theater because
then I'd be no wiser than I already was. Even if I continued along the path and found nothing, at least I
wouldn't be able to condemn myself as a craven coward.''*

He seemed to slump over and draw into himself. Susanna could tell that he was ashamed of his cowardice.
But honestly, she thought suddenly, we're all cowards
in one way or another. Danilo was a physical coward.
Perhaps she might be an emotional one. The good Lord
knew, she wouldn't let herself unbend with Julian for
fear of making a mistake. But how could one know?
Where did prudence end and cowardice begin? It was
all too puzzling. She told herself to pay attention to Danilo.

*''Well, Sedgewick must have heard me following him
and hidden himself, because I hadn't walked another ten
paces before he leaped out in the path in front of me
and challenged me.''*

''Mercy,'' whispered Susanna. ''What did he do?
How did he challenge you?''

Danilo flung his head back. *''I remember it well.''*
His tone was biting. '' *'What are you doing following*

me, Matteucci?' What the hell . . . I beg your pardon, Miss Clement, but the man was a veritable pit of foul language and every other vice imaginable.''

"I understand. It's perfectly all right."

"Magnanimous," Julian whispered in her ear. She frowned at him. She knew he was laughing at her and resented him for it, even as she still craved the comfort of his closeness.

"He said, '' 'What the hell are you doing following me?' I, of course, said, 'I'm trying to find Magdalena, my fiancée, you fiend, and I know you know where she is.' Actually, I knew no such thing, but I had a feeling, you understand.''

"Yes, I understand." Susanna felt Julian nodding at her side as if he understood, too.

"He said with a snarl, 'What makes you think I know anything about your little ladybird, Matteucci? You're the one she's engaged to. It's your job to keep an eye on her and make sure she doesn't run off with other men.' That was the way he talked, you see. Squalid slanders were nothing to him, even when he referred to the woman he himself claimed to have wanted to marry. He was a hound. A demon. A villain.''

Danilo hugged himself. Susanna wished Julian would hug her, then chastised herself for the wish.

"He went on in that vein for several moments. I denied his dastardly accusations. I told him that I knew Magdalena better than he, and that her character was one of sterling merit. He gave me one of his ugly laughs—everything about him was ugly—and told me to get away from him. Said that if I persisted in following him, he would assume my purpose was criminal and do something.''

"Do what?"

Danilo glanced up at Susanna and shrugged. *"He didn't say. I said I didn't believe him. He told me to try anything—anything at all—and I'd find out he meant exactly what he said. He went on to say that the authorities couldn't fault a man for defending himself.''*

"Defending himself? Against what?"

"Against me, of course, Mr. Kittrick," said Danilo, irked. *"Just because I'm willing to admit among the three of us that I've always been a coward doesn't mean that I went around trumpeting the information to the world. I can assure* you *that my reputation in Palmyra, Maine, at the time was that of a gallant, dauntless gentleman."*

"Of course," Susanna murmured, trying to soothe the poor ghost's ragged nerves. She wished Julian would keep his mouth shut. He was about the least diplomatic man she'd ever known. She felt him nod again, and hoped he'd leave it at that.

"Well, from that I understood that Sedgewick would use his alleged suspicion of footpads as an excuse to perpetrate an attack upon my person if I continued to follow him. His meaning was obvious. And, while I had taken the precaution of bringing my derringer with me, I had no idea what kinds of arms Sedgewick carried."

"Of course," Susanna said again, appreciating Danilo's predicament on that long-ago night in the forest.

The ghost laughed bitterly. *"Even I, who knew exactly what sort of creature he was, overestimated Sedgewick's honor that night. Realizing my mission was doomed to failure, I dared turn my back on him and began walking away."*

He paused. Breathless, Susanna urged him on. "Yes? Then what happened?"

"The fiend attacked me with a knife."

"Good heavens!"

Even Julian seemed appalled by this chronicle of Sedgewick's villainy. He muttered a soft, "Damn."

"Indeed," said Danilo, his voice dripping irony. *"He got me in the back and pierced my lung. I didn't know that at the time, of course, but I did know that the wound was a deadly one and that I probably didn't have much time. It's odd,"* he continued, sinking into a melancholy reverie, *"how one's thought processes work in times of crisis. I was lying on my side, bleeding to death, and I*

distinctly recall thinking I couldn't allow Sedgewick to get away with cold-blooded murder, that I needed somehow to show the world that he was the one at fault. I couldn't think of a way to do it except by trying my very best to shoot him. So, while he was still hovering over me—probably waiting until I expired so he could withdraw his knife, clean it off, and hide the evidence of his sin, I pulled the derringer out of my coat pocket and shot him. It was very coolly done, I can assure you.''

Susanna, who had begun to shiver, didn't push Julian's arm from her shoulder when she felt it go around her. In fact, as much as she deprecated the fact as a further sign of her weak nature, she appreciated the support it offered. She whispered, ''How awful.''

''You don't know the half of it,'' Danilo said dryly. *''The ghastly man had the audacity to fall right on top of me, driving his murderous knife farther into my own revered flesh and assuring my own demise.''*

She shuddered. Julian's arm tightened around her shoulder. She could only be glad.

''With my dying breath, I pushed him off me. I mean, can you imagine being locked for all eternity with the very wretch who murdered you? I couldn't bear the thought. At the time I had no way of knowing that our bodies would be discovered the next day when the cast reported my absence to the authorities.''

''Did they ever figure out what happened? I mean, did they piece the scene of the crime together and realize he'd stabbed you and you'd only shot him in self-defense?''

Julian sounded more curious than horrified. Susanna took it as one more indication that his sensibilities were lacking. They'd undoubtedly been undernourished in his youth, when he'd had to fight so hard to survive. That was a pity, but there was nothing she could do about it now. The two of them were utterly incompatible and always would be. It wasn't within her power to undo an entire childhood's teachings. She knew it. Miss Amberly had told her students time and time again that when one married in the hope of altering behavior in one's spouse, one's marriage was doomed to failure from the outset. The thought made her heart throb even harder with wrecked hopes than it had been throbbing for Danilo.

"I believe they did, yes."

"You *believe* they did? What did they do?"

"Nothing. They did nothing."

"Oh, but that's not fair!" Susanna had been told by cynical people, including Julian, that fairness was not one of life's promises—and she acknowledged that they might be right. That didn't stop her from deploring its lack.

"Of course it's not fair," Danilo agreed. *"The citizens of Palmyra, Maine, however—not to mention the constabulary—were not keen to stir up a controversy that was destined to end in speculation, no matter how well they read the signs. There was, after all, no living witness to the tragedy that had transpired in the forest that night."*

"Oh," said Susanna. "Of course not."

"Since Sedgewick was hand in glove with southern slaveholders, there were political implications as well that no one wanted to get in to, much less stir up. You can't imagine the tense climate prevailing in the States forty years ago."

"My goodness." Susanna, who had grown up in the freedom of the relatively new territory, couldn't imagine what life might have been like before the Civil War, and how people's emotions and moral fiber must have been tested almost daily. As much as she deplored the official neglect of Danilo's tragic demise, she began to understand the motivation behind it.

"How close were you to the cabin, Danilo? Could you see it from where you were killed?"

What an odd question, Susanna thought, yet so relevant. It definitely wasn't one Julian could ask the subjects of his journalistic inquiries on an everyday basis: *Where were you when you were killed?* She told herself to control her nerves, or she'd begin laughing in hysterics.

"I couldn't see a thing, anywhere. I've already told you it was dark in the woods that night. It was black as India ink where we fought among all those trees. I have no idea where the cabin stood in relation to where we were, although I believe it was nearby, because I felt something. I felt Magdalena's spirit calling to me."

"And you didn't see the cabin afterward? I mean, after you'd died or anything?" Good heavens, that sounded odd. Susanna wouldn't allow herself to dwell on it.

"All was confusion afterward. You'll discover one day—I devoutly pray not in the way I did—that your entry into the afterlife is accompanied by a cacophony of sounds, lights, colors, and commotion. The lights are blinding, the noise is incredible, and one's emotions and sensations are in total chaos. It takes a while to sort it all out."

"How long?" That was Julian, ever striving to pin down the details.

"I have no idea." Danilo sounded irritated. *"Time ceases to matter much once one's deadlines have all been met."*

Susanna shuddered as the word "deadlines" took on a whole sheaf of new meanings to her.

"By the time I'd come to grips with my new plane of existence, I had lost track of Sedgewick entirely. I'd already lost track of Magdalena. I tried to find her, though. I tried, by every way I could, to determine where she was, alive or dead. Something blocked my search. I don't know what it was to this day, but it continues. I know, because I've never given up my search. I'm sure that it has something to do with Sedgewick. Sometimes evil can be a potent force."

"Yeah. We felt it in that cabin."

"Yes," Susanna said. "We certainly did."

Danilo sighed.

"That's an amazing series of events, Danilo. You've

really been through a lot, haven't you?'' Julian sounded respectful. Susanna was grateful. She knew it had been difficult for Danilo to tell them his story.

"Yes," the ghost whispered. *"And I fear my travails are not yet over."*

Susanna took a deep breath. They'd come to the point, she reckoned. "You think Magdalena was in that cabin, don't you. You think that her captivity and perhaps even her death had something to do with what happened to you all those years ago. Whatever it was took control of me the other day when Julian and I entered it, didn't it?''

She could barely see him nod in the gloom of the graveyard.

"I don't want you going back there, Susanna," Julian said suddenly. "It's too dangerous for you. Maybe I should go alone." This time it was he who shuddered.

"No!" Danilo jumped up from Magdalena's headstone. *"No, neither of you should go there again. Not ever. There's something bad in there. From what you told me, there's an evil aura about the place, as if Sedgewick has erected guards from beyond the grave to keep it secure. If he has, it's as much as your life is worth to go back to that vile place. Don't do it!"*

Shaking off Julian's arm, Susanna rose as well. "But we have to, Danilo. We *have* to. In order to get to the bottom of this, and to prevent Mr. Kittrick from making up awful stories about Magdalena Bondurant—"

"Hey!" Julian jumped up, too.

"—we have to discover the truth. The whole point of our collaboration was to discover the truth! I won't quit now. I *won't*!" She stamped her foot, for all the good it did in the mossy, grassy graveyard.

"I am not going to make up awful stories! I'm as eager to discover the truth as you are, dammit, but Danilo's right. You almost lost your mind forever in that blasted cabin, Susanna. You can't go back there."

"Watch me," she said, feeling as defiant as anything just then. "You just watch me, Mr. Julian Kittrick. I'm not afraid of a blighted, murderous Sedgewick.''

"You should be," muttered Danilo. *"Look what he did to me."*

Whirling around, Susanna thought furiously for a moment while Julian grumbled at her back. She had a sudden brilliant idea and whirled around again. "Why, I'll arm myself!''

"How in the name of Glory can you arm yourself against evil ghosts?'' Julian sounded disgusted.

"With the Bible! With crucifixes—if I can find any. With crosses and prayers and whatever else we can think of to ward off evil.''

"It won't work, Miss Clement."

She turned to find Danilo shaking his head. She considered his desertion most unfair, and told him so. He wouldn't be swayed.

"There's the devil's work afoot in that shack, Miss Clement. It's not a game, and Bibles and crosses and so forth aren't going to be strong enough to ward the evil off unless someone who knows how to use them goes with you."

"Blast it, there must be *something* we can do.''

"Well, for one thing, we should only go in full daylight. That place is too spooky after dark.'' Julian sounded annoyed and reluctant, as if he didn't really want to be adding to this conversation.

"Yes.'' Susanna rubbed her hands up and down her arms. "That's true.''

"Although,'' Julian added, "I personally think you're a fool to go back there—ever.''

"Well, of all the nerve! I am not a fool. I know there's something foul about the place, and I *do* plan to take precautions!'' She added reluctantly, "Going in the daytime is a good idea.''

"It won't matter," Danilo declared. *"Evil doesn't rest just because the sun is out."*

"Right,'' said Julian.

Susanna ignored him and concentrated her efforts on the ghost. Danilo, after all, had a lot at stake in this endeavor. "But Danilo, you said yourself that your own strength is sapped in the daylight. Doesn't that hold true for evil ghosts, too?"

He frowned at her. *"Well . . . perhaps."*

She felt a burst of satisfaction. "There! You see? We'll go in the daylight. Maybe noonish. That's when the sun's at its zenith. Surely we'll be able to plow through the devils at noon!"

Danilo snorted. Julian said, "I don't know about this."

The ghost said, *"I know about it. I know you'd be risking your very lives if you attempted to go back inside that abysmal place."*

"But Danilo, don't you want to know what happened to Magdalena?"

"Of course I do!"

"There! Can you think of another way to do it?"

He paced a circle around the Homstead monument, his head bowed, his hands clasped behind his back. Susanna wondered how he did that, since his hands—like the rest of him—were insubstantial. Yet he managed. She guessed it took practice.

When he finally came to a stop in front of her, he seemed exceedingly peeved. *"No. Quite frankly, I can't think of another single way to find out what we need to know. I'm stuck here, you know, in this nebulous place between heaven and earth, awaiting the resolution of my soul's tribulations before I can go to my eternal rest. I have refused rest until I have discovered Magdalena's fate, and I must say it gets wearying, always hovering between things."*

"I should think it must. I didn't know that, Danilo."

He gave her a good glower. *"Well, now you do."*

"You mean you can't get into heaven until you know what happened to Magdalena?"

"No, Mr. Kittrick, I cannot. It was my choice, of course, but I knew heaven would be no heaven without her. Your parents have been in much the same pickle, worrying about you."

"Oh."

Susanna looked at Julian, thinking surely he'd say something else, but he didn't. It seemed to her that any mention of his parents shut him up like a locked safe, and she decided to bear it in mind.

"Well," she said, "it looks to me like it's settled. We *must* return to that cabin."

"*Egad!*" Danilo turned away from them. His internal agitation evidently stirred up the atmosphere surrounding him, because his cloak continued to flutter even after he'd stopped moving, and there was no breeze.

"I still don't like it."

Susanna frowned at Julian, who frowned back. "Can you think of another way to solve the puzzle once and for all? It's not fair to leave Danilo suffering this way, you know."

"I know."

"You needn't sound so annoyed. Instead of wasting your energy being crabby, why don't you put it to some use and think of a way to approach that cabin that won't get us both killed?"

"We'll have to figure out some way to mitigate the influence it has on you, that's for sure."

"Yes," she said, and shivered. "I think so, too."

"*Lead.*"

"I beg your pardon?"

Danilo turned to face them and repeated, "*Lead. I understand lead implements can ward off evil to a degree, although I doubt their efficacy against such potent evil as Sedgewick's.*"

"I'd never heard that. How interesting."

"I thought you were supposed to use silver bullets or something," said Julian.

Danilo cast his eyes heavenward. "*For heaven's sake, Mr. Kittrick, we're not going to be dealing with fictional werewolves or vampires. We're going to be doing battle with real evil beings.*"

"I know that. I just didn't know lead worked. Why

don't I just take my gun along and shoot any ghosts we find. The bullets contain lead.''

"That won't work. Spirits move too quickly for mere mortal bullets."

"Shoot," Julian murmured appropriately, taken aback.

Susanna knew what he meant, though. It was daunting to consider waging a life-or-death struggle with something that could move faster than a bullet. "What types of lead implements do you recommend, Danilo?"

He shrugged. *"I have no idea. Piping, perhaps? Farm implements? Does your uncle have any lead weights in his fishing tackle box or anything?"*

"I—I don't know. I guess I can ask him."

"I wouldn't," said Julian. "If you ask him specifically for a lead weight, he might want to know why you need it. It's probably better not to tell anyone what we're up to, and I know you don't like to lie."

She examined his expression to see if he was being sarcastic, but he seemed serious. She appreciated his assessment of her character. She hadn't been able to chalk up many points to her credit recently; she savored getting one from him.

"All right. I'll look through his tackle box for lead weights. And I think there's some lead piping in the barn."

"Pencils," said Julian. "We already have pencils with lead points."

"Right. So we'll take lead weights and pencils." She squinted at Danilo. "This actually sounds like a pretty silly catalog of armaments, Danilo. Don't you think it might be a good idea to take a Bible along, and maybe a cross or two?"

"If it makes you feel better, Miss Clement." Danilo bowed slightly, as if conceding an unimportant point.

"I'd feel better with a Bible along."

"Got any lead crosses?" Julian asked with a short laugh.

"I wish."

"I wonder what my rosary beads are made of."

Susanna's eyebrows shot up. "You have rosary beads with you?" How astonishing. She'd believed him to be completely without moral principles, yet he carried rosary beads around with him? She was somehow comforted to know that Julian Kittrick actually seemed to believe in something.

He shrugged. Susanna could swear he blushed, too, but it was too dark to tell for certain. "Old habit," he muttered, but she didn't believe him.

"They were his mother's," Danilo said as if he were imparting information of no particular consequence. *"She twined them in his babyish fingers just before she died."*

"She did?" Susanna stared at Julian.

"She did?" Julian stared at Danilo, who nodded.

"She did."

"My goodness."

"I didn't know that. I only knew they were mine, and that I'd had them since before I could remember anything."

"Well, there you go. Learn something new every day." Danilo sounded bored.

"Look here, Danilo, I know you don't like me, and I know my parents and I are nothing to you, but this stuff is important to me—and I *am* trying to help you out of a fix, don't forget. If you have any other information about my parents and my infancy, I wish you'd just tell me all at once instead of dropping little tidbits into the conversation every now and then. When you do that, it stops me cold. I—I . . ." Julian threw out his arms. "I don't know. It's upsetting."

Susanna put a hand on his shoulder, an unconscious gesture of support that she realized she'd done only when he looked at her as if it had surprised—and gratified—him. She spoke to the ghost. "He's right, Danilo. It does seem unfair of you to keep these pieces of information to yourself. They may seem small to you, but they must be terribly important to a person who never knew his parents."

"I'm not doing it on purpose!" The ghost huffed indignantly and put his hands on his hips. *"I can't remember everything. I only remembered that part when he mentioned his rosary. For heaven's sake, I'm only human, you know. Or used to be."*

"I understand," she said soothingly. "And I'm sure Mr. Kittrick does, too." She gave Julian a look the meaning of which she hoped he understood. They couldn't afford to alienate Danilo now.

Julian had a small struggle with himself; Susanna could see it on his face. At last, however, he said mildly, "Of course. I understand. And I appreciate any information you have to tell me, whenever you remember it." He shot Susanna a glance that told her she'd better appreciate his forbearance because it didn't come easily. She did, and smiled to show him so.

"All right." Danilo shifted his shoulder as if he were getting back to business *"So you'll bring your lead things and your religious things—including rosary beads, whether lead or not—and we'll go at high noon. Better make that elevenish. By the time we get there and figure out where to look, it might take some little time. If it looks like we're going to have a battle on our hands, we want the sun to be at its height."*

"What do you mean by 'we'?" asked Julian.

Susanna looked at him and then at Danilo. "Yes. What do you mean by 'we'?"

Danilo's gaze was steady. *"I am going with you."*

"But you can't go with us! You can't appear in the daylight without hurting yourself!"

"She's right, Danilo. We don't want to have to be worrying about you as well as the evil stuff that's already in that cabin."

"Well, I like that! Do you honestly believe I'd offer you my services if I weren't absolutely positive that my presence would be a help to you rather than a hindrance? What do you take me for, Mr. Kittrick?"

Julian stuttered several syllables but didn't manage to form a word.

Susanna said, "Are you sure, Danilo? We would love to have your help if you're sure it won't hurt you."

The ghost lifted his head, puffed out his chest, and said in a thrilling, Hamlet-like voice, *"I shall join you. We shall prevail."* Dropping the act, he muttered, *"But I'd better rest up and recruit my strength, because it's going to be a terrible ordeal. I'll see the both of you here at eleven o'clock tomorrow morning."*

And with that, he vanished.

Chapter Sixteen

"Blast! It's so disconcerting when he just up and disappears that way."

Julian grinned at Susanna. She had a way with words, she did. He adored her for it, too.

"I had some more questions I wanted to ask him."

"What more do we need to know at this point? We know where the cabin is and what to bring with us. We don't know what's there or what we'll be up against, but neither does he. I imagine when we get inside the cabin, we'll have to improvise, depending on what happens to us there. I expect everything else is more or less gravy."

He saw her shiver, and he put his arm around her again. He wasn't sure she wouldn't fling it away and was prepared for the eventuality, but she didn't. Instead, she shrank against him, as if seeking the succor of his strength. Not that she didn't have plenty of her own strength to draw upon. But he was a man, and physically stronger than she. And as much as he longed to protect and comfort her, she evidently appreciated being protected and comforted—every now and then, anyway.

"What—or who—do you think will be waiting for us in that awful place?" Her shoulders quivered with her shudder.

"I have no idea. Sedgewick, I guess."

"Do you suppose he has—minions?"

"I don't know. At least we'll have Danilo with us. I expect he knows how to battle the forces of evil." At least he hoped so.

He led her to the Homstead monument and sat down there with her, his arm still around her shoulder. They sat in the quiet of the evening, the forest still, dark, and rather comforting around them. The fragrance of pines and oaks mingled with that of the mossy dampness that Julian had noticed when he first arrived here in Maine. The smell reminded him of old things, of historical events, of Pilgrims and Quakers and the first Thanksgiving. The very first settlers newly arrived from England would have smelled that same smell.

Night sounds whispered around them. Julian heard the soft whoosh of a bat's wings and an owl calling to its mate, who answered from a few trees over. Fireflies blinked on and off. The atmosphere, for all they were sitting in a cemetery, was cozy.

"I'm afraid to go back there, Julian."

He gave her shoulders a little squeeze. "You don't have to, you know, Susanna. In fact, I wish you wouldn't."

"I do have to. You know it as well as I do."

He peered down to find her looking up at him, her gorgeous eyes huge and shining. She was such a pretty thing. At the moment she seemed vulnerable. He knew better. Morally, she was as strong as an ox; invincible. She had character. Principles. Ethics. All the qualities Father Patrick had drummed into Julian, and that Julian had pretended to put behind him for so many years.

He sighed, wondering how his careful plan for himself could have gone so completely awry. He never thought he'd regret having succeeded in creating himself in the image he craved, but he did now. He wanted Susanna Clement to know him as he was inside, not as the carefully crafted, audacious journalist he acted for the world's sake. Too late. He was too late.

"Yes," he said quietly. "I know you have to do it."

"Thank you." Her voice was soft, breathy. It feathered over Julian's senses, teasing them, tantalizing him.

"You're welcome."

She sighed and snuggled closer. He tightened his arm around her.

"I'll do my best to protect you, Susanna."

"I know you will. Thank you, Julian."

They sat that way, not speaking, for a long time. Julian thought about that foul cabin in the woods. Susanna might die there tomorrow. For that matter, they both might die. It was a daunting thought, not the less because he and Susanna had so many unresolved issues between them. At least they were unresolved in Julian's mind. For all he knew, she might have already written him off as a miserable wretch who wasn't worth her time.

"I'm afraid of what might happen to me in that cabin tomorrow, Julian."

He gave her another squeeze and this time didn't release it. "We'll have Danilo with us. And I'll do everything in my power to safeguard you from whatever's in there."

"Something—something might happen to you, too."

"Yeah, I've already thought of that." He looked down and saw her lick her lips.

"I really don't want to die, you know."

"Of course you don't. And you won't. Danilo and I will protect you."

"I know you'll try. But it might not be enough."

"Hey, this conversation is getting really gloomy." He tried for a laugh and didn't fail too dismally. "Let's not talk about the bad things that might happen. Don't forget that if we succeed, poor old Danilo will be able to rest in peace with his lady love for all eternity."

After a moment of silence Susanna said, "Yes. Yes, that's true."

"So we should think about that and not about possible catastrophes. Don't forget that good is supposed to be stronger than evil. That's what all the priests and ministers and those folks say."

"I don't know. The minister back home in Artesia is always telling us to beware of the devil because he can get you when your back is turned."

Neither of them spoke again for several minutes. Julian was surprised when he felt Susanna's finger begin to stroke the back of his hand. Her gentle touch provoked his carnal instincts, but he endeavored not to let it show. He didn't want to scare her. She'd get scares aplenty tomorrow, unless he missed his guess.

After several more silent moments Susanna said softly, "Julian?"

"Yes?"

"Do you suppose Danilo and Magdalena ever—well—you know, um, had carnal knowledge of each other?"

What? His senses went on the alert in an instant. He said cautiously, "Er, they weren't married."

"I know that, but theatrical folks are supposed to be— less constrained by society's attitudes than the rest of us."

"Yeah. I guess that's true."

"So do you think they did?"

Damn, he wished she'd stop talking about people making love. Thinking about it—and about what he'd like to do with Susanna—was making him squirm. "I don't know. Probably. I mean, I suppose so. I guess." He shrugged, uncomfortable with the topic.

He heard her lick her lips again, as if she were unsettled by the conversation, too. "Julian?"

"Yes?"

"Julian, um, will you make love with me?"

His body had reacted to her astonishing question before his brain assimilated it. He was hard as a rock in seconds. When his brain caught up with his body, he looked down at her again, dumbfounded. "I beg your pardon?"

She couldn't look him in the eye. "I—was thinking about Danilo and Magdalena, and about how much they loved each other. It seems awful to think they might have died without ever knowing each other in—in—you know. In that way."

Julian gulped audibly. His thinking processes had been knocked askew by Susanna's incredible question, and he didn't know what to say. *Yes* sprang to mind, but he feared that was his lust talking. Susanna deserved more from him than mere lust.

Evidently she took his silence as a refusal or as censure. "It's not as if I'm asking you to commit a felony." She was striving to sound ironic, but her hurt came through loud and clear.

"I know it. But—but—but—"

"Oh, don't worry. I won't make you marry me."

There it was again, the pungent combination of humiliation and sarcasm. The words she'd chosen to fling at him hurt, too. She really believed he was a bounder and a cad. A scoundrel who'd think nothing of seducing and abandoning virgins the country over. How little she knew him. How well he'd crafted the mask he presented to the world.

"It's not that," he said as soon as he could catch his breath and make his tongue work. "It's not that at all."

"No? What is it then? Do you find me repugnant? Is that it? I thought men didn't care what a female looked like as long as she was willing."

"Dammit, it's not that, either! I don't find you repugnant, for heaven's sake."

"Well then, what *is* the matter, Julian? Surely you can't mean you actually have scruples about bedding a lady who isn't your wife?"

Now it was he who was indignant. "I do, too, have scruples about it. A fellow can't just go around making love with any female who comes his way!"

"Why not? I thought that's what men did."

"Dammit, Susanna, I don't know who's been filling your head with such nonsense, but we're not all unscrupulous cads."

She gave him a humph and didn't reply.

"I do have scruples. Strong scruples. And I don't want to do anything that might hurt you. I—I like you too well for that."

"You do?"

He could hear the disbelief in her voice, and it irked him. "Yes, I do! Why do you find that hard to believe?"

"I—I don't know."

"Well, it's the truth, and I resent your doubting me."

"Hmph. It seems to me that these scruples of yours have chosen a rather inconvenient time to rear their heads, Julian Kittrick. Where were they the day before yesterday, hmm? Where were they when you all but attacked me on top of this very tombstone?" She slapped it hard and cried, "Ow!"

Grasping for anything to lighten the atmosphere, Julian said, "That'll teach you to mess with the dead."

Instead of lightening it, his joke seemed to bring darkness down upon them. Susanna stopped struggling in his arms and fell silent. He stilled, too.

She cleared her throat. "We're back to that."

He decided silence was the better part of discretion and didn't speak.

"I don't want to die without having experienced the kind of physical love that happens between men and women, Julian. Although I never thought about it before now, I suppose I always expected to marry and have children. But that might not happen. I might die tomorrow."

"Stop saying that." He shook her lightly in the cocoon of his arm.

"I might as well say it, because it's the truth. And, since I have no idea who might marry me eventually if I live—assuming anyone ever wants to—you and I are here together, and I wish you'd just shut up and make love to me."

"But what if you don't die tomorrow, Susanna?—and I'm sure you won't. What then? Do you suppose your future husband will appreciate marrying a woman who didn't wait for him?"

She snorted indelicately. "What about him? How many men do you know who wait for their wedding nights before sampling the pleasures of the flesh?"

Since he didn't know a single one, he only shrugged. As he might have guessed would happen, his shrug didn't fool her.

"Can't think of any, can you? Well, there you go. I don't intend to allow the world's paradoxical standards to prevent me from doing what I deem best for myself, now or ever."

"That doesn't surprise me at all, somehow."

"So I'm asking you again. Don't take this to mean that I'm begging you to do something distasteful, either. I got the impression you don't find me wholly unappealing—"

"Far from it."

"So if you can think of no other idiotic objections, will you please make love with me? You may think of it in the light of an experiment, or a journalistic exercise, or something along those lines."

As if he ever could. As he sat with his arm around her shoulder on the Homstead tombstone in the Spring Hill Cemetery in Palmyra, Maine, Julian knew that he'd been longing to make love to her since the first moment he saw her, sitting and musing over mysteries to which they were now uncovering answers together. He still wanted to make love to her. He discovered, however, that he was strangely reluctant to do so.

God save him, he didn't want to hurt her. The words he had uttered almost by rote because he couldn't think of anything else to say, he suddenly discovered were the truth. He didn't want to hurt her. Ever. Not physically and not emotionally.

And they both might die tomorrow.

The reality sobered him. It also left him with what he

perceived as only one option. "All right."

She gave a start of surprise. "All right? You mean you will?"

"Yes." He nodded, wondering if he'd lost his mind. Then he decided it didn't matter. They both might *die* tomorrow. "But not here."

He rose, taking her with him. He had no idea where they were going to consummate their passions, but he'd be skewered if he'd do it on a tombstone. Gently taking her by the hand, he led her down the path and farther into the woods. These woods held none of the terror inherent in those surrounding the cabin. These trees and mosses were friendly, welcoming. Julian felt almost as if something were calling him deeper into the forest— unless that was his desire playing tricks on his conscience. He wasn't sure of anything anymore.

She followed him willingly. He thought it was touching that she trusted him enough to allow him the honor of being the first. The notion of another man following him didn't appeal at all, so he didn't dwell on it. He would think only of this evening, and of how he would do his best to make the experience good for her.

His mind touched upon the notion that he loved her, that he wanted this to be the first of many such joinings. Only he didn't want them to be clandestine. He wanted to be able to make love to her freely, their union blessed by God and man. Rebelling violently, his brain thrust the notion aside.

They hadn't walked far before they came to a small glen. It seemed almost magical to Julian that they should have found such a perfect place. Soft grasses grew in an opening among the trees, and the stars shone down upon them so that he could almost see the colors in spite of the deepness of the night.

"Here," he said.

"Yes. It's lovely here. It looks almost like the fairies might meet here."

"Fairies," he said with a chuckle. "Don't tell me you believe in fairies, too."

"I didn't used to believe in ghosts," she reminded him.

He had no answer. They walked to the center of the clearing and looked around. Julian removed his coat.

"Here, use this." Susanna handed him her shawl. "I'm sure you know what to do. I'm new at this, so you'll have to lead the way."

Great. That's just the reminder he needed. As if he hadn't been nervous enough already. He used the few seconds it took him to arrange her shawl and his jacket on the grass to get his wits together.

Then he took a deep breath and turned around. Susanna was peering at the ground, at the place where she was going to be losing her virginity. She looked more curious than frightened. Why didn't that surprise him? He was sure he was more scared than she was. He reached for her hand, and she smiled at him. Her smile pierced the wall his taut nerves had built and soothed his heart. He smiled back.

"Let's sit down," he suggested softly. "And get comfortable."

She complied with grace. She really was a special creature, lithe and agile, every movement fluid. When she wasn't being mutinous, she was lively and charming. And honestly, when he thought about it, she wasn't prickly often—mostly when people were crossing her will and refusing to enter into her sentiments on a particular issue. She got huffy, too, when folks refused to allow her to do things because she was female. That must be frustrating to a lively intelligence like hers. He guessed he could understand her moments of rebellion.

He sat next to her, then drew her closer until they sat side by side. Since he was beginning to get nervous again, he decided to plunge onward.

Gently, because he didn't want to scare himself, he began by nuzzling her ear. She sighed, and her head dropped back. Taking it as a sign to continue, he moved his lips to her throat. Her skin was so damned soft.

He lost track of time and of the nebulous plan he'd

been formulating on how to proceed in this enterprise. Ever so slowly he kissed her throat and her chin and her cheeks. When he got to her lips, they were soft and parted and ready for him. He skimmed them with his own, savoring the sweetness of her, the thrill of her surrender. Surrender? Well, savoring the thrill, at any rate.

The pressure in his loins was building every second. He tried to ignore it because he didn't want his own needs to get in the way of Susanna's pleasure. He tried to keep in mind that this might well be the only time they ever had together; he wanted with all his heart to make it special for both of them.

Susanna had never felt cherished before. She did now, and knew the feeling to be an illusion. After all, Julian had only conceded to her wishes reluctantly. But she couldn't help herself. After fighting the phenomenon for several minutes, she decided to give herself up to it. This might be the only time she'd ever feel these sensations; she aimed to savor every one of them. If the worst happened tomorrow, there would be no time for regrets. Even if they both survived safe and sound, she had goals to achieve in her life. She wouldn't allow herself to waste time that could better be spent achieving them in dwelling on doubts or recriminations. Not that she'd have any. This had been her idea.

And it had been a brilliant one. She knew it when she felt Julian's lips on her bare flesh. Sensations sparkled through her, from where his mouth touched her skin clear to her toes. She wanted to rip her bodice open, to expose more flesh to his seeking lips. Since she'd already shocked him tonight, she didn't quite dare do that. She did, however, bend so as to afford him as much access to the exposed areas of her person as possible.

"Your skin is like satin, Susanna. You're smooth as silk."

Since she wasn't sure what a female was supposed to respond to such flattery, she only said, "Mmmm."

His hand found her breast, and her murmur squeaked

at the end. Then she moaned softly, conscious thought having fled at the delicious feelings he began to create with his stroking, provoking fingers.

"Let's get rid of some of this stuff, all right?"

The question had been asked softly, but Susanna could detect an element of strain in it. She wondered if he wasn't enjoying this as much as she was and decided to ask. She'd taken a bold step this evening; she'd be humiliated if he were acquiescing to her request only out of a sense of duty and not because he wanted to.

Eyeing him closely, she asked, "Do you want to, Julian? You don't have to if you don't want to."

His answer was a low chuckle that sounded even more strained than his prior question. "Yes indeedy, Susanna. I want to continue, believe me."

She did. Something in his voice vibrated with sincerity. She yielded with pleasure as he began to unfasten the buttons of her bodice. His fingers were clumsy, and she wanted to help him, to move the matter along. She held back because she wasn't sure her interference would be appreciated.

A chill struck her when he opened her bodice at last, and she realized she'd become heated in the past several minutes. She'd never had so much of herself exposed before the admiring eye of a gentleman, and Julian's scrutiny thrilled her. Even when she'd been at the pond with her bathing costume plastered to her feminine curves and she'd noticed men watching her, she hadn't enjoyed the experience. She enjoyed this one. She wanted Julian's approval of her femininity more than anything.

For years she'd deplored the wiles of females who sought to make themselves attractive to men in order to snare husbands. Susanna had scorned such tactics as demeaning to her sex. She firmly believed that women didn't need men to be fulfilled as human beings. At the moment, however, Julian's confirmation of her desirability as a woman meant the world to her.

When she felt his tongue moisten the fine lawn of her

chemise, she gasped with pleasure. Merciful heavens, she didn't know men did such things—or that women allowed them to. Or that they could feel so good. If she was ever so fortunate as to find a man who wanted to marry her—and whom she wanted to marry—she hoped he'd do these things, too. Since the idea of another man being so familiar with her person appalled her and made her feel sad, she consigned the thought to the back of her mind.

"Does that feel good, Susanna?"

She licked her lips, embarrassed that he'd asked such a personal question. Then, reminding herself that she was a modern woman approaching a new century, she whispered, "Yes. Oh, yes. It feels wonderful."

"Good. I want to make you feel good."

She wondered if she should thank him.

"Your breasts are beautiful. I want to see them."

Good grief, what was he doing, if he wasn't seeing them? She had her answer a second later when he unfastened her corset, tossed it aside, and slipped her chemise and camisole straps down her shoulders, baring her breasts to the night air and his own avid gaze.

He said something under his breath. Susanna fought the impulse to cover herself with her arms. Because she felt helpless and didn't like the feeling, she decided to put her arms around Julian. The decision was easier because Julian whispered, "Relax for me, Susanna. Please try to relax."

Easy for him to say. She was as nervous as a cat— or a virgin bride on her wedding night. Nevertheless, she tried to do as he'd suggested.

It helped when she concentrated on Julian's body as he seemed to be concentrating on hers. Her hands rested on his shoulders, and she decided to explore what had always impressed her as a rather alarming set of muscles for a man whose trade was journalism. Deciding to be bold, she asked, "Your shoulders are very broad, Julian. Did you ever do manual labor before you took to the pen?"

"Worked my way through college as a blacksmith's helper."

A blacksmith! "My goodness." No wonder he had muscles like steel. Susanna investigated further. She was glad he'd removed his jacket, because it was easier for her to feel his musculature through the cotton of his shirt than it would have been through the heavier fabric of his suit jacket.

She wanted to gaze upon his naked chest, to see if it was hairy and, if so, what color his chest hairs were. Sensation hit her like a blow to her solar plexus when he lowered his head and his warm tongue flicked her bare nipple. Good heavens! Her nipples had hardened into nubby tips by this time, and his attentions were driving her to distraction. Her breasts ached for more. He gave it to them when his hand covered one of them, he crushed her to his chest and kissed her hard on the lips. She whimpered before she knew what she was doing and was embarrassed. Julian didn't seem to mind. He groaned, and it sounded like a mark of his pleasure.

As Julian worked his magic on her body, Susanna began to relax. She stopped analyzing her every reaction to his every move. Before she knew what she was doing, she discovered her hands had taken on an intelligence of their own and were unbuttoning his shirt.

Blast! He wore an undershirt, too.

With his help, she worked his shirt off. They had some trouble with the cuff links, but not enough to matter. Then, nearly mad by her need to investigate his chest, Susanna grabbed the straps of his undershirt and yanked them from his shoulders. They got caught on his muscles, and she stared in fascination.

His chest hair was golden, like the hair on his head, and it curled over the top of his undershirt, tempting her to do crazy, outrageous things. Susanna's fingers gripped his shoulders until her nails dug into his flesh. She wanted to run them through that hair on his chest, but his blasted undershirt was in her way.

He chuckled again. The sound was low, provocative,

and it sent rivers of fire through her body. She looked into his eyes and thought the heat she saw there might consume her if she allowed it to. She wouldn't. She'd meet his heat with her own. They might both perish in the ensuing conflagration, but it would be a spectacular way to go.

"Lie down, Susanna. And take your shoes and skirt off. I'm not sure how much longer I can hold off."

As he spoke, he ripped the undershirt from his body. Susanna stared at his chest for several seconds before the meaning of his words galvanized her into doing as he'd requested. She shucked off her shoes, leaving her stockings until later. Then she unfastened her skirt and wriggled it and her petticoat off. Julian had disposed of her camisole and corset. She rid herself of her chemise.

She heard the breath catch in his throat and looked up to find him gazing at her as if he wanted to eat her for supper. Or dessert. The expression on his face was one she associated with less mundane things than supper. She felt like an exotic and tasty delicacy, something rare and precious and to be savored. Perhaps served with a sauce made with an intoxicating liqueur. The feeling was one she wished she could remember and keep with her.

"God, you're beautiful."

His tone was reverent. Susanna could hardly believe her ears. And here she'd begun to think Julian didn't appreciate anything. She said, "So are you." His eyes widened, as if he didn't know what to make of her calling him beautiful.

Feeling bolder than she'd ever felt in her life, she reached up and drew him down to her. When his chest hair touched her breasts she gasped in pure pleasure.

"You're exactly what a man should look like, Julian. You're not soft, like most men whose employment isn't active. You look like a *man*."

"Thank you. Maybe I should chuck journalism for blacksmithing. Wouldn't want to get soft."

"You're not soft."

"No." He laughed again, low in his throat. "I'm sure not."

And he took her hand and guided it to his arousal. Good grief, he was huge! Were men supposed to be that big? Susanna had grown up in the territory, where women weren't allowed the questionable benefits of being sheltered from the mysteries of life. She was no stranger to mating activities, as she'd seen plenty in various barnyards.

Still, were men supposed to be that big? She whispered "My goodness," because she couldn't think of a tactful way to ask the question.

He didn't give her time to worry about it. Pinning her to the pad they'd made of her shawl and his jacket, he kissed her hard, sinking his tongue into her mouth and teaching her own tongue a thing or two about mating. One of his hands still explored her breasts. The other had taken to more far-reaching exploration. She felt its smooth circles on her stomach and almost swooned.

After she'd become dizzy from that, he moved his hand to her leg, still encased in its sensible summer cotton stocking. He untied her garter, making a production of it and ensuring that Susanna would never do the mundane task again without remembering this evening. With exquisite care he peeled the stocking from her leg. Susanna had to stuff the back of her hand into her mouth or shriek from the pleasure of his touch against the bare skin of her leg. When he got to her foot, he lifted it in his hand and kissed it. When he licked her toes, she wasn't sure she didn't faint for an instant. Then he did the same to her other stocking.

Susanna didn't know if she'd survive this evening or not. She'd had no idea, when she'd begged him to make love to her, how he'd go about it. She hadn't known men and women did these things. This experience might well cause her to amend her attitude about marriage.

Then, when he smoothed a hand up her naked leg and found the soft curls covering the most intimate place on her body, she stiffened, remembering what lay in store for her.

"Don't be afraid, Susanna. This is what you asked me to do."

That's right; it was. But she was afraid suddenly, and grabbed his wrist. His hand ceased its wandering immediately, and he caught his breath.

"Do you want me to stop?" It sounded as if it might kill him if she said yes.

"N-no. But—but I'm afraid, Julian. You . . ." She gasped and held the breath for a second. Then she decided she had to say it. "You're so big—down there. Will you fit?"

He exhaled as if he, too, had been holding his breath. His laugh was low and soft and made heat dance up and down her body. "I'll fit, sweetheart. It looks more frightening than it is. People have been doing this since the beginning of time, don't forget."

"Well, yes, but are all men so big—down there?"

"I don't know. But don't worry. No one's ever complained before."

Stung, Susanna snapped, "You needn't sound so smug. And you needn't remind me that I'm only one of many."

"I'm sorry, sweetheart. That was a stupid thing to say."

"Yes, it was."

"But you're not one of many, Susanna."

"Hmph."

"You're not. You're special. You're you—one of a kind. The only one there is."

Not much mollified but feeling slightly less like a convenient washrag laid out for his use, Susanna said, "Hmmm."

"And please don't worry. I won't hurt you any more than it ever hurts a woman the first time."

"All right." She knew it would hurt. Everyone knew that. Miss Amberly had been very frank about these sorts of things, up to a point. Julian was about to take her beyond that point.

It took him several minutes to undo the damage his thoughtless comment had done. But he was a skillful lover—Susanna didn't know whether to deplore the fact as an indication of his fallen nature or to rejoice in it as it was now easing her into a new experience—and soon she was writhing under him, ready for anything.

His fingers had dipped beyond the curls, beyond the sensitive lips surrounding her intimate secrets, and were now driving her into a lunatic frenzy of pleasure and desire and spiraling pressure. He played her body like a musician played a lute. Susanna moaned in need. She clung to his shoulders and kissed him passionately, longing for the release she knew he was going to give her.

Then it happened. In a burst of aching pleasure, her climax came, convulsing her body with delight and tearing a ragged groan from her throat. While she was still reeling from the newness of it, Julian let go of her and sat up. She hadn't recovered from her own satisfaction enough to register her displeasure at his abandonment when he was back again, stark naked, and poised above her.

"My goodness," she murmured right before his lips covered hers, and she felt him guide his enormous manly thing to the moist center of her womanhood. This was it. This is what she'd asked of him. She was about to participate in the most intimate act a man and a woman could perform together.

He thrust into her. It hurt. Susanna wondered if perhaps they might have done better to skip this part. She knew that would have been unfair to Julian, however, and she was a fair-minded girl. At least she didn't cry out and embarrass herself.

"Are you all right, Susanna?" He kissed her and kissed her and kissed her after he asked the question, his lips skimming her mouth and ears and nose and cheeks and throat. She thought he was being exceptionally sweet under the circumstances.

She wasn't sure she was all right, however. She was attempting to adjust to his invasion. He gave her time, kissing her all the while. After a moment, she began to relax. "Yes. Yes, I think I am."

It was odd, really, but the throbbing from her torn maidenhead was beginning to give way to a throbbing of an entirely different nature. After he'd been inside her for several moments, he moved gently. Susanna moaned when the movement touched the same center of pleasure he'd recently teased into fulfillment.

She realized there was more to this act than she'd suspected. Tentatively she moved under him. He groaned.

Power. A sudden sensation of power filled her. Power and pleasure. It was within her power to render this man, this journalist who presented such a show of jocular indifference to the world, helpless with wanting.

She moved again. He groaned again. Then he took over, and Susanna's brief perception of power fled as her own need began to spiral up once more.

Goodness, what strange and delightful sensations. She felt filled by him. That in itself was odd but not unpleasant. He'd been right about his not being too big to fit. He fit nicely. Quite wonderfully, in fact.

Truly, the feelings were incredible. Her body began to arch of its own accord until she was meeting each thrust on his part with an arch on hers. Her eyes had been closed, but she opened them now, not wanting to miss a single second of this amazing, timeless act.

Perspiration had beaded on Julian's upper lip and forehead. His arms were slick with it, and starshine glinted on his muscles. Enthralled, Susanna rubbed her hands over them, glorying in the maleness of him.

Then he kissed her again, their bodies met, and she clung to him as if to salvation when he sent her over the edge and into blissful oblivion for the second time that night. The second time was more precious to her because, with a hoarse cry, he joined her there.

Chapter
Seventeen

Susanna was surprised it wasn't much later in the evening when Julian accompanied her up the walk to her aunt's front porch. They'd lain together for what seemed like hours after they'd made love, watching the stars and talking in a desultory way about this and that.

Her body still sang as they walked down the lane to the Dexter place. She wanted to cling to his arm, to smile into his eyes, to lean into him with the freedom real lovers enjoyed, but she didn't give in to the temptation. She knew their relationship bore no resemblance to that of couples who were in love, more's the pity.

Still, he was as careful with her as if he loved her, and she appreciated him for it. He held her arm and helped her up the porch steps as if she were fragile, which he knew very well she wasn't. Then he kissed her on the lips and waited until she entered the house before he turned to go back to his solitary hotel room. She wished he could come upstairs with her and share her bed for the rest of the night. How delicious it would be to go to sleep with his arms around her and to wake up in his arms; perhaps to make love again.

How shocking of her! What a scarlet woman she'd turned out to be under her prim calico trappings. She almost hugged herself with delight in this latest discovery.

"Good night, Aunt Winnie!" she called cheerfully as she passed the parlor and saw her aunt and uncle sitting there.

By the light of the lamps on the tables, her aunt was knitting and her uncle was reading, as they did every evening. Susanna, whose heart was light and filled with love for everyone, waved and smiled. "Good night, Uncle Cyrus."

Uncle Cyrus, in his usual taciturn way, lifted his head and returned her smile before going back to his book.

"Good night, Susanna. I hope you had a pleasant evening with your young man." Aunt Winnie beamed at her from her well-padded rocking chair. Winnie approved of Julian; Susanna had known it for days now.

Thrilled with her evening, Susanna said in all honesty, "I had a lovely evening, Aunt Winnie, thank you."

She heard her aunt and uncle chuckle, and grinned to herself. She was sure they'd have a good, long chat after she was in her room—or at least Winnie would talk while Cyrus offered encouraging grunts from time to time. Aunt Winnie would probably begin planning the wedding any day now. Poor thing. Susanna felt a little guilty about leading the two of them on in this way. They were dear people, and they couldn't help it if they were old-fashioned and unused to modern women of Susanna's stamp. She refused to allow herself to dwell on the more-than-slight yearning for a permanent alliance with Julian that troubled her own heart.

Although she was a little sore, she scampered up the stairs and made her way to her aunt's sewing room. From there, by the light of the moon and stars, she could watch Julian's progress as he walked down the road and into town. Blast all the wretched trees that occasionally hid him from her view!

His shoulders were slightly hunched, he had his hands jammed into his pockets, and his footsteps seemed to drag. Susanna was surprised by his posture. She'd understood that men usually felt a sense of accomplishment after they'd made a sexual conquest. She'd expected him to be swaggering down the road, proud of himself. His manner, from what she could judge from here and in the partial darkness, was far from cocky; he looked almost dejected. Even his hat, which most often sat at a rakish angle on his golden hair, now perched there straight and stodgy as if it, too, were glum. How odd.

She watched him until he was out of sight. Then she sighed deeply and went to her own room, where she documented the amazing experiences the day had brought her.

When she'd written everything she could think of to describe her adventures, she went to bed. Exhausted, she slept the night through, untroubled by any thoughts but her own.

Julian felt like a rat. He hated leaving Susanna at her aunt's door. He wanted to go inside the house with her, to protect her from the prying eyes and probing questions she might face beyond that portal. But it was closed against him, and he was powerless to shield her from any queries or accusations her aunt and uncle might hurl at her. She was on her own in there.

Not that Susanna Clement couldn't handle herself under any circumstances. Still, damn it, as a gentleman, he should be there to protect her. Gentleman, bah! He was a brute. Father Patrick would be ashamed of him, and he'd have good reason to be.

Although he was rumpled and grass-stained, Julian stopped at the saloon before he went to his hotel. He wasn't ready to face a solitary bed in that featureless, impersonal rented room of his. He wanted to be lying in that clearing in the woods, holding Susanna in his arms, staring up at the stars, and talking about nothing. Or everything.

Susanna could converse on any subject. Even if she didn't know anything about a topic, she was curious and could keep an endless conversation going just by asking questions.

She was the perfect woman for him. He knew it, and his heart suffered with the knowledge.

What would become of them? Even if they both survived the morrow in one piece, what hope was there for the two of them? Julian's job would take him back to Denver. Susanna had told him time and again that she wasn't interested in marriage. She was going to teach school in Artesia.

He sipped his beer and felt more sentimental and moody than he could remember feeling in ages. Did he care? Did he really want to do something so outrageous as *marry* Susanna Clement? He'd sure feel a hell of a lot less guilty about having made love with her if they were married. On the other hand, did he want a wife? Especially one who'd fight him every time he did something she didn't like?

He sighed heavily, and decided there was no way to win this game by conventional means. Not that there was much of anything conventional in this pursuit they were undertaking together. The wisest thing for him to do, he guessed, was to await events. After tomorrow, the whole question might be moot. If it turned out that they survived, then he could wrestle with the matter and draw a conclusion. Plot a course of action. Plan a strategy. Damn, he was depressed.

He swallowed the last of his beer and turned to leave the bar. He'd taken one step when the word *Sedgewick* diverted his attention and brought his head swiveling around. Two men sat at a table, one of them looking distraught, the other obviously offering what sympathy he could.

"I don't have the money, Joe," said the unhappy

man. "And I don't know how to get it in time. Sedgewick says he won't wait."

"Sedgewick's a bastard. We'll think of something, Sam," said the other in a comfort-giving voice.

Sam's head drooped farther. "He's a bastard, all right. He won't give me any more time. Says it's either pay it all right now or lose the farm. If he'd give me another month, I could come up with the money."

"We'll think of something, Sam," Joe repeated, his heart obviously in the right place even if his conversational skills were limited.

Sedgewick. Julian shook his head. This present-day Sedgewick was apparently as mean-spirited and cruel as the one who'd killed Danilo. And the family's penchant for ruining others financially had prevailed through generations. Damn. It didn't seem fair that the man in town with the least humane instincts was the one who wielded the most monetary power over its inhabitants.

Perhaps after tomorrow he and Susanna could do something to end this current Sedgewick's reign of financial terror in Palmyra. If they survived.

One thing at a time, he cautioned himself. Take one thing at a time and perhaps everything would fall into place.

He left the saloon and went back to his hotel room. In spite of his gloomy mood, he slept soundly and awoke ready to do battle with any number of evil spirits.

"I have an idea about what to do with the proceeds if we ever find the jewels."

Susanna eyed Julian askance. She felt like a million dollars this morning, refreshed, revitalized, her sense of purpose renewed. Astonishing what being loved, even momentarily and illusorily, could do for one. A good night's sleep hadn't hurt her overall state of health, either. She fought the impulse to reach for Julian and walk down the lane with him, hand-in-hand, the way she would do if they were promised to each other.

But his words brought his intrinsic character defects

careening back into her consciousness with a crash. This
morning, the morning after their delicious interlude in
the woods, she didn't think she could stand hearing
something sardonic come out of his mouth about the
gems. Cautiously, not sure she wanted to know, she said,
"What's your idea?"

He scuffed his toe on the path. This morning, like last
night, he had his hands in his pockets and his shoulders
hunched. Susanna didn't like seeing him this way. In
spite of herself, she wanted his old devil-may-care in-
souciance back. At least his hat was back at its custom-
ary cocky angle.

"Well, I heard something in the saloon last night—"

"You went to the saloon?" She didn't know whether
to be dismayed or resigned.

He glanced at her, and something of the old irony
gleamed in his vivid blue eyes. "Yeah. I didn't want to
go back to my lonely old hotel room quite yet."

"Oh." Blast! She could tell she was blushing.

"Anyway, there were a couple of men sitting there,
one of whom was very unhappy. I didn't eavesdrop for
long, but from what I gathered, the present-day Mr.
Sedgewick is going to repossess his farm unless he
comes up with a payment. The poor man sounded to me
as though he knew the matter was hopeless. I heard him
say that he could come up with the money if Sedgewick
would give him another month, but the old miser won't
do it."

"How sad."

"Yeah, I thought so, too. Anyway, it occurred to me
that maybe Magdalena Bondurant wouldn't have considered it a bad idea if some of the money earned from the
sale of those jewels were to be used to help the poor
farmers in the Palmyra area who otherwise would have
to owe their souls to Sedgewick. I gather he's not one
to look charitably upon other people's souls."

"Or even his own," Susanna said darkly.

"Or even his own," Julian concurred. "So what do
you think? We could set up a farmers' trust or some-

thing. Depending on how much money we'd have, of course. If we find the gems.''

Susanna cleared her throat. In truth she was shocked. She'd become so used to thinking of Julian as a man who cared about nothing and nobody that this indication that he might possess a better nature surprised her. ''I think it's a wonderful idea.''

''You don't have to sound so amazed. I'm not a complete wastrel. I'm really not as bad as you think I am.'' His voice held an edge, as if her obvious skepticism annoyed him.

''I'm sure you couldn't be,'' she murmured. He gave her a black look, and she wished she'd phrased her response in more flattering language.

They continued their trudge to the graveyard in silence. Susanna kept glancing around, her gaze all but eating up the scenery. In the back of her mind the thought that this might be the last time she had an opportunity to observe it nagged at her. She tried not to dwell on the possibilities for evil, but to bear in mind that today might also be the day in which all the mysteries associated with Magdalena's disappearance would be cleared up and all the demons dispelled.

''Do you have your Bible?'' Julian asked, startling her.

''Yes. Do you have your rosary beads?'' She glanced at him, marveling anew that this man who had made her body sing, who presented an appearance of cynicism to the world, would cherish the beads his mother had left him. Why, he hadn't even known those beads had come from her until Danilo told him!

What incredibly different lives they had led from one another. She acknowledged this morning that she had begun to hope they might find some common ground and continue a relationship. She wasn't sure what kind of relationship. She wasn't sure how they could maintain it between Artesia and Denver, either. She was no longer sure of anything, for that matter, and decided to ponder it all later, after they'd done what they had to do this noontime.

"Did you bring any lead weights?"

"Yes. I found several in the barn, near the fishing poles, and I also brought a piece of lead pipe. It's all in my handbag here." She lifted it to show him. It was as heavy as—well, as lead. She generally carried a much smaller reticule with her. She'd considered packing all of these ghost-fighting armaments in a satchel but didn't want to invite questions from her aunt and uncle.

"Good. I found some lead stuff, too."

"Oh? What?"

"Bullets." He looked embarrassed. "I stuffed 'em in my pockets. I also brought my gun, even though Danilo doesn't think it will help."

"It was good thinking to stick bullets in your pockets."

He scuffed his toe again. In Artesia the gesture would have produced a cloud of dust and pebbles. In the green, waterlogged state of Maine, it merely left an indentation in the damp earth. "Um, I'd like you to stick some bullets in your pockets and so forth, too. And maybe a pencil or two. Just in case lead really does help to ward off evil, you know."

She glanced at him, but he was looking off into the trees, as if he didn't want her to read anything into his request but the natural concern of one colleague for another. She didn't believe it, and was touched by this evidence of his feelings for her, which, if not exactly loving, were at least tender.

"Thank you. I shall. I think you ought to have your rosary out and in plain sight, too, and I'll do the same with my Bible."

"Right." After a moment or two he said, "Damn, I wish we had some kind of textbook to refer to on how to go about fighting demons."

"So do I. After this is over, maybe we should write one." She managed a light, teasing note.

She could tell he appreciated her feeble attempt at

humor because he smiled, and his eyes lit up. "Good idea."

They had no sooner arrived at Magdalena's headstone than Danilo appeared. He looked washed out in the daylight, even less substantial than usual.

"Gads, I didn't think the two of you would ever get here!"

Julian pulled out his pocket watch and squinted at it. "It's only half past ten, Danilo. That'll give us plenty of time to get to the cabin."

"I know, I know." Danilo took an agitated turn around the Homstead monument.

Julian saw that he was wringing his hands, and realized his initial comment had sprung from nervousness. He didn't take the ghost's overt symptoms of worry as a good sign, and wondered if he could convince Susanna to stay behind while he and Danilo went to investigate that cabin. Julian glanced at her. Fat chance. She'd never go for it. Damn.

"We brought all the things we talked about, Danilo," Susanna offered helpfully, her own manner excited. "I have my Bible, and Julian brought his rosary beads and pencils and a lot of lead bullets. I found several lead weights and some lead pipe, too."

"Trash," said Danilo with a grunt. *"It's all useless trash. I know it. We're doomed."* He lifted the back of a hand to his white brow in a gesture Julian had never before seen in real life—if this could be considered real life.

"Well, really! Why did you tell us to bring the lead things, then, if they're trash? We might as well have left them at home. They're enormously heavy."

Annoyed by the ghost's negative thinking, especially since Julian feared it might infect Susanna, he said, "Stop being so damned gloomy. We have to try this. You know it as well as we do."

Danilo heaved a huge sigh—Julian still didn't know how he did that, since he couldn't possibly need to breathe—and said, *"I beg your pardon. Those things might help. But the forces we're going to be facing are powerful. You need to know that and to keep it in mind at all times. They're evil and wicked and will stop at nothing to keep their secrets."*

Julian walked up close to him and said with a hiss, "Will you shut up? Susanna's got enough to worry about without you telling her how awful everything's going to be."

Danilo's eyes blazed with indignation. He evidently understood the justice of Julian's observation, however, because he ceased his doom-saying prattle. Turning abruptly, he marched toward the boundary of the graveyard. *"Well, let's get down to business, then. We can talk about our strategy as we walk to the cabin."*

"What strategy? Aren't we going to simply go inside that place and see what we can see?"

Danilo shot Susanna a look over his shoulder. *"You are entirely too literal, Miss Clement. Has anyone ever told you that before now?"*

"Actually," she murmured in a tone of apology, "they have, yes."

"I'm not surprised. Follow me." With a theatrical flutter of his cape, Danilo was off into the woods.

So they did as he advised. Because he was as worried as Danilo, Julian took Susanna's hand. He hoped she wouldn't object, and she didn't. She undoubtedly thought he was merely trying to help guide her along the path. He wasn't. He needed to touch her, to remind himself at every step what he had to lose if he lost her, and that he had to protect her, come what may, whatever the cost to himself.

As they neared the McKenzie property, Julian noticed Susanna's hand tightening in his of its own accord. He squeezed it gently, hoping to convey a modicum of hope and trust to her in that way.

Danilo rattled on for some time about what they should do when they got to the cabin. It didn't take Julian long to realize that he was talking to give himself courage. The poor bastard really wasn't very brave. For some reason, Julian considered him all the more courageous for daring to do battle with the forces of evil in the face of his fear.

Susanna cut into Danilo's monologue abruptly when they came to a clearing in the woods. "There's the barn."

They stopped and looked. There was the barn, all right, ramshackle and leaning even farther to one side than Julian remembered. "The well and the wall must be over there then." He pointed northward, squinting to find them.

"I think I see the wall." Susanna walked toward the barn. She didn't let go of Julian's hand, and he followed closely behind her. He wasn't going to allow her out of his sight today.

"Yes, this looks like it."

"I hate this place," Danilo announced suddenly.

"I don't blame you." Julian saw that the ghost was glancing around, as if he expected evil beings to leap out at them. It wasn't a comforting sight.

"All right." Susanna peered around thoughtfully. "This is the wall. So the old McKenzie family plot must be right here, but I don't see the headstones we uncovered the other day."

Again they stopped and looked. Julian shook his head. "How could everything get so overgrown so fast? We were here only a couple of days ago."

"Spirits," said Danilo gloomy. *"They like to keep their handiwork covered up."*

"I didn't think the McKenzies were bad, though."

Danilo cast a jaundiced gaze upon Susanna. *"The McKenzies weren't bad. But the McKenzies have all died out, and their property has been overrun by Sedgewick and the forces of evil."* He made it sound very dramatic.

Susanna said, "Oh."

"I hate this place," the ghost declared again.

"It's not my favorite, either," said Julian, peering around. "All right, so I guess we'll have to rip the vines off of the headstones until we find the right one again. Wasn't Leola's headstone up there?'' He pointed.

Susanna nodded. ''I think I know which one it was. Is.''

She was right. Julian brushed the vegetation aside, read the barely discernible name on the stone, and almost wished she hadn't been. This whole trek was beginning to seem less and less advisable the closer they got to that damned shack in the woods.

''I don't recall which way the path went,'' Danilo said. *''I haven't walked it for forty years. I know it began some ways away from the McKenzie plot.''*

''There's a big old maple tree,'' said Susanna. ''The path starts there, by the bramble bushes. And I know which tree it is.''

Drat. She was going to find the blasted path in no time flat, and then they'd have to follow it. To Julian it seemed as if she were leading them all to their doom. He tried not to think about it.

''Yes, indeed. Here's the tree, and here's the path!''

Julian mumbled, ''Don't know why you should be so damned happy about it.''

She frowned at him. ''This is why we came here today, isn't it?''

Danilo muttered, *''No matter. This is a terrible idea.''*

Susanna turned on the ghost in a huff. ''We're doing this for you, Danilo! At least we are in part. We're doing it for you and for my family's name and honor, so Mr. Kittrick here won't be able to make up scandalous untruths about Magdalena Bondurant and write them in his wretched paper.''

''I won't write anything scandalous about her.''

''What do you mean, you won't write anything scandalous? You said you'd make up something awful if we didn't discover the truth.''

''If it'll keep you from tackling that cabin again, I won't write a single word that you don't approve of first. Promise. On my word of honor.'' He held up his hand, palm outward, in a gesture associated with solemn oaths.

"You mean it?"

Irked and with his nerves jumping, Julian barked, "Dammit, Susanna, will you stop doubting my integrity? When I say I'll do something, I'll do it!"

"You needn't curse at me, Julian Kittrick."

"Children, will you please stop squabbling? My nerves are shattered already."

They turned to discover Danilo, a hand pressed to his forehead, looking as if he might faint. Julian didn't understand how he did that. Maybe it was all for show. "Good idea," he muttered. Susanna's doubt angered him. Hadn't he demonstrated his trustworthiness to her yet? Lord, she was stubborn.

She proved it again when she said, "Well, I don't care. I think it's nice that you won't print nasty made-up scandals about Magdalena, but I need to know what happened. If the two of you are too scared to go to that cabin, I'll go alone."

Julian knew she meant it. He bowed his head, shook it, and muttered, "Damn."

Danilo sighed deeply and said, *"Oh, all right."*

Susanna, of course, wasn't satisfied. "All right what? Does that mean all right, I should go on alone, or does it mean all right, you'll go with me?"

"Don't be a damned fool, Susanna," said Julian. "Of course we'll go with you."

"Stop swearing at me!"

Danilo glared at Julian. *"Speak for yourself, Mr. Kittrick."* Then he frowned at Susanna, sighed again, and said with a growl, *"Oh, very well. I'll go. I'm probably the only hope the two of you have."*

"How encouraging." Julian felt mighty glum when he took Susanna's hand again—she tried to withdraw it, but he wouldn't let her—and they started down the path.

Was it her imagination, or were the woods even thicker and more mysterious today than they'd been three days ago, when she and Julian had walked down this same path? She could swear the brambles were thicker. And they had prickers, too, that seemed almost to reach out and grab at her clothing. Susanna used her free hand to bunch her skirt together in front of her so it wouldn't catch on the thorns and rip.

"I don't like this," Danilo muttered.

Susanna didn't much like it either, but she couldn't quit now. They were on the verge of discovery. She wouldn't quit.

"There's evil afoot. I can feel it."

"Will you stop that? This is no fun already, and it doesn't help to have you telling us we're in for it."

"Don't snap at Danilo, Julian. I'm sure he's doing his best."

"I certainly am." Danilo had been hovering along the path, sometimes in front of them, sometimes in back, often over their heads. That's where he was now. Susanna got the impression he'd like to drop something on Julian's head. Preferably something large and heavy, and with great force.

"Well, this is difficult enough without his being such a wet blanket."

"Wet blanket am I? Just you wait. You'll see. You won't be calling me names when you see what's in store for us."

"I wish you'd both stop this senseless bickering. We're going to have a hard enough time dealing with whatever's in that cabin. We don't need to be fighting among ourselves."

"You're a fine one to talk," Danilo said, his voice gone sharp. *"You and that blond devil have been snapping at each other like rabid dogs ever since I met you."*

"Rabid dogs," Julian said, grumbling. "Good grief."

Dogs in heat was more like it, Susanna thought, although she'd cut her tongue out before she said so. "We're all nervous about this, and I think that's why our tempers are a little on edge. So why don't we just try to get along until this whole thing is over. Perhaps if none of us talked at all, we'd be better off."

They took her suggestion, and it worked for a while.

In fact, when she managed to put aside their purpose in traveling down this path today, which wasn't easy and wasn't often, Susanna found the walk almost pleasant. True, the brambles were thick and the tree branches tangled overhead, thus giving the path an aura of twilight, but still the green of everything appealed to her eyes. They were used to the tans and browns of the desert. All this green was really quite lovely.

The path itself was rather pretty, too. Springy with fallen leaves and pine needles, it cushioned her footsteps and muffled the noise of their trudge. The silence surrounding them was intense, actually. The forest was almost too quiet. No birds sang. No squirrels chattered. No animals rustled through the underbrush. The silence was, in fact, eerie. That wispy mist trailing along the path didn't help to dissipate the ominous impression, either.

Wait a minute. Susanna stared at the path. Where had that fog come from? It hadn't been there before; she knew it.

This was too bizarre. She glanced at Julian and found him frowning at the ribbons of mist. They were becoming thicker, and had begun piling up at the edges of the path like a bank of pea-soup fog. Her heart hammering, she lifted her head, hoping to find that Danilo was unimpressed by this latest weird phenomenon. He wasn't there.

"Danilo!" Her voice sounded shrill to her own ears. "What's wrong?"

She could hear Julian's concern plainly. She cleared her throat and wished she'd thought to moderate her tone when calling for the ghost.

"I, er, can't seem to find Danilo."

"What?" Julian glanced around, his eyes wild. "Where the hell is he?"

"For heaven's sake, I've told you before, you needn't shriek at me."

With a soft floop, Danilo materialized before her. Susanna shut her eyes for a moment and offered up a prayer of gratitude. "I beg your pardon," she said when she could. "I was worried because I couldn't find you."

"And there's that weird mist on the ground. I don't like it." Julian pointed at the path.

The fog appeared even thicker now, and was closing in on them. It curled around their ankles and reminded Susanna of slithering snakes. She shook off the thought. She wasn't supposed to be imaginative, blast it, and they had enough to worry about without her manufacturing trouble.

Danilo scowled at the gathering fog. *"I saw it. I don't like it either."*

"None of us likes it," said Julian. "What is it?"

"Evil emanations."

Susanna looked at him. So did Julian. Julian spoke first. "What's that supposed to mean?"

"It means," Danilo said, sounding more sepulchral than ever, *"that we're in for a lot of trouble."*

Julian rolled his eyes. "We'd already figured that out. So what does this fog mean? Exactly. I mean, where's it coming from?"

"Keep walking and you'll find out," Danilo advised, and shot on ahead of them.

"I wish he wouldn't do that," Julian mumbled.

Susanna couldn't fault him for the sentiment. She wished he wouldn't do that, too.

Chapter Eighteen

"Criminy Jeeze."

Julian held Susanna's hand tightly. Instead of drawing away from him, she scrunched up behind him and put a hand on his shoulder. He felt her body against his, and a primitive urge to shield her from what lay ahead washed through him. If she were only a trace more tractable, he'd force her to stay behind while he braved whatever awaited them.

"I've never seen anything like that before," she whispered, her breath feathering over his ear and neck and making gooseflesh rise on his skin.

"Me, neither."

They could scarcely see the cabin for the fog enveloping it. It wasn't an earthly fog. This was an extension of that blasted fog that had trailed along the path. The cabin was shrouded in it, and it seemed to Julian as if the mass of mist pulsed with evil. Shoot, he had to get his imagination under control.

"Where's Danilo? Do you see him?" Susanna's voice had sunk to a whisper.

"No." So had Julian's. "He's got to be around here somewhere, unless he already went inside that place."

He felt her shudder. "I hope he didn't. I think we ought to go in together."

"Yeah. Me, too."

What he wanted was an armed guard, preferably a whole army unit, to go in that place with him. Or, even better, instead of him. He sensed that two humans and a frightened ghost weren't going to have an easy time of it in there.

"You finally got here."

Julian looked up to see from whence that voice had come. Danilo sat in a tree, parting the branches with a translucent hand and peering through the leaves at the cabin. He looked like he might faint.

"We can't move as fast as you," Julian reminded the ghost.

"I know, I know." Danilo didn't glance at them but continued to stare at the fog-veiled cabin as if he couldn't believe something that awful could exist on the same plane he did.

Julian didn't like the expression on his face one little bit. "You going to stay there and stand guard, or will you come inside with us?" He tried to keep from sounding sarcastic. The truth was that he didn't blame the ghost for being scared. Fear seemed merely prudent in this instance.

Danilo ceased staring at the cabin and glared down at Julian, his eyes blazing red with fury. Julian didn't know ghosts' eyes could do that, and was disconcerted to find it out at this particular moment.

"Of course I'm going in there with you. Do you honestly believe the two of you could handle it alone? You're a fool if you do."

"Julian didn't mean to sound cross, Danilo," Susanna told him. Julian wasn't sure if she believed her own words, but he honored her for trying to mollify Danilo, as Julian himself was unable to think past the bank of fog enfolding that cabin. Bank of evil emanations, rather, if Danilo were to be believed. Unfortunately, Julian couldn't think of a reason not to believe him.

"Stuff these lead bullets in your pockets, Susanna."

He withdrew several bullets from his own pocket and handed them to her. He watched to be sure she did as he asked. Then he handed her two of the four pencils he'd brought along. Their lead points were encased in wood, but Julian figured they were better than nothing.

She crammed the pencils in her pockets. "All right. I've got lead tucked everywhere now." She even dropped one bullet down the front of her bodice. Julian knew exactly where it would remain, too, since her corset snugged her camisole to her body directly beneath her lovely breasts. Lord, he hoped they'd both live so he could see those breasts again, cup them in his hands, caress them, kiss them, feel their nipples pebble under the assault of his tongue.

He told himself to snap out of it.

"Get your Bible out."

"It's out. Where are your rosary beads?"

He reached into his breast pocket. He always kept his rosary there, next to his heart, although he'd never admit to such sentimentality. "Got it." He twisted it through his fingers, much as his mother must have done nearly thirty years before.

"I brought this along, too, just in case."

Julian turned to see where Danilo was talking from now, and discovered him directly in back of them, holding a small metal cross in both hands. Julian lifted an eyebrow in inquiry.

"Plucked it from the inside of a family vault. Figured no one would mind if I borrowed it for a while." Danilo looked self-conscious.

"I thought you didn't believe these religious artifacts would do any good," Julian reminded him, trying not to grin.

The ghost shrugged. *"I'm not sure they will. There are no atheists on the battlefield, however."*

"I suppose not." Julian had heard the same sentiment

expressed many times before, but hadn't truly understood what it meant until now. He uttered a silent prayer
and crossed himself, hoping neither Susanna nor Danilo
would notice. When he glanced at Susanna, her head
was bowed and her lips were moving, and he guessed
she'd had the same idea. When he peeked at Danilo, the
ghost was smirking at him. Julian decided not to object.

When Susanna lifted her head, he eyed her keenly,
searching for any sign that she might be willing to remain behind. He saw none, and he gave up hoping.
"Ready?"

She nodded. "Yes, I'm ready."

Good. He wished he was. He glanced again at Danilo,
who looked as if he were about to collapse. Well, that
didn't matter. Ready or not, they had to do it.

"All right, then. Let's go."

And Julian found himself leading the way to the fog-
enshrouded cabin where, he trusted, all the answers to
all of their questions lay.

If the answers weren't there, he was damned well going to quit searching. He wasn't going through this again
for anything.

The door creaked like a million rusty hinges when
Julian pushed on it. He didn't have to batter it down
today because it gaped from having been kicked out by
him when they were here last. Susanna didn't know if
that boded good or ill.

Her hair and clothing were damp from the ghostly
mist, and her skirt and petticoat clung to her as if trying
to hold her back. She wondered if that was a natural
phenomenon, or if the powers of evil that were so pat-
ently evident in this small shack were governing them.

She held her Bible in front of her like a shield. Julian
had his rosary beads looped through his fingers. She saw
the cross dangling from it when he put his hand on the
splintered wooden door. The cross was made of wood,
too, she noticed, and her heart gave a quick, painful
spasm. If they could afford only wooden beads and

cross, his parents must have been poor. And they must have loved him desperately. Susanna couldn't imagine having to die knowing that a child of her body would be left in the world unprotected. Especially in a foreign country and in a city as huge and cruel as New York.

Stop thinking about it, she commanded herself. She needed all her resources to be alert for whatever lay before her in this cabin.

"Tut, tut, what a mess."

She glanced over to see Danilo hovering above the floor of the cabin, as if he disdained putting his feet on the dirty floorboards. Glancing down, she saw not merely the dust and dirt that had accumulated over the nearly half century since the cabin had last been used, but rodent droppings as well. She shivered, partly from disgust and partly from cold. The atmosphere in the cabin was viciously chilly.

A recollection of the last time she'd been in this place hit her. She remembered the cold then, too, but it had struck them toward the end of their stay, right before that—thing—had taken possession of her.

She braced herself, willing her mental powers to fight off any spirit that attempted to gain control over her today. If she went into this venture knowing what she was up against, she was sure she could ward it off. That—thing—had only managed to subdue her because she hadn't been expecting it. That's all. Today she was prepared. She lifted her Bible higher in an effort to convince herself.

When Julian's arm went around her, she could only be thankful. His expression held grave concern. She smiled to show him she was fine. Just fine. Another shiver racked her.

"Listen, Susanna, if you begin to feel the least bit strange, tell me, and we'll get the hell out of here."

She nodded, thinking how appropriate his wording was. He squeezed her harder.

"I mean it, dammit. I'm not going to risk your life

or sanity for the sake of a forty-year-old mystery. What-ever's in here isn't worth your life."

Susanna wasn't sure about that. She had a feeling that whatever was in here was worth more than her own puny life, however precious it was to her. She didn't say so to Julian, because she sensed he wasn't interested in the larger issues plaguing the world at the moment.

"All right," she said. "I'll let you know if I begin to feel anything. Except cold. It's very cold in here, isn't it?"

"Freezing."

His one-word confirmation of her bodily sensations lifted a weight from her that she hadn't realized was there. But if he felt it, too, then she knew the spirits weren't after her alone. Yet. She shook off the stray thought.

She felt as though they were being followed and kept shooting glances over her shoulder. Except for Danilo, she didn't see a thing other than that ghastly fog. It had followed them inside, and she wished it hadn't. It gave her the creeps.

"Damn, it's spooky in here. It feels like all the de-mons in hell are after us."

"You feel it, too?" She was glad, somehow, that she hadn't imagined that feeling as well. It was odd how knowing someone else shared her uneasiness comforted her.

"Damned right, I feel it. This place is worse than a graveyard at midnight."

"I beg your pardon?"

Julian peered at Danilo. "Sorry. Just an observation."

Danilo hmphed, but it didn't sound very convincing. Susanna could tell he was shaking in his ghostly shoes.

"Where did you find that wretched chest?" Danilo held his cross out in front of him, and waved it in the air around him as if signaling to unseen enemies.

"In the closet over there."

They went over to inspect the closet. The door still hung open. Evidently none of the ghostly influences that haunted the place had deemed it necessary to close it. Susanna deplored their overall housekeeping.

"I don't see anything else to this place. There's this room, that room"—Danilo pointed to the room leading off of the one they were in; there was no door barring their view, and the room appeared to be empty—*"and there's that closet. What else is in here?"*

"I don't know. It sure doesn't look like anything could be hidden anywhere."

"How about an attic?" Susanna suggested.

She thought it had been a bright idea until they looked up and saw all the holes in the roof. Where the ceiling hadn't collapsed completely, eerie daylight shone through huge cracks and holes. There wasn't a single two-foot-square piece of solid ceiling left behind which anything could be hidden.

"Um, I don't think so. If there had been anything up there—anything of any weight, at least—it's fallen through by now."

Julian wouldn't let go of her hand so she could investigate on her own. She'd have resented it if she weren't so scared. She had to acknowledge the justice of his observation. "I suppose you're right. But there must be something in here."

"You're right," said Danilo. *"Sedgewick's spirit wouldn't have gone to this much trouble to guard the place if there was nothing in it worth guarding. He's put on quite a show for us."*

"He certainly has." She shivered again.

"But what is it? Where is it?"

"I don't know, but I think we two living beings need more light." Julian finally released Susanna's hand so he could strike a match and light the kerosene lamp he'd brought with them. The lantern didn't help much. The fog had become almost as thick inside the cabin as it was outside, and beams from the lamp didn't penetrate it but seemed to bounce off of it.

Susanna took a step closer to Julian and suddenly felt

her shin bang against something barring her way. She
fell down with a thud.

"Susanna!" Julian was at her side in an instant.
"Good Lord, what happened?"

She pushed herself up, unhurt but startled. "I—I'm
not sure. I tripped over something. It bumped against
my shin."

Julian peered around, holding the lantern close to the
floor. "There's nothing here to trip over."

Susanna saw the same thing—nothing. There was
nothing on or near the floor that could account for her
having fallen, yet she'd distinctly felt something against
her shin. Uneasy, she pressed her hand on the floor to
push herself up and felt something under her palm. Sure
it must be something grotesque or filthy, she immediately lifted her hand. "Ugh!" Then she peered more
closely at the floor.

It wasn't a dead rat. It was—it was . . .

"Good gracious, look at this!"

"What's wrong?" Julian lowered his head and he
looked, too. Then he waved to the ghost. "Danilo, look
at this."

"What is it?"

"It's a ring. A metal ring. And I'll bet you anything
it lifts a trapdoor."

"Gads." Danilo hovered over them, looking nervous.
*"That's all we need—a trapdoor into God knows what
heathen den."*

"It may be nothing, Danilo." Susanna didn't sound
the least convinced.

"I guess there's only one way to find out." And Julian set his lantern aside, grabbed the dusty metal ring,
and pulled with all his might.

An avalanche of dust and debris showered from the
edges of the trapdoor. The old rusty hinges didn't want
to move, and screeched like all the banshees in hell
when Julian made them work. He could tell the trapdoor

hadn't been lifted in decades. Probably not for nearly forty years.

When he let the door go, it fell back with another rasp of hinges and hit the floor with a hollow thump. He dusted off his hands and peeked inside the hole.

"It's awfully dark down there."

Julian's ears were ringing from the shriek of the hinges, and he hardly heard Susanna's whisper. She was right. Lifting the door had revealed a gaping square hole in the flooring. "That's why we have the lantern."

Cautiously he lowered the lantern into the hole. There was a dust-covered ladder leading to whatever was down there. From the numerous scuttlings and scrapings and squeaks, he knew the rats and mice weren't pleased to have had their rest disturbed. He shuddered.

"Shoot, I really don't think you should go down there, Susanna. It's too filthy and dark."

"I'm not staying up here all by myself, Julian Kittrick, so you can put that idea right out of your mind."

He was out of his mind, all right. He said merely, "All right."

"I'll bring up the rear."

Julian glanced over his shoulder. Danilo was darting glances around the cabin, waving his cross like a white flag. The picture he made might have been amusing if the circumstances had been different.

"All right. I have the lantern, so I'll go first. Susanna comes next, and you'll guard our flank."

Julian wanted to go first for other reasons, too, but wouldn't let on what they were in front of Susanna. He knew she'd object if he admitted he wanted to make sure it was safe down there. She'd assume he doubted her ability because she was a woman. If she only knew. Julian thought she was about the most competent person he'd ever met, but her strength was of purpose and integrity. Physically, he was still stronger than she, and he didn't feel like having to argue with her about it now.

Susanna murmured her consent. Good. He took a deep breath. He really didn't want to go down into that pit.

"I'm going to take it slow. This ladder might have rotten rungs. Wait until I've made it to the bottom safely before you start."

No one objected, so he started down the ladder.

As anxious as he was, Julian wouldn't have been much alarmed if goblins had grabbed his ankles and heaved him to the floor. He was almost surprised, therefore, that nothing hampered his descent into the bowels of that cabin. The unearthly fog that had filled the cabin trailed around his feet as he stepped from rung to rung, but nothing hindered his progress.

As soon as his feet hit the floor, he turned, lifted the lantern, and peered into the gloom. The light didn't penetrate deeply, but Julian sensed the room was small. He knew he'd have to wait until the others climbed down before he could investigate further. Susanna would never forgive him if he did so without her.

"All right," he called. "You can come on down now."

"*Is it safe?*" Danilo's voice quavered with his terror.

"Well, it's not unsafe, at least not that I can tell so far." It was cold. And damp. And dark as the grave. And wildly creepy. Julian didn't bother to relate those attributes, since they were only to be expected.

"What does it look like?"

Faintly annoyed, Julian said, "It's filthy with dust and dirt, and it's dark, and I can't see two feet in front of me, even with the lantern. Fortunately, I brought some candles, too."

"I'm coming down. Lift the lantern."

"All right. Here, let me help you."

Julian held the lamp in one hand and helped guide Susanna down the ladder with the other. She hopped off the ladder and looked around with interest. "My goodness, it certainly is dark. I can't see a thing."

"Yes, well let's wait until Danilo gets down here before we start inspecting it, all right?"

"All right."

Danilo, of course, didn't need the ladder. He wafted

down into their pit, his insubstantial form wavering in the lamplight. Julian sensed that he was shaking with fear and wondered if ghosts' teeth chattered. Probably not.

"All here?" Julian looked at his two cohorts. They huddled close to each other. He took Susanna's hand, and she gripped his with gratitude. "Let's start looking."

They didn't have to look far. As soon as Julian lifted the lantern to shoulder height and took two steps forward, beams of light illuminated a sight grisly enough to make them all stop dead in their tracks and gasp, even Danilo.

Julian thought his heart actually stopped beating for a second. He immediately looked to see how Susanna was. She'd put a hand over her mouth, and her eyes were wide with horror. Danilo quivered behind them.

There, leering at them from a small tabletop, was a skull. The rest of the skeleton sat in a chair. The bones of one arm were chained to a wall. It looked as if whoever had died here had sat in the chair, rested his or her head on the table, and expired in that position. Shreds of cloth hung from the bones in ribbons, rotted from time and who knew what else.

Frozen with shock, they stood transfixed for a moment. Then Susanna spoke in a voice shaking with emotion.

"Do you think they're the bones of a runaway slave?"

Julian glanced at her. "Do you want them to be?"

She nodded. Then she shook her head. She dashed a hand across her eyes, and he saw that she was wiping away tears. "It's not a slave, is it?" Her voice shook even harder now.

He cleared his throat. "I don't know. I suppose we should look more closely."

Behind them, Danilo moaned softly. His ghostly form swept past them and knelt beside the pathetic spectacle of bones and frayed fabric. Susanna rushed to his side and reached out to lay a hand on his shoulder. Her hand went through him, and she gave it up, but she folded her hands in front of her and gazed at him. Julian saw the sympathy in her eyes. He watched them both, wishing he could do something to ease their grief.

Susanna picked up a tatter of cloth. It was a faded blue brocade, much too fine a fabric to have clothed any slave.

"Do—do you remember this cloth, Danilo?"

The ghost nodded somberly. *"It's the skirt she wore that night."*

Susanna sank her head in her hands. Julian didn't know if she was crying. He couldn't stand back any longer; he had to hold her. With a quick movement, he stepped toward her—and his foot slipped on a pebble and slid out from beneath him. He barely caught himself in time to prevent the lantern from crashing to the floor. That's all they needed, was to have the whole cabin go up in flames.

"Damn," he said. "What's on this floor, anyway?"

Susanna lifted her face from her cupped hands. Her cheeks were smeared with dust from her fingertips and, Julian suspected, tears. "Who knows? It's been almost forty years."

"It's been since the night of June 21, 1857," Danilo whispered.

"Yeah, well, why would there be a bunch of pebbles scattered on the floor?"

Danilo didn't answer. He gazed at the skeleton and, hands folded together in prayer, whispered, *"My God, my God. Oh, my precious Magdalena. How could I have let you come to this?"*

Worried lest they have an accident on those dust-covered pebbles, Julian set the lantern down and inspected the floor, thinking to brush the pebbles aside. He wished he had a broom. Damn, they were all over the place. He got out his handkerchief to protect his hands from dirt and began scooping them up. He didn't pay much attention to the job because he was too worried about Danilo and Susanna. They were both really upset, and he didn't blame them.

Obviously, those bones were the last earthly remains of Magdalena Bondurant. Also obviously, she'd perished here all those years ago in exactly the manner Susanna had dreamed about. Julian shuddered, thinking about how awful her end must have been. What a way to go.

These were the weirdest pebbles he'd ever felt. Not that they were any more weird than anything else that they'd seen or done lately. Nevertheless, he was curious and rubbed one of them between his fingers to clean it of years' worth of dust and dirt. Odd little pebble. Strange—

"Sweet Lord in heaven!"

Susanna had been trying to offer some kind of solace to the bereaved ghost. Her head jerked around at Julian's exclamation.

"What is it? What happened?"

Julian stared at the stone in his fingers. It was a deep, rich red. Ruby red. His mouth felt dry. "Um, I think we've found the jewels, too."

"I can't believe it." It was at least the third time Susanna had expressed the sentiment, but Julian wasn't bored yet. He couldn't believe it either.

"She must have had them hidden, or Sedgewick would have taken them away from her. That's undoubtedly why he'd chained her down here—to weaken her resolve. He didn't know her. She'd never have weakened." Danilo broke down again.

His sobs were heart-wrenching. Julian wished he could do something to ease the poor ghost's anguish. Since he couldn't, he continued helping Susanna gather up the rest of the gems. He'd managed to find a hook on which to hang the lantern. From it he'd lit the three tallow candles he'd stuffed into his pocket, and the feeble light helped their search. There must have been tens of thousands of dollars' worth of loose stones scattered on the floor, covered by nearly a half century's worth of grime. And something else. Julian's hand touched it when he bent to pick up another jewel.

"I think this is where she had them hidden." He picked up a small pouch made of plain white calico. It had been stitched with cotton thread, and the thread had given way under the weight of years and karats.

Susanna took the bag and turned it over, studying it closely. "She must have had it sewn onto her petticoat. I understand women used to keep valuables in such pockets."

"Did they?"

She nodded. "That must be why Sedgewick didn't find it. Even he wasn't base enough to search her."

"*Ha!*"

They both turned to find Danilo's eyes blazing at them. The effect was eerie, because his eyes glowed like red embers through the gloom. Julian tried to bear in mind that Danilo was their friend and that this phenomenon wasn't intended to be frightening.

"What do you mean, Danilo? Do you really think he'd have searched her?" Susanna sounded shocked.

"*Have no doubt about it, Miss Clement. The man was vile. He would stop at nothing to achieve his covetous aims. If I hadn't killed him, he'd have gotten around to searching her sooner or later. He was undoubtedly trying to wear her down first.*"

"How horrible."

"*Yes.*" Danilo sniffled miserably. "*The truly horrible part is that if I hadn't followed him that night, Magdalena might still live.*"

They were all quiet for a minute.

Susanna murmured, "I don't know how he could have let her live after he'd kidnapped her and stolen these gems."

Danilo wept pitiably.

Julian, uneasy in the company of such sorrow and self-recrimination, made a last search of the floor. He didn't find any more stones. He and Susanna had stacked those they'd found on the table, beside Magdalena's skull. The skull and gems together presented a grisly picture, and one Julian thought might be used by parents and teachers as a moral lesson against the twin evils of ambition and avarice.

It couldn't be denied, however, that Magdalena's ambition had been for others. Julian considered it mighty unfair of God to have punished her in this way.

Not that God had anything to do with it. As Father Patrick used to tell him, people were given choices. What they did with them wasn't God's fault. Julian sighed, wishing there could have been a happier ending to this story.

At least Susanna wouldn't have to worry about him writing about Magdalena Bondurant in anything but glowing terms. The folks who read the *Denver Post* wouldn't mind. They liked a good sob story as much as they liked a good scandal. And Julian did have some inside scoops, what with Danilo's intriguing tidbits to add to the mix.

They had found a mildewed diary beside Magdalena's skull. Now that they'd recovered the gems, Susanna picked the book up. Julian wasn't sure he wanted to hear what was inside.

"Look at this," she said softly. "She was documenting her last days on earth."

That's what Julian had feared. Now he *really* didn't want to hear. Danilo wept.

"This is so sad." Susanna's voice was thick. " 'My love is gone. I know that's what that shot meant. There is no hope now. No rescue. Sedgewick will wear me down and my resolve will weaken, and I'll have to give up the gems. Then what will become of those poor souls whom we sought to set free? What will become of *me*? Will he let me live after he robs me?' Oh, dear, she obviously didn't know both of you died that night."

The ghost answered with another sob. Susanna flipped farther along in the diary. She gave a little cry of dismay. "Oh, Julian, listen to this."

He didn't want to, but there was no getting away from it.

" 'I don't understand. What has become of my captor? Am I to die here of thirst and hunger, chained to the wall in this cabin that was meant for so much more noble a purpose?' Oh, how sad!''

It was sad, all right. Julian could hardly stand to listen. To be useful, he carefully slid the jewels into Susanna's handbag. They chinked against the lead weights she'd stored in there. What an incredible trip this had been. Bibles, crosses, lead weights, rosaries. And now a fortune in gems, another diary, and the skeleton of a brave, martyred woman.

"This is terrible.''

He looked over to see that Susanna had brought the diary closer to the hanging lantern.

" 'All hope is gone. Trapped. Chained. Abandoned. Sedgewick must have decided to leave me here to die. Even I, who knew his wicked ways, didn't know he was this evil. Good-bye, world. I am now so weak I can scarcely hold the pencil. Oh, Danilo, I am so sorry!' ''

Danilo wailed like a soul in torment, which, Julian imagined, he was. Susanna began to cry audibly.

"Oh, Julian, those words are exactly what I dreamed. This is too horrible to imagine! Look how her handwriting gets feebler and feebler as she nears the end. It's too awful. Too terrible.''

Julian agreed.

Suddenly the atmosphere in the room thickened. A cold malevolence, smelling of sulfur, filled the small space around them. A low moan vibrated through the air and swelled to an ear-splitting shriek. The three of them looked at each other in terror.

"My God,'' Danilo whispered. *"He's come at last.''*

"He? You mean Sedgewick?'' Susanna's voice trembled.

The ghost nodded. *"He won't let us take his gems.''*

"But they aren't his!''

Julian lurched to the table and grabbed Susanna by

the arm. He didn't bother with the lantern or the candles. "I get the feeling he doesn't care about that. Come on! We're getting the hell out of here!"

She grabbed her Bible and handbag, stuffed Magdalena's diary into her skirt pocket, and went with him.

They almost made it.

Chapter Nineteen

Julian all but shoved Susanna up the ladder. She had too damned many skirts and petticoats in the way to make her ascent easy. If women ever expected to equal men in physical endeavors, they were going to have to wear considerably fewer clothes. He cursed his way up the ladder and into the room above. Danilo, who didn't need the ladder, followed in a whoosh, his cross held high.

Clutching her arm in his fingers, Julian dragged Susanna toward the door. Wouldn't you know it? Someone had closed it again. And barred it. And the fog was intense. It stank as he expected hell must smell.

"My God!"

The room shook like an earthquake. Julian couldn't keep to his feet, but he didn't release Susanna's arm. She fell on top of him, and he rolled over so his body covered hers. He would protect her or die trying.

"Julian! My head! Oh, my head!"

Looking down, he found her clutching at her hair like a madwoman. His heart froze in terror. "What's the matter? What is it? Did you bump it?"

"No, no! It's coming from inside. It hurts! Oh, it hurts!"

"*I am the matter.*" The ghastly voice permeated Julian's senses like acid. He looked wildly around but saw nothing but that damned, stinking fog.

Then he saw it. Yellow, shadowy, transparent, the embodiment of evil looming before the door. The long rat-like nose, thin lips, beady eyes, and hunkered shoulders proclaimed whose ghost this was. Julian whispered, "Sedgewick."

The thing grimaced horribly. "*Sedgewick. And I want what's mine.*"

It was huge. Filthy tendrils of sooty yellow fog drifted from it and filled the room. Could evil grow over the years? Evidently it could. Julian didn't know what to do, so he held the cross on his rosary up in a shaking hand. The thing that had been Sedgewick laughed. It was an awful laugh, and it boomed through the sulfurous haze like a foghorn.

"*Did you really think those trumpery gewgaws would stop me? You pathetic creature. You and your woman friend are meddling busybodies, and you aren't getting out of here with what's mine.*"

"Those gems aren't yours, Sedgewick."

Shocked by the strength of Danilo's declaration, Julian turned to gape at him. He'd never heard the ghost sound so firm and resolute. So brave. By God, Julian hoped Danilo had found his courage at last, because Julian himself was at the end of his.

"*You!*" Sedgewick shot a contemptuous glance at Danilo that Julian could see from where he lay on the floor.

Susanna moaned. Julian glanced at her. She still held her head in both hands, and rocked back and forth as if the pain were too great for her to bear. Damn, he had to get her out of here. He tried to inch his way toward the door, but Sedgewick saw him and laughed again. Julian froze where he was. He wasn't about to risk trying to haul Susanna through that yellow foggy thing, reeking of brimstone.

Sedgewick apparently considered Julian no threat. He turned back to Danilo. *"Do you think to stop me, Matteucci? You? An actor? A coward? A pathetic human and an even more pathetic ghost? Ha!"*

"You murdered Magdalena, Sedgewick, and you murdered me, and it's time for you to pay for your crimes."

"Oh? And who's going to make me pay? You? Don't make me laugh."

"Julian. Julian, the pain is too much. I can't stand it. Take me away. Please take me away." Susanna's voice was small, pathetic.

He hugged her hard. "I will, sweetheart. I'll make a break for it as soon as I can."

"I can't take much more. My head is going to explode."

He believed her. He'd never seen her—or anyone else—look like that. Tears streamed down her face. Her eyes were dilated with agony. She pressed at her temples as if trying to hold back a flood. But, Lord in heaven, what was he to do? He couldn't get past that thing blocking the door. Fog clung to them both like tentacles, heavy, cleaving, pulling him down, holding him back.

"Yes," said Danilo. *"I'll make you pay, you blackhearted scoundrel. You murdered my Magdalena!"*

"Try it," Sedgewick barked, his whole being now snapping and sparking like an electrical storm. *"Just try to do anything to me, Matteucci."* Bolts of what looked like lightning shot from him in all directions. One of them struck Julian and felt like an electrical shock. He tried to cover more of Susanna's body with his.

"Damn you for all eternity, Sedgewick!"

And with that, Danilo launched himself at the emanation across the room. The foul thing pulsed and grew larger for an instant before it hurtled at Danilo. Julian shut his eyes, but forced them open again. He had to watch.

Danilo shrieked. It sounded like a cry of anguish.

All at once a fluorescent blue streak flashed across the room. It shot straight through Julian, who felt it like an icy arrow. He doubled over in pain, trying all the while to shield Susanna. She had succumbed to her agony and now lay, groaning beneath him.

He heard a frightful cry, as of shock and alarm, and realized it had come from Sedgewick. Then he heard Danilo's voice, amazed, triumphant.

"Magdalena! My darling, is it you?"

A new voice, one Julian had never heard before, shouted, *"Yes!"*

"It can't be!" Sedgewick cried.

"Oh, but it is, Philip, and together Danilo and I are going to end your evil career! It was love that set me free, and it's love that will spell your doom."

With Sedgewick now occupied with two enemies, Julian seized his chance. As soon as he was sure the door was free from Sedgewick's influence, he grabbed Susanna under her arms and dragged her to it. He had the devil of a time unbarring it, and he had to kick it out again. At last, though, he was able to haul Susanna outside.

Stumbling, his eyes burning with that sulfurous fog and his body still reeling from Magdalena's blue streak, he got Susanna as far away from that evil cabin as he could before he collapsed. Then he held and rocked her in his arms as he watched and listened to the furious battle being waged inside.

He'd never seen or heard anything like it. It sounded like a thousand thunderstorms and looked like sixty Fourth of July fireworks displays. He wondered what had happened to his lantern, and if it would survive the fury of that battle or tip over and set the cabin on fire.

He didn't know what he hoped would happen. Perhaps if the place burned to the ground, all the evil that had accumulated there over the years would burn up with it. On the other hand, what would become of Magdalena's skeleton in such a conflagration? Did bones burn? She deserved a decent burial. In fact, Julian was willing to grant her sainthood by this time.

Piercing, unearthly screams filled the air around him. He clasped Susanna close to his chest, stroked her cheeks and hair, and prayed hard. He couldn't remember ever praying so hard, not even when he was a kid. Back then, he didn't expect anything of the world, much less harbor hopes. The whole of his early childhood had been spent in the struggle for survival.

He wanted to survive this time, too, but now he knew what it was to hope. He held his hope in his arms. Every now and then, when he could tear his attention away from the spectacle of that battle, he glanced down at Susanna. She was breathing, but unconscious. He didn't know what had happened to her, what was wrong with her now, or what to do about it, but he sensed that he needed to remain here until the issues in that cabin were resolved.

Suddenly a noise like a thousand cymbals crashing together tore through the clearing where they lay huddled. A fierce, harsh light filled the sky until it was a blazing, painful white, and Julian was forced to close his eyes against it. Then he heard a long, agonized scream of pain and terror that lasted until he was sure his eardrums would burst. He clapped his hands over Susanna's ears to protect them and hunched his head down, trying to hide his own ears in the collar of his jacket.

And then it was over. Silence sounded like thunder in Julian's ears. When he cautiously lifted his head and looked at the cabin, he saw it standing there, shabby, unpainted, unused, as if it had survived there unmolested for decades. No lights flashed from its boarded windows, no noise came from its shattered door.

Julian blinked into the sunshine suddenly flooding the formerly murky clearing. There was no fog, no smell of sulfur, no stench of hellfire and brimstone.

He crossed himself and whispered, "Thank you, God."

With all the care he could summon, he rose to his feet, cradling Susanna in his arms. His legs were shaky and he was frightened. He wished Danilo would come out of that cabin and explain what had happened. Or was Danilo lost forever? What had become of Magdalena? What about Sedgewick?

He called softly, "Danilo?"

No answer.

A little louder, he said, "Danilo, are you there?"

Again no answer met his query. Susanna groaned softly, and he decided he couldn't wait.

Because he wasn't sure what was going on, he called out, "Danilo! If you can hear me, something has happened to Susanna. I have to get her back to her aunt's house."

After waiting another ten seconds or so, he set out for the Dexter place as quickly as he could. He carried Susanna, her handbag, and her Bible down the path through the forest, past the McKenzie family plot, down the lane, through the Spring Hill Cemetery, and to her aunt's front door. By the time he got there, he was exhausted and scared to death for her.

Hammering on the front door, he cried, "Mrs. Dexter! Something's happened to Susanna. Open the door. Please hurry!"

When she wasn't dabbing her eyes with it, Winnie Dexter mauled her handkerchief with her work-worn hands. She sniffled audibly and made little "Oh, oh, oh" sounds from the foot of the bed as she watched.

Dr. Dunstable frowned as he checked Susanna's pulse. Julian stared down at her with eyes that felt as if they'd been scraped with sandpaper. He didn't know how long the doctor had been there, poking and prodding and pressing various parts of her body. He only knew that his nerves were popping like firecrackers and his skin was prickling and he was about to explode with anxiety.

"It's a brain fever, Doctor," Winnie whimpered, not for the first time. "Mr. Kittrick said she fell down in a fit and has been unconscious ever since. He carried her all the way from the old McKenzie place.'' She gave Julian a grateful smile, which he acknowledged with a brief glance in her direction. He was too worried to smile back.

The doctor grunted and lifted her other wrist, presumably to take the pulse in that one. Julian's temper snapped.

''For God's sake, Dr. Dunstable, what's the matter with her? What can we do? How many times do you have to take her pulse, anyway? Isn't it the same in either wrist?''

The venerable, gray-haired doctor glowered up at Julian. ''Mind your tongue, young man. Medical diagnoses take time.''

Mind his tongue. Julian wanted to grab the medical man by the collar of his shiny black coat and heave him out the door. Then he wanted to lie on the bed next to Susanna, take her in his arms, hold her forever, and whisper to her that they were out of danger, that Magdalena's memory was sacred, that he needed Susanna, wanted her, loved her. Oh, God, would this agony never end?

It seemed like an eternity before Dr. Dunstable creaked to his feet, put his stethoscope back into his black case with infinite care, replaced several other medical implements as slowly as he possibly could, and looked at Winnie. Her expression registered both worry and hope.

Julian was ready to scream. He thought, *At last! Maybe we'll get a diagnosis and a prognosis*.

''It's a brain fever, Mrs. Dexter. You were right.''

Wonderful. We already knew that. Julian held in his temper with difficulty.

''She must have sustained quite a shock.''

The doctor scowled at Julian as if he suspected Julian was somehow at fault. He was right. Julian knew he should have prevented Susanna from entering that blasted cabin, even if he had to tie her up. He said, ''She must have.''

"Do you know what it was?"

After giving a quick thought to the ghosts, the cabin, the jewels, and Magdalena Bondurant's bones, Julian said, "No." He couldn't explain all that. Not now. Not unless he fancied being carted off to a lunatic asylum, and he planned to stay right here, by Susanna's side, until she was out of danger.

"And why did she have bullets and pencils in all of her pockets?"

The doctor peered hard at Julian, who shrugged, feeling helpless.

"Hmph. Well, she's in a bad state." He gave up on Julian as a lost cause and turned to Winnie. "Try if you can get a few sips of brandy down her, and some sustaining beef tea. She's unconscious now and can't take any solid food. Even if she should awaken, don't burden her constitution with solids. Porridge is the most she should take. I'll send over a strengthening elixir of my own making."

"Will she be all right, Doctor?"

Winnie's handkerchief would never last if she kept twisting it that way. Julian sensed she was using it as a means of alleviating her tension and fears for Susanna, and remembered his rosary beads. He couldn't recall what he'd done with them. When he patted his breast pocket and felt them in there, relief flooded him. He was glad he hadn't lost them in that cabin. Even before he'd learned they'd come from his mother, he'd treasured them. While neither the doctor nor Winnie was looking, he withdrew them and clutched them in his fist, feeling vaguely comforted.

"I don't know." The doctor shook his head and sounded gloomy. "I've never seen a case quite like this. She's mumbling under her breath about ghosts and jewels and somebody named Bondurant."

Winnie gave a quick huff. "Oh, that child! I told her to leave things lay, but would she listen to me? No. Had to go digging into ancient family history in spite of anything anyone said to her. And now look what's happened. She probably learned something awful and couldn't stand the shock and shame of it!'' She burst into a fresh bout of tears and put her hankie to the use for which it was intended.

Julian felt so guilty he hardly knew where to look. He knew the emotion wasn't valid; after all, Susanna would have searched for answers with or without him. Still, he felt responsible. He should have protected her.

"May I stay here with her, Mrs. Dexter? May I nurse her? I know you have other work to do. I—I'd feel less guilty if you'd allow me to nurse her.''

The doctor gave him a keen look. "And why should you feel guilty, young man? What have you been doing to that child?''

"Nothing! I've done nothing to cause this. I only helped her dig for answers.''

"Hmph.''

"He's telling the truth, Dr. Dunstable. He's been kindness itself to Susanna. Going with her on her silly jaunts into the woods and the library and the courthouse, and making sure she was safe. He's been wonderful to her. This isn't his fault, I know it.''

As the doctor huffed again, Julian hoped his expression conveyed his gratitude and relief to Winnie Dexter. He was too choked up by her faith in him to speak. No one but Father Patrick had ever delved beyond his carefully crafted exterior to see the good intentions underneath. Not even Susanna. She still believed him to be an unprincipled opportunist. He fought the urge to sink to his knees by her bedside, lift her hand, and confess his heart's yearnings to her. Later, when they were alone, he would tell her everything. If Mrs. Dexter let him stay here.

"She needs constant watching, boy,'' the doctor said in his gruff way. "If you intend to nurse her, you've got to be vigilant. You have to watch her for signs that she's getting agitated or sinking.''

"Sinking?'' Julian's whisper wobbled.

"She might not make it. Brain fever is a perilous condition caused by shock and we know not what else. Sometimes people pull out of it. Sometimes they don't.''

Oh, Lord. She had to get better. She *had* to. Julian needed to tell her so many things.

''You can't slack off. If she weakens, you have to force liquids into her. Beef tea, brandy, the elixir I'm going to send by. Can you do that?''

The doctor's doubt in him rankled, but Julian said merely, ''Yes, I can do that. I'll watch her constantly. I won't shut my eyes—except to pray.'' He could hardly believe he'd added that last part, even though he meant it.

Dr. Dunstable's attitude softened slightly. He surveyed Julian with a keen gaze for several seconds before he nodded once, sharply, and turned to Winnie. ''I'll not offer you false hope, Winifred. She's in a perilous state. How these attacks of brain fever will resolve themselves is anyone's guess. She's strong and was healthy before the fit came upon her. If that young man does his job and sees to her properly, we should know more by tomorrow evening at the earliest.''

''It'll take that long to know anything?''

The doctor was frowning again when he turned to Julian. ''Yes, young man, it will take that long. Possibly longer. We're past the age of miracles, you know.''

After what he'd been through lately, Julian didn't believe that for a minute. He nodded meekly, because he wanted the crusty old man to leave. Then he wanted Winnie to go away. He wanted—needed—to be alone with Susanna.

Damn, he wished Danilo would show up again. Maybe the ghost would know what was wrong with Susanna and what to do about it.

It took forever for Winnie and Dr. Dunstable to quit conferring and for the doctor to stop questioning Julian's qualifications to nurse the patient. Julian refrained from hollering only with the greatest of difficulty.

Then Winnie hovered. She puttered and fussed and tutted and fluffed Susanna's pillows and asked Julian if he needed tea until he nearly wept with frustration. Dusk was falling before he remembered some unfinished business and used it to get rid of Winnie.

"Mrs. Dexter, is there a policeman in Palmyra? A constable or a sheriff or something?"

"We have a police force here in town, yes."

Julian lifted his brows. "A whole force?"

She shrugged. "Well, it consists of two officers."

"I see. I need you to bring one of them here. Susanna and I discovered some evidence that should be brought to the attention of the authorities."

"Evidence? What evidence? Of what?"

"Of the murder of Magdalena Bondurant."

"Murder?" Winnie paled and staggered backward. Julian wished he'd used more diplomacy in imparting the information. He wasn't generally so dull-witted, and chalked up his present maladroitness to being overwrought.

"I'm afraid she was murdered by Mr. Sedgewick's uncle, ma'am. I'm sorry to spring it on you this way. I didn't mean to."

"Sedgewick! Why, that mean old miser!"

"Miser and worse, Mrs. Dexter. Susanna and I found proof of it today. In fact, we found the remains of Magdalena Bondurant and an account, in her own words, of how Sedgewick killed her."

"But—but she was a thief and a runaway." Winnie's eyes were as round as billiard balls as she stared at Julian. "Wasn't she?"

"Magdalena Bondurant was probably as close to being a saint as people ever get on this earth, Mrs. Dexter. She was involved in the Underground Railroad, and was attempting to rescue slaves from the South and transport them to Canada."

"The Underground Railroad?" Winnie's voice had sunk to a whisper.

"Yes, ma'am."

"And she didn't steal those diamonds and such?"

"No, ma'am. Mr. McKenzie gave them to her to finance the Underground Railroad operation. Sedgewick was trying to steal them from her. She wouldn't give them up, and he kidnapped her to get them.''

Winnie looked stricken. She didn't speak for several moments. Then she burst into tears again. ''Oh, my land! You mean we've been thinking ill of her all these years, when she was a good woman all along?''

''You had no way of knowing, ma'am,'' Julian said in a consoling tone. ''But we can clear her name for good and all now. And perhaps put the present Mr. Sedgewick out of the business of ruining Palmyra's farmers.''

''I'll go fetch the constable myself,'' Winnie said, sounding determined. ''And I hope you're right about Sedgewick. That man is a scoundrel!''

''Right.'' *Thank God*, thought Julian. He needed to be alone with Susanna. His gratitude couldn't be measured when Winnie left them together. From the window of Susanna's room he saw that Winnie had thrown on her shawl and bonnet and was almost running toward the road to town. Twilight was falling fast, and she was soon out of sight.

''Thank God.''

He went back to Susanna's bed and studied her face. It was as white as freshly fallen snow. Her eyelids looked blue, like livid bruises against the pallor of her skin. Her breathing was so shallow he could scarcely detect it except in the rise and fall of the covers over her bosom. He fell to his knees on the floor beside her bed and took up her hand.

''Susanna. Oh, God, Susanna, please don't leave me. You can't leave me now when I've just found you.''

''A pretty speech, Mr. Kittrick. Don't you ever think of anyone but yourself?''

On his knees, Julian whirled around. Danilo stood there, his expression the same as it always was when he was talking to Julian. He looked supercilious and disdainful, as if he didn't care to be associating with a member of the press. Julian got light-headed with relief.

"Danilo. Thank God!"

"*Hmph. I should say you should be thanking God, young man. And I also think you should change your tactics when speaking to that dear, brave girl.*"

"*Be kind, Danilo. The poor boy is terribly upset.*"

Julian blinked and rubbed his eyes. There, standing beside Danilo, and as transparent as he, stood the most beautiful woman Julian had ever seen. It must be . . . But he'd just seen her bones! Yet, it couldn't be anyone else. "M-Magdalena?"

"*Mrs. Matteucci to you,*" snapped Danilo.

Magdalena wafted to Julian's side. "*Pay no attention to Danilo, Mr. Kittrick. He's never approved of the press since they gave his first play terrible reviews.*"

Danilo turned his back on the both of them. "*Philistines!*"

"*Yes, darling,*" said Magdalena, her sweet voice full of love. "*But now we must put our resources together to save this girl. It was her faith that saved me, you know.*"

"It was?" Julian's voice squeaked like a mouse.

"*Yes.*" Magdalena slowly ran her hands over Susanna, from the top of her head to where her feet lifted the covers. "*She was the only person who believed in me. Her love rescued me. I had been trapped for so long.*"

Julian watched, fascinated, as a shudder made Magdalena's ghostly form flutter and waver.

"*And then she recruited you in her plan.*" She gave him such a smile as he'd never hoped to receive from a female. He swallowed hard. "*And you and she together—with my darling Danilo—set me free.*"

"Wh-what happened to Sedgewick?"

"*He will never hurt anyone again.*"

"*He's in hell, where he belongs,*" Danilo said darkly.

Magdalena nodded. "*Yes, he is. And I can never thank you and Susanna enough.*"

After he'd almost recovered from her smile, Julian stammered, "Y-yes, you can, Miss Bondurant—Mrs.

Matteucci. You can help me save Susanna's life."

"The truth will set her free, Mr. Kittrick, just as it did me," Magdalena said with another of her smiles. *"You need to tell her the truth."*

"The truth," Julian whispered, wondering what the hell she was talking about.

"The truth. She needs to hear the truth from your lips."

"He's a journalist, Magdalena. He wouldn't know the truth if it bit him on the ankle."

She chuckled. *"Danilo, you mustn't say such things. The poor boy is in terrible distress."*

"He should be."

"Darling, be kind."

The truth. He had to tell her the truth. What did Magdalena mean, tell Susanna the truth? Julian didn't understand.

"We'll be back, Mr. Kittrick. We won't be far away until this crisis has passed. But only you can save her."

Julian felt his eyes all but pop out of their sockets. *"Me?"* Alone? How could he save her?

Magdalena rested her palm on his cheek for a split second and gave him a very tender smile. *"You. You're the only one. You must tell her the truth."*

Magdalena floated back to Danilo, and the two ghosts disappeared. Julian stared at where they had been and whispered a soft, "Damn."

Chapter Twenty

Julian had pulled up a chair next to Susanna's bedside. He was leaning over, holding her hand, and murmuring soft nothings to her—truthful soft nothings—when Winnie Dexter returned with the policeman. He heard them softly open the door and come inside.

"How is she?" Winnie asked in a stage whisper.

"The same, unfortunately."

Winnie sighed deeply. "This is Sergeant Hopkins, Mr. Kittrick. I told him you had some information for him about a terrible crime, but I didn't know what else to say."

Julian looked from Winnie to the policeman, and his heart sank. Sergeant Hopkins was a big fellow who had run to fat years before. His round face was pasty and looked vacant, as if it had been shaped out of bread dough and undercooked. His eyes were almost lost in the creases around them. Lord, Julian hoped the officer wasn't as dim as he looked.

"That's all right, Mrs. Dexter. I'll tell him everything."

He didn't want to let go of Susanna's hand. Nor did he want to leave her bedside for as long as it would take to explain Magdalena's demise to this oxlike policeman. With an internal groan of resignation, he did it. Winnie took his place, and he was grateful to her for it.

"Have you given her anything?" Winnie settled herself into the chair Julian had reluctantly vacated.

"I managed to get a little of Dr. Dunstable's elixir down her, but she hasn't taken anything else."

"Has she said anything?"

"Only something about bones." Julian briefly shut his eyes, recalling the pathetic specter of Magdalena's bones chained to that dank, dirty wall. Every time he thought about how she'd met her end, his heart spasmed. What had happened to her was about as unfair as life got, he reckoned. And here he'd been prepared to write a snide, scurrilous story about her, Magdalena Bondurant, a woman who had literally been martyred for a noble cause. He was ashamed of himself.

"Oh, the poor dear girl." Winnie sank down on Julian's chair and picked up Susanna's hand. She patted it tenderly, and Julian couldn't look.

He turned to the policeman. "Sergeant Hopkins, I'm Julian Kittrick. Susanna Clement and I discovered evidence of a despicable crime that took place here in Palmyra almost forty years ago. It might have consequences today as well."

"Let's hear it, Mr. Kittrick."

Julian started, surprised by Hopkins's crisp tone and businesslike manner. He was encouraged when the policeman whipped out a small pad and a pencil, licked its lead point, poised it over his pad, and looked at him, his expression suddenly alert. Maybe this guy wasn't such an oaf after all.

Armed with the jewels, Magdalena's early diaries, and the small book they'd found at the crime scene, Julian explained everything to Sergeant Hopkins. He left out all references to ghosts and the final battle between the forces of good and evil.

"You'll find her bones there, in that hole of a basement, Sergeant Hopkins. The bones of her left hand are still bound around by that iron manacle, and the manacle is attached to the wall by a chain fastened to a huge metal screw." He shuddered involuntarily. "It's pretty grim."

He realized the policeman had been staring at him with round eyes.

"She was chained to the wall?"

Julian nodded. He didn't want to say it again because it hurt too much.

With a jerk, Sergeant Hopkins resumed writing. "Sounds bad."

"It is."

It occurred to Julian to wonder if Magdalena's bones remained undisturbed. After the war that had raged in that cabin, he'd been surprised to find the thing still standing. Who knew what was left inside it? It might all be a shambles, or those lightning bolts might have incinerated everything. Well, he couldn't worry about that now, although he'd sure feel like a fool if the bones weren't there any longer.

"I'd like it if you could lead me to that cabin, Mr. Kittrick. We'll have to check out this story."

"Of course." Julian had already resigned himself to that probability. It meant he'd have to leave Susanna's side for several hours, but he knew he had to do it. Susanna would want him to. Discovering the truth about Magdalena had become her chief aim in life, and he wouldn't fail her now.

He held up the diary Susanna had stuffed into her pocket right before the demons got her. "Here. You'll want to read this. It's Magdalena Bondurant's record of her last days on earth. It names names."

"Mrs. Dexter mentioned Sedgewick."

Was it merely hope on Julian's part, or did the phlegmatic sergeant look perkier? Peering more sharply, Julian decided it wasn't his imagination; evidently even the constabulary in Palmyra wanted to get the goods on Sedgewick. Well, good. Here they were.

"Yes, sir. Sedgewick kidnapped Miss Bondurant and chained her up in that basement. He wanted to steal these."

He dumped the gems out of Susanna's handbag onto the small table between them. He wasn't surprised when Sergeant Hopkins let out with a low whistle.

"Good glory." The policeman picked up a green stone and held it to the kerosene lamp burning low between them. "This looks like an emerald."

"There are more of them. And some rubies. Not sure about diamonds. I haven't had a chance to look through them."

Hopkins squinted at the table. "And the lead weights?"

Feeling unfit to make anything up, Julian shrugged. The policeman seemed to take his shrug as an indication that he didn't know how the lead weights got mixed in with the gems.

"And you say McKenzie gave these to Miss Bondurant?"

"That's what the records say. Even the papers we found in Sedgewick's house indicate the gems were a gift to Magdalena. After having investigated everything, we're sure she planned to sell them to finance the Underground Railroad operations here in Maine, but I suppose they were hers by right, since McKenzie had given them to her."

The sergeant shook his head and put the emerald onto the pile of glittering stones almost reverently. His fingers looked like grotesque sausages next to the assortment of jewels. "If what you say is true, I expect they did belong to Miss Bondurant. I suppose they should have descended to her heirs, since she wasn't able to use them as she'd intended."

"She didn't have any children," Winnie said from Susanna's bedside. "She wasn't married."

She is now, Julian thought, and wondered if some

ghostly preacher had performed the ceremony. He and the sergeant glanced at Winnie. She wiped her eyes. "They belong to Susanna now. She deserves them. She's the one who found them."

Actually, it had been he who found them. He'd nearly broken his neck slipping on them, in fact. He wasn't about to argue, however. "Absolutely. They belong to her. She's the one who had the faith in Magdalena Bondurant, and who refused to give up until we uncovered the truth."

"Stubborn female, is she?"

Julian peered at Sergeant Hopkins, whose piggy eyes were now twinkling. Julian grinned. "The stubbornest."

The sergeant nodded. "I fancy you don't mind stubborn females much."

Suddenly Julian decided he liked this policeman quite well. He was sharp, much sharper than his looks would lead one to believe. "Not much."

The sergeant winked at him.

"Thank you for helping her, Mr. Kittrick. I worried about her, you know."

As well you might. "I wanted to do it, Mrs. Dexter. My newspaper sent me out here from Denver to find this story, so we actually had the same goal." Sort of.

"Do you mind if I take this book with me, Mr. Kittrick? I think I'd do best to study it, and any other information you dug up about this situation." Sergeant Hopkins frowned at the pile of jewels. "Don't know what to do about those things."

"You probably ought to lock them up in a safe somewhere until this whole matter is resolved," Julian cautioned. "Sedgewick might try to claim they belonged to his uncle."

The policeman held Magdalena's last diary up in a beefy fist. "He's going to have a hard time doing it with this as evidence. Especially after we recover her bones." He tugged at his lower lip. "Maybe I can get Ollie Johnson to take a photograph picture of the scene of the crime."

Better and better. Julian's respect for Sergeant Hopkins shot up like an arrow. "Good idea. I can take you out there whenever you want me to." He glanced over to Winnie. "I guess I can leave Susanna in your care for an hour or two, Mrs. Dexter."

"I should say so!" Winnie's eyes sparkled with indignation.

"Of course." Hell, he had to get his brain working again. He hadn't meant to offend the poor woman.

Julian slept in Susanna's room that night. In fact, in spite of the pallet Winnie Dexter prepared for him next to Susanna's bed, he slept in her bed, on top of the covers, and with his arms around her. He was encouraged when she sighed and snuggled up next to him, but she didn't awaken. Nor did she speak.

Once during the night, she moaned and started to thrash feebly, but she calmed down when Julian held her close and whispered calming words in her ear. She still didn't awaken.

His heart felt alternately light and heavy the next morning. At least she was still alive. But she wasn't conscious. And she hadn't spoken a coherent sentence since she'd collapsed in that clearing.

The doctor and the sergeant arrived at the Dexter house at the same time. Julian was torn between staying for the doctor's latest prognosis or haring off with the sergeant and getting that part of this ordeal over with.

Dr. Dunstable solved his dilemma for him. "Get out of here, young man. You're skittish as a colt, and you're getting on my nerves."

So Julian left. The doctor's grumbles followed him down the stairs and out of the house.

The sergeant twinkled at him. "Don't mind Doc Dunstable, Mr. Kittrick. He's been like that for thirty years now."

Julian managed a small grin.

*   *   *

The cabin remained as he and Susanna had left it the day before, bearing no evidence at all of having been the scene of a terrible battle. What amazed Julian even more than that was the changed atmosphere inside.

Where before the whole place had given off an aura of potent, irredeemable malevolence, it now seemed merely decayed from neglect. He looked around with intense curiosity, but he could see no sign whatever that anyone but he and Susanna had set foot inside the place for thirty-eight years. He shook his head in wonder. Had they both imagined everything?

But no. They couldn't have. The trapdoor stood open, as they'd left it yesterday. And when he and Sergeant Hopkins descended the rickety ladder, there were Magdalena's bones.

"Holy Moses," whispered the sergeant, awed by the sight. "What that poor woman must have suffered."

Julian nodded and swallowed the lump in his throat with difficulty. "I didn't have a chance to read the entire account of her last days, but they must have been terrible."

Silence greeted his observation. When he turned his head, he found the policeman nodding solemnly. He'd removed his hat and pressed it to his heart in a gesture of respect. Julian would have done likewise except that he'd lost his latest hat yesterday. How many did that make? Well, no matter.

Sergeant Hopkins cleared his throat. "I read it. Her statement is clear. Sedgewick murdered her." As if trying to turn from a painful subject, he said, "Because of the circumstances of the case, I checked the old records this morning before I went to the Dexter place. Sedgewick's body was found on the twenty-first of June, 1857, in the woods not far from this cabin. He and another fellow had evidently been in a fight. They were both dead."

The twenty-first of June. "When is Magdalena's last entry in the diary?"

Sergeant Hopkins had to clear his throat again. "The

fifth of July.'' His voice broke. ''That poor woman.''

Julian shook his head. Sedgewick must have been furious to have had his plan to get those gems scuttled. Vicious and vindictive, his ghost had come back here to the cabin and made sure that Magdalena's own spirit couldn't escape after it left her mortal body.

Recalling Danilo's story about how the first period of time after death is one of confusion, Julian imagined that Sedgewick had rallied his resources before her death. Since he knew where she was, he'd been able to return to the cabin before Danilo knew what was going on. Then, after Magdalena herself had succumbed to his brutality and before she could get her wits about her, he'd trapped her. Like a mouse in a cage. He shivered with the horror of it.

''Well, we can give her a proper burial now, and treat her memory with the respect it deserves.''

''Ay-eh. We can do that.'' The sergeant was silent for a moment. ''And we can let it be known what kind of villain Sedgewick was, too.''

''Good idea.''

''Folks here in Maine don't hold with this sort of thing, you know.''

Julian wondered if the sergeant thought folks in Colorado did. He didn't ask.

''Folks won't be too keen on doing business with the nephew of a murderer.''

''Good. Maybe that'll ease Sedgewick's financial grip on the town. Especially if Susanna—Miss Clement— uses the proceeds from those jewels the way I expect she will.''

Sergeant Hopkins left off staring at Magdalena's bones. ''You mean . . .''

Julian nodded. ''I think so. She wants to do something Magdalena Bondurant would approve of with the money. And, given her last days on earth, I expect Magdalena would approve of freeing the town from Sedgewick.''

The policeman put his hat back on. ''Good for her.''

With a last reverent glance at Magdalena's earthly remains, he said, "Let's get out of here. I'll get Ollie to take a picture and have the undertaker collect the bones. Maybe the town will want to do something by way of a memorial after her story comes to be known."

Julian nodded. He wanted to get back to Susanna.

For three days and three nights he hovered over Susanna, praying, despairing, hoping, and loving. For three days and three nights her condition remained unchanged. On the fourth night Danilo and Magdalena came again.

"How is she?"

He turned to see them standing hand-in-hand, like an old-fashioned couple from pre–Civil War days. He rubbed his gritty eyes. "The same."

Magdalena came closer. *"She hasn't improved?"*

His throat felt tight, and he could only shake his head.

She looked at him thoughtfully. *"Have you told her the truth yet, Mr. Kittrick?"*

The truth. They were back to the truth. He nodded again and swallowed hard. "Yes." Lord, his voice sounded like a rasp against metal. "Yes, I've told her I love her. Over and over again." A thousand times. A million times.

"That's sweet," said Magdalena. *"But have you told her the* truth?*"*

Julian had learned over the years that one got more with honey than one did with vinegar. It was useful in his line of work to be patient with people—and even with ghosts. He'd been through a lot in the past few days, however, and his patience had rubbed too thin to withstand enigmas. It snapped like a dry twig now.

"What truth? What the devil are you talking about? I'll tell her anything if it'll save her life. For the love of God, tell me what to do!"

"Well, really!" Danilo said behind them.

Magdalena smiled tenderly. *"Don't be impatient, Danilo. Poor Mr. Kittrick doesn't understand."*

"Tell her what's in yer heart, lad."

That was a new voice, a low, gruff voice, thick with Irish fogs. Julian whirled around and his knees gave out. Fortunately the chair was behind him, so he fell into it instead of onto the floor.

His parents. Those two new ghosts, standing by the window; they must be his parents. His father might have been Julian himself, they looked so much alike. His mother was dabbing her eyes with a handkerchief, and when she withdrew it, Julian knew a mother's love for the first time in his life. He saw it in her eyes, and his own filled with tears.

"Tell her ye have a good heart, Julian," she said in an accent as thick as his father's and brimming with love. *"Tell her what ye want, lovie. Tell her who ye are."*

Julian could only stare for several minutes. Then his brain stirred. *Tell her what I want. Tell her who I am.* He glanced at Magdalena. She looked like a benevolent angel, and she smiled at him with so much tenderness he couldn't hold her gaze. His glance slid to Susanna again.

Tell her who I am. He slipped from the chair and to his knees beside her once more. Picking up her hand, he whispered, "Susanna. Susanna, listen to me, please. You have to know that I'm not what you think I am. I made myself look like a cynical journalist because that was the only way I could think of to protect myself. I'm not like that, really. It's a pose. It's a sham." His breath shuddered in and out. This was so hard. He glanced over his shoulder, oddly unembarrassed to be confessing his innermost thoughts with four entities watching and listening.

"That's right, lovie. Tell her what's in yer heart."

His mother and father were both smiling at him. And they were holding hands and looked happy, as if they were proud of him. He shut his eyes for a minute, overcome with emotion.

"My—my parents are here, Susanna. They and Danilo and Magdalena have come here to help you get better. You saved Magdalena's soul, Susanna. You saved her from the clutches of Sedgewick's evil. It was you, Susanna. You had the faith. And I love you for it. I love you so much. And I swear to you that I know I was wrong. I was falling for my own image and thought it would be cute to write a disparaging article about her.

"No more. No more, Susanna, I swear. I'm going to write the most glowing tribute to a noble woman that the *Denver Post* has ever seen. It will be the truth, Susanna, and it will have come about because of you.

"You not only saved Magdalena, sweetheart, but you saved me as well. You saved me from believing my own creation. But that's not me. The only thing I've ever wanted in my life is a home and a family of my own. I want those things with you, Susanna. Please come back to me. Please."

He couldn't go on. His muscles couldn't hold him rigid any longer, and he collapsed at her bedside, crying like a baby.

For how many minutes he huddled there he could never afterward say. Nor did he know the exact moment he realized someone's hand was resting on his head. He didn't, in fact, even know if he heard the first soft "Julian" that Susanna uttered.

But he heard her at last, and his heart soared like an eagle. He lifted his head. "Susanna?"

"Julian."

"Susanna?"

"Yes, Julian, it's Susanna." She smiled at him with the same tenderness he'd seen in the expressions of two other women, ghostly women, only today.

Because he thought he'd die with disappointment if his eyes were deceiving him, he asked cautiously, "Is it really you?"

"It's really me."

He reached up and touched her cheek. "Honestly? This is really you?"

"Who else would it be?"

"Are you really awake?"

"Well, of course I'm awake," she said with some of her old asperity. "Why else would I be talking to you? Did I hear you say your parents showed themselves to you? I must meet them. You're being terribly rude, you know."

She was back! She was back, and she was cranky! Glory hallelujah! Julian jumped up from the floor and danced a jig around the room. He made a grab for Magdalena, intending to dance her around the floor, but his hands went through her. She laughed and accommodated him. They did a polka so wild it would have shocked her peers. Julian's parents looked on and laughed. Even Danilo left off frowning for a moment.

By the time Julian's joy wore him out, Susanna was scowling fiercely. He flopped down on her bed and gathered her in his arms before she could do more than utter a protesting squeal.

"Oh, my darling! Thank God! I was so worried about you, Susanna. You can't imagine how terrified I was that you'd not come back to us." He abruptly held her at arm's length so he could examine her state of health. She was so weak from her ordeal that she flopped in his hands like a rag doll.

"Julian Kittrick, you stop that right this instant! Are you trying to kill me?"

He stared at her, incredulous. "*Kill* you? I've been nursing you night and day since we were in that cabin!"

"You have?"

He could clearly discern her uncertainty. "I have. I love you, Susanna."

"You do?"

"I do. And I want you to marry me. I want you to come back to Denver with me and be my wife."

"You *do*?"

"Yes."

He watched her with all the hope he'd tried to submerge for thirty years. She didn't answer. And didn't answer. And didn't answer. Julian got worried.

"What's wrong, Susanna? I know you can't love me

as much as I love you, but don't you think we could make a life together? A good life?"

She waved her hand in a dismissive gesture. "Love isn't the question here, Julian. For all the difference it makes, I've loved you for ages now."

His heart soared very nearly out of his chest. "You have?"

Her brows furrowed. "Well, of course I have. You don't think I'd have asked you to . . . Never mind."

For the first time in days her cheeks flushed with color. Julian watched her avidly.

"But we're so different from one another."

"We're not that different."

"Yes, we are. I know you said you're not really the cynical care-for-nobody you pretend to be, but is that the truth? I can't marry a man without compassion, principles, and high ideals, you know, Julian." She sounded very severe. "I have ethics and a philosophy of equality and justice to uphold, you know. I have moral battles against oppression to wage."

She squeaked when he suddenly pulled her to his chest again and buried his head in her hair. "Oh, God, Susanna, I love you so much. I love you for your willingness to battle the forces of evil for the causes of justice. I love you for your passion, for your practicality, for your—I don't know. For everything you are."

"Oh." She was silent for a minute while Julian dropped little kisses on her head and cheeks and forehead and everywhere else he could reach that wouldn't embarrass either one of them in front of his parents. She seemed to lose herself in his adoration for a moment before she could gather her righteousness around her again. "But is it true, Julian? Do you really care about right and wrong? Are you really not the jaded skeptic you try to make people believe you are?"

"No, I'm not." He took a deep breath. This was difficult, especially with an audience. "I've never told another soul this, Susanna, but ever since I left New York, I've been sending a third of my income back to Father

Patrick to help him save children from the streets of New York, as he saved me. I've never told anyone because men in my line of work don't do things like that.

"We're supposed to be hard, to have hearts of ice. We're supposed to sneer at do-gooders. We're supposed to mock charitable people and attempt to expose them all as self-seeking bigots underneath. We're supposed to believe that everyone's black-hearted and depraved under a thin veneer of civilized behavior. We're supposed to believe that if you scratch a saint you'll find the devil.

"But the truth is that some people *are* genuinely compassionate, and they *do* perform profoundly good works out of the kindness of their hearts. No one on the face of the earth is entirely good, but there are plenty of people who, taken all in all, are more good than bad, who try to help others, and who attempt with all their might to right the world's wrongs. You're one of them, Susanna, and I am, too, believe it or not."

He sucked in a huge breath and plunged forward, fearful that if he stopped, he might not ever get this said. "I might not have been if you hadn't happened into my life. You brought me up short and exposed my pose to me as the sham it was." He gazed into her soft brown eyes, alive now with wonder. "Do you believe me, Susanna? It's the truth, you know."

She didn't speak, and Julian began to despair.

"It's the truth, lovie. He's a good boy. He's always been a good boy."

Susanna jerked and looked over her shoulder. "Mrs. Kittrick?"

Julian heard the amazement in her voice. "Yes, Susanna. Please let me introduce you to Mr. and Mrs. Emmett Kittrick, my parents." His voice thickened on the words.

Susanna wriggled out of his embrace and stood. She was unsteady on her legs and had to grab Julian's shoulder to gain her balance. He didn't mind in the least. In fact, he put a hand on her waist to help her. Then she dipped a perfect little curtsy for his parents and clasped her hands at her bosom. Julian was charmed.

"It's such a pleasure to meet you both. Danilo has told us so much about you."

"*And he's told us about you, too, dearie.*" Julian's mother had to wipe her eyes. "*I'm so glad my boy's found such a wonderful girl. He's a good, bright lad, and his heart is pure.*"

"Aye, it is," concurred Julian's father.

"*I suppose it is.*" Danilo sounded as if he begrudged having to admit the truth in this instance.

"*He has a very good heart, Susanna. One of the best.*"

Susanna turned so fast, her knees gave out, and she plopped down on the bed before Julian could catch her. "Magdalena!"

The ghost of Magdalena Bondurant floated over to Susanna and embraced her warmly. "*Yes. It is I, dear, and I can never thank you enough for releasing my spirit and for reuniting me with my darling Danilo.*"

"Oh, well, I—"

"*It was I who tripped you that day in the cabin, you know, so that you could find the trapdoor.*"

Susanna blinked at her. "It was?"

"*Yes. I had just enough energy for that. It took Danilo's willingness to battle Sedgewick on my behalf that released me for good. You facilitated that to happen.*"

"I did?"

"*You did. Your love and confidence in me did.*"

Susanna glanced at Julian. He'd have expected an *I told you so* look from her, but she appeared merely befuddled.

Magdalena went on. "*You saved me from eternal suspension in a hellish void, Susanna. You and your Julian. He has a truly good heart. If you'll take my advice, you'll snap up his offer before some other female snaps him up. He's the catch of a lifetime, dear.*"

"He is?" Susanna looked doubtfully at Julian, who nodded eagerly.

"Yes, dear, he is."

"Well . . ."

"It's the truth, lass. He's my son." Emmett Kittrick's voice rang with pride.

Julian smiled at him, and was happy when his father winked back. Damn, he liked those two. He was glad they were his parents.

"Well . . ." Susanna pondered for another moment or two. "All right, then."

Julian's head whipped around, and he stared at her. "You mean it?"

Her brow crinkled again. "I'm not in the habit of telling falsehoods, Julian Kittrick, no matter what *you* are!"

Before she could say another word, he wrapped his arms around her, lifted her into the air, and danced her around the room, laughing and crying and in a state the likes of which he'd never been before. She beat feebly against his chest in an effort to curb his enthusiasm, but it wouldn't be subdued. He'd never been so happy in his life. She finally gave herself up to enjoying the ride.

A patter of running feet brought Julian to a panting stop in the middle of the room. He and Susanna both stared at the door. When it crashed open, he was holding her as if she were already his bride and he was carrying her over the threshold. She had her arms twined around his neck. Her cheeks were flushed, and she had a happy smile on her face.

Winnie Dexter looked from Julian to Susanna and back again. "What—what—what—"

"She's better, Mrs. Dexter! She's going to be just fine!"

"I am, Aunt Winnie."

Aunt Winnie burst into tears. So did Julian. When Dr. Dunstable finally got to the door, fretful and out of breath, Susanna could only look at him and lift her shoulders as if to say, *It's not my fault.*

Chapter
Twenty-one

The bones of Magdalena Bondurant were laid to rest in the Spring Hill Cemetery three weeks after Julian and Susanna discovered them. They were buried amid much pomp and ceremony and reverent speeches about the distinction of Magdalena's life and the tragedy of her death.

Although he didn't understand the motivation behind it, the funeral director acquiesced to Susanna and Julian's request that the memorial service be conducted at sunset. No one else in town questioned their decision. They were all only happy to pay their respects to the woman who had, from her wretched, solitary crypt in the basement of that cabin in the woods, saved them from the clutches of the last of the miserly Sedgewick clan.

Shamed and vilified as a black-hearted nephew of an even more black-hearted scoundrel, the present Mr. Sedgewick hadn't been seen or heard of in town since news of the scandal broke. The only people who'd been allowed into his home were his housekeeper and the police. Rumors abounded that the authorities had ransacked the place in the face of Sedgewick's vociferous objections, searching for "clues."

However the search had been conducted, the police had unearthed evidence that the same Sedgewick who had murdered Magdalena Bondurant had also gained a great part of his wealth by illegal means.

The machinery had already begun that, with luck and good legal counsel, might wrest a goodly portion of this last Sedgewick's property away from him and disperse it among the families from whom it had originally been stolen. Everyone in town, even those who wouldn't directly profit from a successful lawsuit, hoped Sedgewick would be stripped of his illegally gotten gains—or at least have the decency to pack up and move away from Palmyra.

Now, as Susanna watched and listened to a choir of Sunday-school children sing a pretty, mournful hymn, she took a long look around the cemetery. It was only mid-September, but already the leaves had begun to turn from green to golden, orange, and brown. She glanced up into the maple tree above Magdalena's grave and smiled when she recalled Danilo sitting there, twirling Julian's jaunty straw hat in his fingers.

Julian wore another jaunty straw hat these days. Susanna had given it to him. She no longer decried his trappings, because now she knew what lay beneath them. She hoped he'd always wear a jaunty straw hat. She planned to keep him well supplied with them.

Early autumn leaves drifted down during the ceremony, making fanciful designs on the shiny mahogany coffin in which lay Magdalena's bones. Susanna hoped she and Julian could remain in Maine for a while longer so they might see the state in all its autumnal glory. She'd heard the sight of the fall leaves in the eastern states was one a person never forgot. Lately she'd been storing up memories like the Sedgewicks stored money.

During the memorial service Julian held her hand tightly in his, as if he feared she might run away if he let her go. As if he'd ever get rid of her now! She didn't mind his show of possessiveness, though; not one teeny-tiny bit.

She and Julian had sent a telegram to her parents, advising them of their engagement. Mr. and Mrs. Clement should be arriving sometime next week. Then she and Julian would be married in Palmyra's Episcopal Church, which had been a happy compromise between Julian's Catholicism and Susanna's Methodism.

Julian had written to Father Patrick, who had sent his blessings. They planned to visit him and Uncle Cullen after they were married and before they returned to Artesia to pick up Susanna's things. Then they would go to Denver, where they would settle into married life together. Susanna was eager to see both New York and Colorado.

Julian leaned over and whispered in her ear, "Do you think these people would be so eager to sanctify Magdalena if they didn't get the added benefit of blackening the Sedgewick name beyond redemption along with elevating hers?"

In spite of the solemnity of the occasion, Susanna giggled. Fortunately she managed to cover her mouth with her gloved hand and muffle her giggle before it leaked out. "I doubt it."

"It took nearly forty years, but I guess the Sedgewick reign of financial terror in Palmyra is over now."

"Yes. And I'm so happy we could help."

"I think you were brilliant to establish a low-interest farmers' bank with the proceeds from those jewels, Susanna."

"I had some good advice from an expert," she told him with a look she hoped conveyed her deep love.

"Aw, I'm not really an expert."

"Maybe not, but it was a wonderful idea."

He shrugged. "I know all about setting up trusts and so forth because of my efforts to help Father Patrick's orphans."

She squeezed his hand. "I know it. And I'm very pleased to know I'll be marrying a smart man as well

as a compassionate one. I couldn't abide being married
to a fool."

He laughed softly. "Nor could I."

When she gazed up at him again, his blue eyes
gleamed like stars. They shone with love, and Susanna
felt light-headed for a moment. She hadn't entirely recovered from her ordeal, but she was gaining strength
every day. She could hardly wait until she and Julian
were married. They would no longer have to sneak off
to the woods to make love then.

"Ashes to ashes," the minister intoned solemnly.
"Dust to dust."

All the spectators watched as the coffin containing
Magdalena's bones was lowered into the grave that had
not been dug for her until nearly forty years after her
death. Susanna's eyes filled with tears as she watched.
How sad Magdalena's story was. How sad and yet how
precious. She'd been a noble, brave woman, and she was
finally getting the respect and admiration she deserved.

She felt Julian squeeze her hand and looked up to see
what he wanted. He gave his head a quick jerk to the
left, and she glanced over to see the very, very faint
manifestations of Danilo and Magdalena, more transparent than ever, watching at the edge of the cemetery. Oh,
good! This was why she and Julian had insisted the ceremony be conducted at sunset.

Magdalena was looking on with a sweet, serene smile
on her beautiful face. Danilo, needless to say, was weeping copious tears. His red-lined cape fluttered in the
summer evening breeze, and his handkerchief looked
like it was soaked through already.

Glancing around the graveyard, Susanna realized that
she and Julian were the only ones present who saw the
ghosts. She was glad. She wanted to keep them between
themselves. She smiled at them. Magdalena smiled back
and winked. Danilo was too overwhelmed by his emotions to do anything but nod. Susanna understood.

The town fathers had decided to dedicate a memorial
statue to Magdalena Bondurant. She was to be Palmyra's

martyred saint to the Union cause. Although Susanna suspected Magdalena herself didn't so much care about the Union cause as the abolition of the vile and pernicious institution of slavery, she honored their decision. She and Julian had been asked to return to Palmyra for the dedication ceremony after the statue was finished. She looked forward to another visit to Maine.

"Do you think Magdalena and Danilo and your parents will come to our wedding, Julian?"

He lifted his head and looked at her, then stroked her naked breast. They were both out of breath and slick with perspiration, having just indulged in a spectacular bout of lovemaking in their special glade in the forest. Every time they made love, it got better.

"I'll be disappointed if they don't." He dipped his head and licked her pebbly nipple where his hand had just stroked it. He loved her breasts. They were a perfect handful.

She sighed blissfully. "So will I." She arched her back in order to thrust her breast closer to him. Julian loved her passionate response to his caresses.

"How many children do you want, Susanna?"

Her body was so lovely. He smoothed a hand from her breast to her abdomen, wondering if there might already be a new life growing there. He hoped so. He wanted children of his own. He wanted to be a father like he'd never had, the kind of father he now knew his own would have been had he lived. Children were such precious little beings; even now his heart hurt to think of all the abandoned waifs struggling to maintain life on the streets where he'd grown up.

"I've never thought about it."

She arched under his touch, igniting his responses. He drew her close. "I want a hundred of them."

She laughed low in her throat. "I don't think that's possible, sweetheart, but I'm sure we can have three or four. I've always wanted children."

"Me, too. I guess three or four will have to do."

She caught his face between her hands and kissed him hard. They were both panting when she finally broke the kiss. "Maybe five or six." Her voice had gone husky.

She reached for his sex, which had grown hard again. He groaned with pleasure. "Seven or eight," he whispered as she guided him home.

"Nine or ten," she said breathlessly as she met his thrust with an arch that drove him wild.

They didn't speak again for another twenty minutes or so.

Julian and Susanna insisted on an evening ceremony. They were married on the first Saturday in October, and it was a lovely wedding. The whole town had come together for the event, and the church was decorated with a forest of fall flowers and leaves. Susanna wore her Grandmother Bondurant's wedding gown. The years had dyed its white satin to ivory, but Susanna loved it anyway. If Magdalena Bondurant had lived, she might have been married to Danilo in just such a gown.

The Episcopal priest, Father Tom Billingsly, pronounced Julian and Susanna husband and wife as the church bells began to toll seven o'clock. Miss Pritchard, the church organist, struck up a lovely melody several seconds before Julian and Susanna stopped kissing. Susanna thought she did it to break them apart. Perhaps they had gotten a little carried away, but they loved each other so dearly that it was difficult to curb their displays of affection. She recalled Miss Amberly's admonitions against overt displays of affection and decided Miss Amberly had never been in love.

When they turned to face the assembled guests, Susanna saw that her mother and Aunt Winnie were crying tears of joy. Even her father's eyes glistened with tears. Uncle Cyrus winked at her. She smiled back. She loved her family very much; she only wished Julian had family here to see him take a bride.

Then she saw them. In the choir loft in the back of the church, she saw them: Emmett and Kathleen Kittrick standing next to Danilo and Magdalena Matteucci.

"Julian!" she whispered.

"I see them," he said, and she could tell he was choked up. So was she.

Susanna and Julian traveled to New York after their wedding. Susanna was pleased to meet the aging Father Patrick, although she did get just a little tired of the priest singing her husband's praises. As much as she adored him, she didn't want Julian to get swellheaded.

The best part of their honeymoon, though, was when Julian and she managed to find Mr. Cullen Kittrick, a greengrocer in the Bronx. Uncle Cullen and Aunt Maud lived above their grocery store in a noisy street full of tall, skinny buildings the likes of which Susanna had never seen before.

She and Julian walked into Kittrick's Greengrocers one October afternoon, Susanna holding Julian's hand tightly. Neither of them knew what to expect. When they saw a tall man setting out cabbages, they stopped and stared, neither having any idea what to say or how exactly to inquire as to Cullen Kittrick's whereabouts.

When the man turned around, all three of them gasped in chorus. Susanna thought she might have been looking at the living Emmett Kittrick. Cullen dropped the cabbage he'd been holding. He rubbed his eyes. "Em-Emmett?" he stammered, as if he'd seen a ghost.

Julian shook his head. Susanna saw tears in his eyes. "Emmett's son," he said in a shaky whisper.

Cullen's eyes opened up as wide as platters for a second before he threw another cabbage into the air, let out with a shout of joy, and raced over to embrace Julian.

The newlyweds were welcomed into the Kittrick family as if they'd been part of it all their lives. Susanna had never experienced the exuberance of an Irish family, but she liked it. She liked it a lot.

They settled in Denver, and Susanna decided she liked Denver, too. It was at once both more and less civilized than her hometown of Artesia, the city of Denver being more sophisticated, and some of its citizens being rather less orderly than she considered seemly. They gave her a lot of material to work with in her endeavors as a reformer.

When Magdalena Bondurant's statue was unveiled a year and a half after their wedding, Susanna and Julian took the train to Palmyra, Maine. They traveled with their four-month-old son, Emmett, and took him to the Spring Hill Cemetery one fine March evening. A brisk breeze was blowing.

"Do you think she knows we're here?" Susanna asked Julian, who carried a bundled-up Emmett in his arms.

"I don't know."

"Magdalena?" she called experimentally. "Danilo?"

They waited for several minutes, but no ghostly apparitions appeared to them. Susanna was disappointed until Julian made a cogent point to her.

"I suppose this means that their spirits are at rest together at last."

She liked that idea a whole lot. They walked back to Aunt Winnie and Uncle Cyrus's house, hand-in-hand.

Neither one of them ever saw another ghost.